Hanah's Paradise

Hanah's Paradise

Ligia Ravé

NEW DOOR BOOKS
Philadelphia 2009

NEW DOOR BOOKS
An imprint of P. M. Gordon Associates, Inc.
2115 Wallace Street
Philadelphia, Pennsylvania 19130
U.S.A.

This is a work of fiction. Any resemblance herein to actual persons, living or
dead, or to actual events or locales is purely coincidental.

Library of Congress Control Number: 2009935184
ISBN 978-0-9788636-3-0

Published in Spanish as *El Paraíso de Hanah*
by Ellago Ediciones S.L., Castellón, Spain, 2007

Cover illustrations:

Diagram of the divine world adapted from Moses (Moshe) Cordovero,
Pardes Rimonim, 1548

Detail of the Zodiac mosaic at the Severus Synagogue in Hammat Tiberias,
Israel, reproduced by courtesy of BibleWalks.com

To David, always generous, always in love

The Garden

The garden was divided into sixty-four equal squares, numbered without following any known mathematical progression: forty-nine, sixty-four, thirteen, seven, and so on.

Hanah was the one who brought pink stone from the Petra Valley and, after enclosing the garden within an eight-foot-high wall, numbered the plots like that, unordered. But it was Abraham, Hanah's father, who, trusting that words attract reality, felt compelled to leave a message at Hanah's Paradise. To this end he installed stone tablets within each plot. "*Ani maamin*, I believe," he chiseled on the first square. And it was he who requested that the firstborn from each branch of the family visit the garden and leave behind a message in their own dialect:

Berberic, Amharic, Bucharic, Arabic, Aragonic,
Canaanic, Espaniolik, Catalanic, Derebendic, Esfahanic,
Galestani, Kanshashani, Hamedani, Malayalami, Gruzinik,
Takestani, Haketic, Yevanik, Juhuric, Italkit, Karaic,
Shaudit, Krimchakit, Kunsaric, Tadjikit, Zaraphic,
Siahkali, Provençal, Yazdani, Shirazi, Romaniot, Tatic,
Dzuhurei, Zargon, and Yiddish.

Faded by time, the names, poems, locations, recipes, and personal thoughts were chiseled into the pink stones, one below the other. Even the narrow paths between squares were covered with words. Hanah's firstborn daughter, Tamar, installed the gates to the garden and left her own inscription. "What is mysterious to you, do not seek," she chiseled in the stone.

When Yakov Binyamin Ravayah, the great-grandfather of my grandfather, went to Hanah's Paradise in 1804, a grove of yellow bamboo shielded the view of the garden. Once inside, he followed the established paths, wandering through quotations from the *Sefirot*, apologies, lamentations, and references from the Talmud. Intrigued by the randomness of numbers, he added them up in every horizontal row, in every column, and on the two main diagonals. To his surprise, he came up with the number 260 each time. He then added the numbers on the rising or descending diagonals and came up with equal sums, 260. Consumed by his discovery, he went to the High Rabbinical Tribunal to ask for an explanation.

The most renowned scholars studied the numbers and after several permutations declared "Hanah's Paradise mystical." It was conceived with the numbers 32, 64, and 260, which in the Book of Numbers means *yeladim kerem*, children of the vineyard—symbol of the tribe of Israel. Sixty-four is also twice thirty-two, and God created His universe with thirty-two mystical paths of wisdom and with three letters:

S–P–R.
With E He made *Seper*, Book.
With A He made *Separ*, Number.
With I and U God wrote *Sippur*, Story.

But thirty-two could also mean *derekh*, a public road, which can take you only across town: to the gate of the city, to the market, or to the cemetery. All kinds of people can use it—even prostitutes! "All roads lead to oneself," Hanah wrote and doubled the paths of the garden to sixty-four to spell the word *Nativ*, a personal route, a hidden path, without markers or signs. It is the road one must discover on one's own. "The paths at Hanah's Paradise," the scholar concluded, "are *peliyot*, mystical, individual, and concealed, and one should not alter them. Sixty-four is the sixth power of two, which defines a mysterious six-dimensional space."

Seeking an answer to the mystery of the garden and of Hanah herself, a French visitor in the seventeenth century wrote a message to all women:

Wisdom is the beginning of Separation,
Separation is the domain of Feminine Essence.

Hanah's own inscription, left on square number eight, represented the numerical equivalent of either thirty-two or sixty-four, and the meaning of her inscription provoked many interpretations.

64: *Ve'Bayom* — And on the day
64: *Ve'Habaim* — They that came
32: *Ve'Yhyeh* — That which will be (the Lord)
32: *Hagidi* — Tells me
64: *Hagoyim Ve'Natah Hatemah* — The nations spread hot displeasure
64: *Ve'Bayom* — And on that day
64: *Ve'Iehdilu* — They ceased to
64: *Yieleidi* — Bear children
32: *Lev bohi* — Heart weep for me

Only in the last century, around 1980, did the interpretation by an American poet, Sally Kagan Swift, become widely accepted: "Hanah was a mystic and her inscription, a prophecy describing people sprinkled with chemicals, ceasing to bear children."

> Hanah left her wisdom,
> *Lee, lah, loh*, to me, to her, to him.
> Hanah left her trust,
> *Bee, bah, boh*, in me, in her, in him.

Attached to Sally's letter was a surprisingly detailed article from a science magazine explaining that the number 260 is equal to the size of the wavelength absorbed by DNA.

Then Nathan Ravayah, another firstborn, from Kiev, cleaned the garden, repaired the walls, and recorded by author and location all the inscriptions left on the squares. According to his calculation, 67,600 *bechorim*, firstborn sons or daughters, representing some 2,700 generations, could leave their inscriptions on the stones of Hanah's Paradise.

Nathan's firstborn daughter, Corina Bat Ravayah, came to work at the garden and eventually acquired the land around it. She planted sixty-four *rimonim*, pomegranate trees, along each of the four walls of the garden. She trimmed the golden bamboo growing between the gates and burned the discarded shoots to ensure that they would not fall into strangers' hands. She took pale Jerusalem stone and extended the edges of Hanah's Paradise with a wall in which she set thirty-two gates. She filled the space between the two walls with orange sand and set upon it at various angles black basalt stones from Namibia. From a bird's-eye perspective, one could see a square within a rectangle. A knowing mind would recognize the plan of the Second Jerusalem Temple before the Roman destruction, with Hanah's Paradise sitting in the middle.

> In Their Wisdom,
> God's Thoughts
> Are Geometrical Forms.

Outside the garden, Corina set two-foot-high letters in gold mosaic, a different one on each of the four walls. *P* for *Pshat*, the literal sense, the ordinary, the plain; *R* for *Remez*, the allusive, the hint; *D* or *Drash*, the implicative, the allegorical; and *S* for *Sod*, the mystical, the esoteric. The letters represent the four methods of interpretation of any text—and there are no hierarchical values to the interpretative reading. "Hebrew letters are direct expressions of God's thoughts," Corina wrote. Walking around the garden's walls, a visitor might be compelled to insert different vowels between those letters, forming thirty-two permutations and a multiplicity of words:

> P R D S
> PaRDeS, DiaSPoRa, SePhaRD, RaPSoDia.

Corina's firstborn daughter, Priscille, built a ladder with thirty-two steps, upon which one could climb to approach the Infinite Being. Her firstborn daughter, Masha, cleaned the garden of unwanted weeds and chiseled on the wall under her name an unanswered question:

> Before *one*, what is there to count?

1

"Red hair, black eyes, one meter sixty-eight, female, no distinctive marks, born in Bucharest," the policeman read. "This is not a passport," he said, shuffling my travel documents in anger.

He had prepared himself for the day. On a piece of paper torn from a notebook, he had drawn columns for Name, Country, Color of Passport, Place of Origin, Stamp, and Destination, but I disrupted his system. I did not have a passport. I had a letter of travel issued by the United Nations to *apatrides*, citizens without a country, displaced by the war. He had never seen such a thing. There was no place to put a stamp. My letter of passage didn't fit in any of his columns.

"Sa-lo-meia," he said, separating the syllables, as if he could barely read. "How long were you here . . . two months?" and without waiting for an answer, pointed to my suitcase and showed me into a small, windowless room. He took the only chair, and I stood in front of him on the other side of a metal desk. A lamp cast light onto the wall in front of me, where a large photograph covered the entire side of the office. In the photograph, Ceaușescu, the president of the Socialist Republic of Romania, was shown with a scepter in his hand, his right foot resting on the stuffed head of a boar, a red flag in the background. Gold letters on the frame identified him as "The Genius of the Danube."

"What do people call you?"

"Meia."

"When did you leave our country?"

"Over five years ago. I was allowed to emigrate."

"Why did you come back to Romania?"

"My parents live here. I came to visit them."

"And you are going to Istanbul?"

"No, Istanbul is only a stopover."

"Where do you live?"

"I live in Israel with my grandfather, at a place called Hanah's Paradise."

"What kind of people are you?" he asked with disdain. "Don't you have any shame? You are born here, eat our bread, then you leave. If my daughter were to leave our country," he continued, "I would kill her with my bare hands," and twisting his hands, he showed me how. The officer's brown-green uniform was crumpled, and rings of dirt showed on his neck. His odor of garlic and cheap tobacco filled the room. Could he stop me from leaving? No, I thought, he couldn't. There was no reason to be afraid.

"What is that?" he asked, looking through my bag, knowing exactly what it was. "Mar—ma—lade; marmalade. This is for me," he mumbled and put it into his pocket.

"You can't leave," he said and pushed my bag toward me. "You don't have a passport. You have to wait here until the comrade my boss looks at your document."

He showed me out of his office into the unlit corridor. There was nobody around. The plane to Istanbul had already left. I stared at the empty hall and the immigration booth, trying to control my fear. I could be arrested, abused, interrogated, and kept there for days. I sat down on the cold cement floor, with no other option than to wait. From the corner of my eye, I saw the officer walk to a water fountain. He drank some water, spat into his hands, straightened his hair with the spit, then lit a cigarette. When he passed by me I asked, "Can I have a temporary entry visa to go back to my parents?"

"A new visa? You want a new entry visa? What do you think," he said in a sarcastic tone, "I am here at your orders? *Modmosela* doesn't have documents but wants a new visa," he said, mispronouncing the French word. "Nobody can give you a visa! They are not issued at the border. You have to stay in the airport until my boss arrives. You can take the next flight, if he lets you go. Two days."

My hands grew sweaty and I felt I would faint. As the officer continued talking, his body seemed to swell larger and larger. I could barely understand his words.

"And how much is a car where you're coming from?" he asked.

I looked at him, lightheaded, until he repeated the question.

"*A masina, cit costa o masina?* A car, how much is a car?"

I took a deep breath and slowly said, "I am sorry, *Nu stiu*, I don't know."

"My daughter is your age and needs new shoes," he said, looking at mine.

"May I use the phone to call my parents?" I managed to ask.

"It is forbidden," he answered.

I nodded my head, looking at the floor, thinking of my grandfather waiting for me in Tel Aviv.

"I only want to tell my family about the delay."

"And I want a big house and a roasted chicken. Should I call my parents?"

"I am sorry," I said. I stood up and, with effort, pushed my suitcase toward a glass door on which "International Departure Lounge" was written in red paint in five languages.

The departure lounge was closed. The glass door had been painted the same green color as the walls, and NEPO REVEN was scratched on it from the inside. Through the large patches of peeled-off paint, I could see a jar of pickles prominently displayed on a red Formica counter. On the wall above the counter a plaster bas-relief of a Russian tank draped in flags and flowers caught my eye. Surrounding the tank, people raised their arms in a happy salute and a child was pushed forward to give a flower to a Russian soldier. The soldier waved one hand at the viewer while holding the other one to his cap, on which a brilliant red star was painted. Outlining the bottom of the bas-relief, a short poem in Russian described the scene:

> Gazing at the flag above,
> My whole soul is filled with love,
> And when hand to heart I put,
> Soviet heroes I salute.

From a distance the red star seemed to float above the raised arms, transforming the war scene into a Communist nativity. On the opposite wall, through arches of green droplets spelling the word "Oceanic," an enormous fish sprang forward from an open can surrounded by blue ocean waves. This eye-catcher, made from painted layers of cardboard, was the symbol of friendship between Romania and China, a sign of prosperity that could be seen along the roads displayed on buildings, on tractors, and on bus shelters.

At the airport, the Oceanic Fish floated on the wall, lit by a bare bulb attached to the plaster ceiling, where circles left by water leaks showed a general indifference. Also attached to the ceiling was a row of sticky yellow ribbons covered with dead flies left over from summer. High on the wall and out of reach was the black box of a loudspeaker, from which I could hear a constant stream of revolutionary songs and political slogans. Shadows moved on the other side of the glass, and when I heard laughter, I stepped away.

Not long after, an airport official brought two other travelers to the door of the Departure Lounge. We said hello, I in French, they in German. They looked alike, with the same stern expression and the same rigid walk. Only their clothes were different. While the older man wore elegant shoes and a tie, the younger one looked poor in his worn sweater and old tennis shoes.

The airport official, a skinny man with a sad look in his eyes, pointed a finger at us and in gruff, broken English said, "Visas no! Here stay! Here sleep! Here eat! *Here.*" He stamped his foot on the floor. "Understand? You go no city. Transport *kaput*! Out bad dog; gun, boom-boom, dead! Telephone *kaput*! Good food give here. Two day *avion* go. *Verstehen*? Understand?" And with his arms extended, he stood on one foot and bent his body, as if he were an airplane. At least I am not alone, I thought. If something happens to me, if I get arrested, these two people are witnesses.

"Comrade," I said after he finished his speech. "May I have my travel document? The comrade officer at the immigration booth has it. I would like it back."

"You no spy, document back. You spy, document *kaput*."

"I am not a spy," I defended myself, but the official ignored me. He unlocked the glass door and motioned us to enter. Looking toward the plaster sculpture on the wall, he shouted, "*E o mare onoare*, it is a great honor, to be a guest of the Romanian Socialist Republic!"

"*Ja, ja*," the older of the two men said, "I missed my plane. They wouldn't let me go until I paid for a smallpox health certificate. It must be a scam," he added, trying to restrain his fury.

Resigned, I nodded my head in agreement. "Yes," I said, ready to share my feelings. "We are stranded here."

On this cold January day, the lounge smelled of vomit, urine, and boiled cabbage. In the dim light of the room, a woman dressed in a brown military uniform sat on the floor. Undisturbed by our arrival, she continued to count napkins, folding them into triangles. At the red Formica counter, a short, fat man was separating aluminum spoons from forks, making two piles.

There were no seats in the room, so the two travelers, Karl and Axel, sat on the floor talking while I sat on my suitcase listening to them. I learned that Axel was a West German engineer working for BMW. He was going to Baghdad and had made a stopover in Bucharest to visit the city. The other man, Karl, was from East Germany. He was on his way to Bulgaria to attend a youth conference.

After a while, the short, fat man opened a closet and pulled several chairs into the room. Axel made a desk with his suitcase, then took another chair and sat down drumming his fingers and gazing out the windows at a group of soldiers who were walking their dogs between the watchtowers. The short, fat man frowned in disagreement and said something that made the uniformed woman laugh. He came near us and dismantled the desk, moving the chairs to face the wall. When Axel tried to stop him, the man pointed his finger at us and yelled authoritatively, "*Nein, nein. Nu se poate, kaput!*"

The sordid reality of Romania under the *Conducator*, the Leader, was condensed in those words: "*Nu se poate*, not allowed"—the Romanian answer to everything.

Should I speak Romanian? I wondered. And if I choose not to, can I hide my reactions? Can I fake not understanding? There is no law obliging me to speak Romanian in Romania just because I know the language.

Axel, the West German, could not contain his frustration and, addressing no one in particular, he said, "Look at this gloomy place: water dripping from the ceiling, stained walls, ripped linoleum floors, all Communist countries are alike. There is no incentive. People receive compensation no matter whether they work hard or not at all. People bribe the doctors to get extended sick leaves. Somebody who escaped from East Berlin told me that at his institute there would not be enough desks and chairs if all the employees came to work. Communism is the welfare state."

Karl leaned forward and, with a forced smile, whispered, "*Ist das eine Provokation*, Is this a provocation? Are you insulting Communism? Are you an enemy?"

"*Nein, nein*," Axel answered, standing up. "*Das ist keine Falle*, This is not a setup!"

"*Ich weiss nicht*, I don't know," Karl whispered in a grimace of discomfort. "You want me to criticize my country so you can denounce me to the Party."

"*Ich bin ein Freund*, I am a friend," Axel said several times, looking baffled at Karl. "*Ich bin kein Provokateur*, I am not a provocateur, *nein, nein*," he repeated, shaking his head.

From the speaker on the ceiling, the "Beloved Leader," the dictator elected for life, was delivering a scathing attack on the American Empire. The "Supreme Hero" had declared war on the free market, which was incompatible with the principles of freedom. Child labor, prostitution, human misery, and illiteracy, he told his subjects in an angry tone, support the capitalist economy. The program continued with songs and spirited poems about the Leader's efforts to rid the country of imperialist vermin. Verse after verse praised him and his parents:

> Your breasts are sunflowers,
> Your smile is milk,
> When your feet touch the earth,
> Our corn stalks grow thick.

> Our thanks go to you,
> Mother of us all,
> For the boy you loved
> And raised so well,

> For the child you nurtured
> To give us the light—
> Your son, our Leader,
> We now celebrate.

And to you, Dear Mother,
We all come to say
Forever be happy,
In our hearts you will stay.

Every hour, the radio program was interrupted by the Supreme Hero himself: "Heroic Romanian People, Children of the Revolution, have faith in equality, fraternity, and true liberty. I will fight for our country, for our people, and for humanity."

"Ceaușescu, *Führer*," Axel said, pointing at the speaker on the wall.

The radio could not be turned off, not at the airport, nor in factories or schools. From border to border, the songs, poems, and national news resounded at the same time in every village and every public plaza. Lucky them, I thought, looking at the two Germans. They don't understand Romanian.

THE BAR

In anticipation of the weekly flight from Belgrade that continued on to Geneva, the short, fat man finally opened the bar. Everything had to be purchased in American dollars, but there was nothing other than mustard, sweet white wine, instant coffee, small cans of beans, and salami sandwiches. This last category consisted of a thick slice of white bread, called *franzela*, a smidgen of white grease, and a paper-thin slice of garlic salami. When the flight from Belgrade arrived, several passengers, men and women, were escorted to the lounge. They looked at the food but the bread was already stale, the grease melted, and the round salami edges curled, making room for the flies to land and die. The bartender bowed his head to welcome the passengers, then pointed to the jar of pickles on the counter. They wanted coffee, they said. Yes, as a favor he agreed to make instant coffee, but they would have to buy a pickle also. "They come together," he explained. Making the coffee was a complex operation, and he did it with great pride, describing the action with grunts of pleasure and vulgar little poems.

I will make a coffee cup
For the pretty lonely cunt.

When, slowly and with determination, he had mixed the coffee powder and sugar to his satisfaction, the bartender added several drops of hot water. This was the key to success. Too much water —the sugar would melt and the thick gooey brown paste would lose its foam. The evolution of the coffee powder into coffee paste, then into a drink, was a glorious endeavor, and the bartender was its living expression. He sucked in his stomach, straightened his shoulders, and added a half-spoonful of hot water to the cup, mixing the coffee with rapid movements, always in the same direction. Then he poured in more water while with his other hand he caressed his loins, continuing to praise himself in short breathless verses:

> Only short men, just like me,
> Give you total ecstasy.
> When you kiss my darling dick,
> You will never want to speak.
> Your body will be sore,
> But you'll only cry for more.

Rising to the brim of the cup, the coffee's brown foam gave the bartender an orgasmic delight. In one final gesture of seduction, he stuck out his greasy brown tongue, flanked by a poorly shaven jaw, and slowly licked the spoon. His lips opened slightly to let out a crude sound. "*Puuuuuuuuusssssssssssy, voilà. Danke schön. Prego! Pajalusta! Bitte!* Please! *Ruminul e nascut poet!* The Romanian is a born poet!" he said.

For men, the poems changed to glorify the bartender to the detriment of his customers, who were "small as my asshole" or "tall as my dick," and for whose mothers he felt sorry. The fact that Romanians were not allowed to travel out of the country and that the few arriving visitors almost never spoke the language offered the bartender extraordinary freedom: the privilege of operating a split between the content and affect of his words.

"Of course you want coffee, you bastard born in Hell," he said, in a sweet inflection, smiling at a traveler. "You think you are big shit with your money in your pocket. *Ai un cap de cur*, you have a stupid asshole face." The man nodded his head and smiled back. "You have American dollars, but *cuoaie ai*, do you have balls?" the bartender asked. *"Nimic,* nothing," he answered. *"You* were born with a passport and *I* was born with balls. *Capisce? Panimaiete?* Understand? *Verstehen?* Who is the lucky one, huh? Who is born in the most beautiful country in the world?" he asked pointing at himself, yelling toward the plaster tank where a microphone that used to be hidden was now visible.

"You know why?" the bartender continued, "because we are *saraci da curati,* poor but honest."

The passengers in transit, Swiss working for the World Heritage Committee, gave me a chance to send a message to my grandfather. Talking with them alleviated my fears. At least somebody knew my name and my whereabouts. Axel also promised to call my grandfather once he left Romania. He continued to reassure me that he would resist my arrest, should that happen.

Interrupting our talk, the uniformed woman stood up and shouted, *"Achtung,* comrades!" Then, rubbing her stomach with one hand, she said, *"Miam-miam,* yum-yum. *Mincare, ca la mama acasa!* Food, just like home! *Mmmwoa,"* she said, puckering her lips and kissing the fingers of her other hand.

The kitchen personnel brought out several trays and set up a buffet on the bar counter. The food consisted of cabbage mixed with bacon and garlic, black bread, plum marmalade, and beets. On a hunk of lard, the words *Wilko* and *men*—welcome, we assumed—were written in squiggly lines of yellow mustard. To drink, there was black Russian tea and water. Before we had time to go to the buffet, the workers had filled their plates and returned to the kitchen.

"Look," Axel said laughing. "They are eating the food they prepared for us."

"Why shouldn't the comrades assigned to cooking eat gourmet food also?" Karl said in defense. "In West Berlin, children die of starvation as rich capitalist exploiters gorge themselves on caviar."

Karl wanted to continue talking, but a woman rushed in from the kitchen. She set up a folding table for us and, pointing to the food, she said loudly, *"Poftiti la masa, draga domnilor, tovarasi,"* an expression that conveyed the meaning, Dinner is ready and our Lords are served.

Karl moved his chair and sat down first. Axel sat near me, avoiding looking at Karl.

The woman pushed away several empty boxes to clear a space in front of the table. Then, in the middle of this imaginary circle, she tightened her apron, moistened her lips, and with her hands on her hips and her elbows akimbo, declaimed a poem of her own:

No bird's meat tastes as sweet as . . . piglet,
No flower smells as sweet as . . . cabbage,
No water tastes as good as wine,
And for the Party I bake bread.

I knew that she would ask for money and, indeed, she opened her hand, pointing to her palm. Karl looked down. *"Nein, nein,"* Axel said. "You work for the Party." Seeing me searching for money, he changed his mind and gave her some cigarettes.

Axel tasted the food, put his fork down, then spread some marmalade on a piece of bread. Karl, who had grown up in East Germany after the war, was trained to fake sincerity, and with smiling glances, he complimented the comrade, saying, *"Sehr gut,* Very good."

From the kitchen, we could hear vehement discussions and screams of laughter. The clinking of glasses and the words of the toast made my skin crawl:

Money and good news,
And death to the Jews!

I couldn't eat. I knew the food only too well. I had lived in Romania the first sixteen years of my life. Food was on everybody's mind all the time. It was scarce, and of poor quality. People spent long hours lining up for it. In the winter they built fires on the streets to keep warm while waiting for stores to open. My mother found some scraps of wood and made me a child's chair. I used it to wait in line alone, sometimes for hours, until she could come and take over. Like everyone else, she always carried an empty bag in case she found something to buy. People seen with a package were stopped on the street. "What do you have?" would be followed by "Where did you find it?" and "What do you want for it?" Sometimes you could hear someone calling a neighbor from the street: "Mariano, Mariano, *vino repede,* come fast, they are giving sugar!" *They* were the Communists, and *giving* meant you were allowed to purchase your ration of sugar for the month—*if* you got in line early enough, and *if* there was anything left when your turn finally arrived. People stood in line in a stupor, not knowing what was for sale, hoping for anything.

"What are they giving?" one would ask. "They are giving cheese!" somebody would answer. "No!" another person would correct. "They are giving eggs—half a dozen per person." "Who says?" an angry voice would interrupt. "They are not giving eggs, they are giving coffee!" "Coffee?" a new voice would challenge. "They are not giving coffee! I have not seen coffee in eighteen years! They are giving salami!"

The eagerness to buy was matched only by the eagerness to barter. The reward of spending a day to buy some electric wire lay in the possibility of exchanging it for soap or food. Early in the morning, the city took on a surreal feeling. People walked to work with strings of clothing attached to their shoulders, dishes on their backs, or shoes hanging from their arms. Sometimes they had only a large piece of paper pinned on their backs listing what they had to barter. Everyone was always ready to make a deal.

In Romania, connections had more value than cash. With connections one could obtain anything: a job, an apartment, admission to the university, an appointment with the dentist, or products manufactured for export. A position of power at the carpet factory made possible the exchange of a rug for a radio, a radio for a set of china, a set of china for clothes. Of significant value were products from enemy markets. A carton of Kent cigarettes, a bottle of whiskey, an ounce of French perfume, a bar of soap, or a tube of lipstick could buy a foreigner—at the black market—an antique silver icon, which could be sold outside the country for a nice profit. The cigarettes or the whiskey would, in turn, open the door to the dentist, which, in turn, opened the door to the school's admission officer, and so on. The bottle and the carton were passed on, never consumed. In time the label would start to peel, the cellophane would fray at the corners, and the box would break, spilling tobacco dust from the stale cigarettes. Sometimes the working class would inherit these much-traveled commodities, and the circle would continue. The factory manager would receive them from a worker as a favor for a prolonged sick leave or a gift for a potential promotion.

Every once in a while, however, greed or nostalgia would stop the trajectory. The bottle would be opened with friends for a special occasion, the cigarettes would be smoked at a wedding, and the lipstick would be applied discreetly for a party at a friend's house, then washed off before the return home. In those rare moments, freed from the street banners, the marching music, the heroic children reporting on their parents for listening to the Voice of America, one could, for a short time, feel different. Inhaling the sweet blond tobacco of a capitalist cigarette—far better than the wet, black Communist variety—gave us the illusion of abundance and high-quality living. We felt we were subversive. Soap wrapped in delicate paper smelled sweeter than boiled fat and made us feel elegant and dignified. A drop of perfume made us forget the smell of our bodies jammed into open trucks—cargoes of mandatory enthusiasm delivered to the train station on our only day off to applaud visiting "heroes." A glass of brandy and a cigarette were an equation for existence. We felt a semblance of happiness, alive and free.

After dinner, Axel, still vehemently opposing Communism, made Karl an offer. "Why don't you cross the Iron Curtain into West Germany and see which system is better. Take my passport —I'm sincere."

Karl's face went white. He covered his ears with his hands and shut his eyes very tightly. Beads of sweat formed on his forehead. He tried to stand up, but Axel grabbed his shoulder and pushed him back down.

"This is not a trap, Karl," Axel said. "Trust me! Take my passport and see for yourself."

Karl screamed in terror.

The bartender saw Karl contorted on his chair and called to someone in the kitchen.

"*Otet! Adu otetul ca moare omu!* Vinegar! Bring vinegar, the man is dying!"

Axel shrugged his shoulders and retreated into himself.

The cook brought out vinegar, which the bartender massaged on Karl's forehead and arms. The acid smell made Karl cough.

The bartender moved away from him and, with a look of compassion, said, "He needs some pussy."

From his chair Axel nodded, "Ah, so!" and having no clue about the meaning of the words, ordered some sweet wine. I was reading nearby, and from the corner of my eye, I noticed the bartender bringing Axel the wine. He smiled at me, slowly moving his tongue over his lips, and left telling a final poem in honor of the Oceanic Fish:

> If you eat fish from the ocean
> And drink water from a well
> You will never dream of pussy
> And your prick will never swell.

As dusk fell, we moved the chairs over by the windows. The soldiers were walking their dogs in the rain. Slowly the night hid the airport. The lights from the watchtowers started sweeping the sky. At regular intervals the bright lights flooded our room, keeping us awake. When the airport official burst into the room, only Karl was sleeping. He had opened his suitcase, propped it upright against a wall, and put his head inside, to hide from the lights.

The airport official came over to Axel, waving his arms and talking loud and very fast.

"*Avion* Istanbul?" he said. "Two day. No two day; now go Tirana, Albania. Chinese *avion una ora. Eins.* One." He pointed to an imaginary wristwatch, saying, "Go, go, Chinese friend. Tirana *avion* Istanbul, O.K.?" I understood that there was a special flight to Tirana on a Chinese airline. Axel could fly with them and catch a flight to Istanbul. I also understood that I would not leave and I stopped a scream of fear by covering my mouth with my hand. Then I started to cry. Not sobbing and not weeping—trickling lament from my breath and tears from my eyes. The sorrow was equal to the weight of my fear, and Axel understood. "And she?" he asked the official. "She also has to go," and he took my hand and motioned toward the door.

"*Nein, nein, document kaput.*"

"*Document sehr gut,* you understand," Axel said in anger. "Get her document. Now!"

The man shook his head, "*Nu se poate*, not possible."

"Of course possible," Axel yelled at him, his face red and his fist in the air. "I refuse to leave without her. Go tell that to your comrades."

Karl woke up, and when he understood what the commotion was about, he too tried to help me.

"I represent the Communist government of the Democratic Republic of Germany. In the name of the workers I declare that you do not have the right to detain the documents of a stateless person. You have to let her go. It is in the Geneva Convention. If you don't let her go, I will send a report to the Central Committee in Moscow. It will be an international incident."

My mind was blank. I couldn't understand their words. While Axel was cursing Communism, Karl took the airport official by the shoulders and walked with him to the windows. When I heard them laughing, I knew I would leave.

"*Repede, repede*, hurry, hurry," the official yelled, handing me the document.

Axel and I picked up our bags. As we were leaving, Karl said, "Death to Capitalism."

"Good-bye, Karl. See you in Berlin—on the other side of the wall."

"Thank you," I muttered.

IN TRANSIT

The plane was almost empty. Thirty or so Chinese passengers dressed in dark blue Mao-style jackets were going to a ping-pong competition in Albania. A white curtain with Mao's face embroidered in red separated the main cabin from the cockpit. At his chest Mao held a smiling child. Each time the curtain opened, Mao's face grimaced comically. When the curtain was only half-open, his mouth seemed to be biting the child.

Axel and I were given the front-row seats. Axel could not take his eyes off Mao's face. He studied it for a long time and then, pointing at the folds, started to laugh.

The Chinese flight attendant distributed red booklets and took our attention away from the curtains. "It must be the menu," Axel said. I was giddy with anticipation. I had never seen Chinese food.

The flight attendant pushed the curtain aside and the copilot passed through to our side of the cabin. Mao's eyes winked at us. The loudspeakers blasted a cheerful Chinese melody. Then the copilot and the flight attendant opened their red booklets. Stroking the air with chopsticks, they began conducting an imaginary orchestra, and all the passengers started to sing. Eventually, Mao's name became discernible.

Realizing the function of the red booklets, Axel started laughing loudly. He turned his body to the window, covered his eyes with his left hand, and with the other, slapped his leg in rhythm to the music. Seeing his body shaking with laughter made me laugh, also. Embarrassed, I turned the other way. I managed to contain myself for a few minutes—until a plate of food was handed to me. Cut into small squares, the salami sandwiches from the airport had been transformed into Chinese food!

Axel turned back to look at me, and when he caught my eye, we both burst into laughter again. Across the aisle, a young man started laughing, and after him, in a split second, everyone on the plane was laughing with us. Encouraged by this sudden camaraderie, Axel and I—laughing now without restraint—shook hands above the empty seat between us. During our final descent into Tirana, the Chinese copilot handed us red buttons with Mao's profile on them.

We were met in the terminal by Albanian soldiers wearing the same uniforms, holding the same machine guns, and tethered to the same dogs as the Romanians. "You do not have an entry visa," a bored soldier told us in Russian. "You must stay in the international transit lounge." He then read to us from a book:

In Albania there is no unemployment, no corruption, no foreign debt. Women have been freed from the veil, and thanks to our glorious leader, Comrade Enver Hoxha, our country is self-sufficient. Please do not engage in conversation with our citizens. You and they will be arrested. Singing is forbidden in bars and restaurants. Thank you for visiting the only atheist country of pure Communist ideology. Have a nice stay.

Waiting for the next plane, we talked about Karl and his decision to help me. What could he have said to the Romanian official to make him laugh? And how did they understand each other?

"Maybe they both know some Russian," I offered—"surely Karl does."

"He must have promised him something. They all take bribes."

The short flight to Istanbul brought us into the city as the sun was rising from the Asian side. With a few hours to spare before our next flights, Axel hired a car and invited me to visit the city. The bridge over the Bosporus, the minarets, and the blue tiles of the mosques were glowing like supplicants of light. On a corner street children were singing around a man and his dancing bear. Axel felt poetic. Pointing at the wooden houses on the other side of the Bosporus, he declared that Istanbul was a flower with open petals that envelop you in sweet smells and curved lines. We had lunch at Pera Palace, a musty, charming place where Mata Hari, Agatha Christie, and Greta Garbo—women whom Axel admired —had once stayed. As I listened to him, I made the mental calculation that Israelis always do when they meet a German. How old was he? Had he been a Nazi? Had he seen the Jews from his city being deported? Where was he when my parents and their friends were being sent to concentration camps? He was the first German I had met, and I began to feel uncomfortable around him. What did he think about Jews and Israelis? Perhaps, stored on my retina, the despair that burned in my parents' eyes whenever Germans were mentioned was visible to him. I looked down to protect my parents. Why didn't I dare to ask him anything about his past? Because I knew that whatever his answers might be, I wouldn't trust him? Perhaps he was guilty, perhaps he was brave, and perhaps he was sorry. No matter what, I knew that Germans were to be kept at a distance and treated with cold civility.

After lunch, we headed back to the airport and went our separate ways. For years afterward we sent each other postcards from our travels, and once we met in Cyprus by chance. But I never asked him what he had done during the war or told him my parents' stories.

2

As the Germans were being defeated, refugees of war trailed in the wake of the Russian army, crossing the devastated countries of Europe. My parents were among them. They did not know each other then, but both went south hoping to break the British blockade and join their families in Palestine. They met in Romania during their long wait for travel documents. I was born there.

Norah, my mother, was from Adah Kaleh, an island on the Danube. It was a small Turkish colony whose Jewish population numbered some forty families. The inhabitants were known for their rose gardens and their sweet tobacco. My mother spoke Turkish and knew how to make rose-petal jelly.

Aram, my father, was born in Vienna and grew up in Budapest. But my grandfather, Rafa'el, his father, Nathan, Nathan's grandfather, Yakov, and Yakov's great-grandfather, Abranel, had all been born in Palestine under Ottoman rule.

Earlier records, saved by other generations, show that before moving to Palestine, my father's family had lived in Morocco. They were traders on the caravan route that in the 1200s brought gold from Ghana into the Iberian Peninsula. They named themselves *Ravayah*, hoping that the name, "overflowing" in Old Hebrew, would bring them abundance. The word also means saturated, as when a field has immeasurable bounty. "My cup is *ravayah*," King David says in the Psalms, and the word is even more mystical because its numerical value is equal to King David's cup: 221 measures. It was a good name; it began with *Resh*, which due to the mystery of its two distinct pronunciations is the most important letter of the Hebrew alphabet. Soft *Resh* is rolled from the tip of the tongue, while hard *Resh* is pronounced with the tongue down, spread out between the teeth. The hard pronunciation of this consonant indicates peace and was deliberately concealed in all words by the High Rabbinical Tribunal to recall the destruction of God's Temple. The Sanhedrins of Tiberias knew its original pronunciation, but they sacrificed its sound with the promise to give it back in time of peace, when the Temple will be rebuilt.

The curious phonetic history of the proper pronunciation of *Resh* is an ongoing debate. Anyone who speaks Hebrew knows that the strong *Resh* refuses to come out the right way. To this day, since nations are always at war, many scholars are waiting for peace so that they can hear its true sound.

The name Ravayah pronounced with a soft *Resh* was chosen by our ancestors, who lived in the lower hills of the Atlas Mountains at the end of the Zíz Valley in Morocco. Several families named Ravayah are still living there today. They are jewelry makers. The trade involves little fixed capital and easily transportable tools. It is a mobile skill that one can take anywhere, and a way to secure convertible investment—one can pack up a fortune at a moment's notice.

The records also show that from Morocco, some family members went to Andalusia, where they prospered for several generations. In time, as the Catholic kings started to persecute the Jews and the Inquisition put pressure on them, the Ravayahs converted to Catholicism and sought refuge in Portugal, where they lived in the mountain village of Belmonte. They were called *Conversos*, Converted, Pork-Eaters, *Nuevos Cristianos*, New Christians, *Marranos*, Swines, or *Anusim*, the Forced Ones. After a short stay in Portugal they escaped to Sabbioneta, a city-state in Lombardy. Surrounded by *lulavim*, curved palm branches, the family's name is still carved on the houses in Sabbioneta where they once lived. The presence of the palm tree—symbol of man's vertebral column—shows that the family believed in a divine omnipresence. They bent their backs to serve God, just as a palm tree bends in the wind.

The family members who went to the Yizra'el valley in Palestine arrived there in the summer of 1264. Only Hanah, her father, Abraham, and her husband, Dawud, left Morocco. First they sailed to Ancona, then to Haifa. There, they received protection from Baybar, the sultan of Mamluks, who allowed them to set up a trading post at Endor in exchange for a tax on gold. Endor, as the name says, was a natural spring, at a major crossing point, where the road between Africa and Asia met the one to India and Spain. From the four cardinal points, caravans arrived at the trading post to exchange travelers, news, and merchandise with other caravans going in the opposite direction. From Baghdad, Damascus, and cities as far east as Cochin, caravans bearing spices, silk, and choice rugs, as well as sacks of grain, amber, and salt, passed through the valley. Through the arriving and departing caravans, Hanah sent messages to her family urging them to keep close connections with her and with their relatives from other lands. In time, and as the trading post prospered, her father established rules of family conduct, asking that before marriage every firstborn come to the trading post at Passover time. He believed that keeping family ties would ensure worldwide connections and prosperity. Working at the trading post also meant that all firstborns knew the physical place to which they belonged. It was their home. "It is so that they know where they are coming from," Hanah's father said. "It is so that the family finds continuity in the future. When money for passage is necessary, the closest family on that land should help, and I will reward them myself."

From wherever they lived, each firstborn came to the trading post and girls as well as boys were trained in the rules of lending and gold exchange. They were also taught writing and the mysteries of the Books. Each of them chiseled in the stones a personal message under their names. Each of them wrote the story of their family on large sheets of parchment that were attached to a scroll. The information was updated as the links were maintained and news from other relatives arrived. This tradition of *Pasquar*, going to the Holy Land for Passover, ensured an abundance of connections to far-reaching destinations.

Returning to one's own home was permitted only when the next firstborn arrived. But since the Jews were not always allowed to travel, and the ships of the Italian republics were sometimes late, one could wait many months, stranded, until a boat or a passing caravan brought a new relative. Disrespect of the ancestral law was punishable by the family's rabbi, and *herem*, a ban, was put on those breaking the link. They were excommunicated, invisible to their family, and forever abandoned. As the records show,

Pulssa di Nura, the Whip of Fire, a ceremony conferring a terrible curse, was performed with great success against several members of the family.

In time, the trading post became known as Hanah's Paradise for the exotic trees and flowers growing there. Visiting family members would take home a shoot of the golden bamboo that grew between the gates of the garden and would chisel into plaques of stone a thought by which their stay at Hanah's Paradise could be remembered. From their countries they sent back donations for the grove, along with descriptions of their lives and other family stories. Only the Inquisition and, later, the Nazis interrupted this tradition. During such times, the burden of keeping up the garden and the trading post fell to the family branches from Palestine. But in times of peace, every firstborn and his or her firstborn made the journey to Hanah's Paradise. Even those of us from Communist countries, like my father and me, who weren't allowed to travel and for whom Hanah's Paradise was a mystical place, dreamed of going there not only because it was our obligation but because we needed to make the myth a reality.

As was done before him, my grandfather, himself a firstborn, compiled many of the family records. The information was entered on a scroll, and births, death, visits, marriages, financial transactions, travel journals, letters of credit, wills, deeds, complaints, promissory notes, and stories were kept chronologically and transcribed exactly as received, in the language and spelling of the author. The text was written in the center part of the scroll, leaving large margins for newly revealed details and for references to other family ties. This cross-reference system enabled my grandfather to find and read the story of his remote cousin Don Simeon and tell it to my grandmother, who wrote it down and left it on her dresser. My father found it and, after reading it, told it to his sister, then both of them told it to me. When I was able to read the story for myself, I felt drawn to this man, Simeon, and to the events of his life. He was passionate and curious, solitary and sentimental, attributes that I recognized in my father and grandfather, and perhaps also in myself. My father was a firstborn and wanted nothing so much as to write his name in the family records. But he never did. I wrote his story, and then mine, because I, too, am a firstborn and live at Hanah's Paradise.

3

In the summer of 1498, after his cousin from Yemen arrived at Hanah's Paradise to replace him, Shimon Ben Ravayah did not return to the city of his birth, Zaragoza. A caravan brought a message from his father informing him that while Shimon was at the trading post, the rest of his family in Spain had been converted and was now Christian. Ridiculed for their transformation, fearing that redemption was not sufficient to save their lives, they had fled to Portugal where King Manuel's Edict accepted the Jews, offering them protection for 20 years. They joined distant cousins established from around 1300 in western Beira. They paid an entrance tax to the Portuguese king and a tax to the Church to validate their new names. In Portugal they believed they could be considered true Christians; only the family would know that they were *conversos*, converts. Since Shimon was not converted, his father had sent him strict written instructions about how to dress, what to carry in his bags, what language to speak on the road, and where to stop for food and rest. To obscure his origin, his father recommended that he modify his name from Shimon Ravayah to Simeon Raveyra, still keeping the first letter, *Resh*. The name made Don Simeon think of a river, and he envisioned within himself the strength of a rushing mountain stream. He was also told to remove *la rota*, the yellow circular piece of fabric sewn *en un lugar visible del petcho*, on a visible place on his coat, which identified him on the road as a Jew. Finally, Simeon's father suggested that he cut his hair and beard, to *arapar*, alter his image.

"For the time being, and as you, my son Simeon, can see for yourself, a beard is not a sign of intelligence—otherwise, goats would speak. *Nahon? Isn't that so? Nao e verdade?* Is this not true?" his father wrote to him.

Don Simeon carried with him a shoot of the golden bamboo—
a gift sent to his parents by the family at Hanah's Paradise. He
traveled by land from *Yerushalayim* to Cairo, stopped in Alexandria, then went by boat to Tangier, where another cousin gave him
money and instructions on how to reach his parents. The letter
he had to show on his journey read that Don Simeon Raveyra, of
age seventeen, coming from Alexandria, was to go to Belmonte in
Portugal. He was summoned there to teach gardening and astron-
omy at the house of Senhor Pedro d'Albeu Arcozelo y Amanda
Oxian Cabral Da Cunha.

After seven months on the road, Don Simeon reached the fortified hill town of Belmonte and found the thirty-six members of
his family leading a new life in a house overlooking the Zêzere
Valley. They had altered their names and their clothes to imitate
those of the Christians and were not afraid to put forbidden foods
on the table. His father, Abravanel Ben Ravayah, was now called
Don Alfonso Raveyra da Silva; his mother, Malkah, called herself Reina, and his sisters, Sarah, Rebecca, and Lea, were called
Susanna, Rafaela, and Laeticia.

The house was in the part of the village called *Marrocos*. The
inhabitants, with the exception of the *Senhor* and several peasants
living in the woods, were Jews from Morocco who must have felt
safe enough in 1296 to build a synagogue, which still existed. But
recently, Senhor Pedro Cabral Da Cunha, the owner of the village
and the valley, had returned from a long voyage to the newly discovered continent to find his village inhabited by more Jews fleeing the Spanish Inquisition. The *Senhor* called for a census of his
population. The new residents went into lamentations. Jewish law
forbids equating Jews with numbers. Taking a head count, num-
bering them, could bring affliction to the land. After many arguments, it was agreed that each person would give one silver coin
to the *Senhor*. This particular manner of counting convinced Senhor Da Cunha to allow the Jews to stay. After the money was col-
lected, he converted all the Jewish families living on his land to
Catholicism. Anyone who opposed him was forced to leave without any protection or property. Don Simeon's family, who had
already been converted while in Spain, converted again. They
didn't want to move from place to place, to take new names in new
countries and adopt new habits. They wanted to stay.

In Portugal, Don Alfonso's skills in drawing maps of the world and charts of the sky were well respected. From his family's connections he received requests for new maps of the Mediterranean harbors and trading routes. Crisscrossed by thirty-two lines showing the directions of the winds, Don Alfonso's hand-painted portolan charts were based on realistic descriptions from people who sailed the coasts. His life was his work. He loved to shape the continents, to color the countries and the harbors, to draw, lions, camels, sea monsters, cherubs holding trumpets and squeezing winds out of a bag, and unusually clothed inhabitants. He was also agreeable in changing the names of places at the patron's request.

The Greeks called the North African coast, the land of the Copts, *Aiguptios*. The Arabs called it *Misr*. The Jewish merchants referred to it as *Mitzraim*, the narrow place. The Spaniards called the area *Egypto* and its inhabitants *Egyptanos*, from the word *gyp*, a wild flower that grows in North Africa. Seen from the Persian Gulf, Tunisia was called *Ifriqiya*. Viewed from Rome, the Mediterranean Sea was called *Mare Nostrum*, Our Sea.

Doña Reina kept the family connections with merchants roaming the seas, invested money in nutmeg and pepper from the coast of Malabar, and traded gold and precious stones from Africa. The family was affluent and felt integrated into the Portugal of the late 1490s. Secretly, they kept kosher dietary laws in their household and lit candles on the Sabbath. They spoke French, Spanish, and Portuguese in public, and a mixture of Hebrew, Turkish, and Arabic among themselves.

On the first Sunday he arrived in the village, Don Simeon was taken to Mass to be introduced to the Catholic priest. Simeon liked the church; it resembled a synagogue with round walls and painted windows. His mother's delight in singing the Christians' songs came as a surprise to him. She sang *"Cordeiro Senhor quem cuida los pecados dao mondo, por nossas compaixão,* Lord, our Lamb who in your compassion forgives the sins of the world," in a clear and pure voice, like an angel sent from Heaven. To her son's dismay, Doña Reina ignored her obligation to receive God's words standing up. Instead, she knelt and prayed in the manner of the Christians. Not only did she respect the *hukkath hagoi*, the Gentiles' ways, but she wore a golden cross on her dark skin. When Don Simeon asked his mother about the prayers to the new God, she looked at him with love and answered with reassurance: "They are only words, *djanim*, my soul, and words don't have to mean what you think or feel. Speech is an act of faith, translating universal feelings."

Simeon thought his family had betrayed their God and wondered what price they would pay for it. He felt an immense solitude. There was no place for him. He was a Jew who had changed his name and who had to feign love for a God for whom he felt only indifference. Accepting the Christian faith meant punishment from his own God and from the new one as well, since his belief was insincere.

"Simeon," his Mother told him, "you studied the Talmud at Hanah's Paradise. Do you remember the passage where God said, 'Although he had sinned, he must be considered a Jew?' And pay attention my son, He didn't say 'he must consider himself a Jew,' He said he must *be* considered one, meaning by others. And Simeon, I am your Mother and I consider you a Jew."

Don Simeon felt sad and confused. After several months of questioning his sins, he went to speak with his father.

"Here I have to live in deception. I have to believe in my own lies, then free myself from them enough to go to church and cry for my misfortune. For me this is not possible. Father, I am scared."

"Simeon," his father said, "you are not the only one who is scared. We are all living with conflicts and contradictions. We do not want to betray or to lie, but neither do we want to die. We are Christians with the awareness that we are also Jews, and with the fear that this might be discovered. No matter what, we will always be Jews because we were born that way. This can never be changed."

"Seniyor Baba," Simeon answered after some thought, "I feel that I am two people. One is Simeon who feels guilt and pain, and the other is Simeon who feels shame and fear. Let me go back to Hanah's Paradise; there I can be myself and can live peacefully with the Turks."

Don Alfonso listened to his son, then, using words from the Hebrew prayers, said, "You may go if you want to but remember that *Baruhu, Baruh Shemo*, praised be His name, gave Moses the written laws, and you are not Moses. The words you say, think, and feel do not have to coincide. The most important thing is to say what is appropriate for each situation. And that depends on the audience."

"But, Father, if I can think like that, others can also think the same way, and therefore I cannot put my trust in what I hear around me."

"Words, my son, can both reveal and conceal! Saying a Christian prayer in Portugal does not mean you are betraying your God in Jerusalem. Do not feel *merkeiyozo*, anxious. We are simply adapting to circumstances that we cannot control." Don Alfonso believed that God was aware of the dilemma his children faced, and that it was better to be a *Marrano que vive*, an alive swine, than a dead Jew. As the proverb says, "A lion in a cage is better than a dead cat."

Don Simeon took his father's advice and considered with curiosity his encounter with the new God.

Doña Reina asked her family to remember Purim, the holy day described in the Book of Esther. "On this most joyous day, we tell jokes and laugh at each other. We even make fun of our rabbis. We dress in different clothes, put masks on our face, and take other identities, hoping to ward off fate. Appearance is deceitful. We are living in a Catholic world and should disguise ourselves as Catholics. We have to keep an invisible Christian mask on our minds and on our faces and behave as if every day were the carnival of Purim. God's ways are sometimes mysterious, but we know that *Baruch Ha'Shem*, blessed is He, wants us to keep our traditions for ourselves and teach them to our children. God is asking us to live as Christians, *le Ade lo yada*, until I don't know when, until nobody can distinguish anymore who we are. We will live like them, but in our minds we shall remain like us! The doubt that comes from the belief in a belief is not a lie. We live on Earth and should enjoy every day of this carnival because this is our life. Whenever it is possible, we should put the masks aside and act in accordance with the covenants made with our own God."

Don Alfonso leased an olive grove in the valley, and bought a piece of land in the village to build a large house for his extended family. The rooms, arranged around an interior hexagonal courtyard, had large windows to welcome the breeze and potted trees on the roof to provide shade. In the courtyard, Don Alfonso shaped two vines into an arch and made an altar from a piece of white stone. On the altar he engraved a saying he knew from his father:

With Wisdom, a house is built.
With Understanding, it is established.
With Knowledge, its rooms are filled.

From the roof terrace Don Alfonso could see the entire olive grove and the road climbing to the village. In front of the house he built a well. On its north side he inscribed, in Latin, *"Felix qui potuit rerum cognoscere causas,* fortunate is he who is able to understand the causes of things," and on the opposite side, *"Credo quia absurdum,* I believe because it is absurd." A small metal cross with the inscription, *"Sol lucet omnibus,* the sun shines on everyone," floated in the air above the fountain. Don Alfonso was hoping that this would please the Catholic king and his informers, should either be passing by. Above the front door in colored-glass mosaic, he wrote his personal belief:

Understand with Wisdom.
Be Wise with Understanding.

Doña Reina planted several palm trees in the courtyard to remind her family that just as the palm tree bends in the wind, so, too, should they "bend their backs" to serve God. Golden bamboo from Hanah's Paradise grew in a big pot near the entrance to the kitchen. Inside the house Doña Reina covered the floors of the rooms with rugs from the Atlas Mountains. In the main room, facing the large mirror, she hung a painting of Jesus entering the Holy City of *Yerushalayim.* In the background, the painting showed Mount Zion, the Pool of Siloam, Gethsemane, the Mount of Olives, and *Shaar HaRakhamim,* the Golden Gate—which will open only when the Messiah comes. Doña Reina liked the painting. Jesus on a white horse was just another pilgrim, and if the Christians loved him and believed he was their Messiah, she had no objection to having him in her house. The painting's reflection in the mirror gave Doña Reina the illusion of walking in the streets of the city of David. Surrounded by the beauty of Jerusalem, she felt holy. "The meaning of life," she thought, "entails a circular understanding. The answer has many parts. I, on my own, I found a way to make the loop a straight line."

Her greatest difficulty was concealing the menorah. A Jew has the obligation to pray for *ner tamid*, light to be eternal. The menorah is a specific Jewish ritual object supporting seven oil lamps in a row, always lit on Fridays for the prayer. Doña Reina's menorah was made of a simple straight column topped by a horizontal piece of wood into which seven small copper cups for burning oil were inserted. To make it acceptable to the Christians, Doña Reina asked her husband to add seven extra cups to the existing menorah and extend the column above the line of cups to form a cross. On the horizontal arm, Doña Reina hung fourteen medallions depicting scenes from the Stations of the Cross. Embossed in copper, Jesus walks on the Via Dolorosa, falls, meets his mother at the fourth station, then Veronica, a friend, wipes his face. He falls again, stands up, admonishes the women of Jerusalem, talks with Shimon, falls again, stands up and walks, gets nailed to the cross, gets taken down and put in the sepulcher. Suspended in the air, the copper plates moved each time someone passed or a door was opened. The place of the menorah was changed according to need:

> He who wishes wisdom let him face south.
> He who wishes wealth let him face north.
> He who wishes health let him face between.

At the church Doña Reina praised the glory of Jesus with the congregants, but in private she called him "*um altro ebreo*, just another Jew; a *BenAdamlik*," she said, nothing more than a son of Adam, to which the Turkish suffix "*lik*," meaning "small," was added, just to show how *minim*, insignificant, he was. When everybody else in church was singing "*Em Jesu Cristo creio*," Doña Reina followed along in Portuguese, replacing the words of the prayer. "*Em Jejum Crista' creio*, I believe in clear fasting," she shouted guiltlessly, timing her words with the original song and mispronouncing them to respect the rhymes.

To communicate with her family in front of other people, Doña Reina inserted Turkish, Arabic, Greek, Castilian, and Hebrew words into the Portuguese. This lingua franca became a code that only family members could understand. *"Bom dia* Senhor *Dnlm,"* Doña Reina would say to the priest, mumbling the Hebrew words *"Adonai ulam,* my Master of the Universe," from which she eliminated the vowels. "Only my family knows the vowels of my words," she thought, "so I am safe. After all the Torah scroll is written only with consonants; we supply the vowels when we read it."

They draped the Portuguese over the fusion language of their thoughts like a silk shawl. The irony, the distance, the nuances, the devastating humor of a language with double meaning allowed Doña Reina and her family to conserve their Jewish identity. Words on loan from other languages, false friends—words that sounded alike but had different meanings—gave Doña Reina a range of possibilities for communicating. She said what *she* wanted but let the world hear what *they* wanted. *"El Senhor dichiya muntchos palabras,* the Lord told me many words," she would say to the priest. Only her family knew that *palabras,* Spanish for "words," means "lies" in Turkish.

For Don Simeon the connection with Jesus as the Messiah remained unclear. He agreed that Mary, a sorrowful-looking woman, could perform miracles, because he believed women capable of that. But how an eternal God could look old and how Mary could give birth and still be a virgin were mysteries to him. Don Simeon prayed for a miracle:

> God Almighty, who, in Your wisdom,
> Allowed Mary to give birth without knowing man,
> Allow me to know women
> Without them giving birth.

Don Simeon studied the paintings on the walls of the church. The Virgin was floating on a celestial throne and the saints around her stood in a hierarchy of height. They carried golden round plates on the backs of their heads, which Don Simeon found absurd. The same Virgin, a painted plaster statue, was also seated in a niche overlooking the assembly. People kissed her plaster feet and the inscription below her purple dress: "What have I done, my children, to deserve such insults?"

Don Simeon put his forehead into the Virgin's hand as if he was kissing it, and whispered that "Suffering is not noble, and turning the other cheek only brings more pain."

"Senhora Madre," Don Simeon said, "you may not know this, but in the Book of Numbers 'nothingness' has the same numerical value as the name Yieshu. I believe the Catholic Son of God is an empty image, *bli-mah*, without anything. *Alenou le shabbeah*, it is our duty, to tell this to the priest."

In Don Simeon's view, he and all the members of his family could not conceive that a plaster image could change one's life, but God's words could, because with them, He created a world.

God made the letters of the Hebrew alphabet
And with them He created the universe.

First He made man and gave him magic.
Then He made Woman and gave her illusion.

Next He gave man wisdom, and woman understanding
And with them, man and woman coupled.

He then gave them a square to build a house,
A circle to mark the time, and a triangle for stability.

"When we talk, we invent our world," Don Simeon told his mother. "God put his spirit in every letter, and his lust in every thought. The priest prays to an idol, and he can say, 'I look like God; He made me in His own image.' But I don't have an idol, so I have to say, 'I think like God because He made me with His understanding.' This is the difference, Mother. And since an argument is not a contradiction, I would like the priest better if he wouldn't say that the Talmud is a work of blasphemy and that Jesus is the true Messiah. This is *uma babacada, uma tonteria*, a stupid thing!"

"Simeon," Doña Reina admonished him, concerned that somebody might hear her son's impertinence. "You show disrespect. Our priests talks like the great *Maymunidis*." Don Simeon stared at his mother in disbelief. She had combined the Turkish word *maymun*, monkey, with the Greek patronymic *idis*, belonging to.

She had just insulted the priest. The newly invented word *maymunidis*, monkey, sounded like Maimonides, the Jewish philosopher also respected by the Christians.

Doña Reina tried to prove to her son that going to church was akin to going to see the poets, the gypsies, the singers, and the jugglers when they passed through the village. Didn't he remember the famous yearly carnival on the streets of Zaragoza? People in costumes were reciting poems, or singing; bears and horses were dancing, giants swallowed swords and spat fire—he used to love the carnival. "Same thing in the church," she continued. "People in priests' costumes recite stories, have oratorical disputations, we sing with them, we light candles and pay at the door when we leave."

"*Si*, Senhora Madre," Don Simeon answered sadly, "but the priests praise their own glory, and burn Jewish books."

At the Church, his mind wandered and he imagined himself at the pulpit, dressed in the costume of the priest, telling stories from Hanah's Paradise, telling the worshipers, "The Talmud was there before Jesus and the Bible; why not believe in both of them." He also imagined that a column of light could replace the crude statue as he couldn't bring himself to kiss the plaster dress of the Virgin Mary.

He discussed the matter with Don Alfonso, who directed him to learn medicine from his uncle Botarel before he was deemed a nonbeliever and tortured to death. But Don Simeon didn't like to be around sick people. Secretly, he would have preferred to be a poet, singing the glory of love.

"Father, I find myself in a dilemma," he confessed. "I can pray without believing but I can't make poetry without loving the words. I can sing a hymn to Mary but I can't write a poem for her."

To reconcile his own uncertainties, he began writing biblical commentaries, offering examples from imaginary events. He made *kemeos*, amulets and charms, which he believed had the power to induce prophetic dreams in which Adam himself disclosed the future.

When Don Alfonso heard that his son was rewriting the Bible, he took him for a walk around the ramparts of the village. "Simeon," his father said, "I understand that after you returned from Hanah's Paradise you felt confused about our new life here.

Please keep in mind that even though we were baptized and changed our names and way of life, for the Church a new conversion is a false conversion. The priests are watching and the neighbors are spying. *Il Nuovo Cristiano* is bitterly hated, subject to suspicion and harassment, despised and reviled as heretic by the Church. Should we come under the suspicion of the Church, it will not be difficult to prove that we do not have the required *limpieza del sangre*, clean blood. We gave up our Jewish identity for the right to live, but to the Church, we are still Jews. You are my firstborn, and it would pain me to see you hurt, or to see us wandering the roads in search of a new place to live. If we are punished with exile, we will not survive. I want you to understand, Simeon, that every nation has a fable. And the Christian's fable is about the Virgin Mary and Jesus who ascended into Heaven. Not only does every nation have a fable but each family and each individual has one, too. Please promise me that you will keep your fables to yourself. Do not put our lives in danger! We are foreigners here, and it is only right to keep our differences to ourselves. Learn to live within the secret. Our God, *Elohim*, teaches us understanding, which is what divides *tohu mi bohu*, chaos from void. Tell your fables to the wind or the trees, to the pigeons on the roof, but never tell them to your Christian sisters and brothers. We struggle to free ourselves from oppression and go from darkness to light, but as long as we live in Portugal, my son, we are Catholics."

After this conversation Don Simeon went to church but spoke only about the Virgin Mary's joy in having a child. Otherwise, respecting his father's request, he kept his thoughts to himself. But at dusk he moved his bed to the roof and as the night became darker, he explained to an imaginary audience the nature of Original Sin, the use of words, and his thoughts on women. Later on, he wrote his commentaries on parchment and sent them to Hanah's Paradise, where they were kept under his name, Simeon born Ravayah, converted Raveyra, a firstborn living in Belmonte, Portugal.

He confessed that contrary to what he was told at the church, he was no longer afraid of the primordial sin, hoping to experience it soon, *Deo volente*, God willing, advising his cousins to love and respect women, just as he would do, *Inshâ-Allâh*, God providing.

Dear cousins at Hanah's Paradise,

I hope that my letter finds you well and that the garden is abundant. I want to inform you that here in Belmonte almost everyone used to be Jewish, but now we are all *Conversos* and go to church not to the synagogue. A priest from the town comes to our village every first day, which here some call *Domingo*. He is teaching us about saints, virgins, and sins like being with a woman or eating too much, or wanting something that we don't have. He also said that love of women is the devil. Only love of God and of one's parents is true love. If a priest comes to Hanah's Paradise, you have to know that there is no primordial sin, there is only primordial pleasure. The priests are afraid of women because they can't resist their own temptations. I am ready to love a woman with my body, with my words, and with my imagination. A selfish man loses the trust of his wife. A generous man receives many favors. The priests are married only with their God and can't have children. I am sending you my own understandings so you can be prepared should a black-dressed priest come to Hanah's Paradise to convert you.

DON SIMEON'S COMMENTARIES

On *Tisha be Av*, September 9th of the year 3761, as counted by the Jewish *calendario*, God created the first man, Adam, right in the middle of *Urussalim*. He made him from the *adamah Har Ha Moriyya*, the dust of Mount Moria, whose name means teaching. One by one He made 613 organs, ligaments, and limbs, just as many as the commandments given by God to Moses. After God, blessed be His actions, made Adam, He blew life into Adam's nostrils. This made him *differente*. It gave him a soul. A soul is a long, straight line that runs between good and evil, linking them, with no in-between. Then God looked at Adam and said,

> *Adam ha-Rishon*, Adam, the first!
> I put in front of you
> Life and Death,
> Benediction and Malediction.
> Do as I say!

U'vachcarta bachayeem,
Choose Life and Benediction.

God spoke to Adam in the first language of man, which nobody knew. Once Adam discovered that he could understand God, he used the words to think for himself and said,

The Universe is in a sentence.
God could betray Himself and deny it,
After all, He is the measure and the measurer.
I will do as He says: "Choose Life and Benediction."

Then God said,

Adam, look back! What you see is the past.
You should call that Memory.
Adam, look ahead! What you see is the future.
You should call that Hope.
Now look straight in front of you
And look back over your shoulder.
The time it takes to look ahead, then back, that, Adam, you
    should call Life.

God spoke first; Adam simply answered Him. Then He, in His generosity, gave Adam the privilege of naming things. Adam recognized the essence of animals and named them according to their mission. Then He in His glory told Adam to name action, and Adam called that "verb."

Eternal be His love gave Adam three sounds from one single *shoresh*, verb root. With them, Adam made seven *binyanim*, verb patterns, to describe the many actions that happened to him. Then God put Adam in His garden and said, *"Adam Kadma,"* which means Elemental Man, "even though your place is here, this is *makom sheli*, my place! You must not eat from the Tree of Knowledge of Good and Evil. This is my personal tree."

Adam called Him *Shem*, because he didn't know how to address Him and *Shem* means name and God has no name but Name. "How can I have knowledge without eating the fruit? Please, *Elohim*," which also means understanding, "there is a fallacy in the argument. You must remove the tree from the garden so I will not eat your fruit by accident."

The One named Name, also called *Ruah*, Wind, because He is like a breeze when His love embraces us, thought about this for a while, then answered: "Adam, you can't give me orders just because you call me Name. I was the one who spoke first."

And Adam said to *Shem*, "I don't want to eat any fruit. Right now I just want to know the essence of a She-being. It is getting dark, so I am going to the well to see if I can still find some *hayyot*, some beings, there."

Women Are Desire

In the Garden of Eden, at the evening market, Adam came upon a She-being who had named herself Lilith of the Night. Other She-beings considered Lilith a *mefotzetzet*, an explosion of pleasure and laughter, a real *hatihah*, a beauty, a woman of good decisions, *uma alma generosa*, a generous soul. She had long, curly, red-orange hair, black eyes, and long legs, and she was *orgolliosa*, proud.

Adam took Lilith to the olive grove where he lived and made her repeat after him: "Adam is my master. Say it, Lilith, say it: I really, really, really obey my only master, Adam. Remember those words and repeat after me: Adam *celebilik*, master; Lilith *argat*, daily servant." Lilith repeated the words, and Adam made her his wife.

Lilith liked to sport with Adam, and knew the sounds for how to tempt and seduce a man, how to fire his desires and how to show her passion. "Adam," Lilith said to him, "move your body very slowly when you enter my place. Please, don't rush! Let me feel your limb until I lose my head and I can be delighted. I want to know your stick in my seven openings, just move slowly when you enter my cave."

"It makes me feel good if you rest there when your limb is strong."

"To rest when I move . . ." Adam said, leaving the words to fly around him for a long time. "I don't know how to call that, and if it doesn't have a name, it doesn't exist."

"*Ain adam nolad lamdan*, no man is born a scholar," Lilith said. "Listen to the sound that your stick makes when it enters my half-moon, and call it like that, *foohkh, foohkh, foohkh*. I can teach you how to do it," Lilith answered eagerly.

"You will see for yourself that if, without losing the grip, you go in and out through my open star, there is more delight for both of us."

"*Ha'Shem* asked me to name His actions, not the sounds of your lust, Lilith! *Alavay el Kriyador*, for the glory of God, He said that you will invent delicious meals, repair my clothes, clean the house, bear children, keep family ties, remember everyone's birthday, amuse me with your charms, and always have a cheerful disposition. He told me to use your body as I want. This is why I took you for my wife when I met you by the well at the evening market."

Lilith wrote down the list, then said, "I am your wife, but I will not give you children. Ask God to make them for you. I don't want my body to get fat. I will not take your seed into the opening of my cave. No children."

"And I will tell God that you disobey me."

"Adam, *motek sheli*, my sweet, God has an agreement with *you*, not with *me*! He didn't ask me to have children."

Adam looked at her in irritation and said, "He put His spirit in my seed so I can make life, and He gave me a servant to carry it for me."

"Let us be clear, Adam. When He decided to speak, He did not converse with me! I cannot speak in accordance with His nature. Had the Name addressed His emanations to both of us, I would also be responsible. But He spoke to you, not to me. I don't have to obey His words—whatever He told you about His primordial language, magical songs, or children. Please don't lecture me about your Procreator and don't complain that I do not make the right sounds when you mount me."

Adam went to *Ha'Shem* to ask for advice. After He listened to him, *Ha'Shem* said, "Adam, you must understand. *Lo kol she'elah ra'uyah le teshuvah*, not every question deserves an answer. I taught you how to speak to glorify my name, not to bicker about Lilith. For the sake of my glory, please keep words only for me."

Lilith built a house open to the breeze, overlooking the garden. She situated the kitchen in a quiet, removed place. She planted beds of green vegetables, bunches of sugarcane, clumps of the fig tree, the mustard plant, the fennel plant, the garlic plant, the common beet, the eggplant, the cucumber, and *xanthochymus garcina*, yellow berries, which she used as a dye and a purgative. On the path to the house, she planted *andropogon muricatus*, the tall grass that sways in the evening breeze and is used as a sedative. China roses, yellow amaranth, parsley, and *jasminium magnificum* grew under the windows. She made a labyrinth of laurel trees and put a small pool in the middle, in which a pair of carps played and multiplied. Lilith built everything with her own hands. One hand has five fingers, five fingers have fourteen bones, and in Hebrew fourteen is the addition of two letters, *yud* and *dallet*, which together make *yad*, hand, and with her two hands Lilith built the house:

> Two stones build two houses,
> Three stones build six houses,
> Four stones build twenty-four houses.

Adam was very particular. God hadn't taught him this word yet, so he couldn't say it, but he wanted everything to be done his way, perfectly:

> Lilith of the Night,
> I want my house with seven rooms,
> Not six!
> I want my house with seven rooms,
> Not eight!

After Lilith finished building the house, she put a *mezuzah*, a scroll of prayers, on the left side of the door. And just before they moved in, she let a black rooster walk through the house to bring her good luck. Then she killed it and made a nice meal.

Adam liked the food but not the house.

"It is not perfect," he said.

"Adam, perfection is a measure. Ask the Name to give it to us."

"*You* ask Him," Adam replied, in the whining, boyish voice that she detested.

Lilith was disappointed with Adam but stayed with him, cooking and cleaning, presenting him with her body and caressing his stick as often as he wanted. She even combed his hair. Meanwhile, Adam admired his stick, whistled at the young girls passing by, and waited for God to tell him what to say.

When Lilith of the Night went to the well, she complained that life with Adam was only work and no pleasure for her. "I am disenchanted." One of her girlfriends who was more experienced said, "Before you get married, be sure that you know whom you are going to divorce. Love can be easily replaced by hate. Adam is *imaturo*, egotistic, and pompous. He needs to prove that he is the best. You should be on top of him."

"You are right," Lilith answered.

When she returned home, Lilith said, "Adam, if you can be on top of me, I can also be on top of you."

"Never!" he replied. "And for confronting me with such an ungrateful request, you must write a hundred times, 'Adam is number one.' I want that written on the front wall of the house so everyone can see it."

Lilith wrote it thirty times before she ran out of beet juice. Then she looked at the wall and said to Adam, "Why should I stay with you? You never bring me fruit, never make me a bracelet from flowers, and never tell me nice words. You didn't help with the house; you don't work in the field; you don't feed the chickens. You talk with flowers and play with animals but not with me."

> Build your own house,
> Get your own room.
> From here on,
> Go out and calculate:
> That which the mouth
> Cannot speak,
> And that which the ear
> Cannot hear.

"*Ay un mankamiento*, are you missing my limb?" he asked, pretending to read *Sefer Raziel*, a book about the secrets of Creation given to him by an angel. "Or is it the *kostumbre*, the time of your monthly?"

Adam is rude, Lilith thought, but *agora mijor de estar de kayada*, it is better to remain silent. Why *diskutir*?

But one afternoon, after she had obeyed him with her mouth, she looked at him napping and said, "*Maspik conyorar*, enough lamentations! Men never change! *Tyempo de partensya*, it is time to leave."

When Adam woke up from his rest, Lilith wasn't there. He looked over his shoulder, to the past, and remembered that just after he took his meal, he felt that the universe was sending him a message. The air was warm and pure; the food Lilith cooked filled his stomach; and God's special gift to him, his *aber min*, the limb for sex, felt ready to say some words. Lilith was seated at his feet, cleaning his toenails, and he said to her, "Now you should embrace my head and make it grow." And she did. After he filled her speaking mouth with his pleasure, he lay down and fell asleep. He didn't sleep for very long. When he awoke he whistled for her, even called her name, and when she did not come immediately, he understood that she had gone.

"It was a good embrace," he said out loud. "She was fast with her tongue and her lips were tight. She even knew how to tease my stick with her teeth. Why did she leave?" He could still picture the strands of her orange hair covering his body and could see his celestial foam on her lips. After she had drunk the last drops of his water, Adam had stood there, unable to move. Her small breasts were touching his knees, and in that light of day, looking at her, Adam felt close to God and thought to tell Him about this new embrace, which he named *Amor*. His fingers were still squeezing a nipple when slowly, with his hand, he pushed Lilith's head toward his magnificent organ, still erect from the pleasure of his horniness. He felt her cheek against his wet flesh and with a surge of affection, grabbed her hair, pulling her head backward. She was on her knees, her back straight, and her chin slightly up. He looked into her wide-open eyes and, remembering the feeling of her ruby lips on his straight one, he said lovingly, "Lilith! How was I?"

Adam screamed many sounds and called them *za'am*, fury, then drank the wine reserved for prayers. Several nights later,

Lilith came into his dream. She had fled to the Red Sea and would never return. The following morning Adam sent three seraphim to Lilith with a message. "Return," he said, "and I will make you mistress over the barnyard. I will let you eat the feet, wings, and tails of all the animals you cook for me."

Lilith received the seraphim on the large tiled terrace of her summer house, which overlooked the Gulf of Aqaba. She looked at the angels and admired them one by one. Each had six wings: two to cover their faces when God talked to them, two to cover their feet when they talked to people and animals, and two to fly when they went from here to there. To show hospitality, Lilith offered them something special to eat.

Lilith's Caldo Freddo

Steam your favorite vegetables.

Spread the orange flesh of a mango over the *legumbres*.

Sprinkle with *langues d'oiseaux*, fiery red peppers that arouse good feelings, named that way because they look like little red birds' tongues, although really they are peppers that birds drop while flying over your house.

The angels kindly thanked her for the meal, then delivered Adam's message. As they spoke, they couldn't help noticing the red silk dress that Lilith was wearing. It made her body look so appealing that the angels got erections. Looking at her curly orange hair and her big black eyes, they started rubbing their wings together, caressing themselves under their linen robes.

Lilith considered Adam's message as she listened to the noise of their debauchery. Then, moistening her lips, she said, "Man is selfish. Tell the proud, self-promoting liar that I am busy building a white marble house for me and the Sheikh Al-Satan. He gives me everything and plays with me all day. Soon we shall get married, here in Sharm El Sheik."

The cherubs felt happy for Lilith and offered a congratulatory prayer for her and her new keeper: "Blessed are You, Our Lord, who makes the bridegroom to rejoice with his bride." Then the angels moved their wings, dancing and singing: "*Ay sinyora novya, ke soch namoroza,* ah, *belle fiancée,* may you be in love."

Lilith of the Night smiled politely but ignored the song. "Adam lost his chance," she said, "he acted like a *tembel*, an idiot. He is an *imaturo* mean-spirited man. Tell him to breathe the golden air of Jerusalem. It gives brains even to an ass."

The angels felt a bit stunned since, until then, nobody had ever called Adam such things. So after ejaculating some words, they left.

When the angels told Adam that Lilith was not returning to him, he said, "She is jealous because I look like God and she doesn't. Go and get me another She-being," he commanded them. "Lilith didn't have any fire, even if her hair was like a flame. Make sure this one has lucky marks on her body. I want her to have good hair, good nails and teeth, good ears and eyes. Make sure that her breasts are neither bigger nor smaller than they ought to be." The angels went to inform God.

God looked down.

Adam was drinking from the wine reserved for prayers, and He of light and bounty said to Himself, "Even in Heaven it is better to have a companion. I am alone because I am God, but a man can never live well alone. Adam will be bored and will start to argue with me. This time I will not let him choose. I will make a companion fit for him, one that will obey him."

God waited until Adam had named everything before He of blessed joy gave him a companion. "No need for them to quarrel about the meaning of words," He reasoned. But God didn't want to spend His time to make all organs and ligaments for her as he did for Adam. He took a rib from Adam, put a hole into it, and kissed it to give it a soul.

In the beginning, the creature did not move. Adam touched her body and said, "She looks like me but is *differente*. Her balls are up on her chest, easier to squeeze; her big brown nipples are easier to suck; and she can take my stick inside her, just like Lilith did." Adam pulled apart her legs and pushed aside the dark clouds of her half-moon to peek inside. He named her after him, bone of his bone, flesh of his flesh, wo-man that we call *ish-shah*, made from the word *ish*, or man. He made her *immah*, the mother of everything that lives, and named her Eve, from the word *hawwah*, love.

When Eve woke up and started moving, Adam told her how to look after him:

When you hear the sound of my footsteps coming home, you should get up at once and be ready to welcome me. After you wash my feet, you must be ready to obey me. You should cook only the meals I like. You should always serve me first, sit down after me, get up before me, and never wake me when I am resting. You should never scold me, and you should avoid sulky looks, bad expressions, and standing in the doorway. You must till the fields and take care of the grain; feed the rams, cocks, quails, cows, and goats; then look after and repair the things that I like. You must amuse me with your dances, play the strings, and tell me stories that make me laugh. You should clean and perfume your body with sweet-smelling oils, then obey my magic stick's wishes. You must practice with me the sixty-four meanings of pleasure given by God, and grow my seed inside you for the glory of our Creator. On the days of your indisposition you must take me into your talking opening, or find me another woman with whom I can practice the sixty-four positions.

Adam didn't promise Eve anything in exchange. His pleasure should be her pleasure; serving him well would be her reward. "Man is the norm," he told her. "Woman is the other, and just as the name of God is not separated from God, so it is that my name, Adam, means Man."

Eve nodded her head in approval at each of Adam's demands. She didn't say a word. She already knew everything. Lilith had talked to her in a dream.

"Adam's God doesn't know anything about women. He doesn't have a mother, a wife, or even a sister," Lilith told her. "No one ever held him, no one ever caressed him. He strongly believes that women are necessary only to multiply His sons. Eve, they are taking advantage of you! Have you noticed how they speak their own language and never include you in their decisions? Be aware, my sister, *kol adam cozev*, all men tell lies."

But Eve didn't mind. "I must confess to you, my sister, that I am very happy here in the Garden of Eden. I feel sometimes lonely but I can speak with the flowers and the animals. As for Adam, he has never lain over me. He told me in great secret that he used to have three stones, but lost one after you left. Now he is afraid to come near me."

"*No me diga!* You don't say!" Lilith replied with mischievous delight. "He lost one?"

"You've heard how Adam tells everyone that he had to sacrifice one of his ribs in order for the Name to make me. The truth is that I wasn't made from a rib, a *tzela*, which means side, but a *sela*, which means a stone. I was made from one of Adam's cullions, and Adam is mispronouncing the word deliberately, so people believe that he still has three.

"He also said that women tempt men into the indulgence of the flesh, only to result in the loss of their gonads. Now he diddles around with some boys. They put their stones together, and two and three makes five."

"Less work for you, sister!" Lilith replied.

But Eve felt lonely, and when the fallen angel Samael, the wicked *nahash*, the serpent, asked, "Did God perhaps say, 'You shall not eat of a certain tree of the garden?'" Eve shook her head. "Unh-unh," she said, "God never spoke to me." Then Eve looked at the snake out of the corner of her eye, moved her lips as if to scorn him, and yelled to Adam, "*Mira mira*, look, look, *anguis in herba*, a snake in the grass!" But Adam ignored her. He was *apanayar mouchkas*, catching flies in the shade, waiting for God to give him things to name.

Meanwhile, the serpent, who was infatuated with Eve, noticed that she had blushed when he addressed her. Encouraged, he pushed her toward the *Etz Hadaat*, the Tree of Knowledge, and said, "Have one of these." But Eve turned around to leave. Afraid of losing her, the snake said, "*Hawwah motek sheli, ulai at lo yodaat*, Eve, my sweet, perhaps you don't know, *ve ulai Adam lo amarlach*, and maybe Adam didn't tell you, *aval at meod hushanit*, but you are very sensuous. *Mamash hushanit*, real sensuous!"

"I feel like eating strawberries," she said and bent down to pick a few that were growing beneath that very tree.

But Samael, the snake, wanted Eve to have pleasure with him, as Adam had with Lilith. When the snake saw Adam with Lilith, just like that—naked in a field of yellow flowers, her knees up to keep Adam close to her, him peeking at the red flower between her legs, her white breasts touching his chest, her nipples large and erect, Adam moving his body in and out, in and out, into the half-moon, moaning, biting her hair, kissing her mouth, her eyes, her ears, screaming *yes, yes* while she herself was laughing—the snake became jealous. "Now it is my turn," the snake said. "I will keep this woman for myself, to give *me* the pleasure. I will not let her keep two places in her heart— one for Adam and one for me. For it is said in the Book, '*Aain mal'akh ekhad oshtey she'elot,* not even an angel can fulfill two missions at once.' If an angel had two missions, then it would be two angels." The *nahash* was so sure that she loved him too that he stared at her, singing,

> Soon you will hear
> In the city of Jerusalem
> The voice of gladness—
> And the happiness of my bride
> Rejoicing in my embrace.

As Eve lay down eating the strawberries, the snake circled her breasts and licked her nipples. He licked her orifice with his slippery tongue, aimed to make the guardian of her orifice grow, and inserted his tail through the small opening of the universe. He turned around like a mad dervish until her warm, velvety orifice couldn't stop closing and opening. Then the cunning creature entered Eve all the way, astonished to find her insides *matukah ve raka,* sweet and soft.

Eve had felt something, but not knowing what it was—and it being so pleasurable—she moaned with delight and fell asleep. When she awakened, she was famished. The snake immediately pointed to a fruit and said, "Here, eat this." He pushed a branch lower so she could reach the fruit, knowing that if she ate it, God would chase her from Eden to *Sitra Ahara,* the Other Side. Once God exiled Eve from eternity into history, the *nahash* could become Eve's savior and proprietor.

Eve took the fruit, smelled it, played with it, and then, to the snake's surprise, she gave it to Adam. He put the fruit in his mouth and took a bite. But when he swallowed, a piece of apple got stuck in his throat. Ever since then, all men are born with an Adam's apple planted in their throat. The priests call it apple, but it was a sweet *igo*, a fig, velvety pink like the breast of a young girl, and so smooth you just had to take a bite. After he finished eating most of the fruit, Adam said, "Here, I am not selfish; have the last bite and cover your shame."

When God returned from His Sabbath he went to His garden and said, "Adam, *eifo atah*, where are you?"

"When I heard the sound of You, I immediately told Eve to cover her shame, then I hid."

"How did you know that she was naked?" God asked. "Did you eat from the tree?"

"The woman whom You made to be with me, she gave me the fruit of the tree. I didn't know what it was, but I ate it anyway. It is her fault, and also Yours, for giving me a woman like Eve."

"I will curse both of you for disobeying me. I give you *milah sheli*, my word," God said after he listened carefully to Adam. "All Eves shall suffer great pain in childbirth, and all Adams' limb for sex shall be cut to bleed on their eighth day after birth. Messiah will come only when men are born circumcised."

Dear cousins,

The priest will tell you that all is Eve's fault, that we are born with the guilt of Eve's primordial sin. Don't believe it. The priest will also tell you not to trust women because they are evil. But look at our sisters, look at our mothers; women are wonderful. Remember, my cousins, that Eve is *innocenta*; it is he, Adam, who was ungrateful to God and deceived Eve. I, Simeon Raveyra from Belmonte, inform you that if we do not love women here on earth, we may lose our minds before we enter Paradise. We should prepare ourselves to always love our wives. Even when death will separate us, we will still rest together *en el luguar*, in the cave of Makpélah, just as Adam lies next to Eve, and Abraham next to Sarah.

4

Doña Reina, who took note of her son conversing on the roof and spending the early hours of morning writing to his cousins, brought him *aqua y dulse boyicos*, water and sweet biscuits. Sometimes she stayed to keep him company, encouraging him to seek universal understanding.

Don Simeon felt grateful to his mother. Often they conversed together late into the night, reading from manuscripts in her collection.

"The essence of God is unknowable," Doña Reina said. "'Thou canst see my face,' is what Moses heard. Moses couldn't see God's face, because God—like His children—is in exile from His own creation. Before the beginning, God filled the stuff of nothingness with His luminous essence, and there was never night. But, to create the Earth, God made His luminous emanation smaller and squeezed himself out of His own creation. He sacrificed Himself and left the world that He, Himself alone created so we can have more space. God went into exile, may His sacrifice be rewarded, but He left us Light."

"*Madre,*" Don Simeon said. "I also am in exile. I don't understand my life here. I feel alone."

"*Mi kerido,* my precious son, the One Named God gave you two ears. Listen with one of them and agree with what you hear yourself saying. Then listen with the other one and disagree. Now you can have an argument."

Don Simeon found his mother's advice most helpful. A woman is also a God because her essence is unknowable. He noticed that in his bed *ante luce*, before daybreak, when he sometimes whispered the word *mulher*, woman, her warm body covered his, and on his arms he could feel her form and her delicate hands explor-

49

ing his body. "Alas, *amigos*, words talk about things that are not there, and a word is not a woman, even though I can see her presence in my mind. But, *dum spiro spero*, as long as I breathe, I hope," Don Simeon said out loud.

Don Simeon noticed that often when he thought about the company of a woman, a certain tremor came to his *membrum*. Whenever a young woman was around, Don Simeon felt a strong desire to pull up her dress, cross his hands between her legs, lift her up, and kiss her on the lips. It was a sensation he could not control. He could almost feel the tenderness of a woman's flesh in one hand, and the voluptuousness of a peach in the other. Alone on the roof, he would close his eyes and follow the line between the two halves of the peach, moving slowly, until one finger finally touched the other side and entered into a cave of wonders. "*Be amet*, in truth, one woman is all women, and I love them all. I will imbed my body into my wife and whisper words to impregnate her with my love."

Don Simeon went to church and explained to the priest that a specific part of his body moved out of his control when he thought about women. Unexpected things happened to him. "I looked at them *kada una i una*, one after the other, and I believe that they know what to do with the fire burning within me." Simeon feared that *eyem harim*, a bad spell, had been placed on him and released the tears from his lower body with his own hand. Did the Christians, perhaps, have a remedy for this? The priest told Simeon to stop playing with his cullions and to save his seed for God. Otherwise warts would cover his hands and pimples his skin and he would risk becoming deaf and going to Hell.

Con malenkolía, with great sadness, Don Simeon fasted and prayed for several days, then tied a rope around his waist to separate his thoughts from the unholy stuff below. But his *spermary* ignored the separation and flooded Don Simeon's bed each time he thought about women.

One Friday, when secretly he took the ritual bath, he prayed to the *tevilah*, the purifying virtue of water. That night he received a message from God: "Love and honor all parts of your body." *Con bueno korazon y alegria*, with light heart and happiness, Don Simeon concluded that his emissions were directly connected with the one who is called Name. "*Mersí muntcho*, thank you,

Ha'Shem, for giving me the privilege to emit for You. I am Your servant. I will obey You like Elijah did, *anima et fide*, courageously and faithfully."

Ey'Li'Yahoo, Elijah, went to the top of Mount Carmel and took off his clothes. He looked at his blessed organ and felt the *darshana*, the illuminating glance from his master, the eye of the Eternal Grace gazing back at him at the place of his circumcision. His bosom was filled with joy. He felt ennobled by his *membrum* and thanked God that the barrier standing in the way of beneficial results—his foreskin, the *orlah*, as it is called in the Scriptures—had been removed from him.

Elijah sat on a stone and placed his face between his knees. He moved his head up and down, as God had instructed His people to do during prayer, and the *milah*, the circumcised word in his mouth, made him feel closer to Heaven.

From the valley one could see Elijah's naked body moving back and forth. "There goes Elijah again, eating his words, bending his back to serve the Infinite Being with his prayers," those who saw him would say.

Elijah felt open to the love of God, and the sweet taste of his own words filled him with happiness. An intense spiritual energy descended upon him in conjunction with the mark of his circumcision. In this position, Elijah brought together his ten fingers, his ten toes, his *membrum*, and his tongue, and they numbered twenty-two, as many as the letters in the Hebrew alphabet. He put his living God in his mouth, he held his toes with his fingers, and, as he moved up and down, his body became a book of spiritual essence.

And so, we have learned from Elijah, *beatae memoriae*, of blessed memory, how to concentrate our spirits into the sexual organ. Elijah showed us how to gain complete control over our sexual activities, even in the midst of intercourse. Meditate over the ten toes and sanctify yourself during copulation, and you will be able to determine the qualities of the child to be conceived.

Don Simeon believed that touching his penis pleased God. If *milah* meant both word and circumcision, caressing his *membrum* was truly a form of prayer. He recalled Rabbi Hillel's questions and agreed that they were meant for him:

> Eem ain a'nee lee,   If I am not for myself,
> Mee lee?   Who will be for me?
> V' eem lo achshav,   And if not now,
> Aimatai?   When?

"I will love my wife *le olam vaed*, forever and for eternity. I will respect her as I respect our matriarchs," Simeon concluded.

Esteemed Heroines of My Heart

As they were about to enter Egypt, Abraham said to Sarah, "*Sarai hanum*, Sarah my dear princess, you are a woman of beautiful appearance, and when the Egyptians see you, they will say, 'This is his wife,' and I will be killed. But you, the Egyptians will let live. Please say that you are my sister so that it may go well with me, and that I may live for you."

When the Egyptian officials saw Sarah, they lauded her beauty and took her to the house of Pharaoh. Abraham, who loved her sincerely, was very chagrined but had no choice. He had to let the Pharaoh believe that he could have Sarah as his wife.

For Sarah's sake, the Egyptians treated Abraham very well. He acquired many gifts, because he could not refuse them without arousing suspicion. Sarah, for her part, never told anybody that she was indeed Abraham's wife—and his niece as well. When she lay down with the Pharaoh, she did it only for the love of her husband: to save his life.

But Abraham had committed a sin. By allowing his wife to be with another man, he had put her in danger. He was ashamed of himself. God the Merciful took pity on him, afflicting Pharaoh with *katurize*, an illness that made it impossible for Pharaoh to lie with Sarah.

When Abraham heard about Pharaoh's illness, he said, "*Mersi muntcho Atyo*, thank you very much, God, for inflicting Pharaoh with *katorze*. You assured the chastity of my Princess." And God looked at him from above and said, "Abraham, I didn't give Pharaoh *katorze*; that means fourteen, in French. I gave him *katurize*, diarrhea in Espaniolikos."

Pharaoh couldn't understand why this illness had seized him. He consulted his astrologer, who told him that his affliction was caused by Abraham, who was united with Sarah. So Pharaoh summoned Abraham to his palace. He made the accusation that Sarah was Abraham's wife. Abraham didn't answer. But *qui tacet consentire videtur*, silence is consent, so Pharaoh told him to take his *hore* and to leave Egypt immediately. And so they did.

And how can anyone forget the sacrifice of Lot's daughters? Realizing that there were no men around to ensure the future of their family, they went to bed with their own father.

> Consider Oedipus Rex:
> A myth about
> Addition,
> Multiplication,
> & Substitution.

First they got him drunk. Lot, who was as nice as a little lamb, became aggressive as a lion while drinking, behaved like a pig when he got drunk, and chattered like a monkey when he awoke. They never told him anything. They knew what had to be done and accomplished it, because women have the doorway into the mystery of life. It is called *igul*, a womb, and we men must espouse it. Whoever does not marry lives without joy, benediction, or spirit. Even God, who is alone, encourages us to find pleasure in our wives. For every time that we miss the opportunity to enjoy the company of women, God will punish us. There is nothing in life higher than *oneg*, delight, the Name thinks so, blessed be the love of women.

> God loves women.
> He concerns Himself
> With the creation and study of Beauty.
> It is a science, one could say.

The life of Don Simeon and that of his family was the best-documented story in the Hanah's Paradise records. He lived a long time, wrote in many languages, and kept a close connection with his cousins. Despite the maddening commentaries he wrote to conceal his resentment or his desires, he became a much-respected businessman. He knew how to arrange vast expanses of land into dreamlike gardens with grottos, labyrinths, aquatic features, statues, underwater galleries, and arches. His gardens dotted the landscape from Iberia to Lombardy, and his knowledge of plants made him famous. He designed gardens for the Church and for the prince, for notables and for his friends. In each of them, clumps of bamboo prohibited the visitor from seeing the garden at once. Simeon forced the eye to anticipate the miracle of his design and be surprised by the drama of the landscape. He left several manuscripts with strict instructions on the geometric disposition of plants according to color, texture, smell, and season, and the design of a fountain surrounded by columns and arches forming an ornamental structure. His wedding, his travels, his poems and drawings were well-documented. I searched for his name and those of his children in every footnote and in every entry in the records at Hanah's Paradise. I couldn't stop myself from liking him. He was a much-loved son, and his mother sent a letter to Hanah's Paradise asking for a special prayer and amulet so she could find a good woman to be a wife to him. *"Lo tov heyot ha'adam l'vado,* it is not good for man to be alone," Doña Reina wrote her family at Hanah's Paradise. "We must find a wife for our son." Don Alfonso asked a *shadhan*, a matchmaker, to find his son a *kalla*, a bride, from another *converso* family—to make a *shiddoukh*, a match, and a marriage.

5

The marriage broker, himself a *converso*, no longer allowed to display the distinctive sign of his trade—the red scarf with white dots—found the Mass a perfect place to mingle with other *conversos*. At the church in Coimbra he noticed a young woman who, to enter into the grace of the new God, embroidered white lace for the Virgin Mary.

At twenty-two, Isabel, the oldest daughter of Senhor Piedraverde, *um físiko*, a doctor, was still virtuous. She kept the books for her father, knew about remedies, and had a lovely face. Isabel was quite slim, with long reddish-black hair, dark skin, and big black eyes. Converted in Lisbon together with two thousand other Jews, Isabel had been baptized on a rainy night in 1492 in the Plaza Rossio, just after her fourteenth birthday. Her given name was Bavat Einaym, Apple of My Eye, but the priest had renamed her Isabel. Bavat Einaym did not like her new name. It sounded like Jezebel, the wicked, shameless wife of Ahab, the ancient king of Israel.

Isabel had a way of isolating herself from people, even when sharing the same bench. Her mind always seemed to be somewhere else, but once she understood that someone's words were addressed to her, her two black eyes would follow every sound and her gracious smile would ask forgiveness for being lost in her thoughts.

> I rested a bit
> Between my feelings,
> And went to some
> Unknown place,
> To choose
> My own words.

After all,
The risk of talking
Is mine.

Following the *shadhan*'s recommendation, Doña Reina sent word to the *fíziko* that she was interested in a union with his family. On the appointed day, on her way back from the market in Coimbra, she stopped by the *fíziko*'s house to meet the family and to take a look at Isabel. She had to see the *shadhan*'s choice for herself, since, *"Mi she'aino m'shaker aino yachol lihiyot shadhan,* whoever cannot lie cannot be a matchmaker." Only her own eyes would tell her the truth.

Isabel was not yet married because, as Doña Reina could see for herself, she was not fat enough. She had never been. Her mother had fed her seeds of the fenugreek plant in an effort to help her gain weight, to achieve the double chin and the required body padding that would make her desirable. But Isabel had remained thin, and without a corpulent body, symbol of beauty, wealth, and voluptuousness, nobody had offered to marry her. The *fíziko* assured Doña Reina that despite this flaw, Isabel was in perfect health and of fine disposition. He would not offer to her as a daughter-in-law some chipped piece of pottery!

Doña Reina considered the matter and consulted with her husband. She had to agree with the *fíziko* that Isabel lacked physical appeal, but she was clearly *eshet chayil*, a woman of virtue, and, being almost three years older than Don Simeon, more mature. She would be a good choice for their son. *"Sheker hachain v'hevel hayofee,* charm is deceitful and beauty vain," she told her husband, as her own mother told her when she got married.

Don Alfonso verified Isabel's personality according to the day of her birth. For it was well known that whoever is born on

Sunday shall have distinction;
Monday, anger;
Tuesday, wealth and voluptuousness;
Wednesday, intelligence;
Thursday, benevolence;
Friday, *Mazzal Tov*;
Saturday, piety.

Then he looked into the stars to determine the influence that the bride's name would have on his son's life. He wrote the letters in Hebrew characters, added them up, and determined the numerical value of her name. He divided the sum by twelve to find the sign of the zodiac. Isabel was of the sign *Bethulah*, Virgo. He took this remainder, forty-nine, and divided it by seven. The resulting number was a good sign, *siman tov*. With it he searched the skies. Isabel's celestial sign was the moon, and that made her queen over action, descendant from the tribe of Zebulon. Don Alfonso thought Isabel to be a good addition to the life of his meditative son.

Finally, Don Alfonso asked permission from the landowner, Senhor Cabral Da Cunha, to marry his son and bring the bride's family to his house. The *Senhor* was willing to accept them, as long as they promised to be good Catholics, to respect the Church's rituals, work on the Sabbath, and pay the Church a yearly tax of gratitude, as all new Christians were obliged to do.

Isabel arrived at Don Alfonso's house with her parents, her four brothers and their wives, and her parents' parents. On a mule she brought two dresses, several books, pots of herbs, two goose-feather pillows, a copper bowl for making fig jam, a canary, and several jars of black pepper, salt, and sugar. Because she was not fat enough, two gold bracelets had been added to her dowry. Don Alfonso welcomed the family by the fountain in front of his house. The men kissed each other on the neck, as Jacob had done when he greeted his brother Esau. The women touched one another's heads. "*Ma Bruch*, be blessed," they said, as Naomi had said to Ruth.

Isabel was put in a room, far from the eyes of Don Simeon, and when Doña Reina went to see her, Isabel bowed and kissed her hand. "*Ke seyach mazaloza*, May you be fortunate," Doña Reina said. "Come to us with a good heart and be a good wife to my son."

In the days before the wedding, Don Simeon found excuses to linger around the courtyard, trying to capture his bride's voice and her laugh. Whenever he thought about Isabel, a nervousness he had never before encountered warmed his body. Although he had not seen Isabel and would not see her until the wedding, his mother had assured him that she was the right wife for him. In anticipation of the ceremony, he repeated an Aramaic incantation to anyone who approached the subject of his wedding: "*U chavruta u meetuta,* Either companionship or death."

The couple would be married first in the church, united by the priest and welcomed by Senhor Da Cunha. Their families agreed that, in keeping with Jewish tradition, the blessing at the church would be considered a pre-wedding reception, to be followed next day by the nuptial ceremony, a private affair at their own house.

Doña Reina set tables in front of the church and invited the village to enjoy her son's wedding, making sure that Doña Isabel's face remained veiled. She showed her generosity by offering the guests olives, cheese, jam, and boiled eggs. She also served a dish that her mother had made for her own wedding:

Pão dao Abuela, Grandmother's Bread

Mix chopped almonds with various *aromatos.*
Add sliced oranges, boiled onions, and parsnips.
Mix in green and black olives; add day-old bread.
Sprinkle with olive oil and let sit for the afternoon.

The next day, for the private Jewish wedding at their house, Doña Reina offered her daughter-in-law a *kamea,* a gold charm, to bring her good luck. Her *Ketouba,* marriage contract, written in Aramaic, asked that all her possessions be given to the Church in the event of divorce, which would ensure her a long marriage. Don Alfonso paid Senhor Piedraverde two hundred *zuzim* to keep for her in the event of need.

Isabel looked frail under the sumptuous ceremonial Great Dress. A *fusta,* an ankle-length fan-shaped skirt, and a jacket with flaring sleeves, hid her body completely. A gold-mesh belt, adorned with natural leaves and flowers to bring magic potency to her husband, marked her waist. A velvet plastron embroidered with gold-threaded palm leaves and a stylized pomegranate—symbol of fertility—was a reminder to those who could read the signs that this woman belonged to the tribe of Yizra'el. Isabel had asked Don Simeon for a pearl for their engagement, an aquamarine stone for the wedding, and another stone of his choosing after their first night spent together as husband and wife. Now, suspended from her headdress of silver wire and enameled ornaments, the white pearl rested on her forehead. A black pearl on her left ear was a reminder of the destruction of the Temple of Jerusalem, which the Jews were always mourning.

Around his shoulders Don Simeon wore an embroidered *akhnif*, a cape. A hat covered his long hair, and a gold pearl glowed on his ear. To show that he, too, was mourning the Temple's destruction, a black band hemmed his white trousers.

Doña Isabel and Don Simeon were married for *ra ve tov*, bad or good, in the courtyard under the arch formed by a grapevine. Don Alfonso said the prayers, and the families were united. As required by the Jewish law, Isabel and Don Simeon said to each other "*Ashamnou*, we have sinned." This ensured that in this world their past would be forgiven. For taking a new name, making a new union, or simply moving is considered by God to be a new birth. The bride circled seven times around her husband, slashing the air with a silver sword to ward off evil spirits. Don Simeon circled her three times. He then moved to the altar, stood on one foot, put his arms up to keep his balance, and with his raised foot crushed a glass on the floor. This gesture, required by Jewish law, is a reminder of the sound of the smashed alabaster windows when the Temple was destroyed. The grin on Don Simeon's face made one believe that, in his mind, the breaking of the glass meant something more personal and immediate.

For the wedding dinner, Doña Reina had made several dishes, inviting Doña Isabel's family to prepare some, too, so they could learn from each other.

Bacallao Dao Reina

Keep a slab of dry cod in water for one day and one night.
Keep the pot covered and change the water many times.
At nighttime, Angels use uncovered pots to relieve
    themselves.
Boil the fish until tender. Boil some parsnips.
In a mortar, mix the fish with the *legumbres*.
Add garlic, parsley, olive oil, and lemon.
Serve with salad.

Taking a risk that her mother-in-law noticed and admired, Doña Isabel showed her skills by inventing a dish that had never before been attempted.

Vanilla Red-Cabbage Pie

Cut a red cabbage into small pieces and simmer it.
Make it soft, but not too soft.
Mix in pepper from Aleppo.
Add vanilla from Ceylon, quail's eggs, and soft goat cheese.
Put everything in a crust and bake until done.

After Don Simeon and Doña Isabel were lifted up on chairs and danced around the courtyard, the women set the tables and served the men. Doña Isabel and Don Simeon retired to a room on the second floor terrace to wish each other *terbhou o tseedou*, luck and happiness, and to share their first meal together. Doña Isabel washed her husband's hands and offered him *el Hmam del Aaroussa*, the wedding pie.

New Bride Pie

Mix the meat of a squab with *aromatos*.
Cover it with light dough and bake.
Sprinkle it with cinnamon and cloves from Zanzibar.
Serve it hot with honey sauce, white pepper, and *Zaafrane*.

Don Simeon followed Isabel with his eyes as she served the meal, trying to guess the form of her body under the layered dress. He looked into her blue kohl-painted eyes, and when she smiled, he said, "We will be happy together." The sight of a woman in his room filled him with delirious happiness, and looking through the open window, he started to sing a love song that moved Doña Isabel to tears. She sat next to him on the floor.

> *Decilde a mi amor*
> *Alta alta es la Luna,*
> *Ah el mundo es dolor.*
> *Durmi durmi Kurazon,*
> *Cerra tus lindos ojicos,*
> *Durmi durmi con sabor,*
> *Kriatura de Sion.*

The lingering Ladino words surrounded Isabel's body. Her husband's voice was soft and warm, and his large hands were caressing her. She moved even closer to him and put her head on his lap. *Go to his tent tonight, uncover his feet, and lie down,* she remembered Naomi telling Ruth, and without even thinking, she started to caress his thighs to the rhythm of his song.

> I told my love,
> The moon is high,
> The world is full of pain.
> Sleep well my sweet
> My pretty eyes,
> Sleep with my love in your heart,
> My woman of Zion.

Doña Isabel's breasts felt big and hot. Her nipples hurt under the heavy dress, and her secret flower moved uncontrollably as a wave of heat passed through her body. Don Simeon was caressing her neck and shoulders when Doña Isabel guided his hand toward her *corazon.* As his fingers felt for a nipple between the folds of the fabric, she put her head up and a thrill of pleasure filled the room. Don Simeon kept singing, then folded his body over hers and slowly moved her onto the floor. Doña Isabel was now lying on a Berber wedding carpet, a gift from the family in Morocco. Her hair spread over the red-and-brown geometric motif, and her henna-painted fingers slowly moved on the finely embroidered silk. She felt her body floating above the floor as her husband, hovering over her on his knees, slowly peeled away her layered dress.

Moving his hands around her body, Don Simeon was now singing a different song, a more rapid tune that made her shiver. She felt like *uma alcachofra,* an artichoke, her clothes on the floor like discarded leaves, her husband opening the fruit to find the precious, delicate heart. The thought that Don Simeon could eat the artichoke heart made her burst into laughter. She imagined him moving his head between her legs and drinking her juice. She could not stop laughing at the silly idea as she held onto her husband's body, pulling him toward her on the floor until he himself started laughing. He covered her with his body and, as Doña Isabel put her arms around his shoulders, they started rocking left and right on the rug while his Adam, trying to escape from under his clothes, touched her right at the place where a girl knows she is not a boy.

Don Simeon started to undress himself with one hand, removing Isabel's camisole with the other. When he looked at her naked body lying on top of her clothes, he felt an immense gratitude toward Isabel. He bent to kiss the painted red flower decorating her belly button, and with his hand, covered the triangle of red hair between her legs, caressing it slowly. When his finger circled the bud between her lips, just at the beginning of her mysterious opening, she felt she was falling from the sky.

Don Simeon pushed her legs slightly apart, moved closer, and put his place of circumcision on Doña Isabel's swollen bud. He let her feel the weight of his body, gently moving up and down, one way and the other, so they could start to understand each other's mysteries. He held her very tight, and as he entered her, she felt her body losing shape. She opened her eyes and a sharp cry of pain lingered on the floor as Don Simeon continued singing to her:

> Embraced by the arms of the Universe,
> I ascend along a diagonal path.
> To meet the love of my wife, Isabel,
> *Bavat Einaym*, Apple of My Eye.

When the morning light arrived from around the mountains, Bavat Einaym first said her prayer to God then told her husband that a marriage is when two are united to make one:

> Me over you,
> Or you over me,
> It is not the same thing,
> Though neither of us has changed.

That morning, Don Simeon went to the roof and told the pigeons, "*Nes gadol hayah sham*, a great miracle happened." Then, in front of his parents, he gave Bavat Einaym a third ring, a blue *HaSappir* stone, a reminder of their first union.

To everyone's surprise, Isabel's love brought her husband down from the terraced roof and into the house. Every morning they looked at each other, saying, "*Mode ani Elohim*, I thank God for keeping me alive and sending back my soul from the night it spent with You." Sometimes Don Simeon would take his wife out onto the terrace to show her the stars and to teach her his songs, which filled the courtyard with love and kept the pigeons awake.

Don Simeon looked at Doña Isabel with so much lust that she would blush and smile, happy to feel loved. This did not go unnoticed by Doña Reina. *"Kol adam ohev, kulo same'ach,* everyone loves a happy man," she said to herself, then taught Doña Isabel how to protect herself from pregnancy.

"I believe that you should let your body know your husband for some time before you start to bear children," Doña Reina said. It was a discussion between women, and Doña Isabel put her trust in her mother-in-law, who herself believed in pleasure and happiness.

LESSONS FOR DOÑA ISABEL

Don Simeon, who liked to spend time with his wife, took it upon himself to instruct her in the learning of Christian prayers, just as his father had instructed him.

"Should we ever be questioned by the Church and have to flee, you should be able to say the prayers in different languages," Don Simeon told Isabel.

> *Nosso Pai que estais no ceu*
> *Bènit soit Ton Nom*
> *Venga a nosotros Tu Reino*
> *Fiat voluntas Tua*
> *Wie im Himmel so auf dem Erden,*
> *Give us this day our daily bread,*
> *Amen.*

"I can be Christian," Doña Isabel assured her husband, "but when I am alone I shall light a candle and say my own prayers:

> *Barukh Ha'Shem Adonai,*
> *Eloheinu Melekh Ha'olam,*
> Blessed be Your Name,
> *Eloheinu,* King of the Universe,

Who delights in our pleasures,
And transferred unto us
The wonder of seeing Light.

"It is not for us to tell other people about our God," she continued. "When you run with the wolves, you howl."

The game of double-life and double-talk, the separation between private Judaism and public Catholicism, was not a tool for deception. It was a tool for protection. They were not deceiving the Church, nor were they lying. They were surviving through the rights, laws, and customs that identified them by birth as Jews. They were happy to eat their food kosher, to cease work, and to light candles on the seventh day. They believed that on the day of Sabbath, every Jew is endowed with *neshamah yetera*, an additional soul. God chose them to reveal His wisdom. He asked them to separate milk from meat simply to teach them about order. He asked them to let the Earth rest every seven years, so they would learn not to be greedy. "I was born Jewish, and I shall remain Jewish. And I shall send my firstborn to Hanah's Paradise," Don Simeon concluded.

So much did he like to spend time with his wife that, every Thursday, Don Simeon brought Doña Isabel to listen to the storytellers in front of the church. He would then join her at the market to look at the silks from Damascus, shawls from Kashmir, carpets from Persia, and spices from India and Ceylon, the two of them dreaming together about foreign lands and commenting on the manners and ways of life of other nations.

Slowly Doña Isabel took charge of the household, leaving Doña Reina to concern herself more with the trading business. Happy that Isabel was a good wife for her son, Doña Reina entertained the young pair, translating poems or short stories from the Arabic, Latin, and Hebrew manuscripts in her collection. She would choose them especially for Doña Isabel, whom in private she called Bavat Einaym.

Listening to Doña Reina inspired Doña Isabel to write, and after several attempts at poetry, she wrote a description of her life and of the people in Belmonte, along with cooking instructions for her most interesting meals. She recorded the recipes she learned from her mother and from Doña Reina for all the foods they had eaten in all the countries where they had lived. She organized her book alphabetically—*alcachofras*, artichokes, *al kapares*, capers, *zucca*, zucchini—with special descriptions and drawings of the spices used in cooking broad beans, cabbage, and parsnips. To avoid arousing suspicion for not including pork, Doña Isabel mentioned no meat at all. This vast collection would become the first vegetarian cookbook in the Western world. "Adam ate only *zarzavat*, vegetables, and lived for many years," she said in the book's introduction. "But on special occasions, to improve sight and fertility, we also cook *dagim*, fish," and she provided several recipes.

To Stuff a Fish

Take a small mountain trout or any other *pichkado*.
Poach it in white wine.
Gently remove the whole skin and the bones.
Chop the *pichkado* into small cubes.
Marinate them overnight in lemon juice.
Add chopped herbs, dill, *kolantro*, tarragon, chives,
Whatever you like.
Put the mixture back into the fish skin.
Cover the fish eyes with *al kapares* and serve cold.

Doña Isabel often fell sick on Fridays and would stay alone in her room, eating only a piece of bread with a glass of red wine. When the servants began spreading rumors that she might be blessing the bread and lighting the candles before Sabbath, her father-in-law put an end to the illness. Doña Isabel, who was indeed praying and lighting the candles, consulted with Doña Reina, and, in a very private ceremony, they moved the day of the Sabbath. They informed God that from now on, their week would no longer start on Sunday. *Yom rishon*, the first day, would be Wednesday. Therefore, the seventh day, the Sabbath, would always fall on a Tuesday, a very auspicious day for the Jews. After all, the Church condemned Sabbath, not Tuesday. They could rest, bless the wine, light candles, and read their books without anyone noticing. The entire family embraced the idea, happy that now they could work on Saturday, go to church with the Christians on Sunday, and celebrate Sabbath on Tuesday.

To further prove they were not *Judaisando*, Doña Isabel hung a *Jamon dao Sierra*, a dry ham from the Sierra Mountain, in the window of the kitchen. The family often invited the priest and other Christians to share their meals. Doña Isabel prepared the foods in the Jewish tradition but always served the Christians first, covering up their food with pieces of lard, slices of green limes, and leaves of coriander. With so many people eating, no one ever noticed that the Jews were not being served the lard. She called these dishes *tapas*, covers.

Not eating the lard saddened Don Simeon, for a Christian had told him that eating pork excites the sexual appetite. He tried to imagine his "universal insight" transformed by eating the flesh of the animal, but Doña Isabel found the idea repugnant. She cooked mostly fish and refused even to say the word "pork," instead calling the animal *davar aher*, the other thing.

Doña Isabel served cheese with olives and butter at the end of the meal, rather than at the beginning, as the Jews did. She washed the *farfuri*, dishes, with hot water and ashes and said prayers without vowels between the words of the conversation. She believed that her conversion to Catholicism was complete and, when asked, told everyone that she was from an old Christian family from Capo Verde, "*legitima, entiera e limpia Christa velha*, completely legitimate, with clean old Christian roots."

LESSONS FOR THE CHILDREN

> *Passo tyempo, vino tyempo,*
> Time goes, time comes,
> And all things *a la ora orada,*
> At the right time.

Bavat Einaym gave birth to nine children, none of whom died. At the right age, trusting that they would be able to keep private their Jewish origin, Don Simeon taught them, one by one and in secret, the laws of Abraham.

"There is the world and there is us. The world believes in something, and we believe in something else. What do we do?" he asked his children.

"We can keep secrets," his oldest son, Amadeo, answered.

"Yes, we can, but it is not good to live with secrets. Secrets make one sleep badly and feel guilty. Somebody might discover them, and then what do you do? Never live in secrecy—live in the privacy of your soul! If you are eating a piece of sugar and somebody asks you for some and you say, 'I don't have any sugar,' is this a lie?"

"No," his son answered. "You ate the sugar."

"But you have the sugar in your mouth! You can feel its sweetness on your tongue. Nobody can see it, nobody knows about it, but you have it. Inside ourselves, we can be whatever we want. Sometimes I am a lion! Am I lying? No! Is this a secret? Absolutely not! It is a matter of privacy. It belongs only to me."

Doña Isabel took it upon herself to instruct her children on the dietary laws and certain other prohibitions. "We are not allowed to mix milk with meat," she explained. "This is how God teaches us control of our sensual urges. Only by mastering our desires can we rise from the animal kingdom to our human nature. Restraint separates us from animals. If we do only what we want, we are beasts."

Doña Isabel taught her children *Lutera'i*, an idiom from Persia that was used in the presence of strangers, to talk secretly. She taught them how to convey intricate messages to each other by dropping out vowels when they spoke in public. This habit of hiding the vowels resulted in a very complex communication system, with proper words from Djidio, Judeo-Berber, or Ladino, Judeo-Spanish, inserted into the local dialect of Portuguese. Words such as *shashe*, borrowed from the Romaniot dialect, meant that danger was imminent. The custom of sharing private information in public stayed in the family. It was also useful, for example, when a piece of food was stuck between one's front teeth. On those occasions, one would insert the word *gazelle* into the conversation without pronouncing the vowels. Why *gzl* was chosen to warn of an embarrassing situation was not recorded in the scrolls at Hanah's Paradise.

LESSONS FOR THE *CONVERSOS*

Don Simeon went to church every Sunday, as required, but often left humiliated. Invariably, the sermon ridiculed the Jews. When the priest quoted the famous professor Quiñones, Don Simeon knew that the words were only lies.

This treacherous and rebellious population, this cruel, dishonored, infamous, stubborn nation is recognizable by the rush of blood that every month afflicts their males' behinds as punishment given to them by our Lord as a sign of disgrace and shame for the persecution they inflicted on our true Messiah, Christ our Savior, by nailing him to the Cross. Some of them bleed once a month from the hands and the feet, as God our Father has punished them to suffer into eternity the agony and pain of our Lord. They do not need to eat pork to prove their conversion. They are already *marranos*, swines!

Nonetheless, searching for some reassurance on this point alone, Don Simeon asked his father-in-law, the *fíziko*, about the bleeding. His father-in-law told Simeon that if once a month Jewish males were bleeding from their behinds, Simeon would have known it by now. "Jewish people are not *uma raza maldita*, a cursed race, and the Catholic priest does not know our books. Don't believe in the sayings of the idiots," his father-in-law advised.

Don Simeon felt compelled to inform his cousins about Jesus and Mary, should they, at Hanah's Paradise, fall into the trap of believing that Jesus is the Messiah.

He wrote "*O conto do Maryam y de su Kerido Ijo, Hamudi Jesu dao Nazareth*, The tale of Maryam and Her Dear Son, Sweet Jesus of Nazareth," in Portuguese but left out all the vowels, so no strangers could read it. He covered the parchment with a fine silk paper, filled in the gaps, then read the story to his father, his mother, his wife, and his wife's father and brothers.

Cnt d Mrym y d s Krd Ij Hmd Js d Nzrt

Mrym, whch mns rblls, ws jst lk tht. Maryam, which means rebellious, was just like that. *Th Chrstns chngd hr nm, nd nw sh s clld Mry.* The Christians changed her name, and now she is called Mary. She heard voices, talked to angels, and had uncommon dreams. Other people believed that she was *meshoogah*, crazy. But she was just a fallen woman, and some Christian God showed her mercy by making her a saint.

Her son, Jesus of Nazareth, was *un mamzer*, a bastard child, who was born in Bethlehem from the adulterous love of this

Jewish woman, Maryam, and a Roman soldier. Jesus had many friends who followed him everywhere. They were all men, and he spent a lot of time with each of them to open their eyes to some *mirakolos*. One of his close acquaintances told the Romans that Jesus liked young boys and lay with each of them as a man lies with a woman. The Romans did not care because they themselves used to lie with whatever was around and moving: man, woman, or beast. They kept little boys under the tables to caress their *membrum* with smooth little hands while they were discussing matters of state and war, as one Gaius Petronius told us in his book. Other people believed that Jesus liked to sleep only near men, otherwise—at his advanced age—he would have been married and had children.

A Torah student followed Jesus around the city. He saw Jesus take a man named Saul into his arms and whisper sweet words into his ear. He caressed Saul's dark hair and moved his body so he could feel the flesh growing under his robe. When the Grand Rabbi found this out, he became very upset. The one named Name had commanded His children not to unite themselves in flesh by choosing something other than what their parents had chosen. If men chose men and women chose women, if His children contaminated their flesh and did not choose well, His land, too, would be contaminated. *HaKohen HaGadol*, the Grand Rabbi, asked to speak with Jesus.

"Yieshu of Nazareth, born in Bethlehem, bastard child, son of Maryam," he said. "What are you doing to your people? The one named Name has asked that on His land we not uncover the nakedness of a man and lie with him as one lies with a woman. His land is holy and He, blessed be His gaze upon us, can recall the land, as He did before when He expelled the Canaanites. If His land becomes contaminated, He can recall the iniquity and disgorge its inhabitants."

But Jesus was arrogant with the *rabbino* and disrespectful to the Name. "You are discussing my private parts," he said, "and I shall use my ejaculations as they please me. Nobody loves me," he said with tears in his eyes. "*Abah, lama atah sabashtani?* Father, why have You abandoned me?" he cried to the sky, then left the room laughing, promising to kill himself.

The Grand Rabbi thought carefully, then said to the assembly, "We don't believe in death, we believe in life. We don't worship a star, we worship its light. In a unique event, the Name gave us light. It happened only once and will perhaps never happen again. Some things happen that way, *mustar*, for hidden reasons.

"Joseph brought Maryam in front of me to unite them in marriage," the rabbi continued. "She told me then that 'a Roman soldier came into the pool while I was still washing, and his water entered me,' she said." The rabbi also mentioned that she had used the Sanskrit word *semen*, for water, letting everyone determine the nature of the fluid that had penetrated her.

"'This soldier will come after her, to make her a slave in his house,' Joseph told me then. 'To save her, I have to marry her now.'"

"'*Rayon tov*, good idea,' Maryam said in front of me."

"You are telling lies," Jesus yelled, bursting into the room, for he had been listening by the door. "She didn't say *rayon tov*, good idea; she said *be-herayon tov*, good pregnancy, meaning advanced. My mother told me the truth. When she was bathing, *um andjeló* came to her. '*Noli me tangere!* Don't touch me! *Anokhee lo petukhah*, I am not open,' she told him. But he whispered in her ear, a secret message. 'My God Priapus is sending you His own essence. You will conceive the Son of God.' And that is me," Jesus said, opening his arms and laughing with happiness.

"And because I am the Son of God, I don't want to learn carpentry. And you see," and here Jesus pulled up his robe to show his legs, "I shave the hair from my body. Father doesn't like to feel wood dust on my limbs when he caresses me. I am a special son. I bathe myself in perfumed oil and have smooth skin like a virgin," he said, laughing again.

"We know," the rabbi answered. "We also know that you and your friends set up a mock marriage with a Torah scroll."

"We did," Yieshu answered, smiling, "Father gave me permission. I was dressed in a majestic robe. My short round beard framed my face, and my eyes lit with pleasure as I kissed the scroll under the bridal canopy. I looked divine. After I danced with the scroll, I took it to my bed and read it with my third eye. My *membrum* cried at the beauty of my bride, and now the scroll is written on my own body."

"*Aveenu Malkheynu*, Our Father, Our King," the Grand Rabbi said. "Yieshu of Nazareth, born in Bethlehem, you committed sacrilege and you are cursed, excommunicated from the Temple. If you are contaminated, the one called Name can no longer be your God! You will have to separate yourself from Him and find someone else to love you," the rabbi told him. "You have no choice now but to leave God's land!"

His disciples heard that a curse had been put on Jesus, and they abandoned him. They made themselves invisible and stole the water from the Sinai. In fact, they are still rubbing their hands with pleasure because now the water is a Dead Sea, full of salt.

Alone, in an act of self-indulgence, Jesus went to the desert, praying to idols, which is forbidden by God. From there he went to *Mitzraiym*, the narrow land of Egypt, where they worship cats. There he learned witchcraft and practiced it with devotion. He returned to Jerusalem with secret formulas, praying to *paxaritos*, little birds made of *adamah*, clay. He would say *Abra K'Adabra*, which means, "I will create as I speak," giving the clay life, which is repulsive *avodah lezara*, devil's work. The rabbi could see the work of Satan and told others that Yieshu was *un minnim, un heretico*. They hit him with a whip of fire and put on him *kherem*, a curse of excommunication, and then ignored him, as if he weren't there.

Yieshu felt very much alone. He walked around the city of Jerusalem, telling people that they were all brothers and that they should love him. He also said that if someone hurt them, they should not strike back but should turn their other cheek.

One day, fearing he might be punished for provoking a fight at the Temple, Yieshu hid in the hills of Jericho. There he talked with animals and learned about magic herbs and desert truffles. For many days he ate only those mushrooms and smelled those herbs. Then, in the stupor of the midday sun, he returned to Jerusalem and went to the palace of Pontius Pilate.

"Roman Centurion, Pontius," he called out. "It's me, Yieshu, talking. Pontius, listen to me. You are more ambitious than intelligent, *atah mevin*, you understand?"

Pontius Pilate, who hated to be interrupted from his afternoon sleep, ordered his soldiers to arrest Yieshu. That evening, before the Sabbath began, he sentenced Yieshu to death.

"You cannot kill me," Yieshu said. "I am the Son of God, I am the King and I will never die."

Ignoring his words, the Romans made him carry a wooden cross all the way to the hill called Golgotha, the skull. The soldiers nailed Yieshu to a cross and let him hang there to die of thirst and hunger. Then they put a crown of thorns on his head and called him *Rex Judeorum*, King of the Jews.

While Jesus was on the cross, a woman whom he had known passed by. She looked at him and said, "Yieshu, I am the woman you once knew. You gave me some money, even though you didn't know me well. Your limb for knowing women cried before even it could see my *nymphi*. Here, have some water to quench your thirst," and she passed a wet sponge on his face.

Maryam saw the woman giving water to her son and said to her, "Go to my house on Pulgat Hakotel near the Dung Gate, boil some poppy seeds, and bring the drink back for Yieshu." The woman did just that. She brought the brew to Yieshu, who drank it and fell asleep as if he were dead.

The Romans were surprised to find that Jesus had died so quickly but were too lazy to verify it. They let his mother, his friends, and the woman take him off the cross to bring him to the grave. The women covered him in cloth washed in salamander blood so it would never burn. Then his mother and her friends waited for the night to fall. In the darkness, they took him out of the tomb, resuscitated him with some wine, and sent him to hide in a cave at Khirbet Qumran, near the Dead Sea, or *Yam Hamelach*, the Salt Sea, as we say.

When rumors that Jesus was still alive reached the Romans, they opened the tomb and found it empty but for a shroud. "He is the Son of God and his body went to Heaven," people said. "He is a saint protected by the fire of God; his shroud does not burn."

When things settled down, Jesus' mother sent him in secret to Al Qayrawan on the shores of *Ifriqiya*, and from there by boat to Gaeta, south of Rome. Was there any better place for him to hide? One by one, all of his friends, some of whom were also his brothers, took the boat to Genoa. From there, *per pedes Apostolorum*, *à pieds comme les Apôtres*, traveling by foot like the Apostles, they joined him in Rome. There they told the Romans that

Jesus could perform *mirakolos*. He could fly, he could speak every language and make gold from stone and wine from water. Since everyone enjoys getting something for nothing, many people in *Roma* abandoned their own Gods to follow Jesus. They stopped working and asked for free wine and free bread, but their emperor threw them to the lions.

And there in Rome, he, *um ebreo*, ate pork and prayed to another God, like *a dönmeh*, a turncoat. Because of him, whose name means nothingness, I have to go to his church, eat his flesh, and drink his blood like *um cannibalo*. *Y eu tenho Yieshu poko en los ojos*, I hold Jesus in low esteem. For this much *konosko yo*, I know is true:

> The opposite of nothing
> Is nothing.

Don Simeon's parents, wife, and father-in-law had all listened to his *comentario*. Doña Reina said that, indeed, the true story of Jesus was *Tov Beeshvil Ha' Yehudim*, favorable to the Jews. Don Alfonso asked Simeon to keep the story secret, to curb his arrogance in judging others, and, within his strength, to behave with humility.

"Simeon, my son-in-law," Senhor Piedraverde, the *fíziko*, told him, "please remember who we are! *Al ta'amod al hamekach b'sha'ah she'ain l'cha demim*, don't bargain when you don't have any money. The *familiares* are stopping by our house all the time. They are traveling Catholic spies, verifying whether the *conversos* are respecting the Church rituals. If we are investigated, if the Saint's Office of the Inquisition declares us suspects, we will have to confess imaginary rituals and risk our lives. Please, Simeon, learn to live in the secret. Keep the secret, secret—even from yourself! Believe in what you must believe as if it were true, just as we must belong without belonging."

"*Senhor Padre*," Don Simeon answered back, "I cannot believe without trusting."

Doña Isabel told her husband that she enjoyed the way he told the story and asked him to write stories for the children. Then she washed the ink from the parchment and gave it back to him to use anew.

"We must prepare to leave," Don Alfonso told his wife. "Rumors that we are respecting the Jewish laws are circulating in the village. The New Christians are once again damned, accused, and banned from office. In Bragança they set up tables on the streets and eat pork publicly, while being ridiculed for doing it. In Lisboa the citizens were more fanatic than ever and on the first day of Passover the hatred exploded. More than 2000 *Maran Atha* were killed. I am afraid." To avoid the insulting word *Marranos*, Don Alfonso said *Maran Atha*, an expression from the New Testament, which sounded almost the same but meant the Lord had come.

"I beg you all to understand," Don Alfonso said, addressing his family, "that the secret practice of Judaism means death. New Christians are forbidden to leave the country. To flee would be an admission of guilt. I am asking all of you to trust our God and not bring calamities upon our family. We will never forget our God, even if in these times we cannot celebrate Him. We will keep our traditions and say *Le Shanah Habaah be Yerushalayim*, next year in Jerusalem, only when we are alone. I am also asking you, Simeon, to protect our family and to leave Jesus alone, whatever he did. God asks us to preserve our lives."

Doña Reina offered salt to the Virgin Mary and cinnamon to the priest. Doña Isabel cooked pork with clams and chicken with shrimp, sprinkled them with *kolantro*, and served them whenever strangers came to their house. She never again offered a repast to a friend undertaking a voyage. Yet she sometimes managed to drop the meat on the floor or to spill something on it, to have a reason to wash out the blood. When they went to church, they received Communion, kissed the crucifix, and silently exchanged in the benediction each *Ave Maria* for *Eva maminah*, Eve believes. Nevertheless, every morning, as they walked from the house to the olive grove, they sang quietly:

Quando viene el Sabbath	We believe in Moses' pact
En la olivada veo	And drink wine on Sabbath.
Con mi padres bino beo	At the olive grove we stay
En la Ley del Muysen creo.	And to our God we pray.

After the rumors that they were *Judaisando* had died down, Doña Isabel consulted with her mother-in-law, and together they spoke with Senhor Piedraverde, the *físiko*, Isabel's father. He sent word to his relatives in Italy, asking permission to join them. *"Aki no es bom de falar, e no falar es afilu male*, to speak is bad and to keep silent is even worse," he explained. "We are in the wrong place, and fear for our lives. Once again we have to leave." The household of the two families—some forty members—sold their houses. With a letter of travel from the owner of the city of Sabbioneta, inviting them there, they left the land, joining the exodus of New Christians who around 1507 were asked to leave the Iberian Peninsula. From the King of Portugal, they received permission to leave the country with their possessions. *"BeSem Asem Nase Onaslia*, in the name of the Lord, we will do and be successful," Don Simeon remembered the saying of Amir Avraham, a cousin from Isfahan.

"Adieu, *Sephard*," Doña Isabel said.

"Adieu, sound of the water-carrier at dusk, view of the village, morning dew on the path behind the church. Adieu, almond trees, olive trees, orange groves, gardens, beautiful house, land where our children were born, Iberia, adieu!"

6

A *converso* from Lisbon and an educated woman, Doña Isabel's
cousin Beatrice Piedraverde Colonna wrote poems and col-
lected musical instruments. Her husband, Duke Francesco Colonna, considered himself a humanist. He recognized the right
of asylum and abolished the slave trade. Yet when his wife approached him on behalf of Doña Isabel's extended family, the
duke, a man of well-known fits of anger, refused. It is known that
the Jews don't work the land, he argued. They occupy themselves
with commerce, and commerce was what the duke was doing
himself. He didn't want any competition. But after giving it some
thought, he determined that it would be beneficial to invite the
Jews to Sabbioneta, the city-state that he owned. He could use
their skills.

"*Uomini de negozio,* the Jews have connections over the entire
known world. They bring prosperity wherever they settle, and
their knowledge of medicine, geography, cartography, cosmology,
and navigation is vast. They speak many languages, they finance
the discovery of new countries, and they invest their money in
trading spices and gold. As long as they share the wealth and pay
taxes in *La mia Republica,* they may come," he said.

They were forty-two people, including the servants. They traveled for two years before arriving in Lombardy, in the valley of the
River Po. First they joined a pilgrimage trail, moving between religious monuments with groups of seekers returning from Santiago
de Compostela. They purchased travel letters from the Church
for protection on the road. They dressed in pilgrimage coats and
wore pilgrims' symbols: the leather pouch on the hip and the scal-
lop shell on the coat. They told each other that *cucullus non facit*

monachum, clothes do not make the priest. Church steeples and castles were road maps in the sky. They spent the nights in the open markets or in the churches that received travelers. They walked most of the time.

In the spring of 1515, they crossed the mountains of the Sierra da Estrela, stopped in Viseu, and continued north to Oporto, from where they sailed to Tangiers. The family stayed for a time in Morocco, crossed the sea to Genoa, then walked over the Apennines and arrived in Sabbioneta in late 1517, where they were welcomed by Beatrice Piedraverde Colonna and Duke Francesco Colonna.

After gifts were exchanged as tokens of trust, friendship, and protection, the duke renamed them Raveo. The family received the right to ride horses, use swords, wear purple clothing, and write music. The duke, a very diplomatic man and a *condottiere*, a prominent businessman of his time, put the Jewish *fízikos* on his account and established free medical care for his citizens. He put the rabbis in charge of translating his manuscripts and of teaching the classics. The duke, who needed money to build a new city, asked Don Alfonso to use his family connections to sell the duke's boats.

Don Alfonso sent letters describing the merchandise to his firstborn cousins, and after several of them showed interest in the boats, he sold them to the highest bidder. In exchange, Don Alfonso was entitled to live free and exempt of taxes in Sabbioneta. His family was granted commercial and industrial privileges and freedom of religion.

The duke hired Samir Ben Yakov Raveo, a first cousin of Don Simeon's and *um mimar*, an architect, to draw up plans for a new city. The architect presented the duke with plans for a hexagonal town with no main thoroughfare. Emerging from the plain of the river Po, with only one bridge over a deep moat for ease of defense, an ideal fortified town with massive ramparts would replace the medieval village of Sabbioneta. A labyrinth of alleys would end in a square central plaza from which no one could escape. On the streets of the new city, inhabitants could wander among harmonious, well-proportioned buildings. The duke's palace, church, and private chapel would be decorated with portraits and busts of the

Colonna family. Figures from Greek and Roman mythology would embellish the assembly hall, and a majestic column in honor of Minerva, goddess of wisdom and warfare, would be raised in the center of the plaza. This return to a neoclassical iconography allowed the architect to embrace pagan themes without offending the Church.

Pleased to change his activities from war merchant on the seas to scholar at home, the duke approved the plans for a "new Athens," which he envisioned as a center of arts and philosophy. The reconstruction of the city occupied the citizens, the peasants from villages around the valley, and the monks of the cloister on the other side of the river. The duke himself arrived on the construction site early each morning, supervising the masons and giving daily instructions to his artisans.

In the euphoria of reconstructing the city, the duke allowed Don Simeon to build his own house several streets away from the palace. In exchange, the duke requested that the entire family live there, and that a small chapel facing the street be built to prove their love for God.

Simeon built a house with large windows around a half-octagonal garden. He chose this shape because the number four is found in the Divine Torah and refers to the Messiah saying, "I will come." He enclosed the garden with high walls, then planted several exotic trees and the golden bamboo from Hanah's Paradise. At the entrance, under an arch and facing the street, he built a small chapel, triangular in shape and narrow in proportions.

The duke was pleased with the result and asked Don Simeon for a large contribution to build an unusual theater, something that not even the Pope or the emperor in Rome had seen: a theater with a roof. The *Teatro Olimpico* would be the first enclosed theater ever built in the known world. As soon as a major part of the town was completed and the architect had finished the theater, the duke issued a proclamation forcing his subjects to reside within the city's walls.

The Jews of Sabbioneta received the proclamation with much enthusiasm and dedicated a house to be their synagogue. For the first time, instead of being forced to leave, they were being forced to stay! The irony of the situation put the Jews at ease, and the ritual of lighting the Sabbath candles began once again, with Beatrice Piedraverde Colonna herself conducting it. Beatrice declared in public that she was of Jewish origin, published her poems in Italian and Hebrew, and sent her firstborn son to Hanah's Paradise.

The duke allowed Don Alfonso Raveo the privilege of printing songs and prayer books for his family in exchange for printing the manuscripts in his collection. With Don Alfonso's knowledge of languages and the duke's printing press, they published the first multilingual marine dictionary, which brought them much success. Don Simeon, almost forty-one years old, wrote lyrical songs praising the river Po and designed several gardens connecting the roofs of the duke's palaces.

Doña Isabel, who was now named Isabella, printed a book of romantic fantasy, exalting the beauty of women and giving lessons in seduction. It was believed that she wrote it with her mother-in-law. The book was printed in the Old Style Venetian typeface, with contrasting low strokes, diagonal stresses, and bracketed serifs. It taught young brides how to enjoy their first night, how to cover a lost virginity with a drop of pigeon blood, and how to make their husbands love them. "Women love words. Ask *Signore*, your husband, to take you into his arms and tell you nice things. The *Signore* will be wise to massage his wife's pudenda twice a week, using oil of lilies or oil of *azafraan* before inserting his finger inside her mysterious opening. A good wife needs to learn how to talk to and play with her husband's *membrum*. She need not be afraid of it but should introduce it into all her openings to make it strong. Some foods, like juniper berries, black truffles, and wine, make men more loving."

Along with her advice, she also included recipes. Her special meal of spinach and artichokes, *Torta alla Giudia*, is still cooked in Sabbioneta, as is a delicacy of goose meat and spices.

Torta alla Giudia, Pizza Ebraica, Green Tart

Steam spinach, baby artichokes, green peas, and green onions.
Stir in two eggs and fresh goat cheese.
Line a plate with slices of bread.
Fill with the vegetable mixture, cover up, and bake.

Salami de Oca, Goose Sausage

Mix big chunks of goose meat with the *aromatos* you prefer.
Muito, pepper, enhances the mood.
Add bread, eggs, and herbs.
Add *fistiks*, or pistachios, as you call them, *limon* peels, and
  juniper berries.
Fill a bag with this mixture and squeeze out all pockets of air.
Skin a goose neck and string the end.
Stuff the neck carefully with the mixture.
Tie up, then boil or smoke and let dry.
Slice the salami thin and eat with mashed parsnip.
You will know a feeling of pleasure.

The Jews received new privileges when Ehud Raveo, a *mediko*
who knew how to fix bones, devised a way to improve the duke's
vision. The duke had lost his left eye in a battle off the African coast. The *mediko* asked permission to cut out a portion of
the bone from the bridge of the duke's nose. "It will give the re-
maining eye greater range of vision," he explained. But before he
proceeded, he informed His Excellency of the Name's singular
prohibition against approaching *binah*, the altar, while missing a
segment of that bone. "A man whose nose has no bridge and can
apply cosmetics to both eyes in a single stroke shall not give offer-
ings to *Ha'Shem*." The duke had no intention of approaching the
Name's altar so, to his delight, once the protruding bone was removed, he could roll his right eye to the left and see without having to turn his head. Happy that, from the corner of his right eye,
he could see again the left side of the world, the duke bestowed on
the Jews a personal *cavaliere* to accompany them on their travels.
The *cavaliere* was to ride his horse in front of them, displaying the
duke's coat of arms as they passed through cities.

Don Simeon's firstborn son, Amadeo, who inherited his father's
eloquence and visionary bent, felt that in Sabbioneta his Judaism
was an accepted curiosity. After he came of age and celebrated his
Bar Mitzvah, he felt a strong desire to teach his Christian friends
the Jewish laws, the path that one walks: the complete body of
rules and practices that Jews are bound to follow, including comments, commandments, and binding customs from the Torah.

He worked with his father in the gardens of the duke, preaching to the peasants not to gather grapes that have fallen to the ground, not to eat a worm found in fruit, not to wrong a stranger in speech, not to have intercourse with a woman without marriage. He explained to the glazed eyes of the village folk that to indulge in familiarities with relatives, such as kissing, embracing, or winking, may lead to incest. He asked them not to tattoo the body or make incisions of any kind on their flesh; not to consult *ovoth*, ghosts; not to practice *kisuf*, magic, using herbs or stones; and not to cast spells over snakes and scorpions. On Wednesdays, the market day, he would enter into conversations with men from different parts of the country to inform them of the prohibitions against wearing women's clothing and against mixing milk and meat. He petitioned the duke for a rule that would free a newly married man from the army and from public labor for one year, to allow him time to rejoice with his wife. He also informed the duke that a daughter of Israel is prohibited from marrying a eunuch.

Satisfied that in Sabbioneta he no longer needed to keep his religious beliefs secret and without knowing that, around the same age, his father had tried to convert the priest in Belmonte, Amadeo wrote a letter to Pope Clement VI asking for an audience, with the intent of converting him to Judaism:

Illustrissimo Padre Clementius Sixto,

Spero que la mia lettera, I hope that my letter will find you in good health and *buone disposizioni* toward your humble servant Amadeo, son of Simeon Raveo de Sabbioneta, in the service of the Signore Duca Gonzaga Colonna. *Celeste Carissimo Padre,* my name, Ama Deo, is my parents' testimony of their love for God and I am writing you now to ask *una audienzia* with Your Grace, to inform you of the good deeds that *il Dio degli Ebrei,* the Hebrew God, can offer you. *Primo,* you will never have to cook on Saturday, as it is well known that *Ken kozina vyernes kome Chabad,* he who cooks on Friday eats on Saturday. You will also live longer and have better digestion if you separate milk and meat and do not eat them at the same meal. *Secondo,* if you are a rabbi you can have a *moglie,* a wife, and she will give you children. They will love you much more than this Jesus can love you, and you will be proud of your *bambini* as they grow up. There is, of course, the matter of circumcision, but you will never miss the foreskin. Your Highness could drink some vino with poppy seeds before the circumcision and sleep through it all, just like Jesus. You already believe in God, and it will be easy for your Highness to learn Hebrew and to say *Mode Ani*, the morning prayer of thanks. I am not asking you, as the Portuguese asked us, to change your religion or your name. I am suggesting, with your permission, the possibility of accepting who you are: a Christian, but also *un Ebreo*. You can be both! On Christmas you can pray in Latin, and on Yom Kippur, in Hebrew. The dates never coincide. You will also have to give money to charity, rest on the seventh day, and light *candelas*. I would be honored to be Your Sanctity's guide. This would please everyone. Perhaps you didn't hear it yet, but in Morocco some people say that this Jesus, when he went to Egypt, took his mother to bed. *Que tragedia!* Then he found out that the woman was his mother. *Barmynan*, in horror, he ripped out a golden pin from her clothes and mutilated his eyes, not to see himself ever again. *Que barbaridad!* Why would God want a son like that?

Before Amadeo could finish his letter, Don Simeon discovered the draft.

"Amadeo," he said, remembering that at the same age his own father had stopped him from rewriting the entire Bible. "It is not up to us to change the world. It is for us to adapt to the circumstances of life. Pray that God keeps us alive in a safe place, and forget about converting the Pope, whatever he does and whatever his name is."

Everyone lived peacefully and prospered in Sabbioneta—until one Friday evening when the duke caught his wife with Samir, the *arxitekta*, in the act of *Kabbalath Sabbath*, lighting candles to receive the Sabbath. Beatrice had just blessed the *arxitekta* after the prayer and was embracing his eyes to bring them light when her husband discovered them. He accused his wife of adultery. In his demented fury, the duke—a ferocious man known for his bad temper—wrote a murder story lamenting the approaching death of a hero. Distorting reality into a fantasy of original splendor, the duke staged his play in the *Teatro Olimpico*, inviting to the performance both his wife and the architect. It is believed that at this event, covered by the sound of the music and hidden by the fumes of burning perfumed oils, during an extraordinary effect of torch lights passing through glass balls full of colored water, the duke murdered the architect. He then held Beatrice prisoner in the palace, poisoning her very slowly with almond paste. "*Ktzar koma maleh chema*, short men are bad-tempered," Isabel said.

The Jews buried Samir Ben Yakov Raveo in the Catholic cemetery and prayed for him to be magnified and sanctified, blessed and praised and glorified. Then they went home and said the same words: "*Yit'gadal v'yit'kadash, Yit'barakh v'yish'tabach*, Magnified and sanctified, blessed and praised."

When Beatrice's son returned from Hanah's Paradise, he tried to poison his father and free his mother. Although the poison was very strong, Colonna lost only his hair. Later that year the duke killed his wife and his son, then married his widowed daughter-in-law. Then, fearing that his grandson might one day kill him, he sent him to be raised by the Jews.

"Your majesty is well protected by God," Don Simeon told the duke. "We will raise the child as our own son, never revealing his origins, as we renew our vows to serve you as well as we have done in the past."

"It is true that *B'ra cara da'abuha*, like father, like son," Doña Isabel told her family. "But *Hashalom hashuv min ha'emet*, peace matters more than truth, so we will take care of the child." Don Simeon contributed a large sum of money to the Church, then built an imposing funerary monument celebrating the memory of his cousin, the architect.

When the duke, at an older age, lost his mind completely, Don Simeon donated money for a fountain to be built in the main plaza, dedicated to the love of Beatrice and Samir. This scandalous display of the duke's misfortune was nonetheless accepted by the Church and the population because it was a celebration of love.

After the duke's death, his successor gave the family reassurance that they were welcome and free to stay. Still, they asked themselves: "Should we stay or should we leave? Should we join other relatives in distant places? Could Sabbioneta become inhospitable to the converted Jews?"

Don Simeon remained in Sabbioneta and died at the ripe age of 99, only months after the departure of his beloved wife, Isabel, who lived until 102. Their funerary monument was designed by an artist of the time and their names were remembered in prayers all over the known world. Cousins who knew Simeon or had heard of him sent letters, money, and blessings to everyone in the family, and each generation sent a request to the Grand Rabbi to pray for Don Simeon in perpetuity.

The duke's grandson—not knowing his real origins and having grown up with a cosmopolitan outlook—moved to Hanah's Paradise. He sent gifts and news through travelers, encouraging his entire family to join him there. Part of the family did, and those who remained in Sabbioneta, although converted to Catholicism, sent their firstborns to Hanah's Paradise to keep the tradition and leave their name chiseled on the garden's stones.

Older relatives from other parts of the world felt a calling for the Land, and nearing the end of their lives, chose to go to Hanah's Paradise. But traveling to the Holy Land was long, dangerous, and costly. Wars or family crises made travel more difficult—and since, of course, some people died suddenly, a controversial custom, one that still divides the family, emerged. A number of people from far away, who wanted to be buried in the Land of *Yisrael*, asked that after their death, the bone at the end of their vertebral column, the tail bone, be sent to Hanah's Paradise. First to simplify the task of going to die in the Land of their ancestors, the family branch from Kaifengfu, China, sent a letter to Hanah's Paradise:

> . . . You will understand that it is too difficult to come from such a great distance, so it makes good economic sense for us to send the principal bone of the body, the *louz*, for you to take care of. When Messiah comes he will resurrect his people from this most important bone. We are not able to send you the entire body. Our great *Chao*, the mandarin judge, gave us his

permission to remove the last vertebra of our much-loved dead great aunt. We are sending it to you, together with some of her precious objects and a jar of honey.

The belief that from this single bone, named *louz*, almond, in Hebrew, the entire body would be reconstituted contradicted the rabbinical rule of keeping the body intact. The family argued about the mandarin's decision and considered the mutilation of a dead body an insult. An esteemed rabbi was sent to Kaifengfu to explain the gravity of the act. But when, after several years, he failed to return and the bones of relatives kept arriving, a special prayer called the "Impossible Curse" was written to forgive the separation of the bone from the body. In time, with or without rabbinical permission, other families, as well, sent the *louz*, the almond, to Hanah's Paradise, where the bone was *norah*, revered. The name of the deceased was recorded in the family book and each almond was kept in its individual box, awaiting burial on the Mount of Olives.

The only known confusion occurred when Yi'Shak Rabban, a trader from the coast of Malabar, sent the almond of a family member who later arrived at Hanah's Paradise—alive. The letter he had attached to the vertebra described the Judaism of this branch of the family as infused with Sufi thought. They built sumptuous synagogues and respected strict alimentary laws, refusing to eat the meat near the back sciatic nerve, since Jacob in his fight with the Angel of God was wounded there. The Maha Rajah of Mangalore granted each of them the privileges of using a parasol, owning a drum and a trumpet, and resting on the Sabbath.

Another branch of the Ravahias from India were traders and musicians. They ate refined foods, dressed themselves in magnificent apparel, and lived in large houses with many servants. They, too, sent their firstborn children to Hanah's Paradise for *Pasquar.* At the end of the visit, each firstborn would take a bamboo shoot to plant in his or her own land. Only members of the family could receive the bamboo, and they did so with the obligation to burn it if their line of the family died out. The bamboo had started from a single seedling and blossomed every fifteen years. The fascination with the bamboo is that every shoot of it and every shoot of

a shoot—whatever its age, wherever grown in the world, and regardless of climate—flowers at the same time. Every fifteen years,
when small yellow-orange flowers blossom, strangers find out that
they are related. In national and local newspapers one can read
the list of the families to whom the bamboo belongs. Everyone
whose golden bamboo flowers at the same time is part of the same
family and belongs to Hanah's Paradise.

7

Some four hundred years after the first vertebra arrived at Hanah's Paradise, my paternal grandfather, Rafa'el Amador Ben Nathan Raveo, who pronounced his name with a Sephardic accent, *Raphayïel*, had taken it upon himself to argue with the *Dayan*, the chief judge and rabbi of Jerusalem's tribunal, on behalf of those bones, as every generation had done before him. He had wanted to bury them in the oldest Jewish cemetery, on *Har Hazeitim*, the Mount of Olives, looking toward the *Shaar HaRakhamim*, the Golden Gate, ready to be awakened on *Yom HaDin*, the Day of Resurrection. The rabbi had declared that the almonds could not be taken to the cemetery. The Jewish God forbids tattoos, lacerations, deformities, and any type of mutilation.

"The burial ground has to be big enough," the chief rabbi had explained, "for a soul."

"How big is a soul?" my grandfather would argue.

"Can a Jewish soul live in a *louz*, a bone as small as an almond; is it big enough to hear Elijah sounding the *shofar* when Messiah arrives?" the rabbi retorted. "How can a body be resurrected if it doesn't hear the horn?"

The controversy about the dimension of the Jewish soul joined the question about *Shi'Ur Komah*, God's measure of height. Nobody knew how tall God was nor, by extension, how big was a Jewish soul.

My grandfather showed me the records that came to Hanah's Paradise along with each almond-shaped bone. Written on paper, silk, leather, and sometimes on silver or clay tablets, a myriad of dates, locations, and family ties became apparent. With them, the story of Hanah's Paradise and the people who passed through there emerged.

The bones were kept in small boxes stacked alphabetically on the shelves of the library at Hanah's Paradise. They were my connection to the past. Touching the clean yellowish bones and transcribing the information left by people who lived hundreds of years ago proved to be an extended study in geopolitics, sociology, economics, sexuality, and family ties. Generation after generation, names had been changed to adapt to the culture and language of their land of exile. There were Kapor and Mehta from India, Teixeira from Brazil, Pérez from Argentina, Piedraverde from Portugal. There were Ravayah, Rav, Raweh, Raveo, Ravel, Ravinov, Rabinov, Rabinowich, Roven, Ruven, Rubin, Reubeni, Rava, Ramban, Rachba, Rabbat, Riba, Raavan, Ravhania, Revayra. There was a Rahab who had been born circumcised. There was a Rav who traveled from Portugal to Kitai, China, in search of the *para adouma*, the tenth red heifer that the Messiah would need at the Temple for the ritual of purification. There was the well-preserved almond of a *shtadlan*, professional lobbyist, who was king of Poland for a day and a night in 1594. There was a vegetarian cookbook written by Reina and a book of advice for women written by her daughter-in-law, Bavat Einaym, Isabel.

To understand the origin and migration of the vertebrae, I covered the walls of my room with maps. On one side was the map of the world as it was known in the 1500s, and facing it on the opposite wall, a map of the world as we know it today. Walking in the room was like passing between oceans and living between continents. Red dots with family names covered the maps, and blue lines connected the dots with cities, crossing over countries before returning back to themselves, some going around the same city several times as if, in their migration, those Jews did not know where to go. Other lines and dots remained suspended in one country, the connection with Hanah's Paradise forever lost. They died. They converted. They were excommunicated. After one, Antonio Vieira, a Catholic priest, put forth to the king of Portugal the argument that the absence of the Jews had resulted in great economic loss for the country, some were asked to return. The last known link there was with Manuel Torres Raveo, an archeologist still living in Lisbon in 2006.

The information arriving with the bones revealed complex family relationships in Spain, North Africa, India, Russia, Europe, and China. From these far-reaching destinations, my cousins had traded the most precious commodities of the time: exotic medicine, long swords, spices, gems, furs, silks, perfumes, silver—as well as news and, sometimes, people.

A letter informed someone named Asher that Shalom Rahabi, who had an olive press in Cochin, visited the family of Binyamin HaGadol in Bombay. HaGadol could draw perfect circles and was believed to be a great rainmaker. None of them ever arrived at Hanah's Paradise, and the family link was lost after 1620.

After a quarrel with a rabbi who put on him *kherem*, a curse of excommunication, Hayim Moise Luzzo felt his end approaching and sailed from Venice to Hanah's Paradise but died on the road in 1746. His almond arrived in a small leather box, his name recorded as Moise Meshoumad, the One Who Changed. Written in Italian, the story sent with the almond describes his mystical revelations, his conversations with Adam and Eve and with Messiah, requesting a faster return, "*kivet yakhol, kivet yakhol,* if at all possible." A manuscript bearing his name, titled "*Messilath Mecharim,* Road of the Righteous," contains bizarre magical beliefs, the means to attain *rouah HaKodesh*, spiritual elevation, and the precise scale for measuring it.

Along with the almonds, loving wives or husbands often sent letters, money, gold, objects of ritual use, books, musical scores, drawings, maps, cooking recipes, silk, and sometimes descriptions of their lives and the places where they lived. Some told horror stories of pogroms and killings, of burned villages and synagogues. Sometimes a *kemea*, a talisman, was put around the almond to protect the body in *olam habaa*, the next life. Protective amulets had been in everyday use since earliest times. No one would leave the house without invoking protection from the three angels: Sanvi, Sansanvi, Semangelaf. On special occasions protection was requested directly from their superior, the archangel Rafa'el:

> Against the evil eye
> Against highwaymen
> For success
> For a newly married couple
> For profitable trade

To have a sweet voice
To dissipate a mirage, or a hallucination
To cause an enemy to suffer
To confuse a person's mind
To win a favor.

But the amulet's protection could be a double-edged sword. It could turn against the person that it was supposed to protect, and in many cases one could end up

With a high-pitched voice
With a lost umbrella
With an increase in taxes.

A talisman that proved beneficial on three occasions received a superior status. To dress in red and put salt in a pocket would melt another person's heart for your benefit. To ensure success, a house was to be entered with the right foot first. To find a lost object, it was recommended to put a glass upside down in a prominent place. To cut a sick person's hair or nails resulted in their immediate death. It was possible to stop the rain for several hours by placing two knives on the threshold of a house. Because this was dangerous, only people of belief could do it. If the knives were not pointed in the right direction, a tornado might blow you away. As for cursing, it was mentioned several times by different people that *Maldisyón sin razón toka a su patron*, a curse without reason returns to its owner.

8

The life of Amador Raveo, an ardent Catholic and the oldest son of Don Simeon's oldest grandson, was never recorded at Hanah's Paradise. He is known only because his wife left a detailed account of their encounter. What we know is that without any explanation he said, "Adieu, Lombardia," sold his house in Sabbioneta, and took the twenty-six members of his immediate family to Haifa. He then wrote to his father and friends,

> Leave your country, your kinsmen,
> And your father's house.
> And go to a country that
> I will show you.

In Haifa he changed his name from Amador to the Hebrew *Almagor*, which means fearless, bought land and built two houses: one to live in with his family, the other never to be entered—"To remind me of restraint," he would explain. Each house had four windows to look inside, plus one to look toward Jerusalem. Each house had two doors to get out, plus one for the Prophet Elijah to enter. As a reminder of the destruction of the Jerusalem Temple, one wall was left unfinished but inscribed with a proverb that Almagor particularly liked: *"Tivo shel olam aino mishtaneh*, the nature of the world does not change."

The conversion of Almagor Raveo, once a well-respected Catholic who left a fountain in his name in the public square of Sabbioneta, is astonishing. There is no written explanation for his sudden *egzilo*. What had been going on in his life at the time? How had he made the decision to return to Judaism? How had he persuaded half of his family to leave with him, and what had he felt when separated from the others? Of all the stories that I compiled at Hanah's Paradise, his was the most unusual. He established a list of things to do:

Learn the glass-blowing trade
Build two large octagonal houses
Decorate the interior and landscape the exterior
Purchase clothes, perfumes, and jewelry for future wife
Purchase books, clothes, and toys for future children
Purchase musical instruments for wife and children
Find maids for the house and educators for the children

When everything was done—when rugs, paintings, and furniture filled his houses, when the children's rooms were filled with clothes, books, and toys, when fresh flowers were spread out in vases and the baked bread was on the tables, when pots, dishes, and goblets filled in the shelves—he drew a line under his list and wrote, "I don't need to get married; it is enough to know that I can."

But he changed his mind when he met a Romaniot woman, a distant relative from northern Greece. I learned their story by reading a letter she had left for him. Before she ever met Almagor Raveo, the man who fell in love with her and would become her husband, Arina Persephone HaLevy had a vision. She had seen him once. Secretly, she was standing naked in front of the mirror, combing her hair at midnight. First the mirror showed a boat filled with many people in all manner of dress, speaking many languages. A man's face was rising above the others, and when he caught her eye, he took off his hat and smiled at her. Then she saw him walking on the road toward her house, looking very happy, his hat in one hand and a music box in the other. He opened the music box and seven children came out of it. He embraced them all and told them to look for the house of *la novia de las siete fustanelas*, the bride with seven skirts. Then the candlesticks on either side of the mirror started to flicker, and the last thing Arina saw in the mirror was an image of her first child, a daughter with twin children. When Amador Almagor Raveo came to do business with Arina's father, he brought him a gift—a music box—and Arina Persephone HaLevy recognized his face and knew that he was her destiny.

Arina came from the village of Ardhella, from a Jewish community established there in the second century before the Common Era. They belonged to the Second Roman Empire of Byzantium, and were called Romaniot. She spoke in the *Aroman* Jewish-Greek dialect, which requires the addition of the letter *A* in front of all words beginning with an *R*, protecting this most important letter of the Jewish alphabet from the curse of the evil eye. When her husband brought her into his family, only *ararely* did she *arealize* that people made fun of her. Every Friday night, she invited people to her home and sang old songs about departure, separation, and beautiful women from other countries:

> Ared Sea, bring my love to me
> Arelieve my pain from the lost delight
> Aroyal palm grew in my heart
> Aremember you, aruby in the night.

She was famous for her *ared* fish soup, which she served every Friday. Family members left congratulatory notes in the margins of the scroll, under her name.

Arina's Ared *Fish Soup*

Chop up carrots, tomatoes, oranges, and *ared* peppers.
Chop up garlic and any *ared* fish. Steam them.
Add a spoon of brandy, salt, pepper, and *azafraan*.

She was called Arinel by her husband, who loved her immensely and encouraged her to study music and dance. She gave birth to one daughter and three sets of twins, all boys, bringing the number of their children to seven. At a certain age she told them in private how she saw her destiny: "*Ta'amod arom lifnai ha'rei*, stand naked in front of a mirror at midnight, flanked by two lit candles. You should be alone. As you comb your hair, look into the mirror and your future will be unveiled." Arina's much-loved husband died on a business trip to Portugal. A small painting that arrived with his vertebra shows an elegant man dressed in the fashion of the time, with short hair and the distinctive family dimple on his chin. His list of things to do, with annotations on what he had accomplished, was attached to the painting. Everything was addressed to his wife, Arina Persephone HaLevy, *la novia de las siete funtanelas*, the bride of the seven plagues.

Not able to identify his writing, Arina refused to believe that the letter came from her husband and that the vertebra belonged to him. She continued *arogar*, to pray to God to bring him back to clarify for her the confusion between *fustanelas*, skirts, and *funtanelas*, plagues.

9

Disappointed that he could not see his destiny in the mirror, Arina's son, my great-grandfather Nathan Raveo, bought land from the Turks and built a glass factory to make his own mirrors. By 1910, *Avoda Na'a*, Nice Work Glass Factory, was producing mirrors and glassware. The plant was housed in a long building where several Arab children worked and also lived. They roamed the harbor of Haifa, rummaging through the trash for amber- and green-colored beer bottles, and for blue and clear glass of all kinds. The glass would then be smashed, heated, and transformed into paste for hand-blown vases, small pitchers, water bowls, and spice jars. The resulting glass was a colorful random mixture of spots, lines, and blotches, depending on the finds of the day. There was little concern for shape or dimension—no two glasses were ever alike—and pebbles or small pieces of shell were often trapped in the thickness of the glass.

Nathan, who was skillful with his hands, would purchase expensive glass paste from Austria to make beautiful, delicate, thin drinking glasses for special occasions. He would decorate each one with a colored glass snake that wandered between fruits and flowers and curled twice around the glass. Two light-blue or green snake's eyes observed you from between the glass flowers. The flowers and snake became a trademark of the factory, with each generation adding further embellishments.

Among Nathan's sons, only his youngest, my grandfather Rafa'el, refused to learn how to blow glass. As a young man, Rafa'el defied the commandment, "Ye shall not walk in the manner of the nations," and adopted the Turkish style of dress.

A photograph from 1925 shows him wearing white Turkish pants and a long embroidered *kamiza*, or silk shirt, beneath a black cape. He looks majestic. He is smiling at the statue of a nymph covered in snow. He is quite tall and has curly dark hair, salient cheekbones, and a very high forehead. His appearance is handsome, with an air of remoteness lingering in his eyes.

Records left by others describe him as a thoughtful young man who liked to sing, was knowledgeable about plants, spoke slowly, and smiled unexpectedly. It is also noted that he wanted to marry his grandmother's cook, Aishe, a slender Turkish girl who had— he would tell everybody—three wonderful breasts and three lovely nipples. The girl returned his love and would make, especially for him, eggplant stuffed with black walnuts and lamb with raisins in a dark-brown tamarind sauce. She stuffed apricots with minced meat and coriander and baked them in honey and pomegranate juice, covering them with sesame seeds and pistachios. She stuffed figs with goat cheese. She made rose-petal jelly, which he ate on a flat piece of bread, covered with the sweet *gvina levana*, the white cheese that his mother, Sal'it, made for him.

Tuesday was his favorite day because, on this third day of Creation, God stopped His work, looked twice at what He had done, and found it to His liking. In Rafa'el's mind, God's own recognition of a job well done was a display of extraordinary emotional maturity—God's first lesson in marketing. Fluent in several languages, Rafa'el made friends easily with Arabs, Turks, and Christians from all countries. Trained at an early age to recite poems and stories from the Passover legend, he developed an exceptionally good memory. He also had an uncanny talent for evaluating people and adapting his conversation to the listener. Whenever appropriate, he introduced into his conversations quotations from prayers, verses from popular songs, and political slogans.

Rafa'el spent most of his time with his cousins Or'Tal and Carmel, the daughters of his father's brother, a merchant with trading posts in India. They dressed in exotic Indian saris, ate uncommon foods, and lived in an extravagant home of red marble. The house sat on the French side of Mount Carmel, overlooking the Mediterranean Sea. In the interior garden, a stone marked the exact place where it was believed that Elijah used to pray—"naked," the inscription reads, "to feel closer to God."

Rafa'el's talent for conversation and his knowledge of languages got him invited to all sorts of events. Everyone found this young Hebrew man attractive and helpful. He guided people around town, offering his assistance to merchants, military officers, archeologists, and Bible-lovers alike. Through these visitors, he sent letters and small gifts to members of the family dispersed in other countries. In addition, he had many connections in the Arab villages and was always able to find anything that anyone was looking for in the Holy Land. No one ever had come to suspect that Rafa'el and his two cousins were spying for the British.

The Jews who believed in Dr. Herzl's utopian state tried to help from inside, with the hope that when the British defeated the Turks, they would favor a Jewish state. A young man like Rafa'el, and his two Indian cousins in their exotic costumes, could travel, observe, and ask questions easily. They would gather information that the girls' mother then radioed to another cousin, who served as a British intelligence officer in Cairo. To Rafa'el, for whom pleasure and risk were synonymous, collecting information for the British was a way of feeling part of a bigger world.

After the Ottoman Empire was finally dismantled, Rafa'el turned against the British and, along with his cousins, joined the Jewish Defense Force, smuggling weapons and illegal immigrants through Lebanon. The arms were hidden in specially prepared caves at Hanah's Paradise. Building and stocking a cave was a dangerous operation, but since Rafa'el worked only with his cousins, the British never discovered a single weapon or a single informant.

When it was feared that Rafa'el's subversive activities had become too risky, and when, at the same time, Aishe, the Turkish cook, had become pregnant, Rafa'el's parents decided to send him out of the country. Rafa'el went to study and work in Vienna, in a Europe that was safe again after the Great War. The Viennese architect Edgar Frank, who had designed his uncle's red marble house, offered Rafa'el, a promising young man of twenty-four, an entry-level position in his office. His mother had a cousin in Vienna, and Rafa'el went there gladly, planning to study landscape design. Aishe delivered a stillborn baby, then left the family to work for a French singer in Beirut.

RAFA'EL IN VIENNA

After the war the Austro-Hungarian Jewish community of Vienna was trying to forget its losses. By 1925, chased by pogroms and by the Bolshevik Revolution, Jews from the small villages of Transylvania, Russia, Poland, and Slovakia were fleeing. Those who came to work in Vienna provided cheap labor for the textile factories and the sugar refineries. While helping to rebuild Austria after the war, they were also changing their status from peasants to factory workers, organizing themselves into political and social groups, beginning the process of emancipation.

The students Rafa'el met in Vienna were mostly from Poland and Russia. He was unable to make friends among them or among the other immigrants he encountered. Like him, they were foreigners, and the gap between their cultures proved unbridgeable. They were living in different linguistic dimensions—family life in Yiddish, friendship and ideology in Russian or Polish, utopian dreams in Hebrew, and cultural life in German—that converged in a mystical place called Zion. He felt that the Viennese-born Jews were arrogant if they were rich, fearful if they were poor, and Germanized if they were educated.

Rafa'el couldn't identify with any of the European Jews. He felt a spiritual separation between himself and them. They were strangers to each other's way of thinking. They did not speak the same language. Even if they believed in the same God, *their* religion felt stuffy, unreal. It had neither color nor intimacy. It lacked warmth and gaiety. It was an orthodoxy that he did not know. "*N'tzor l'shon me'ra u sfatecha m'daber*, guard your tongue from evil and your lips from telling lies," he told himself.

Rafa'el didn't hide his strangeness, choosing extravagance over anonymity. He dressed only in colorful Oriental clothes, thereby separating himself from the Europeans and even more from the black-garbed Hassidic Jews living in Vienna.

Housing was hard to find in Vienna, and Rafa'el was happy to share a room with his cousin Otto. A literary mind with an extraordinary memory and intelligence, Otto Rosenfeld Rank, who exuded the spirit of the time, was a disciple of psychoanalysis. He went to meetings at Dr. Freud's house and explained to Rafa'el the return of the repressed, the Oedipal complex, and the concept of repetition. Not the least bothered by the return of the re-pressed, Rafa'el showed his affection for Otto by telling him his night dreams and stories from Hanah's Paradise.

Working for Herr Frank and going to school left Rafa'el only enough time to observe the city from the windows of cafés. He became a regular at the Café Bijou, where he sat sipping choco-late and looking at the women passing by. In Vienna women were blonde and pale with watery blue eyes. He wondered if their tri-angle of infinite sophistication was also pale. He remembered his lover Aishe, her olive-colored skin, laughing eyes, and long dark hair and the elegance of her almost perfect dark triangle.

Rafa'el believed that every woman was a cousin and he treated them with the same camaraderie. An opera singer who grew up in Jericho, a cousin of an Arab friend from Palestine, became his comrade. She gratefully shared with him the dried fruits and the sweet *lukum*, Turkish delights, that his mother would send. Once a month, they would meet at the park, speak Arabic, and, savoring the tart taste of quince, feel closer to home. The way she laughed at his jokes made him feel intelligent, and the way she held his arm while walking on the street made him feel important. Women's company brought him pleasure.

At the architect's office, Rafa'el's task was to color the drawings and to render the gardens. The firm was building new villas for the rich, houses for the middle class, and thousands of new apart-ments for the growing working-class population. Coming from Palestine, where time is considered private property and details exist only in the ingredients used for cooking, working in an office felt unnatural to Rafa'el. At first, he tried to change the rules—coming in late, staying up all night, initiating conversations. He then ventured to introduce his colleagues to the pleasure of slowly sipped Turkish coffee and the water pipe for smoking tobacco. Rafa'el encountered only indifference and was soon discouraged. As his cousin Otto pointed out to him, his life at the office was a game played to satisfy a rigid father, his love of details, a form of masturbatory obsession, his Turkish costume a disguise for con-trolling people's attention and putting distance between him and everyone else, a sort of rejection of the other. Not only that, but the choice of his profession, the desire to transform the physical world, involved some degree of rejection and was based on delu-

sion. He, Rafa'el, did not yet understand that architects are pro-
miscuous. Each project is a new mistress; each new idea a form of
seduction; each line drawn on paper, a link to a utopian world. Inventing all modes of life is motivated by a fundamental illusion:
the persistent hope that, one day, an imagined drawing will become reality. This world anticipated on paper is deprived of meaning; like coitus interruptus, it crumbles layer after layer, under the
demands of reality. What is negated, Otto told Rafa'el, is not talent
but imagination. What is castrated is not satisfaction but desire.
Rafa'el felt the remark to be unjust.

Rafa'el walked around the streets thinking about his father and
his own identity. He made mental lists of his own qualities and his
faults; he remembered the good things that his friends had said
about him. He looked back on his life and realized that he could
not remember any time when he had said, "This is what I want."
Events decided for him. His life was an accumulation of situa-
tions into which he had fallen by chance. Every day was the same,
except when something happening outside of himself obliged him
to react.

Rafa'el was at a very delicate point in his existence. He understood that his good nature and humorous ways were a defense
against the wish to be left alone, to do nothing, to feel bad. His
eagerness to help other people made him feel that something of
their life was rubbing off on him. Readily identifying with other
people, Rafa'el imagined himself a musician, an artist, a banker,
or a politician. He felt Arab when he spoke with the Arabs at the
glass factory. He ate with his right hand when he went to their
homes. He felt loved whenever they said, "You are one of us." He
would walk with them across the Jordan to smuggle alcohol and
cigarettes. On the way back he would stop and spend the night
with the Bedouins, sleeping on the sand like them, eating from
one big dish, and helping them sell their hashish to the British.

After his conversation with Otto, Rafa'el hid his loneliness, focused on his work, and made an effort to change his personality. He went to work early in the morning, organized his drawing
table to the strict specifications of Herr Frank, and finally understood that his colleagues were not his friends. He stopped asking them to join him for coffee and exchanged stories only about

the emperor, the mayor, and the performance at the opera. He focused his interest on his work, learning how to draw the plans on crisp linen. Soon Rafa'el's imagination and lust for ambiguity overcame the rules. Giving free expression to his desires, Rafa'el drew terraced gardens for the villas, covering them with caper bushes, cactus plants, fig trees, cypress, artichoke bushes, palm trees—everything that normally grows at a different latitude.

The first time Herr Frank looked at the drawings, he stood there spellbound. Drawings are notations of an imaginary reality at a specific scale. In the elegant landscapes where Rafa'el drew gardens and clouds, the viewer felt drawn into the vanishing point. Painfully rubbed with light-gray charcoal, shadows gave movement to the landscape and depth to the enclosing walls along the gardens. The drawings were indeed beautiful. Only after looking very closely and for a long time, only then, did one notice the Hebrew letters drawn among the flowers and the leaves of trees. Seen from a specific angle, the dot marking the center of a flower and the curly line that turned inward to form a spiral became an *aleph*. From right to left, the grass was talking, and every flower was a message, a measure of Rafa'el's secretive life, of his loneliness and incapacity to adapt to a different culture.

> God made the letters of the Hebrew alphabet
> And with them He created the Universe.
> Should God withdraw His letters
> For even an instant,
> The Universe would cease to exist.

Vertical lines of cypress branches would inform a knowledgeable reader of Hebrew that

> Wisdom is silent, knowledge has voice—
> The alphabet links them.

After Herr Frank studied the drawings, he realized that the bizarreness of the exotic plants gave his buildings a dreamlike quality. He smiled at a softness he associated with the Germanic love for the Mediterranean landscape of Italy and Greece. A most romantic Hebrew man, Herr Frank remarked.

The story of Rafa'el's family as it had been told to him started in the dark-brown center of a sunflower. With the self-centered interest that only a young man could have about his own life, Rafa'el described himself as a tall, good-looking man, twenty-four years of age, with dark eyes, olive skin, and dark hair. Proud of his name and the place it occupies in Heaven, Rafa'el drew elaborate waterfalls and wild landscapes.

> Rafa'el is the archangel who brings good news. I am called *Israfil* in Arabic, and I shall be there on the *Yawm al Quiamah* for the Arabs, on the *Yom HaDin* for the Jews, and on the Day of Resurrection for the Christians. I am a unified angel with an enormous hairy body, covered with many mouths and tongues so I can speak all languages.

Other flowers described the languages Rafa'el could speak and how he had learned them.

> Arabic from my friend Sinan; English from the British when they entered Palestine and from my Indian cousins; French from the *Alliance Française Universelle* in Haifa; German from school in Vienna; Greek from my father; Hebrew from the synagogue and from the first Hebrew newspaper in Jerusalem, the *Levanon*; Ladino from my mother and grandmother; Italian from the Dante Alighieri Literary Circle and Library in Jerusalem; Turkish from Aishe and from the Turks at school.

Rafa'el was the first in his family to be born in Palestine at a time when the Hebrew language was being restored. Around 1880 a poet, Eleizer Ben Yehuda, revived the language by composing new words from the religious vocabulary. An oak tree, drawn on the east side of a villa near the Danube, informed the experienced reader of Hebrew:

> We descend from our patriarch, Ya'aqov. At the stream of Sbbok, after an all-night fight with an angel, he changed his name to Israel.

An entire rose garden blossomed with Rafa'el's descriptions of people, events, and dreams:

When the people of Israel lived in their homeland, they created their own laws, the *Tannah* and the *Mishnah*. Then came the separation of land and people. The law left the land, along with those who created it, and the land acquired other laws, changing from time to time. For more than five thousand years the Jews took their law with them wherever they went, submitting to it whenever they could enjoy any measure of freedom. But they didn't speak Hebrew.

Landscape design is an abstract form of giving texture to contour, and the drawings Rafa'el made for Herr Frank's office were exquisitely crafted works of art. The lawn, the trees, the flowers, the sky, even the light and the shadows—all made of minuscule dots and curly lines—gave the stark modernistic buildings a contrasting luxuriance. The drawings looked intimate and strange at the same time. Feeling that after more than a year working day and night at the office, he had learned all that he needed from Herr Frank, Rafa'el set a date for his return to Palestine.

Before his departure, he asked Herr Frank to help him draw a building praising progress and modernity—a much-needed opera house for the city of Afula, where his grandfather had some land. Afula is known for its *garinim*, roasted sunflower seeds, which people eat constantly as they talk. Because *F* and *P* are the same letter in Hebrew, the city is jokingly known as *Apula*, slang for penis. This simple phonetic distortion made the inhabitants display a certain irritation when asked where they lived. "So what if I am from Afula?" they answered argumentatively.

Rafa'el told his cousin Otto of his plans for the opera house. Otto talked to Rafa'el about *la folie des grandeurs*. Rafa'el made a set of preliminary sketches, and Herr Frank designed an imaginary opera house for a city he didn't know, on a site that was not yet chosen. Rafa'el had not been able to provide him with much information about the city, except that it was situated in a pine grove, that north was on the short side of the land, and that Afula had no major monuments. To his credit, Herr Frank understood the situation and designed a low structure with an impressive top forming a crown upon which "Almagor Ben Yakov Ravayah Opera House" was written in gold letters. Rafa'el placed the building in a formal garden with waterfalls, fountains, ponds, and a ceremonial entrance. He used the occasion to draw the story of his family, exactly as he had heard it from his grandfather at every Passover dinner:

> At Passover, each generation is told that a man must feel as if he himself were a slave. This is to learn not to enslave others. Oppression is evil! The Name took us out of bondage, and in 1296 our name was in the register of Erfoud, a fortified town in the lower Atlas Mountains at the end of the Ziz Valley in Morocco. The family was prosperous and received the right to build a synagogue. Later on, the Jews expelled from Spain by the idiotic Queen Isabella, *La Catolica*, joined them, and there they lived peacefully with the Arabs. They traveled as far east as Persia and China. This is written by Rafa'el, the first native speaker of Modern Hebrew in our family.

The drawing showed a luxurious landscaped garden in which the names of Rafa'el's entire family were inscribed in flowers, trees, birds, statues, and droplets of water. Names of cities, important dates, and words of a prayer formed a pattern around the edges of the opera house drawing.

Av HaRahamim, let us also remember
The communities of *Yehudim*, Jews who have been killed
Because they believed in Your name, O *Père Miséricordieu*.

10

While preparing for his departure, Rafa'el appealed to the Jewish Fund to donate trees to plant in Palestine. For it is written in the Old Testament, "When you come to the Land, plant all manner of trees." When his parents received the news that Rafa'el was returning home, they promised to help him open a school to teach landscaping and gardening to the new immigrants.

All was proceeding as planned when Rafa'el witnessed a most extraordinary event. On the spur of the moment he decided to go to a Zionist meeting, with the hope that he would see someone he knew from Palestine, and with the desire to hear what the people who believed in a Jewish state had to say. He took his time walking there, stopping to drink a hot chocolate at the Café Central, crossing the street, and stopping again—this time to eat an apple cake with honey. He passed by the Art Center, a Secessionist building with an elegant gold dome, glanced at the inscription—"*Der Zeit ihre Kunst, Der Kunst ihre Freiheit*," "To Each Time Its Art, To Art Its Freedom"—and turned the corner to the Hotel Beethoven, where the meeting was being held. The streets were full of people at this time of the day, and Rafa'el noticed how beautiful the trees and the buildings looked under the drizzle of late September. "Autumn is here," he sighed. He hesitated for a moment, looking at the street as if he wanted to count the cobblestones, and with a final feeling of regret, entered the lobby.

Rafa'el wrote his name in the register and was directed to the balcony. Some two hundred people were loudly convening in the ballroom below. It was not a good idea to have come, he thought. The meeting had already begun. Looking around, Rafa'el noticed the Jews from Poland dressed in their ridiculous black coats, with short pants, big hats, and unkempt beards. They were laughing and shouting to each other across the room, arrogantly disrupting the speaker.

Facing the audience on a raised wooden platform, several people sat at a table talking among themselves. From among them a man with a goatee, dressed in the Viennese fashion, stood up thrusting a clenched fist at the audience:

Our previous speaker believes that assimilation is the way to ameliorate the *Volksprofil der Juden*, the profile of the Jewish people, in image and reality. Not to offend him, but I cannot stop myself from asking a question: Is assimilation also a conversion? Our eloquent friend has well-founded reproaches on the morality of the Jews. But has he analyzed the historical circumstances that provoked and, by necessity, produced the decadence of the Jewish character? Should one convert in order to become a moral person?

The question circled the room, and after some hissing and nodding, a man sitting near the speaker shouted unexpectedly: "This is not possible! The subject of conversion goes beyond the limits of reason. It is a question that one addresses to the heart, to filial piety, to the fidelity of parents, who are themselves loyal to *their* parents. This question touches something fundamental in our spirits, which will reveal itself impossible to uproot."

The speaker looked at him and nodded his head in approval. In the front rows, a group of religious scholars sat motionless, their arms crossed, their fur hats projecting large shadows on the walls. They seemed small in their oversized black coats, their pale faces framed by two long strands of hair. On the other side of the room, an older rabbi was trying to calm some children. The speaker looked disturbed by their laughter but continued:

Our illustrious colleague is asking us to raise our children as Christians before they are able to make personal choices, at an age when a conversion could be seen as a sign of opportunism or cowardice. Dissimulation and double life makes for dissidents, libertarians, and freethinkers. Many of the converted Jews are attacking us with more vehemence than the Catholic Church, and some have written horrible books about Jewish life. *Jüden* brothers, how many pogroms should we witness, how much humiliation should we accept, how long should we live in fear? We have no home, and whenever difficulties arise, we are the first to be blamed. Yes, we can ignore anti-Semitism; we can assimilate or convert to different religions, as many of us have done over the centuries.

"Yes!" a voice from the audience erupted. "Even our language is lost in exile! It has been permeated by outside influences. We no longer speak Hebrew, but Yiddish. Remember, brothers, assimilation means annihilation. We cannot assimilate! A Jewish soul is always a Jewish soul, even when converted!"

People were walking in and out of the room, moving chairs, standing up and yelling at each other, ignoring the speaker.

"Dr. Herzl was an assimilated Jew!" somebody shouted.

"Indeed he was!" the man on the podium retorted. "But after he discovered the true face of anti-Semitism at the Dreyfus trial, he changed his position."

"No he didn't!" someone countered.

"Yes he did!" boomed a voice in the back of the room. "He pleaded our cause with the sultan of Constantinople, and with His Majesty Wilhelm the Second as early as 1898!"

"What cause?"

"The cause of political Zionism," somebody from under the balcony answered.

"*Lieben Jüden!* Dear Jews!" the speaker said. "Go home, go to your wives, speak with your neighbors, write letters and tell everybody that we must go home and rebuild our lives and our Temple. The Land of Our Fathers is waiting for our return. Even before Napoleon went to Galilee, Hassidic Jews from Poland settled there in 1777. Moroccans went to Haifa in 1817, and the first *aliyah*, the first migration from Russia, was in 1882. Go to every village. Tell everybody that there is a British mandate for a Jewish homeland. We do not have to fear drunken Polish or Ukrainian soldiers anymore. Go tell our brothers that there is a place where all of us are welcome."

His face red and his hair disheveled, the orator started coughing, moving his arms in circles, gasping for air—the scattered pages of his discourse floating onto the floor. Somebody from the table gave him a glass of water and helped him to a chair. The man took a sip and tried to calm his coughing by slapping himself on the back.

In the second row, a Hassidic rabbi stood up to address the audience. "With your permission, young man, while you catch your breath, I would like to remind everyone in this room that we are not simply Jews without a home, without a language, accepting with joy and humility the leftovers of other nations. We are not just Jews. We are the People of the Book. We are the Chosen People, we are God's children, and there is no *Eretz Israel* until the Messiah comes and leads us all to the City of David. Are you the Messiah, my son?" he asked the speaker. "Are you David's son?"

The man at the table shook his head.

"So, if you are not the Messiah, how dare you upset our hosts and risk bringing more fury on our people! How dare you question a nation that lets us print our prayer books! How dare you insult their leaders by comparing them with drunken soldiers! Yes, people have been killed. But not only Jews! Yes, some have been raped and *geschasst*, chased naked, by dogs. It is true! But this was a mistake. The king's prime minister apologized. This will never happen again. Aren't we free to walk the streets of Vienna? Don't we have Yiddish theaters? Don't we live peacefully with our hosts? Why is this not enough for you? Even our sons returned from war with decorations. They fought against the French, and sometimes the French were their Jewish cousins. We have been guests here for almost four hundred years. Nobody is going anywhere! There is no *Eretz Israel* until Messiah arrives. All of you should be ashamed! When need be, a Jew must die for the sanctification of the Divine Name. Is survival more important than identity?"

His voice now trembling with fury, his fist in the air above his head, his body bent, the rabbi stamped his foot in anger. His fur hat tottered on his head. "Is survival more important than identity?" he shouted again. "Shame on you, shame, shame! You shall be cursed!" He kept shouting until his words became a hoarse whisper and, in the silence of the room, a woman's voice emerged, covering his mumbling.

"Rabbi," the woman began, "I don't think you are aware of the irony of what you just said. Do you really believe that being chased out of a village and losing everything you have is a gift? Do you, Rabbi, believe that being raped is a favor? Do you think that people have to be beaten or murdered to glorify God? And don't you think that when people are so often chased away, it might be a better idea to leave than to return?"

After the initial surprise of hearing a woman confront a rabbi, people were now stretching their necks to look at her.

"Rabbi," she continued, "you are living in a world of superstition and delusions. Persecution will not end, Rabbi. For four hundred years we have been tolerated here. It is time for us to leave. A good guest doesn't stay such a long time, Rabbi. A good guest finds a place to settle."

The voice belonged to a young woman dressed in a blue suit, a bright orange scarf draped around her shoulders. A hat completely covered her head. She moved from her chair, walked up the aisle toward the second row where the rabbi stood, and aimed her finger at him.

"Go home, Saul Ben Levy, rabbi of Danzig," she said with a dramatic slowness. "Go home! Pack your books and your prayer shawl. Leave at once and tell everyone that there is no place for the Jews but *Eretz Israel.*"

As the young woman moved closer to the platform, the previous speaker tried to dismiss her with a flick of his wrist.

"Excuse me, *meine liebe Dame*," he said. "I was interrupted, so please let me respond to our guest, the rabbi, since it was on my time that he spoke."

The woman ignored him. "And there are medals in the *Yishuv*, the settlement, also, along with theaters and libraries," she said, with more than a hint of sarcasm.

From the podium, the speaker tried to stop her. "As a matter of fact, young lady, you talk like those people who frequent Dr. Freud's lectures. What delusions! Keep this pseudo-science in your kitchen—if you know how to cook. This Freud was baptized in secret. He is an assimilated Jew, ashamed of his origins. He believes in a religion born from the same superstitions that he is trying to sweep away. Isn't this Freud the one who believes that everything in our life is about . . ." he said, then started laughing, glancing with complicity at the other men on the podium. "Go to Dr. Freud. Don't mingle in affairs that you don't . . ."

The rest of his sentence was lost in the room as Rafa'el stood up and shouted from the balcony.

Youuuu! You, German Jew! You are insulting our Matriarchs! You are being disrespectful of Sarah, Rebecca, Leah, and Rachel. Watch your tongue, you German Jew! You are talking to a Jewish woman! You speak like a woman-hater! In Palestine, women fight against the British shoulder-to-shoulder with men. In the *Yishuv* they give life to the Balfour Declaration. On *moshavim*, our farms, women use the tractor and the rifle. We respect women. We love them. Have you heard about Operation NILI, a famous spy ring organized by women? They gathered military information and sent it to the British in Cairo to help them get rid of the Turks. Have you heard about it? The acronym stands for "The Eternal One of Israel will not lie." When the Turks discovered them, everyone was arrested and tortured. How many of you have been in a Turkish jail? How many of you know how difficult it is to be a woman? We should all unite and be happy to have women around us because they are intelligent and . . . uh . . . so beautiful.

Rafa'el had only a vague idea of the relationship between Zionism and Jewish mysticism and could not understand this sudden impulse to talk. Hearing his voice floating in the silence of the room, he became confused. From downstairs people looked at him with curiosity. His words were difficult to grasp. He spoke with an accent and rolled his *R*'s. This tall young man with a black cape on his shoulders, a richly embroidered tunic, and long black hair was perhaps an Oriental prince, an emissary of the sultan. As he paused, not knowing what to say, an older woman stood up and addressed him with reverence.

"Thank you, Your Highness, for the kind words, but you don't have to defend us. United, we can speak for ourselves. Women are abused by fearful, small-minded Jews, obsessed with Messiah. It is time for them to stop treating women as slaves."

"And *you* are one of these women who wants to teach us a lesson?" a young man from the back interrupted. Other men in the audience burst into whistles and shouts.

Undeterred, the older woman continued. "Little Jews from small towns, this is Vienna in 1926! We have to stay here and improve our social status. We have to build training schools. We have to demand that Jewish women be admitted to the university. We cannot just get up and leave."

"Of course we can," came a voice from someone Rafa'el couldn't see from the balcony. "We can also build schools *there*." All heads turned toward the man. "Yes," the voice continued. "We need doctors and teachers and rabbis there—and everybody else—to build our country."

The women applauded and the men stamped their feet on the floor. Then the room calmed down, becoming almost silent. The woman with the orange scarf turned her back to the speakers' platform to face the room, and in a calm, clear voice said, "I am Adah Cohen, the granddaughter of Joseph Cohen Meir, rabbi of Zurich. I am a photographer and have documented Jewish life in Serbia and Romania, in Russia and Moravia. Fear and poverty are everywhere. People in the villages speak Yiddish but hardly a word of Russian or Polish. Few of them are able to travel, and there is not much work. Zionism is our fight against Diaspora. United we can determine our own destiny. It is time to go home, to build *Eretz Israel*."

As she continued to speak, the Hassidic rabbi, who now looked rather frail, suddenly shoved the chairs out of his way and stormed in her direction, his eyes fixed on her. She didn't move. When the space between them diminished, he extended his arms, and opened the palms of his hands outward to ensure distance between them. Still staring, he circled around her at arm's length, one way, then the other. He stopped to catch his breath, looked her up and down several times, pushed his fur hat up on his forehead, stretched his neck to get closer, and then, without uttering a word, spat in her face.

Immobilized by the shock of this crude gesture, everyone forgot to breathe. The room felt empty of life. The yellow spit on Adah's face looked like the scar of a wound, a reminder of the pain of the disagreement, a rupture between Jews. Frozen, Adah continued to look in front of her, ignoring both the rabbi's outstretched arms and the saliva on her face. Seen from the balcony, the rabbi's large body was a grotesque form. With his short legs hidden under his black coat, his arms still extended in front of him, and his wide fur hat hiding his face, he looked like a fat black beast moving around a statue.

In a silence that seemed without end, Adah grabbed the end of her orange scarf, wiped her face twice, then wiped off her hand, paused for a moment, and ever so slowly took off her hat. When she shook her head, an enormous orange-red mane spread in the air, capturing the light from the ballroom windows and turning everything to orange.

The rabbi bowed to the assembly, put his hands into his pockets, and said, "We go when Messiah tells us to return from exile. We go when He comes." Turning his body away from Adah, he started to walk—his left foot in the air, his eyes already fixed on the door—a black puppet dancing the *Hora*.

A terrifying cry pierced the room, and Adah leaped forward, pushing the rabbi to the floor. In a second, the old man disappeared under a bolt of orange hair. When people in the room realized what was happening, it was too late. Adah—her knees on the rabbi's chest—had taken hold of his hat and was tearing off pieces of fur, pushing them into the rabbi's mouth and face. It took four men to pull her away.

"*Le Shana Tova*, Rabbi, Happy New Year," Adah said, as she stood up and put on her hat.

Rafa'el felt that his soul had left the balcony and wrapped around that orange hair, orange scarf, blue velvet miracle of a woman, covering her with layers of profound admiration. Still standing in the balcony, he felt lightheaded and, without full awareness, began applauding the woman as she moved away.

The room became alive with shouting people. "She hit the rabbi!" "She had the right to speak." "He spit on her." "Is the rabbi afraid of a young woman?" "A learned man should know better!" Women were forming a circle near Adah, and some men were yelling, nearly at blows. From the podium, a speaker declared the end of the afternoon session.

THE BEDOUIN SONG

Rafa'el walked to the nearby Café Sans Souci. His exotic Oriental clothing made people turn their heads after him. They walked slower as he approached, leaving space around him, letting him pass, and Rafa'el, indifferent to hidden smiles and gazes, observed the Viennese observing him. He sat at a table, looking at the pretty *nekevot*, young girls, passing by. He could not understand what had stirred him to speak. "Happy New Year, Rabbi," he said, then burst into laughter and mumbled to himself, "One should listen only to his own truth! Isn't that what Maimonides said?" Rafa'el decided to return for the evening session. He took the same seat in the balcony and caught himself looking for the woman with the orange scarf. He spotted her unmistakable blue hat, and kept glancing at her back as a new speaker stood up.

"From Zion will come the law, and from Jerusalem the word of the Eternal," the man began. "I came from Tel Aviv to bring you the word of the Eternal. He needs you there. Do not think that if you stay here you will save us from ourselves. We need you in Palestine to increase our Jewish population. We need you, as never before, to unite and dedicate your life to the establishment of our country. You already think about the land of Yizra'el. Don't you pray to be *Le Shanah Habaah be Yerushalayim*, next year in Jerusalem? Why stay here? Why? You live in Poland or Russia, but your life revolves around holidays and events from a different place. Come back to the land of the Talmud! Now you look at snow and see sand dunes. You walk around a lake and think of the Red Sea. Your imagination is full of events and pictures divorced from reality. A Jewish child in Russia is reading Hebrew books and looking at pictures that escape him completely. Who has ever seen a pomegranate, or a camel, in his village? This anomaly makes you have a life in two places. You are always there, while surviving here. Zionism offers you the chance to bridge the gap, to transform the images of the Book into reality. Live your Jewish life in Palestine!"

Seeing the woman in blue and orange getting up to leave, Rafa'el grabbed his cape and rushed for the stairs. When he arrived in the lobby, the concierge was opening the heavy glass door for her. Rafa'el caught his breath.

"I very much admired your courage when you confronted the rabbi," he said. "Congratulations!"

The glass door was already closing when Adah turned around and from outside—taking in the details of his costume—said, "Congratulations to you, too." They were both smiling from opposite sides of the hotel door, until the concierge opened it again and Rafa'el found himself on the street next to her.

"I am Rafa'el Ben Nathan Raveo and I am from Palestine."

She moved a strand of hair from her eyes, waited a second, and replied, "I am Adah Cohen and I am from Budapest." They stood there looking at each other until Rafa'el said, "Maybe I can walk with you, if you don't mind?"

"I am going to my studio, not far from here."

"Why was the rabbi so angry with you?" Rafa'el asked.

"This is not the first time I have argued with him. I went to the meeting to show support for the foundation of a Jewish state. He is a foolish old man. Every morning he thanks God that he was not born a woman. He does not believe in emancipation; for him to be Jewish means to be religious and to fulfill the required daily *mitzvoth*, good deeds. And there are 613 of them."

"As many as the seeds of a pomegranate," Rafa'el said, smiling.

She stopped walking, turned her head to face him, and clearly amused, said, "You didn't count them!" And without waiting for an answer, she said, "The rabbi knows that men could lose control over a free labor force if women become educated. To him, a woman is less important than a cow. A sick cow is treated. A sick woman is lamented. When I photographed the Jews of Eastern Europe, I saw men getting drunk, beating their wives. 'You have to beat your wife every week,' they say. 'If you don't know why, she certainly does.' I see those desperate, hungry women and children—the orphans, the prostitutes—all those people who never learned dignity. I encourage them to join the *Yishuv*. There are organizations that give money for people to make *aliyah*, to immigrate there; to ascend, as the word says. The rabbis are opposed, of course. They are waiting for Messiah to lead them to Jerusalem. For the Hassidic Jews, emancipation means the end of Judaism. The men are obsessed with their mythical past and are waiting for a redeeming future."

"*Bidyiuk*, precisely," Rafa'el said. "Don't believe that we need more of this fanatical, mystical Judaism there. We have our own."

Adah was walking briskly, paying no attention to the street as she cut through the crowds. Rafa'el kept pace, his face turned toward hers.

"And how successful are you," he asked, "in convincing them to go to Palestine?"

"In general," Adah said, "people are looking for an opportunity. The old people are harder to convince. They are afraid and ask the rabbis. But the young, if they are unmarried, are happy to leave home."

"Have you ever been to Palestine?"

"No," said Adah, "never. But I plan to go soon. There is work for me there, too."

"And what are those young people going to do in Palestine?" Rafa'el asked. Adah glanced at him for a few seconds, then said, "Let's forget what they would do there. What do you think they are doing here?"

Before Rafa'el could answer, Adah continued. "Here they move to the city to escape pogroms and to search for work. They change from peddlers and day workers into proletarians. After a while they get organized and support subversive parties, hoping to influence the political regime. Whenever the monarchy feels threatened, the police and the instigators go after the Jews. They are not spared religious and ethnic prejudices. And this is if they are lucky, because in the villages they get killed."

Rafa'el watched her as she went on vividly talking about the Zionist dream. Passersby separated them momentarily; when he caught up with her again, he said, "And there—in Palestine—what could they do?"

"They can work the land, build roads and factories. They can prepare the country for the arrival of the middle class, the merchants and the professionals. After them, the intellectuals will bring cultural life. When we have theaters and museums, art schools and architecture, the wealthy financial class will also arrive. This is how you make a country. The Balfour Declaration calls for a Jewish state for the Jewish people."

Rafa'el shook his head. "Your view is idealistic. There are other forces that will fight against Palestine's becoming a Jewish state. The British will have to leave, and the Arabs will have to agree for the Jews to come. This will never happen!"

Adah stopped walking and turned to face Rafa'el, looking straight into his eyes for a long moment. People flowed around them. When the sound of the tramway wheels screeching on their rails died away, very softly Adah said, "And why not?"

That is when Rafa'el fell in love.

Something about the way Adah said those words reminded him of a night he had spent hiding in the desert near Masada. As that event unfolded in his mind, mist covered his eyes. The dark clouds of the Viennese sky became the night sky of the Negev when the *Hamsim*, the sandstorm from the Arabian Desert, blew in. Rafa'el and two other friends were waiting with their ears glued to the cold rocks near the road to listen for the arrival of a British convoy moving weapons to Jerusalem. The wind grew stronger, the sand bit into their faces. It entered into the eyes, the ears, under the nails, and between the teeth. It struck their leather coats with the sound of rain on a metal roof. Rafa'el turned against the wind and looked at his friends—unrecognizable forms covered with sand.

They waited all night. They couldn't talk or smoke for fear that the Bedouins would see them and inform the British, who might have sent out patrols before the convoy. Rafa'el was cold. His legs were numb and he tried to move. He pulled himself up on the other side of the rock, rolled over, and stretched his body. He stayed there for several minutes, listening to the silence.

The wind had broken the clouds. In the light of the moon the desert took magical forms. Above him, the road to Tel Arad cut into the purple cliffs and rock formations. He saw the ruins of the Roman legion encampment in front of him, and the ice-blue salt islands floating on the Dead Sea. The fires burning on the other side seemed very close. When a heart-breaking Bedouin song ruptured the night, Rafa'el felt a desperate nostalgia in the lilting voice:

> *Va vainou va isefra,*
> A voyage in the night,
> *Isefra va vainou va,*
> Come with me
> To the land of love.
> Ask the wind,
> To bring me to you,
> When doubts arise,
> Where can I hide
> But in your heart?

The tone of Adah's voice brought back the memory of that song.

"And why not?" he repeated her question. "Because the assimilated Jews, the professionals and the middle class, will not move to Palestine. They are well established here, and in Palestine we are constantly at war. The Arabs living in Palestine do not welcome you there. They don't want your theaters and art galleries. They don't want Jerusalem to be a Jewish city and their land, a Jewish state."

Adah shook her head. She took several steps in front of him and stopped by the window of a photo shop. She unlocked the door and entered, leaving Rafa'el in the darkness of the doorway. Unable to see inside, waiting for her to turn on the lights, he followed the swish that the silk lining of her skirt made against her legs. When she turned on the lights, she motioned him to enter and, with the same spellbinding voice that had ripped him apart, she said, "Never underestimate the desires of a woman."

After several months of keeping company and going around the city together, Rafa'el and Adah became friends. His plan to return to Palestine was postponed. On her birthday, he stopped by her studio to bring her a gift.

He sat on a chair near her small stove listening to the rain outside, his eyes following her hands as she opened the long box. It was an ivory cane with a rounded silver top. Engraved in the burnished silver, the temple of Luxor dominated the horizon and a *felucca* sailed on the Nile. On the bank, two men led a camel between groves of bamboo. A flock of storks dotted the sky where a garnet stone radiated its soft light. It was a beautiful object, made even more so because it was, for Adah, useless.

While Adah was admiring the cane, Rafa'el began humming a song. For some reason, it had come to his mind. It was an old Ladino song about love and faith and people leaving for faraway destinations:

> *Nao mi fala de amor,*
> *Fala me tamben dao fado.*
> Do not cry about love!
> Better pray to destiny.
> When the palms move
> In the night wind
> And my lover says good-bye,
> I lend him my heart
> To make the road light.

Her gift in one hand, Adah lit a cigarette with the other and moved closer to him. Rafa'el smiled at her as he sang, then extended his hand toward her. Adah felt a surge of affection for this slender, almost timid young man and put the cane next to him on the table. Then she lifted up her hair, bent her head toward him, and put her lips on the words of his song. Rafa'el took her in his arms. She put one arm around him, holding the other one in the air to keep the smoke away from them, and they stayed like that, kissing, until they could breathe no more. When she felt the cigarette burning her fingers, she disengaged from the embrace. Rafa'el let her slip away but at the last second held her back. "I wanted very much for this to happen!" he said.

"Do you think it has?"

He took the cigarette from her fingers, moved with her slowly to the kitchen, and put some cooking oil over her burn. She turned toward him and kissed him again.

"Now it has," he answered.

They rented an apartment near Rafa'el's office and were married five months later, on March 16, 1927. Rafa'el's parents came all the way from Palestine. His cousin Otto sent a gift from Paris, where he was working as a psychoanalyst. Adah's grandparents arrived from Zurich, bringing with them their cook.

The wedding was celebrated at the Moorish-style Dohány Synagogue in Budapest. For good luck, they chose to be married on a Tuesday. After the ceremony, they went by boat to Pest, where dinner was held in the fashionable Gellert Hotel. Adah and Rafa'el spent the night drinking champagne at the bar, listening to jazz until early morning. They danced, just the two of them, on the empty floor by the bar. They made an attractive couple, he in an elaborate white-embroidered coat, she in a dark-green silk dress. Her orange hair was gathered up, held with a *mahdour*, a headdress of silver wire and enameled ornaments from Morocco, a gift sent by Rafa'el's sisters.

At the end of that fall Adah, eight months pregnant, assumed her new role with patience. Rafa'el admired her courage and studied her transformed body with affection. He drew flowers on her swollen belly, photographed her in profile, and wrote songs and poems for her. Adah delivered twins, which didn't surprise anyone in Rafa'el's family. There were twins in every generation on his father's side. Adah let her mother and a nanny take care of Aram, the boy, and Bilu, the girl. Rafa'el had to stay in Vienna for his work, and Adah stayed with him, making the three-hour trip to Budapest every weekend to spend time with the children.

Three more children followed over the next four years—Rina, Ruth, and Oded—all born in Vienna, all brought up by Adah's parents in Budapest. Adah was hired by the Jewish Joint Distribution Committee, a relief organization that had been helping the poor since 1914. The agency was keeping records of significant historical events and Adah was hired to take photographs of Jewish villages. Adah and Rafa'el bought a car and traveled through Europe. Adah would take pictures, then talk with the women.

"If you want to go to Palestine to work the land, I can find you free passage. In Palestine the air smells like fresh bread and cloves. And it never snows there," she would often add.

IN THE SETTLEMENT

By 1932, after Egypt and Iraq had gained their independence, people from the entire Arab peninsula started moving between the borders of the newly formed states. An air of progress and development swept over the countries around the Mediterranean. From Palestine came increasingly strong requests for new immigrants. People were needed to work in the new port of Haifa and the copper mines in the Negev. Jewish settlements were established and cities started to grow. In Jerusalem, the Hebrew University enrolled its first students. In Haifa, the Technion University finally opened. Conflict over its official language had delayed the classes; Hebrew eventually prevailed over German. In Tel Aviv, Jewish musicians formed the Palestine Symphony Orchestra.

From his sister, Rafa'el received a poster for the Levant Fair: a panorama of products from all over the world would be presented in Tel Aviv. The poster featured a Pegasus flying above the main pavilion of the Settlement, with products from the Jewish colony on display.

The Jewish International Fund helped purchase land, and waves of immigrants from Germany brought European flair to the new cities. Wider streets, apartment houses, parks, gardens, and art galleries were all being built. In 1936 Arturo Toscanini conducted the opening concert of the Palestine Symphony Orchestra. Tel Aviv was the symbol of fun, youth and progress. The first city in the country to be illuminated by electricity, it had a casino by the sea, a wide boardwalk, and fine beaches. "Tel Aviv is never quiet. People stroll, dance, conduct business, and supreme gaiety lasts all night," Rafa'el's younger sister, Karina, wrote. She was teaching at the Gymnasia Herzeliya, the first secular school in the country, where instruction was only in Hebrew, the forgotten language that after more than three thousand years was finally being adapted to modern times. Names and terms for things not known in the biblical time were invented as needed. Hebrew, the language stripped of its life, subdued to liturgy, was being revived. "In Tel Aviv," Karina wrote, "even street signs are in Hebrew."

Helped by recommendations from former clients and connections established in Palestine during his first visit, Herr Frank had won a competition to design the Belingson Hospital near Tel Aviv. When, near the end of 1937, the building was almost completed, Herr Frank offered Rafa'el the opportunity to travel to Palestine for several months to design the landscape surrounding the hospital complex. Rafa'el felt a strong desire to show Adah his home, and Adah felt compelled to see the Settlement in the making.

They left on September 12, 1937, and took with them the three younger children and their nurse. Aram and Bilu, the twins, now almost ten, remained in Budapest to attend school. The travelers took the Orient Express to Istanbul. They stayed at the Pera Palace and, for five days, walked around the Bazaar and the city, then sailed to Greece. They visited Athens and, before taking the boat to Haifa, made a side trip to meet Rafa'el's family in Thessalonica.

Thessalonica was a modern and prosperous city where Jews from France, Spain, Turkey, Greece, and Lebanon worked in the silk and metal businesses. It was, for Adah, an immense surprise. Everybody, including the Christians, spoke Ladino, the language of the Spanish Jews. The harbor and the post office were closed for Sabbath and the entire city respected the Jewish holidays. When two weeks later they sailed for Palestine, Adah was convinced that she could live only on Mediterranean shores. It was a landscape of pleasure, she told Rafa'el. It was sensuous. "Like you," Rafa'el said. "*Hushanit* is the Hebrew word."

Bouncing off the white stone houses of Haifa, the blue light from the Mediterranean gave the city an almost purple cast. "The colors of the sand dunes, the hills of Galilee, and the Mediterranean are constantly changing," Adah wrote to her mother. "I never imagined that there could be so much light on Earth. I've never seen colors like these. The smell of spices, the hot humid air, the mixture of people and languages, the women's camaraderie— all of it makes me euphoric."

Adah found the Settlement exhilarating. Tel Aviv was a miracle. The town, with a population of almost 150,000, was the cultural and commercial center of the country. It was also the harbor for unloading illegal immigrants from arriving ships, the political center of the Settlement, and the hub of the fight against the British.

Rafa'el discovered a new prosperity in Palestine, advanced by the citrus industry, now the most important sector of the economy. The potash mine near the Dead Sea was a major employer. New immigrants brought with them large sums of capital, advanced technology, and professional skills. Haifa, too, was a big city with much industry. His father's glass factory was producing windows, doors, and mirrors for the new housing market.

Even the family was now larger. Cousins and cousins of cousins —from Syria and Iraq, from Poland, Russia, Yemen, Persia, and Turkey—gathered for Sabbath dinner at the home of Rafa'el's parents. New foods, exotic dress, and different languages were all integrated into the new life. Rafa'el visited with his friends, met the newly arrived cousins, and went to Hanah's Paradise to show Adah the garden, walk between the stones, and read the inscriptions left by so many generations.

Adah left the children with their grandparents and took a trip around the country with Rafa'el and his two Indian cousins. She photographed the ruins of Caesarea, searched for Roman coins on the beach, and visited old churches, archeological sites, and Arab villages. Her pictures of the people and the new cities, farms, and orchards reaffirmed her faith in the Zionist dream.

As Adah fell in love with the land, the customs, and the language, she discovered a different Rafa'el. Here he knew instinctively how to act. He made decisions quickly. He talked at length with people he had just met and did not feel as reserved as he had in Vienna. Even his body seemed taller. He walked differently—his pace more relaxed. He looked like a European dressed in Arab clothes. He was more sensuous, as if the humid air or the view of the Mediterranean excited him. He would stop in the street and pull Adah into a doorway to kiss her. He was at home and in love again.

Adah and Rafa'el, determined to aid in the establishment of a Jewish state, agreed that finally they could move to Palestine. They would return to Vienna for a short time to settle their affairs. Then, in the summer, after the twins finished school, all of them, including Adah's parents, would sail to Haifa. Rafa'el would open a school to teach landscape design, and Adah would photograph the country in the making. It was a good plan, supported with much enthusiasm by everyone in the family. Before their return to Europe, Rafa'el bought a piece of land north of Haifa, on Hula Lake.

They left Haifa on March 8, 1938, driving first to Beirut. While waiting for the boat to Piraeus, they took a side trip to the Beqa'a Valley. They visited the Temple of Bacchus, the ruins of Baalbek, the Temple of Jupiter, and the Phoenician harbor of Tyr. On March 11, the BBC announced the German invasion of Austria. The next day they sailed to Piraeus. Two days later, Hitler declared Austria a province of the Reich.

From his cousin's house in Athens, Rafa'el phoned Herr Frank in Vienna. He was politely informed that there was no more work for him. Adah talked to her mother in Budapest. Julia forbade them to return, describing the horrifying pogrom that had just taken place against the Jews in Vienna. There were anti-Jewish laws in Hungary and Romania, and discrimination against Jews in Polish universities.

Adah and Rafa'el disregarded the news and sailed to Istanbul, hoping to take the train to Budapest. They waited there until April 10, when alarming news reached them. Over 97 percent of Austrians had voted for the National Socialist Party. Austria was annexed to Germany. Racist legislation was passed in Italy. Adah and Rafa'el booked tickets on the Orient Express for Adah's parents and the twins. They called her parents in Budapest, talked with them and with the twins, cabled them the tickets, then sailed back to Haifa.

ADIEU, BUDAPEST

In the *Yishuv*, the economic situation had changed overnight. Immigration was again restricted. A blockade throughout the Mediterranean stopped ships carrying Jewish immigrants. The British became less favorable toward establishing a Jewish state, and the political balance of power shifted toward the Arabs. Arab extremists began infiltrating Jewish villages, and acts of terrorism directed against the Jews were praised. A general strike paralyzed the economy for over six months, and people started leaving Palestine. Jews who had arrived earlier tried to go to America.

For Adah and Rafa'el, the country's turmoil became their cause. They were participating in an event of extraordinary consequence; doctors, writers, professors, and students were building the country, literally, with their own hands. Those *haluzim*, pioneers, who while in Europe had been constantly told, "Go to Palestine, Jew," were now fighting the British and the Arabs for the right to settle there. The land of Israel smelled more of gunpowder than of fresh bread and cloves.

In Austria and Czechoslovakia Jews were given one week to leave. In Budapest Adah's parents could not obtain travel documents. The blatant anti-Semitism of the German newspapers that arrived in Palestine reminded Rafa'el of his colleagues' snide remarks—and their enthusiasm for Hitler.

"Adah," he said, "do you remember when we went to Berlin and saw 'For Aryans Only' written on some of the benches in the park?"

"Of course I remember!" Adah answered, annoyed at the question. "There were also the signs on billboards: *'Jüden ungewunscht!* Jews not wanted here!' and 'Germans, do not buy from Jews!' There were children's games: 'Go to Palestine' and 'Jews Out!'"

"Adah, I can't figure it out! In '35, when the Nazis passed the Nuremberg Laws, we didn't think much of it."

"We didn't. They were absurd laws, and they were in Berlin, not in Budapest!"

"We ignored the propaganda. We believed in a social utopia of enlightenment and tolerance. If the French could elect a Leon Blum, a Jewish prime minister, and the Spaniards just elected Juan Negrin, a pro-Communist, then Hitler is a joke, we said to ourselves—and we drank champagne."

"No, we couldn't see it," Rafa'el sighed, after a moment of silence. "And when we heard '*Deutschland erwache, Juda werrecke*, Germany wake up, Jews perish,' we ignored it."

"You know, Rafa'el," Adah said, raising her voice in frustration, "you may not understand this, but there is also an emotional tie that we in Europe have to our homeland. My grandparents and my parents were born in '*Judapest*,' as the Viennese say. They survived pogroms, *numerus clausus* or quota, and anti-Semitic laws. My mother supported the theater and the orchestra—and she still heard curses, even from educated people. It was normal. It had always been like that, and nobody paid any attention. Even the *Judische Rundschau* and the *Judische Arbeiter*, the newspapers of every Jewish family from Krakow to Vienna, advised the Jews to 'wear the yellow badge with pride.' Add to this the Jews who believe only in the heavenly power of God to tell them what to do, plus the fiercely anti-Zionistic orthodoxy of the rabbis, and you will perhaps understand our indifference to anti-Semitism. It was nothing new, just beer-hall agitators in Berlin."

"Adah," Rafa'el said, "this is bigger than the usual burned Polish *shtetl* and a few slaughtered Jews. This is hatred. Hitler's purpose is to destroy the Jews—and any other culture he deems inferior. I'm trying to tell you that we cannot return. . . . I am also telling you, Adah, that it may be a long time before we see Aram and Bilu again."

"What is it you're really telling me, Rafa'el? That I should say, 'Adieu, Budapest, adieu, the hills of Pesta, the Margaret Island where we used to swim, the market where my mother bought the ducks; adieu, the smell of drying paprika, the pleated skirts of peasant girls, the blue shadow of the Parliament building, the synagogue where we married, the hospital where my father worked, the school where I learned how to read, my garden, my memories, my friends, my children, my parents, adieu!'?"

11

Cable: Adah Cohen Raveo at Hanah's Paradise, Palestine
From: Anton Cohen, Bucharest, Romania, 12 January 1942
Urgent STOP Left Budapest STOP All safe STOP Send
residency certificate to British Consulate STOP Need entry
visa approval STOP Letter to follow STOP Papa

Bucharest, 18 February 1942
Dear Adah and Rafa'el,

We had to leave Budapest. Hooligans took over the streets,
searching for Jews. People were dragged in the street and
beaten up, houses were looted and books burned. We feared
for our lives. We tried to go to Zurich but we were not allowed
passage. A connection we made was able to smuggle us into
Romania with a group of Turkish refugees. We closed the door
and walked away separately as if we were going to take a walk.
We left the house in the hands of our connection that organized the passage. There are riots in Bucharest also, but the
situation here is less desperate. Jewish schools are still open.
For the moment, we feel safe. We will wait here for you to
obtain permission for our passage. We found a small apartment and share it with other refugees. For the moment we have
some money and your father is helping a doctor here at a private clinic. We need a letter of sponsorship from you and copies of your legal documents in Palestine to obtain a British
visa to join you. Only when we have the entry visa will we be
allowed to purchase passage to Haifa. There is a boat leaving
in six weeks and by that time we should receive the documents
from you. We are full of hope. The children are healthy and are

waiting to take the boat, excited to be with you. Cable immediately when you send the documents. We love you and send you all our blessings.

Mother

Bucharest, 9 May 1942

Dear Adah and Rafa'el,

I am devastated. We all are. My dear Adah, I am sorry that you were not able to say good-bye to your father. By the time we sent you the cable, he was already buried. He loved you very much and was proud of you and of Rafa'el. He was a good husband and a good father and I know that you will miss him. He was tired when he woke up that morning and wanted to rest a little more. When I went to see him later, I found him unconscious, breathing with difficulty. Emil, a refugee here who studied medicine, gave him some intravenous medication, but it was clear that his heart was weak. "Say good-bye to him," he told us. "His body is tired, give him permission to go." I sat on the bed and put his head on my lap. His eyes were closed and his face looked young and peaceful. I stayed with him all day. Bilu and Aram took turns being with him. Just before he died, he opened his eyes, looked for a long time at the children, and tried to say something. We were with him until the last moment. Bilu and Aram are very much affected. Bilu cried, after the burial, thinking how much her grandfather will miss the taste of cherries from our garden. "When you are dead you do not miss anything," Aram said. "You miss something only when you are alive." And I am missing Anton with all my being. I cannot yet grasp the day-to-day immensity of the loss. I thank God that he died a natural death and had us near him. We found ten men to say the prayer and we buried him at the Spanish Jewish cemetery. I am lost, I am desperate, but even more determined to find a way to join you. We send you all our love.

Mother

Yit'gadal v'yit'kadash   magnified and sanctified
Yit'barakh v'yish'tabach   blessed and praised
v'yit'pa'ar v'yit'romam   glorified and exalted

v'yit'nasei v'yit'hadar extolled and mighty
v'yit'aleh v'yit'halal upraised and lauded

Bucharest, 12 August 1942

Dear Adah and Rafa'el,

I used to believe that I could not live for a day without Anton. And I can't! I don't know how to make decisions. I turn around to ask him something and realize that he is gone. It is awful! When I go to sleep I put my blanket on the bed and try not to move. I know that if I move I will not find his body next to mine. We were together in sleep, embracing each other, waiting to enjoy the next day together. All I have of him is a doctored photograph on a fake travel document. I have lost my best friend. He was a wonderful, generous man. Even here, he was giving German lessons. It was so elegant of him to dissociate the language of terror from that of the heart. I miss him with every breath. We did not receive the sponsorship letter from you. Don't send it to the British Consulate. The lines are very long and it is dangerous for us to be on the streets. Cable us at the clinic address, and use the name of our friend, Dr. Daniel. It is safer. We are in a hostile foreign country, don't speak the language, and are alone. How do we escape from here and where should we go? Our thoughts and all our blessings are with you.

Mother

Bucharest, 15 September 1942

Dear Adah and Rafa'el,

Last week Aram was arrested for subversive activities and sent to jail for two years. He was picked up at a Communist rally against the king. He didn't have any documents on him and didn't give his real name, but our friend Doctor Daniel found him at the police station. Aram confessed that he is a Communist. Today, along with thirty other people in convict uniforms, and their heads shaved, he was escorted by the police and put on a freight car. They are being sent to a labor camp. We went to the train station with the doctor and his family. People were shouting, crying, and cursing the king. Aram caught my eye and started crying. It was horrible. Bilu called his name and when he looked at her she waved your orange scarf and screamed, "Aram! We'll wait for you here!" The angry crowd pushed us closer to the convoy. Bilu got next to one of the prisoners, grabbed his hand, and said, "Give this to Aram; Aram from Budapest." Tied up in your silk orange scarf were some money, sugar, and lemon. When the train pulled away, Bilu kept screaming, "Aram, we'll wait for you here." Bilu and I walked after the train in a stupor. We felt helpless. You entrusted Aram to me and I was not a good keeper.

Aram is not yet 15 and has no idea what Communism is. There is no evidence against him so he may be released. As soon as possible I will send Bilu alone to Hanah's Paradise. I will stay here to wait for Aram. He was arrested by mistake. He could even return next month, Doctor Daniel told us. He is not a Communist. Our love and our thoughts are with you.

Mother

Bucharest, 28 May 1943

My dearest Mama and Papa,

Beside drawings and little poems that I used to give you when I was little, this is the first letter I ever wrote you. Grandma asked me not to complain because it will upset you, but I am very angry with what is happening with us. I don't understand why Aram was taken away. He didn't do anything wrong. He was never a Communist. He would have told me. We never kept any secrets between us. He never lied to me. Never! I am scared here. I don't understand the language and we no longer can go out on the street. We have to hide. Why is Papa not coming to take us away from here?

The new anti-Semitic legislation now requires that we register at the police station. All Jews are doing forced labor, cleaning the streets, painting walls, washing windows, working in factories. Emil, the medical student, from Antwerp, with whom we share the apartment, went to register. We were afraid that he would be arrested like they do in Budapest, in Vienna, in Warsaw; we read in the paper. I stay up late in the night waiting to hear his steps on the stairway. Besides the doctor who is bringing us food, Emil is our only friend.

Although he has to report to the police station every morning, he is allowed to sleep at home. Grandma and I are hiding. Here, too, there are riots against the Jews. The Iron Guard, a paramilitary organization with a radical anti-Semitic program, leads the window-smashing, rioting, and killing. Jews in Romania do not have equal rights with the other citizens, but so far we do not have to wear the yellow star. When will this nightmare end?

Bilu

12

Letters, diaries, requests for help, memoirs, and other news of our branch of the family had been arriving at Hanah's Paradise throughout the war. Some came through international organizations, some were smuggled across the borders, and some were brought in by the few travelers that managed to get out. Once I had become familiar with the records at Hanah's Paradise and I could find my way among generations of names, dates, and locations, Grandpa Rafa'el put in my hands the task of documenting the disjointed life of my parents. It wasn't much; a shoe box filled with papers and some photographs. I added to the records the story of my parents—fragments only, told here and there by my Aunt Bilu, and my parents' friends. The task of recording the stories was a sentimental one. Family events, disagreements, short visits, departures and separations, betrayed friendships—all came rushing back to my mind. But together, my grandfather and I reconstructed their story and set up a place on the shelves at Hanah's Paradise that belonged to me.

The story my grandfather was most eager to hear from me was how my father and my Aunt Bilu finally found each other after being separated for fourteen years.

"First we received a Request for Identification from the police station. Bilu sent it from Moscow, asking for information about her brother."

Request by	Bella Emilianova Neter, a.k.a. Bilu Raveo
Person sought	My brother
Complete name	Aram Amador Raveo
Male or female	Male

Other names used	Aram Naharaim
Date of birth	November 18, 1927
Place of birth	Vienna, Austria
Last known address	Andrassy Utica, No. 104, Budapest, Hungary
Father's full name	Rafa'el Ben Nathan Raveo
Mother's full name	Adah Cohen Raveo
Ethnic group	Jewish
Source of last news	I have seen him in a cattle train going from Bucharest toward the Russian territory.
Additional information	My brother was arrested in Bucharest in September 1942, and sentenced for subversive activities against the King. He then was sent to a forced labor camp, Vapniarka. We have had no further information about him since that time.
Purpose of search	I want to know my brother's fate.

"It arrived in the spring of 1956," I told Grandpa after looking at the stamp. "Then we received some letters and monthly telephone calls until 1963 when Bilu was allowed to visit us."

Grandpa read the letters in silence first and then again aloud, asking for details. He had not seen his children for almost thirty years.

Aram Ravea, Strada Florilor 28, Bucharest
July 18, 1956, Moscow

Dear Mr. Ravea,

The Red Cross notified us that a certain Aram Ravea lives in Bucharest. We believe that you are the same person as my twin brother, Aram Raveo, from whom I was separated by the war in 1942. His is a very uncommon name, and we hope that you are really my brother. If this letter reached you and you are not him, please answer immediately so we can continue our search. I will be very grateful to you and perhaps I can help you also if you are searching for people here. Aram, I have put my entire hope in this letter. I believe that you are alive. This is so important to me that I beg you to answer immediately. I

am now in Moscow, married to Emil. We have a nine-year-old
daughter named Tania, after Grandpa Anton. I am sorry to tell
you that Grandma Julia died in December 1955 of lung fail-
ure. Her grave is marked in the city of Bidjhan, in the Jewish
Autonomous Republic. Emil finished the university and works
now as a doctor in a hospital. I teach arithmetic at the pri-
mary school. Emil lost his entire family and I haven't had any
connection with our parents since 1943, after Grandma and
I crossed the border into the Soviet Union. Just to make sure
that it is you, please remind me of the name of our cat. We are
happy here and grateful to the Russian people, who are very
welcoming. We have many friends who are here alone and now
they are our family.

Thank you in advance, Mr. Ravea, for informing me immediately upon receiving this letter.

Bilu

P.S. Aram, I knew all the time that you would survive!

Neter Family
8 Ulitza Sadovaya, Moscow, USSR
Bucharest, 22 August 1956

Dear Bilu, and dear Emil and Tania,

Your letter reached me. It is *Ness gadol*, a great miracle that
you were able to find me. I am so grateful that you are alive. I
am very sad about Grandma's death and I am sorry I couldn't
say good-bye to her. At least she didn't die alone in a concentration camp. She was with you and with your family and as
much as she suffered for not being with Adah, at least she had
food. The pain I saw in her eyes when I was arrested is still
with me. I am very sorry that she died without knowing that
I survived. I don't understand. How did you end up in Russia?
Why did you leave here? Why didn't you write to Hanah's Paradise? Where have you been for 14 years? I am happy, angry
and also confused. You said that you would wait for me and I
returned here to find you and go to Hanah's Paradise together.
I could have gone there alone, but I stayed here looking desperately for Grandma and you, until the borders were closed and it
was too late. I couldn't leave Romania. If only I had known. For
all these years I have lived with an enormous loss that I can feel

even now, with your letter in my hand. Every year on our birthday I went to the cemetery to sit by Grandpa's grave and talk to
you. I mourned you with tears, with words, with anger. I paid
to add your name and Grandma's on Grandpa's stone and now
you are alive. If we were near each other and I could see you,
perhaps happiness would replace the void and the fear which I
feel now. But what really counts is that you are alive and well,
and when we will see each other, our feelings are going to
mend. I am healthy except for stomach pains, but here we have
food. Nothing happened to me in the labor camp and I have
a normal life. I am married and have a four-year-old daughter
named Salomeia. My wife, Norah Yamit, is of Turkish origin.
She was born on an island, and her name means "Revered Sea."
She comes from Bergen-Belsen and she is alone and works at
the post office. I am a student now. The Party has sent me to
the University to study economics. We share an apartment
with two friends, Clara and Mendel. Clara comes from Flossenbürg and Mendel from Dachau. We met here. Bilu, thank
you for finding me! I am very happy. The name of our cat was
Moka. I have no means to inform Adah and Rafa'el that you are
alive. Contact with the Capitalist world is forbidden. I will have
to inform the political commissar about your letter. Perhaps he
could inform them about you. I hope we will be allowed to visit
each other.

Norah and Salomeia, together with our friends Clara and
Mendel, send you their best wishes.

Your brother Aram

Dear Emil, often I have thought of you. I remember how
you helped us when Grandpa died, and how we spent many
nights looking at maps, trying to find a way out of Romania. I
am very happy that you are now my brother, and I am also very
thankful that you took care of Grandma and Bilu. We share
memories from the past, and I hope that we will be able to be
together again. Please receive my best wishes.

Dear Tania,

Your mother has told you stories about your Uncle Aram
and soon I will see you and tell you more stories. Your aunt,
Norah, and your cousin, Salomeia, together with our best

friends Mendel and Clara are waiting to meet you. We all love you very much.

Uncle Aram

September 19, 1956, Moscow

Dear Aram,

When I opened your letter I could not recognize your handwriting. I saw words in Russian and Hungarian—and there was your name! My hands started shaking, my vision blurred, and I just could not believe that your letter had reached me. I put my head on the kitchen table and cried. Grandma and I thought about you every moment; day and night. When Emil arrived home I ran to him waving the letter, shouting, "It's from Aram, Emil! He is alive!" We stayed up all night making plans. It will be wonderful to be reunited. You couldn't find us because we were sent to Asia, in Birobidjhan, the Jewish Republic. When we received mandatory identity cards, we were taken off the lists of displaced persons. For security reasons, we were not allowed to send or receive mail. Now at least we can write. I am looking forward to being together. I want you to tell me everything. How did you become a Communist without telling me? What happened at the labor camp? And how did you survive? Why are you in Romania? Please write back immediately. My dear brother, please convey our love to your family and friends.

Bilu, with Emil and Tania

9 January 1957, Bucharest

Dear Bilu, Emil, and Tania,

Happy New Year! We wish you good health. Let us hope that the Party will allow us to visit with each other soon. Bilu, I recognized your voice immediately. I couldn't say much on the telephone but I will write you. I am sending the legal forms for the visas. I signed that I will be responsible for you while you are here. I was told that it would take only a few months to obtain the approvals. After all, you are coming to visit family in a Socialist country. There shouldn't be any problems. It is unfortunate that Emil and Tania cannot visit us at the same time. We have the same rules here. The family has to stay behind as a warranty for your return. The form I signed is valid for two years. If, in that time, you aren't able to get the visa, we can renew it. Looking forward to talk to you again next month, I send you all my love.

Aram

Grandpa's stories and anecdotes about two happy teenagers were for me impossible to believe, while the two adults I spoke about were people he didn't know. A playful, funny, curious Aram, an emotional and sensitive young man, was in no way the person I knew as my father. And a cold, disengaged, unemotional man—a man who brought his mistresses home, punished his daughter, and spent most of his time in silence—was not the son he knew. The fragments that Grandpa and I pieced together formed the disjointed narrative of a disjointed family. The names were the same, but the people were different. When he spoke about Bilu, he identified her with me: a teenage girl with red hair and black eyes. This is how she was when he last saw her. The Bilu that I referred to was the tired-looking woman in the black-and-white photograph that I had brought with me. Grandpa used my stories to get closer to his irreclaimable children, and I used his to fill up the void into which I was born. Grandpa was assigning me a place in the family, and I was giving him a link to his firstborn twins.

It must have been around the time when I was four or five years old—I recalled the event for my grandfather—that the first letter from Bilu arrived. I remember because everyone around me was excited that I had a cousin, that I was not alone in the world. Later Aram talked with Bilu on the phone every month. Before the first letter arrived, I didn't know that I even had an aunt. One morning we woke up early, and all of us, including our friends Mendel and Clara, put on our best clothes—as if she could see us over the phone—and went to the post office to wait for Bilu's call. When my father's name was called, he was directed to a wooden cabin with a glass door. I remember the sound of the door when it closed and how hurt I was when my father turned his back to us. I wasn't allowed in the booth with him. I would have liked to be with him and see my aunt in his voice. My mother was always agitated when my father talked on the phone with his sister. I don't know why; maybe she felt like me, upset that his sister was not someone he shared with us. Relentlessly, my mother walked back and forth between our group and the cabin, saying the same thing each time.

"I should go listen to the conversation. After all, she is my sister-in-law."

"This is not your conversation, Norah," Clara would answer. "Stay where you are."

The first time he talked with Bilu after almost fifteen years of separation, my father turned to us and said sheepishly, "We didn't say much because she was crying, but she is doing well." He offered very little information. We understood that he didn't want to talk about Bilu. He took a walk—alone. When he returned home he was angry. My mother made him a pot of tea, put some fried dough sprinkled with sugar on the table, and went to bed. That night he didn't sleep. I remember because he paced the room all night. I could hear him whispering near the curtain that separated my parents' room from mine.

I did not betray you, Bilu. Not when you had the incident in Budapest, nor when I was arrested in 1942. I know you were angry with me. You made a fist at me at the train station. When I was arrested, people whispered, "Nobody is Jewish," so yes, I lied. I had no documents, I didn't speak Romanian. I gave the police a fake address in Budapest, and I said I was Luca Senesz, a Communist who smuggled printing equipment for the comrades in Bucharest. It was the first name that came to mind. I know he was our friend and helped us escape from Budapest. But I gave a fake address and if he or his comrades were arrested, I did it to save you. Should I have told them I was a Jewish refugee and given them your name also? It was better to betray Luca than my sister and grandmother. I don't regret it. Communists were sentenced only to forced labor. The Jews were sent to the concentration camp. You thought that I had become a Communist in secret, that I did something foolish. If I told them I was a Communist and not a Jew, I must have had a good reason, right? You have always been selfish, Bilu, this is the truth. Once they took me away, you turned around and left with Emil. Did you ever think about me?

My father's monologue went on for hours. He was agitated, talking to an imaginary Bilu.

I was not even fifteen, Bilu, when I was arrested. I was judged, put in jail then on a train, and not knowing where you are being taken is a sophisticated form of torture. For four days the train went slowly, moving only in the night. We crossed a bridge over a large river, and in early October 1942 we arrived at a stop in a forest. We were in Russian territory occupied by the Germans, in a place called Vapniarka. After we walked for some three kilometers we climbed a hill, and once on the top, we saw the camp—a rectangle defined by barbed wire. Three buildings faced a courtyard, and watchtowers controlled each corner. In the early morning light, the camp looked banal. What took my breath away was a field of flowers growing outside of the barbed wires. It was a large square of red carnations—the color of my fear of death.

We were in a Nazi camp guarded by Romanians. We slept in barracks, received some food once a day, and worked in a factory not far away. There were some fifty other camps in the area, and German officers went from camp to camp to supervise and kill. The Germans called the Jews *Figuren*, meaning numbers; it is easier to kill an abstraction. The Jews in the camp spoke German, but it was a different language than the one you and I learned. Even the vocabulary was adapted to life in camp: the word for "tomorrow" was "never." To "organize" meant to steal. "Achtung" meant that a soldier was shooting randomly, and those slow to run would be killed. But where I was, people didn't talk much in any language.

> Walk! Walk! Walk!
> *Schnell, Schnell.*
> Work! Work! Work!
> Don't think!
> If you think,
> Don't talk!
> If you talk,
> Don't say anything!
> If you say something,

Be surprised at nothing.
I am a *Figur*—a number,
I have no name.
Whisper!
Death! Death! Death!
Achtung, Achtung.

To get to work we had to cross a field of sugar beets. Sometimes I was able to pick some, and this is how I survived starvation. Then in January 1945, after two years and three months,
the Soviet Army entered the camp and told us to leave. They
opened the gates and pushed us out, pointing toward Romanian territory, themselves trying to escape the retreating German columns. I walked toward the border of Romania for almost
ten days. What kept me walking was thinking about you. But
my feet couldn't carry my body and I collapsed under the bridge
crossing the border, wanting to die, asking you to forgive me for
being weak. And then in the languor of death I heard, "Run, run,
Germans are here!" I clung to others and pushed myself over that
bridge into Romania, looking into your eyes at every step to get
the strength to move. I saw your face, I imagined you waiting for
me on the other side and I crawled on my knees. The Germans
killed those who didn't get across the bridge.

You said that you would wait for me in Bucharest. I looked for
Grandma and you everywhere. You can never imagine the pain
of thinking that you were both dead. I contacted refugee organizations, I filled in forms, I sent letters and requests and I waited.
I could have gone straight to Hanah's Paradise, but I returned
here to meet you. You could have left a message for me at the
Portuguese cemetery. You could have scratched it on Grandpa's
grave. You abandoned me; you disappeared without a word, without any thought of what might happen to me. After you shouted,
"I will wait for you here," you left. You left to be with Emil. He
is the one who always wanted to go to the Soviet Union. I was
able to send a letter to Hanah's Paradise to let them know that I
had survived and was in Bucharest looking for you. By the time
I started to believe that you were no longer here, there were riots
in Palestine, and the British closed the borders.

I was lost, alone and desperate. I sent letters to our house in
Budapest but I never got an answer. I even tried to go back there
hoping for a miracle, but I didn't have any documents and I was
turned away at the border. I returned to Bucharest hoping to get
an entry visa to Palestine. While I was waiting to find you and
a way to leave, I made three friends: Guido, an Italian, Clara,
his Hungarian wife, and Norah. They helped me search for you.
Guido was allowed to leave, but without Clara. She was given a
visa to go back to Hungary. He left but she preferred to stay here
with us. He sent all of us letters of sponsorship to go to Italy.
Guido wasn't even my family, but he cared. He even sent a gold
bracelet for us to sell and pay for our trip. Guido was able to send
messages, only you couldn't. The Italians gave us the entry visa,
but the Romanians said, "Nobody gets a visa, comrades. It is forbidden. The borders are closed!" We stayed here. Then Norah
and I got married. She wanted a commitment to life, not to her.
She understands my feelings. She knows that love, for us, is a
dictionary term. You betrayed me, Bilu. You knew that I couldn't
go to Hanah's Paradise without you.

Aram's pacing kept me awake. After a while, Norah also became
restless. I heard her rearranging her pillow, then saying, "Aram,
you are talking out loud. You are keeping me awake. What do you
want from the Italians?"

"I just remembered when we went there for the visa, and Clara
talked with Guido on the phone," he said, continuing to pace the
room.

"The Romanians didn't care that Clara and Guido were married. So what if the Italian consul did sign the documents. After
killing the intellectuals, the opposition, and anyone else that
helped them get into power, the Romanians needed workers here
and the Russians closed the borders."

"I remember a vine of purple morning glories blooming on the
gate of the Italian Consulate," Aram said, still pacing the room.

"I remember the coffee and the biscuits."

"You ate them with grace," Aram said.

"I fought with myself not to take more. And *tu sais quoi*? You
know what? I was shocked to see that *après avoir été*, after being,

just a number in prison garb, in that room I could again feel elegant."

"I really like that about you," Aram said. "You can put the past aside."

"You must be dreaming. I just don't think about it but I don't put it aside. The consul gave us soap, remember. *'Maggari cari amici che mi piacceva aiudare, ma io, non c'è la juridizione,* I would like to help you, dear friends, but I don't have the jurisdiction to interfere on your behalf. I will send the information to *miei superiori a Roma, per vedere che cosa possono fare,* to see what can be done. *Sonno sicuro que il lasciate-passare,* I believe that a letter of passage, *e possibile.'*"

"No, Norah, he never said that. That is what the Turks said when we asked them for visas."

"Not at all—at the Turkish Consulate I didn't speak Italian. But the Turks said more or less the same thing. They just smiled more and talked with their hands. *'Anlariz,* we understand, Madame *est ebrea,* is Jewish and of Turkish origin. Thanks to our neutrality in the war, Turkish subjects were protected and sent to a privileged camp in Bergen-Belsen,' and he stood up to shake my hand. 'There should not be any problem. It will be done very fast. As soon as the *Effendi Monsieur,* General Consul, arrives. Yes, Madame, the *Effendi Monsieur* will sign the documents. Madame has no reason to be *sabirsizlamayin,* anxious; *merci de votre visite.'* He gave us a box of sugar and some tea, remember?"

"And the Romanians," Aram said. "'We will write you, don't worry! You will be notified.' Then they sealed the borders."

"I never told you but Clara got crazy," my mother said from her bed. "She read the Tarot cards every day and each time saw Guido dead. She tricked her mind. Separation from Guido was not acceptable, death was."

"What was she supposed to do? Wait for Stalin to open the borders?"

"Remember how we laughed when we were taught the slogans?" my father said.

> Who do we thank for milk and bread?
> Who gave us a flag so red?
> Sta-lin! Sta-lin!

"I remember the other one," my mother answered, giggling:

> My father has a big brown bitch—
> Who wants to kiss her ass and twitch?
> Sta-lin, Sta-lin.

"Romanians cover suffering with jokes," I heard my father saying. "They should just give us the exit visa, a stamp on a piece of paper."

"I am thirty and every day I think about the visa and about my death."

"It's too late to die, Aram," my mother said from the bed. "You did that once. Now go to sleep."

13

The university was four hours away, by bus, but Aram came home only on official vacations. He called Norah every Sunday from the public phone in his dorm, saying very little, asking only banal questions. Communications were monitored. To Mendel, he described the classes and the books he was reading and thanked the Party at the end of each conversation for giving him the chance to go to school. Every month, he sent his laundry home. Norah would wash it and send it back to him. The month when she didn't receive it, Norah knew that Aram had a mistress.

Clara, Mendel, and Norah decided to go to the university to speak with Aram in person. Norah tried several days in a row to let him know they were coming, but the phone in the dorm was always busy. Finally, when somebody picked it up, Norah left a message—for Aram, Room 24—"Your family is coming to visit." They packed some food, took several buses, and were soon on the campus. Aram was happy to see them. He introduced them to his colleagues and showed them his books, and all of them went into his dormitory, sat on his bed, and ate the food they brought.

Norah was right to be suspicious. Aram had a friend, Alisa. They studied together, but she was not his mistress, only a comrade, a sister.

"Notice his hands," Norah told Clara when Aram left the room. "Look at the way he moves his fingers."

Aram was a good-looking man. He had high cheekbones, slanted eyes, and copper-red hair. But people always noticed his hands. He moved them with an Oriental slowness, his palms always opened, his long, thin fingers rotating in the space, mesmerizing with their elegance. People stared at his hands.

"Your fingers are curled, Aram," Norah said. "You must be afraid."

Clara took it upon herself to talk to Alisa. Norah refused to meet her. She felt betrayed. "Students," Clara said. "Men," Norah said.

In response to Aram's supposed infidelity, Norah stopped using her married name and made herself a bright red dress so everyone would notice her. When several months later Aram arrived home for a short vacation, he brought Alisa with him. With everyone in the kitchen, Norah confronted him.

"If you and Alisa need to be together, you have to say so. You don't have to stay with me, and I don't have to suffer."

"Norah, Alisa and I are good friends. We are more like brother and sister. I don't want you to suffer and I don't want to be with anyone else but you."

Alisa went to Norah, took her hand, and started crying. "Don't you want to be my sister, Norah? I lost all of them."

Norah shrugged her shoulders and said, "You can stay as a good, trusting neighbor, but you can't be my sister and I don't want to be yours. Sisters fight and, in any case, if I *were* to have one, I would like her to be older than me—much older, almost like a mother."

Waiting for Norah and Clara to include her in the family life, Alisa was careful not to create jealousy and interfere with their relationship. Mendel, who liked her company, asked her to help with his French translations for the Language Institute. All textbooks were being rewritten. Lenin's commentaries on music and Stalin's articles on linguistics were now included in every book. At the Language Institute, the students used those texts to practice their vocabulary and to learn French. Alisa was amazed by the choice of the text, an article by Lenin: "Left-Wing Communism: An Infantile Disorder."

"Why can't they learn French by translating poetry, for example?" she asked one day.

"Because when we bring our *révolution prolétaire* to Paris," Norah said, never missing an occasion to be cynical, "and liberate the French masses, our students will know the slogans in French."

The Party monitored the field of translation very closely, since linguistic false friends could mislead the workers. Mendel's translation was meant for publication, and he was afraid of making ideological mistakes.

"Communisme de Gauche: Une Maladie Infantile, Left-Wing Communism: An Infantile Disorder, poses two structural problems," he asserted. First, there isn't a right-wing and left-wing Communism—there is only Communism. And second, 'infantile disorder' sounds pejorative to me. I don't think it is good to apply it to Communism."

"'Infantile' means immature and 'disorder' means weakness, so clearly the left-wing Communism that Lenin is referring to is not a good thing," Clara said, entering their discussion. "This specific left wing appears to be weak, unformed, and dependent, whereas Lenin wants it strong."

"No sympathy there," said Norah.

Alisa proposed the title, "Communism, Healer of Early Left-Wing Disorders."

After that evening, Alisa and Mendel worked together on every translation, while Aram, Norah, and Clara gave their opinions. Mendel struggled to understand Stalin's intent in another article, "Marxism and Problems of Linguistics," and Clara helped him with the French translation.

Question to Comrade Stalin: Many linguists consider formalism one of the main causes of the stagnation in Soviet linguistics. We should very much like to know your opinion about what formalism in linguistics consists of and how it should be overcome.

Comrade Stalin answers: N. Y. Maar and his closest colleagues brought theoretical confusion into linguistics. To put an end to the stagnation, both must be eliminated. The removal of the plague spots will put Soviet linguistics on a sound basis, leading it onto the broad highway of World Linguistics and enabling it to occupy first place there.

Mendel had some difficulty with "the removal of the plague spots." It was not clear from the context whether "plague" meant the literary formalism, with "spots" being Maar and his closest colleagues, or if "plague" referred to the stagnation.

"But didn't you say that this man, Maar, had recently died?" Clara asked Alisa. "Then blame him, both for the confusion and for the stagnation."

Clara was clever, in a practical way. Even though her Romanian was still elementary, she understood its structure. She made herself a dictionary of slogans and used the words approved by the Party to write lyrics for the songs she composed for the children's choir at the orphanage:

Men are stronger than mountains,
Women have smiles as rich as the sea,
Children forever will honor the Party
That showed them the path to Democracy.

Although this happened before I was born, years later I learned Clara's poems and songs. They were transmitted on the radio, taught in schools, and sung by marching workers on festive days.

LETTER FROM THE ENEMY

Exit visas still did not arrive. At the post office, Norah spotted a letter from Guido addressed to Clara. She had recently found out that anyone receiving mail from outside the country was accused by the secret police of collaborating with the enemy. People were interrogated, and some had been arrested as spies. Out of fear for Clara's safety, Norah destroyed the letter.

"You should have asked me to come to your office to read it there! I was hoping that our friendship was as important to you as it is to me, but you don't really care," Clara said in anger.

"You are angry and not thinking about what you say," Norah shot back. "What if the Party found out? What if they arrested you? Also, didn't you say that Guido was *dead*?"

"You don't think that I believe in fortune-telling, do you?"

"Yes, I do! You said he was dead, so I never mentioned his name again."

"What should I have done?" Clara said. "Wait for the visa? Make plans for the future—wait for him to move to Romania? I said Guido was dead so I could be free of my wishes. I am here with you and Aram and Mendel. I like Mendel, and I am alive now. Guido is from before; Guido is not here."

"You mean to say that you love Guido but stay with Mendel because he happens to be around?"

"Listen to me, Norah. Do you think I am capable of falling in love after what I've witnessed? If you were ever in love before, you know that this feeling is not possible anymore. Guido and I were trying to revive something that was dead for both of us. Besides, unlike me, Guido has a family. The last thing they wanted was for him to bring home a survivor, a woman left without a womb by the Nazi sterilization program!"

"You don't know that," said Norah.

"You think he is different from us. You think that he can face his past. I am sure that he, too, hid his ordeal from his family."

"Maybe, but he married you regardless of his family, and of his past."

"Yes he did. We were together in Vienna, we were arrested, sent to death and we survived. He married me when we met again only because I lost my family and I was alone. He said, 'Clara, I want to help you, I owe you this.' He didn't say, 'Clara, I love you.' He said, 'I owe you this.' He said it twice—once in Italian and once in German. He felt sorry for me, but pity is not a substitute for love, as you well know. It would have been difficult for us to be together. Too much pain! Without me he will be able to have a normal life, you know, with a wife and children and birthday parties. What more can I say that you don't already know?"

"That we are all crazy, and that we ended up in a crazy place," Norah shouted. "Happy are the ones who are dead. That's what you can say!"

After this discussion they avoided each other for several days. Clara started making her own German-Hungarian-Jewish food. Norah started making her own Turkish-Spanish, Greek-Romanian-Jewish food. The distinction was only in the spices. Besides potatoes, onion, garlic, cabbage, and—rarely—a bit of meat, there was nothing else at the market.

ALISA

Aram arrived home for summer vacation and brought Alisa with him once again. She had no other place to go. Aram believed that if he and Norah shared the apartment with Clara and Mendel, there was no reason for Alisa not to be included.

Alisa slept on a folding bed in the kitchen. She was shy, modest, and helpful. The new arrangement sparked a friendship among the three women, obliging Clara and Norah to reconcile and cook together again. They understood Alisa's need to be with people like themselves, those angry at hiding their past. Alisa had been only a young girl when deported, and she was abused and beaten many times. She still shrank in terror if someone touched her. When people were nice to her, she cried. The intense gratitude she felt toward Clara and Norah developed into near-total devotion. Alisa, too, had been left an orphan by the war. All she had now were these people. She could care about them and they could care about her, and this, in her mind, made them a family. To counter-balance her feelings, she could love Aram and then hate herself for betraying Norah.

Alisa cried all the time. Norah, frustrated at her tears, taught her how to cook grape leaves stuffed with lamb, grilled quails with fresh figs, and Turkish *borekytos* with goat cheese and fresh mint. The fact that none of these ingredients could be found at the market, and that the meals were made from words alone, was not a problem. Norah described their taste in detail.

Aram's affection for this skinny girl with red hair was a mixture of rivalry and camaraderie that no one could understand. He treated Alisa with the detached interest one might have in a sister. They clung to each other for reasons that neither of them was able to articulate. Alisa called Aram *Ahi*, my brother.

Norah looked upon all this with a sense of duty. She believed that giving this girl a place in her home was a *mitzvah*, the good deed that every Jew must accomplish. She was confident that Alisa would have killed herself had it not been for Norah, who accepted her into their home. It was the Jewish thing to do.

Norah was a machine. She could not stop moving. She did the job of living: always advancing, always looking for a new challenge—no time for introspection. Of all of them, Norah was the best at covering her past. She was living on Earth, she said, and could not stop what she was doing to remember the past. "If I started thinking back, I would disappear," she often told Clara.

Norah had no aspirations, no desires, no vanities. Along with milk and chocolate, breathing was a gift given to her by the British when they entered the Nazi concentration camp. Life was equated with existence. She believed seeing light was enough. Beyond that, food and shelter were all she needed. The split in her life was extraordinarily well guarded. Cynicism was the tool she used to detach herself from emotions and from desires, like waiting for the exit visa. Life for her was nothing but a stopover before suicide. Alisa meant nothing to her. She treated her with scientific interest. A subspecies made of tears, a receiver of good deeds.

Clara and Mendel were also attached to Alisa. Clara was constantly feeding her. Mendel treated her with a fatherly affection, editing her texts, giving her books to read. Not that she could replace the daughter he had lost to the Nazis, but she evoked in him some softness.

Whenever Aram and Alisa came home from school, Norah and Clara organized small parties, and everyone stayed up late. In the evening the women sang and the men played chess. During the day Aram and Alisa worked on their assigned papers. Their conviction that Communism was the answer to a democratic society translated into long hours of reading aloud from Stalin's books:

> Ousting the capitalist element in the countryside is an inevitable result and component part of the policy of restricting the capitalist elements, the policy restricting the kulaks' exploiting tendencies. Ousting the capitalist element in the countryside means ousting and overcoming individual sections of kulaks, those unable to bear the burden of collectivization and the Soviet government's system of Socialist Measures. Victory will be ours. The power of the landowners and profiteers will be overthrown.

Norah and Clara, who after work had to take mandatory classes on the history of Marxism-Leninism, refused to be immersed in the subject in their own home as well. When Mendel, Aram, and Alisa decided to write a book about the agrarian reform and the role of collectivization in rising productivity, Norah and Clara felt overwhelmed. Mendel tried to explain to them how the subject was important for society: "In a Communist economy, the whole produces more than its parts," but neither of them was interested in the discussion. After several evenings of listening to Aram reading Stalin's article "Concerning the Policy of Eliminating the Kulaks," Norah said, "I don't think I have to be concerned with that." Clara looked at her with admiration and declared that she, too, found the subject boring.

As I was growing up, Norah and Clara often referred to those evenings. Proud of their attitude, they explained to me that Communism was oppressive—but this was something that I wasn't to tell anyone.

"Before you were born," one of them would start, remembering a past event, "such and such happened." By sewing their stories together, I learned how they lived and adapted to life in Romania.

"Remember how scared we were to listen to the Voice of America?" one of them would volunteer.

"That was after we rebelled and refused to read Stalin every night," the other would say. "Mendel and Aram were discussing Communism, and we were listening to the Voice of America to learn how to fight it."

I learned through their conversations that, in the fall of the year when I was born, seven years after Norah was freed from Bergen-Belsen, they got their first radio. My birth coincided with their first attempt to connect with the world. They listened in secret to the Voice of America and learned that the other world was different. As required by Jewish law, I was named after a deceased relative. Norah's mother, Salomé, would have still been part of my life if the Nazis had not killed her in 1945. Murdered, she was only a name—the grandmother I didn't have. A photograph would have been a certificate of presence. It could have proved to me that my grandmother and her own image had both been present at the time of the picture. But having left no trace, she remained an abstract link to a past of which I was deprived.

Aram and Alisa left the university to come home for the occasion of my birth. Clara had told me the story many times, proud of how she defended me in front of everyone.

"She has dark skin and looks like a kitten hidden under a layer of soft red fur," Clara said, when my mother brought me home.

"No she doesn't," Aram said sadly. "We had a kitten once. It didn't look as scary."

"She's not pretty," Alisa told them accusingly. "For sure, she is not."

My mother, who had endured her pregnancy with stoicism, felt betrayed by Aram. She had fulfilled her biological function. Women have babies, and she had one. What was all this talk about how pretty the baby was or wasn't? Why weren't they talking about *her*, how wonderful she was to give them the gift of a child? It didn't really matter how the child looked.

"She may not be pretty, but she is very distinguished. This child has a lot of class," Clara replied haughtily. At that moment in the story, Norah looked at me, laughed, and proud that she could hurt Alisa while defending me, said, "Right now, Alisa, she looks just like you. She has the same disheveled red hair."

My mother called me Meia, short for Salomeia. In Romanian it sounds like the possessive pronoun "mine," and in Hebrew it means "hundred."

Norah had never thought of babies in terms of beauty, but once Aram and Alisa told her that I was ugly, she refused to show me to the neighbors. She had never seen such an ugly creature, she would later tell me, complimenting herself for being able to take care of somebody she didn't really like.

Alisa bought me a Russian doll. From the black market, Aram bought a bright blue Turkish shawl for Norah, and for me, a red wooden wagon attached to a string. Mendel wrote a poem about birth and new life, bought a bottle of Cognac for them, and a white plastic swan for me. The gold bracelet from Guido, the family's communal wealth—to be sold on the black market when the exit visas arrived—was hidden and put aside for me. The Party did not approve of women wearing jewelry, so the bracelet could not be worn in public in any case.

My family kept me warm between blankets and hot-water bottles. Clara sang Hungarian ballads. Norah nursed me, and Mendel looked after me when nobody else was home. A month after my birth, I was registered at the police station. My family's legal status was that of minority: she, Turk; he, Austrian; Clara, Hungarian; and Mendel, not clear. He had been born in Russia, but his little village had changed hands several times since then and he wasn't sure whether he was German, Moldavian, Polish, Romanian, or Russian. In contrast to them, I was not a suspicious foreign element, but a Romanian citizen. I had full rights. I qualified for food stamps and more milk. With me around, they could get more sugar, more bread, and more clothes.

By the time of my first birthday, when Aram and Alisa came home for the summer break, I had gained some weight. My skin was pale, my eyes dark green, and the red hair was only on my head. Norah invited neighbors and other people they all knew to a party. She bartered a book on dream interpretation by a forbidden author for a case of eggplants. She was able to find eggs, which she stuffed with bread and spices. To make coffee, Norah mixed dry chicory flowers with burnt corn meal. Some friends brought prune brandy, homemade.

Bolshevik Eggs

Take as many eggs as your friends can spare.
Boil them for three minutes.
Cut them in half. Set the yolks apart.
Mix leftover cornbread with the soft yolks,
Add mustard, herbs, and spices.
Fill in the whites with this paste.
Decorate.

Eggplant

Take as many eggplants as you can find.
Remove the skin.
Cut them into small pieces and boil them until soft.
Let them drain overnight to lose their bitterness.
Mix them with chopped tomatoes, peppers,
Zucchini—whatever you can find, or with nothing.
Add any herbs—mint leaves, dill, or basil.
If you are lucky and have some oil, mix in several spoonfuls.

Exit visas did not arrive. Mendel was asked to edit a version of *Das Kapital* and *The German Ideology* for young readers. For this task the Party gave him the right to use a typewriter. Its serial number and font type were registered at the police headquarters. Being granted a typewriter was a high form of trust. In the wrong hands, it could be used to write antigovernment propaganda.

With Mendel's help, Aram worked on an article, "Understanding the Five-Year Plan and the Job Market." His analysis showed the direct relationship between the number of first-year students at the university, the number of people retiring from the labor force, and the incentive to accomplish the five-year plan in only four and a half. By the end of the article, the theory was reduced to a single mathematical equation.

Norah, whose Romanian improved, had also learned some Russian and was promoted to manager of the city's postal distribution system. Meanwhile, Clara was declared official composer for the orphanage. But most astoundingly, Alisa wrote a cookbook—desserts only! Elaborate cakes, fruit tarts, and exotic soufflés with unheard-of sauces were not only explained in detail but also illustrated. Alisa invented the desserts, and we gazed for hours at her exquisitely colored miniature drawings, trying to imagine the taste of those sweets. She described lemon-basil ice cream, chocolate soup with caramelized orange peels, angel cake with rosemary syrup, and wild cherry soufflé with thyme sauce—all things that she herself had never tasted. By mixing chestnut puree with vanilla and light cream, she was taking us away from the dreary oppression of rationed flour. Alisa's book gave us something that she herself did not have: pleasure, refinement, excess, and elegance. It was a real gift. From it, I learned the great-sounding word *zabaglione*. Floating above reality, we imagined savoring the refined mousse as we took a piece of stale bread and sprinkled on it some tap water and a half-spoonful of rationed beet sugar. Years later, when I first ate real chocolate, I still believed that the chocolate in Alisa's watercolors tasted better.

The Party gave us a bigger apartment on the third floor of a villa that had a large garden in the back. There was a kitchen, a bathroom, and a large terrace, all of which we shared. Clara and Mendel chose the library for its built-in bookshelves and alcove, where Mendel put a desk. Norah and Aram took the master bedroom. My room was a glass-covered verandah that could be entered through a glass door from the terrace or through a pointed arch from my parents' bedroom. A thin piece of fabric separated my bed from their room. Alisa's bed was installed at the end of the corridor between the library and the bedroom. The radio was set up in the corridor for common use. United by circumstances, the five people that raised me were beginning to feel a sense of domesticity.

I grew up speaking a mixture of Hungarian, Romanian, French, Ladino, English, Italian, and Turkish. At school we were required to learn Russian. At home we spoke French when all of us were together, borrowing words from other languages for nuances that the French could not convey.

When I was seven, the Party sent Mendel to a translators' conference in East Berlin. He returned with a bicycle for me. On the fender, Marx, Engels, and Lenin were drawn in profile in gold paint. He also brought back a lace-like vinyl tablecloth for Norah, a pen with Lenin's head floating up and down in a clear liquid for Aram, and a bouquet of red plastic roses for Clara. The same year, the Party asked Aram to teach Marxist economics at the university and approved the publication of his new book, *The Fall and Anguish of Capitalist Economy*.

Alisa finished school and was asked to work at the Institute for the International Alliance for Communism, a propaganda office that kept track of economic data. She lived with us and taught me Yiddish. She still cried all the time but never told me why. She would hold me on her lap and whisper in Yiddish, "*Mamale, mamale*, little mother. You don't know, *mamale*, how hard it is. It is very hard." I thought about this, and one day I said, "If it makes you so unhappy, why do you want me to know? You want me to cry, too?" Alisa looked confused, then kissed my face with her wet lips, saying, "I have no one to love me; no one to love now."

Only a year after she had officially moved in with us and had made the bed in the corridor her home, the Party sent Alisa to Warsaw to establish a Bureau of Cultural Exchange. She was chosen because she knew the language and had no family left there. Alisa sent us photographs from her trips in Poland, along with small gifts of amber, marmalade, and vodka. When we stopped receiving news from her, Norah went to the political supervisor of the regional workers union and, in secret, inquired about her. The official found out that Alisa had made illegal contacts with nationals from enemy countries. When accused of treason, she had defected to Sweden with a fake passport. We knew that we would never see her again.

Norah was the most affected by Alisa's disappearance. Actually, she was enraged. Here was Norah, still hoping to receive an exit visa, after fourteen years of waiting, and there was Alisa, once again finding somebody to take care of her—this time to smuggle her to freedom. "I am sure she found a married man to help her,"

Norah commented more than once. But Clara defended her, even though she, too, felt betrayed.

"You didn't expect her to give up the opportunity to defect to the West, did you?" she asked. "What did you want her to do? Return to Romania to go to jail? It takes a lot of courage to cross the border illegally; if found, she would have been shot. I am happy that she succeeded. I believe that any one of us would have done the same thing."

"If you really want to know," Norah told Clara, "I feel like the fly from the Russian poem:

Muha siela na varen'e,
Vot ivs'e stihotvorenie.
A fly lands on the marmalade,
This is how the story ends."

14

A t the post office, hidden between the files in her desk, Norah found a letter from Guido. It was a blue envelope with small red lines around the edges and *Posta Internazionale Via Areo* written on the bottom left side. The stamps showed the statue of a woman with a laurel crown on her head. Below was written *Republica Italiana, 400 Lire*. Norah made an exact drawing of the envelope, copied the words, studied it front and back, smelled it, held it to the light to see if she could read the letter inside, smelled it again, and handed it to the commissar supervisor without opening it.

"You don't believe that anyone would have taken the risk to give me in secret a letter from the outside. It was addressed to the three of us, and was hidden on my desk because it was a setup, a pretext to check me out."

"You gave the letter to the Party without reading it?" Clara asked.

"What was I to do? It is irresponsible of Guido to put us at risk with his letter. I was scared!" Norah yelled, "Scared for you, for me, for my job. You can't trust Italian men; they are mama's boys," she shouted in disdain.

"I didn't know you had such vast experience with Italian men. I wonder if perhaps you are referring to Guido," Clara said calmly.

"No, my dear, that was a general statement."

Clara gauged her gestures, her words, the inflection in her voice and said, "So you don't know what was in the letter?"

"I do. Your marriage with Guido was annulled," Norah said, indifferently thrusting her chin forward.

"My marriage was annulled," Clara said. "This means that Guido wants to get married again. I wish I could feel something more than sadness."

"Since I turned in the letter, you are not at risk. I was even congratulated for my loyalty to the Party, and told about a letter from Hanah's Paradise received several months ago."

"I see," Clara said, faking indifference.

"Clara, there was nothing I could have done to bring the letter home."

"You did the right thing," Clara said, and started to cry. Norah put her hands over her face, not to see Clara crying.

They didn't talk to each other again until late that night, when Aram and Mendel came home. After dinner, Norah apologized for bringing home bad news but informed Aram that a letter from Hanah's Paradise had arrived several months earlier. She had never seen it. Aram kept his head down, waiting for the news.

"Another letter?" I started to ask, but Clara signaled me to be quiet.

"Your mother has died," Norah said, looking at no one. Only Aram had a mother still alive, so clearly it was his. "She died four months ago. That is all I was told. I wasn't allowed to read the letter."

My father stood up. "Thank you, Norah," he said, "I don't know how to feel about the news," he said and left.

I didn't know what to feel about my grandmother's death, either, but I cried. Not for her death but because I would never meet her.

My father sent a telegram to his sister in Moscow, and for eight days my mother obliged all of us to pray. She mourned the death in the strangest way. She covered the mirrors, sat on the floor, cut a hole in her dress above her heart, didn't touch leather, didn't cook, didn't wash. She only prayed:

Yit'gadal v'yit'kadash   magnified and sanctified
Yit'barakh v'yish'tabach   blessed and praised

I don't know whether my father ever talked about his mother's death or how he felt about it—I never heard anything—but after that day, the look in his eyes was more distant and his face more rigid.

The Party commissar told Norah that the working class forbade all contact with enemy capitalist countries. The letters should stop arriving, he advised. Norah didn't know how to stop the letters if she wasn't allowed to contact the people who sent them; nevertheless, she apologized. She wrote a confession, denouncing as provocateurs the people who wrote to her family, and promised the Party to fight against them.

When Mendel was sent again to the Conference of Russian Language Translators, this time in Bulgaria, discreetly he asked a British colleague to mail two letters for him from England. They had no return address.

THE PIANO

Clara considered music an important part of my education and took it upon herself to teach me how to play the piano. Twice a week I met her at the orphanage, after school. She showed me how to place my fingers on the keyboard, how to touch the keys and recognize the sounds. But at home I had to practice on a long piece of paper on which Mendel had drawn a keyboard. Clara would supervise me by singing the notes and pointing to their location. With my two hands on the paper, I played arpeggios and octaves until I was able to play Czerny, the father of piano exercises. In time I learned how to play complex musical pieces, sonatas and mazurkas, singing the melody and moving my hands on the black-and-white drawing. Norah was very proud, and when she found an old piano in an abandoned movie theater, she asked permission to take it.

My mother arrived home one day standing next to a small upright pianoforte in the back of an open truck. As she neared our house she became so excited that while the driver was waiting at an intersection she started to play the piano. Hearing music in the street, Clara looked through the window and recognized Norah. She ran to the intersection and climbed onto the truck next to her. Startled neighbors came to their windows. Screaming in delight, children ran into the street, clapping their hands, singing, whistling, and dancing around the slow-moving truck. The truck rumbled down the street toward our house; Clara played a popular tune; Norah, filled with joy, banged on the keys; and the driver honked his horn to the rhythm of the melody, singing at the top of his lungs:

> I love you-ou-ou, I love you-ou-ou,
> Va-len-tiiiiiiiii-no.
> I will wait for your kiss until the ni-iii-ght.

> You are mine and I am youuur true luuuuver,
> And forever I will giiiiiiiive you my heart.
> O Valentinooo, Valentinoooooo!

The truck halted again, forced to stop by a horse-drawn cart carrying wood. There was fun in the air, and everybody laughed as if fancy foods and clothing were floating in the sky, ready to be snatched and taken home. In the midst of all the noise, the horse got scared. He raised his front legs, neighed, and to everyone's delight, broke into a gallop. His driver jumped up and, whirling his whip in the air, shook his hips obscenely to the rhythm of the song. When the truck arrived in front of the house, Mendel, who had witnessed the entire scene from the window, rushed out and in a stern but low voice scolded, "The last thing we need is a display of wealth, alliance with the cultural values of a class society, and jealous neighbors!"

"Remember," he went on, "we are not from here. People are watching to see if we conform to the Party line, if we have a double life. The piano has to be returned!" The driver, meanwhile, helped by some neighbors, had brought the piano inside the apartment. Norah thanked the neighbors, paid the driver, and after everybody left, turned to Mendel. "Go to hell," she said.

"You don't know what you're doing," Mendel shouted. "This is bourgeois affectation, intellectual pursuit, and alliance with the immorality of a manipulative, upper class."

"I am a musician!" Clara shouted back. "I know exactly what I'm doing. I am composing stupid fucking Party songs. This piano is the working tool of a proletarian composer. What do you think the Party condemns most, Mendel, lipstick, hair dye, silk stockings, jewelry—or the piano?"

"Mendel," Norah said, "music has nothing to do with class status and exploitation."

"It does, Norah. It has to do with values."

"So," Clara said, "do they have to be my values?" She and Norah then grabbed my hands and the three of us started dancing around Mendel and the piano, singing with affected passion:

> My beautiful country,
> I love you from my heart.
> For your wealth

I give up my health.
I march to the rhythm
Of the Communist drum
Until the enemy is weakened and dumb.

We sang on, praising

My Pioneer scarf,
Red as the blood of the Communist heart,
Red as the dream of a brand new start,
Red as the fire of pioneers' hopes,
To deliver us from Capitalist dopes.
We are the Party's allies best,
We've made this country our nest.

Transformed by their first attempt at freedom, the two of them, united in this dance—having only each other as sister, mother, and friend—started to cry. Life was continuing to offer them emotions for which they were not prepared. In each other's arms, Clara and Norah remembered what they had lost: the arms that had held them, the hands that had caressed them and taught them how to tie the laces of a shoe, the love not of a man but of a sister, of a friend with whom they could share their memories. There is no solitude more desperate than the loss of affection for your own past. They had only the present, and Mendel was trying to take even that away from them.

The piano was Norah's first attempt at a better life. Abundance was inappropriate. Leftovers were unavailable. Bringing home the piano was a mark of stability and also a gift for Clara and for me. But a piano is beyond necessity. It is an object acquired for the luxury of being delighted by music. Only Clara understood Norah's desperate gesture. The piano was her tacit acknowledgment that the exit visa would never come.

WORKERS' DAY

The celebration of workers on May Day was mandatory for the entire city. A grandstand was erected in front of the Communist Party building, and red flowers were planted in a sickle-and-hammer design. Groups of young gymnasts moved in formation, displaying slogans, and dancers in folkloric costumes performed for the dignitaries, waving small red flags above their heads.

The orphans performed revolutionary songs in front of the official Party delegates with Clara conducting the orchestra. The children, dressed in white shirts with red Pioneer scarves around their necks, stood in the sun waiting for their turn to sing. There must have been fifty of them, between seven and thirteen years old. To protect them from lice, the orphanage supervisor ordered that everyone's head be shaved. Clara was upset. Her orchestra looked "like prisoners going to the gas chamber," she said.

> Ta RA-TA-TA, the horn will ring
> Ta RA-TA-TA, one voice will sing
> On May Day, all workers bring
> Their flags, to show their honoring.

They sang in unison, looking straight at Clara.

When, by late afternoon, the first measure of the international workers' anthem was heard, people knew that the celebration was ending. They dispersed without waiting to applaud. The orphans' voices followed the population, and the song reverberated through the alleys and streets.

> Arise, ye prisoners of starvation
> Arise, ye wretched of the earth.

The melody obsessed us, and we fought it out of our minds, but there was always somebody around to whistle it.

A few days later, Clara was requested to appear in front of the regional Party supervisor. He received her in his office, in a former bourgeois house requisitioned for the Party's needs. The comrades had taken away everything of value. The Party leader had used his authority to keep the ceiling lamp and a carved oak desk too heavy to be stolen. A drape covered half a window and a bookcase without shelves had been transformed into a broom closet. A small Persian rug was nailed to the floor. A wooden crate, previously used to carry charcoal, served as the chair for visitors. The supervisor pointed to the crate, leaving Clara to sit there in front of him while he looked through some papers. Without warning he stood up, banged his fist on the desk, and yelled at her: "Sabotage!

You are sabotaging the Party!" Afraid that he would hit her, Clara recoiled on the wooden box, shielding her head with her arms. The political commissar waved his fist in the air, went around her, and screamed, "You idiot! You stupid whore! You Hungarian gypsy! Do you want to end up in another labor camp?"

Thinking that it was about the piano, Clara said, "The piano is only to compose songs—" but the commissar cut her off.

"I should send you to the canal to dig dirt! You will be singing all day with the other prisoners, you dumb, smelly cow!" Clara covered her face with her hands, shielding her eyes from the image of people in prison uniforms singing on the road.

"You thought the Nazi camp was bad?" he continued. "We will send you to the enemies of the people camp. You will see how we treat them! You will feel sorry for the milk you sucked from your stupid mother's breast! You will be sorry the Nazis didn't finish you!"

Clara fixed her eyes on the Persian carpet under her feet. She felt as if the red lines on the carpet were her veins, from which blood was slowly draining, following the pattern of the rug to form the design of the central medallion. She swallowed the knot in her throat and, in a wounded animal wail, asked, "Why?"

This infuriated the commissar even more. "You don't have the right to ask why! I have to ask why! How do you think I felt on May Day, on the most important day in our country's revolutionary history, with every one of the official Party delegates on the podium? How do you think I felt when the orphans started singing?" Clara looked blank. "I'll tell you how I felt!" he screamed. "They sang those nice Pioneer songs, with melodies that everybody has learned. My own children know them. Even *I* know them. So why did the orphans have to sing those songs with a stupid fucking German accent? Are you crazy? Don't you know that the Germans lost the fucking war? Can you understand the problems you created for me? You could be shot!"

Clara was sobbing, and the reference to her mother's milk had made her dizzy. She was not aware of the Party's mistrust of foreigners. Clara had grown up speaking Yiddish and Hungarian. At the music conservatory in Vienna she had learned German and Italian—she was still learning Romanian. It was not Clara's accent that was disturbing. Her accent was fine. She was a musician and could reproduce sounds. It was the way in which she mispronounced the letters that people found odd. She would say "va-da-r" rather than "father," holding the r between her lips for a second. Then, as she swallowed the letter, she would let out a harsh, rapid sound that, if you knew the word, you recognized as the missing r. The orphans reproduced her sounds without her realizing it.

But the commissar was not through screaming. "Everyone thought those were German songs! One of our guests asked whether the orphans' performance was an act of subversive irony against the Party. You know how 'The Internationale' was heard at the delegates' tribune? You know what the orphans were singing? 'Ass, and, pussy an ovation.' I had to show the delegates the written words before they believed me. The only thing that saved you was having the orphans sing in Russian—with the right accent. From now on you can write the songs but you cannot sing them. Is that clear? If I see you again in my office, you will be singing songs while digging the Danube, you idiot! We'll be keeping an eye on you. Go now and thank the Party for forgiving you this time!"

Clara understood the reference to the Danube–Black Sea Canal. "The Supreme Hero" had asked the people to show their love for the Party by performing an impossible task. Hundreds of thousands of people were sent to dig the Danube's bed for some four hundred kilometers so that Bucharest, the capital, could become a city on the shores of the Black Sea. Building the canal was Stalin's advice to the Romanian president about ruling the country. "The masses must be kept occupied. Give them a big project. We are now building the Moscow–Volga Canal. Take our example. It is the only way to get rid of the opposition." Clara knew a French teacher who had been sent there when the secret police found out that she had borrowed books from the French Consulate. She received a five-year sentence for having contact with foreigners. She would probably not return. Very few returned from there.

Clara told the story to Norah first, who advised her to get a doctor's note and stay home for several weeks. Aram and Mendel disagreed. After hours of discussion they decided that meeting with the commissar would be best.

We all went with Clara. We stood in line in the corridor, waiting at his door until our turn arrived and he let us in. Clara, who had been in his office before, stood against the empty bookshelf and we stood near her, none of us daring to sit on the wooden crate. Mendel, who knew Romanian best, spoke first.

"Thank you for meeting with us, Comrade. We appreciate your advice. We've come to assure you that we are very grateful to the Party and to our comrade workers for giving us a home in Romania. We are very happy here building Communism. We may sometimes make mistakes, but we are loyal people."

"If you are loyal and want to show your gratitude, then why don't you become members of our Communist Party?" he asked.

Nobody said anything. We couldn't tell him, "We don't want to become Communists, Comrade, because we want to leave and are waiting for our visas." To say this would have sent us straight to prison as enemies of the state. We looked at each other first, then Aram, Mendel, and Clara turned to Norah, one by one, not only with hope but with the assurance that she would know what to say.

"Why not, indeed!" she blurted out. "We should join the Party!" She knew from her own job that the comrade had to show an increase in membership in his monthly statistics. Norah believed that the comrade was stupid and that Mendel—with all his explanations—would only make him feel inferior.

"The comrade is right!" she continued. "We are here. We have work, a room, and food coupons. Our life is better than in the Nazi labor camp. We should join the workers. The comrade will lead us to success. He will set an example for the entire free world." She made a sweeping gesture toward the world outside the window.

The comrade listened, mesmerized. A smile of pleasure appeared on his large face. I applauded my mother as she detached herself from our group and sat down on the wooden crate in front of the potential leader of the free world.

THE RED CARD

The election meeting for prospective Party members took place at the People's Palace, a former officers' club. The ballroom had retained its grandeur, despite losing the panels of dark wood from its walls and the chandeliers from its ceiling. The unexpected proportions of the space gave the room a festive feeling. Three columns defined the dance floor—a platform in the shape of a heart.

This area was reserved for the Party delegates, who sat at a table facing the room. A red cloth covered the table and a plaster cast of a Russian tank hung on the wall. The room was clouded by cigarette smoke. Some fifty people, already members of the Party, had been enlisted to listen to each candidate's self-criticism and to vote afterward for or against membership.

The regional Party delegate gave an introductory speech. In a self-assured voice, he commented on Comrade Stalin's article "Against Vulgarizing the Slogan of Self-Criticism."

"The slogan of self-criticism must not be regarded as something temporary and transient," he began. "Self-criticism is a specific method, a Bolshevik method of training the forces of the Party and the working class in the spirit of revolutionary development. Karl Marx himself spoke of self-criticism as a method of strengthening the proletarian revolution, as a specific revolutionary act in the working-class movement."

One by one, the candidates rose and walked to the platform to state their name, date and place of birth, profession, and social origin. A lengthy critical speech about themselves and a brief patriotic explanation of their desire to join the Party accompanied each presentation. On a blackboard that had been pushed against a column, a comrade was writing the information given by each candidate.

Norah was the first from our family to be called to the podium. She thanked the Party for giving her a job and a place where she could raise her children. She was then asked to answer questions from the floor. "Was it true," somebody asked, "that your father was a rich merchant, one of those *porc murdar*, dirty pigs, who suck the blood of our peasants?"

"Yes," she answered. "It is true, but he left my mother after I was born. My mother moved to a little island with some relatives and I grew up there. He was killed in a concentration camp, along with all his family from Thessalonica. I was not raised by him."

"*Da ia spunetine si noua tovarasa*, but tell us, Comrade, is it true that your mother was a bourgeois who had servants and exploited the working class?" the same person asked.

"No," Norah answered. "That is not correct. My mother was beautiful and generous. Members of our extended family lived with us. Of course they helped at home, as we all do. But my mother sent them to school and made sure that they brushed their teeth and got good grades. She transformed their lives, and if she were here today, she would be working for the Party and for women's emancipation, just as all of us do."

"If such was the case," the political supervisor asked, "then why did you ask for a visa to leave? Do you not believe in the success of the Communist Party?"

Norah was taken aback. She had not expected them to know so much. Perhaps they also knew that she had lied about her parents and that she had lived on the island only in the summer. She composed herself and answered in a tone that conveyed modesty and induced sympathy. She pronounced the vowels of every word in a very soft tone, separating the syllables and giving the words a sensuous French-like accent.

"We-ll, my dear Comrades, I was not eee-xactly leav-iiing the countree-y," she said, opening the palms of her hands in a sign of sincerity. "I was here in traans-iit. Hundreds of people were pas-seee-ing through Romaniiià. When I askee-d for the eee-xit viiisà, I was only conteen-uing my jour-ney." Norah was nervous. Not only did she move her head and hands in rhythm with the words, she also rolled her eyes, raised her eyebrows, and puckered her lips. "Yo-uu, Comrades, can verify that I made maa-ny, maa-ny, maa-ny requests. I was confuuuse-d, I didn't know where to go," she said.

"This is correct," the Party delegate said, "but none of the visas you requested were for Socialist countries. You speak Turkish. You could have asked to go to Bulgaria or Albania to join the Turk minorities there in building Socialism. But you asked to go to Italy, to Palestine, and Turkey—all imperialist countries that exploit the workers."

"Ohhh, Comrade," Norah said, fluttering her eyelids, "I could have, but I wasn't thinking. I was s-ooo lonely—" and, tracing in the air the contour of her body with her hands, Norah continued, "—and so-ooo youu-ng. Now I am s-ooo s-ooorry!"

When a delegate nodded at her, Norah looked more confident.

"Comra-aades, it is not that I didn't wa-aant to build Sociali-iism. I just didn't know what it wa-aas!"

Norah glanced at the delegates, moistened her lips, and turned slightly to face the audience, from which laughter could now be heard.

"Comra-aades!" she yelled, finding the occasion ripe for repeating the slogans she had learned. "Not all of us knew about Socialeeism and about class tensee-ions! The capitalist oppress-ors controlled the means of production and the type of production. I didn't know that our exploited working class was forced to exchange life for materi-aaal goods. Comraaa-des, this is baaa-d!" Norah got carried away until, from the front row, Aram signaled with his hand, *enough already*, and she began looking for a way to end. She raised her arms and without hesitation shouted, "Long leee-ive our leaders and our revolutionary heroes—Marx, Engels, Lenin, Stalin, Molotov, Dimitrov, Zhdanov, Rosaaa Luxemburg, Jawaharlal Nehru, and Dolores Ibárruri, La Pasionaria!"

Conditioned to show enthusiasm when hearing the names of heroes, the people applauded mechanically, never interrupting their private conversations.

Pleased with herself for having achieved this effect, Norah continued: "I know that the Paa-rty trusts me, and I trust the Paa-rty. With loyalty and haaa-rd work we will rebuild the country; we will clean the windows of the orphanage. Long live—" she wanted to say Mahatma Gandhi but became confused and shouted, "—Mata Hari." The audience applauded. Norah was elected a member of the Communist Party.

Aram went next. He acknowledged that his parents and siblings had not joined the Party's cause. His father had been born in Palestine but lived in Vienna. The war started while he was visiting Palestine, and he stayed there. "But, Comrades, I personally deplore the aggressive actions of the State of Israel and the aggressive role Israel plays in the Middle East. The Party asked me to sever all relationship with my family, and I did. In my work I demonstrate that the economic model of the Communist system can bring prosperity to the world and eradicate poverty. This economic model is based on the work of our great leaders, Marx, Engels, and Lenin!" The room applauded and Aram sat down. There were no questions from the floor. When the assembly was asked to vote, Aram was accepted into the Communist Party.

Mendel was called next. With his calm voice and well-chosen words, he gave a modest presentation of himself and his achievements. Before the war he was a poet and a Communist and now, a translator. He was arrested by the Gestapo and spent ten months in a concentration camp until liberated by the American army. He insisted that his request to join the Party was a renewal of membership, not a new candidature.

"You can say what you want," a delegate said, "but how can we know that you are not a traitor, a conspirator, or a spy? Why didn't you wait to be liberated by our Russian brothers?"

Mendel nodded his head in agreement. "Comrades, I am a poet, not a spy. American troops entered Dachau first and I was asked to assist with the interrogation of the German prisoners. I speak German and English. I just wanted to be helpful. Now I am here to ask forgiveness from the Party. It was an error of judgment. But please take into account that I was a Communist before the Nazis arrested me. Now I am translating for our working class the complete writings of Comrade Lenin and—" the room burst into applause before he had finished his sentence. Mendel's Communist past was taken into consideration, and the comrade workers renewed his membership. When Mendel sat down, Aram shook his hand vigorously.

Clara was visibly nervous when her name was called. The orphans' performance was still on her mind. She spoke carefully, trying to conceal her German accent, avoiding any words with the letter *r*.

"Budapest was my home. I like music. I went to the music academy in Vienna. The fascists took me to a camp. Eleven months I was a slave to the Nazis. Communist people took me out of the camp. They sent me to Budapest, but my whole family was dead. I met a man who had been in school with me. He asked me to be his wife and go with him to his family in Italy. We left Budapest. We walked and took buses. When we came to you, he abandoned me. He went to Italy alone. He was not a bad man, and I stayed with you. Now I am happy. Now I have food. Thank you."

Clara looked around, but nobody said anything. From the front row, Norah nodded looks of approval. Clara remained tense. She crossed her arms over her chest as if to protect herself and grew pale. She continued speaking in a soft voice, with the greatest effort, confusing *v* with *f*, and *b* with *v*. In the struggle to conceal the *r* and pronounce each syllable clearly her accent became increasingly strong.

"Now I'fe lea'r'nd 'omanian! This is a vutivul language," she said, "A language that has the st'r'ong will of 'r'ussian, and the soft melodious sound of Italian. I compose songs fo' the next gene'r'ation of Communists. Music can uplift people and instill in them mo'r'al justice, love fo' the count'r'y and pat'r'iotism. Take, fo' example, Beethoven's *Thi'r'd Symphony*, the He'r'oica! Listen to the vi'r'st pa'r't and you will hea'r' Napoleon's t'r'oops ma'r'ching." Clara launched into a music-appreciation lecture on meaning, passion, and expression, until a man in the back of the room interrupted her enthusiasm with his own.

"Yes!" he shouted. "We Romanians love music. We sing all the time, even when we are hungry."

"Of course we do! Romanians are born poets," a woman in the middle row said.

Encouraged by the diversion, Norah stood up. Trying to help her friend, she said in her most charming and seductive voice, "Romanian is the language of poets and of democracy." The people burst into applause. "Yes!" somebody shouted. "All Germans should learn Romanian!"

"That's right!" an older man said. "Fuck those mothers! Whoever doesn't learn Romanian goes to Auschwitz!"

Waiting to go home, tired after the day's work, the people needed only this spark of diversion to change the course of the meeting. The laughing from the back of the room increased and, carried by the tobacco clouds, the boredom exploded, diverting the self-criticism into a restless chant:

> Ausch—Fritz, Ausch—Fritz!
> For the Nazis to learn speech!

"*Da Domnule*, yes Sir! Let Fritz go to death camp, to shit in his pants from fear," someone shouted.

"Better to have them work in our factories so we can go fishing!" another said.

"*Mama draga*, dear mother, I haven't gone fishing for a long time," a comrade added.

"What with all these political meetings and the extra work we have to do for the Party . . ."

"Comrades!" shouted the political leader, who had come in from the capital for the occasion, "we are not here to judge the Germans. Remember that half of them are our brothers. Their lives, too, have been destroyed. The American imperialist brutes are occupying their country. Families are separated. Brothers and sisters cannot visit their parents. They also suffer. Our Communist brothers from Eastern Germany were not on the side of the Nazis. They suffered as much as we did, even more. The Americans reduced the city of Dresden to ashes in the last weeks of the war— the last weeks, Comrades, the last weeks! People are still suffering. It was only West Germany—*Vaterland, Naziland*—that was *a cuib de serpi Fascisti*, a nest of Nazi snakes. The rest of the country had nothing to do with the Nazis. They hated Hitler and tried to stop the war. They are heroes!"

The political leader shouted to be heard, but laughter from the back of the room interrupted him again and again. During the entire time, Clara remained standing in front of the assembly, crossing and uncrossing her arms, straightening her skirt, waiting for the meeting to end. From the table the Party leader shouted for silence, then addressed Clara.

"Is it true that you are hiding gold from the Party?"

A frightened look twisted her face. She moved her lips without saying any words and her shoulders sagged, as if she had been hit from behind. All citizens were required to donate their gold. Clara never thought about the bracelet as gold, only as her link to Guido. She knew that anonymous letters to the Party denouncing someone's hidden gold or foreign currency often resolved neighbors' disputes. People's houses were searched. Furniture and valuable objects were confiscated. If jewelry was found, the people were arrested, their children taken to the orphanage, and their apartment given to a deserving Party member. If nothing was found, the person was beaten, threatened, and put on the black list as a potential enemy. It was clear that the Party was well informed. How could anyone have known about the bracelet? Clara's face remained terribly contorted. She looked at us desperately, her lips moving uncontrollably. At first no one noticed, but after a while people rose from their seats and a whisper went through the room: *She is crying.*

Mendel stood up, then my parents pulled me up from my seat.

"Comrade Clara Rombauer," the commissar said harshly, "tears are the weapon of the hypocrite, of the weak, manipulating bourgeoisie."

"I am so'r'y! I don't want to hafe any gold, com'ades. I want to 'r'aite music. Efen in the camp I w'r'ote zongs. In Mauthausen ou' *Kapo*, Alma 'ose, played fo' Himmle'. I was in the women's *o'r'kest'r'a* and I composed zongs: sho'r't zongs, simple melodies, without o'r'namentation, zongs of despai' that people sang to send messages. Please veliefe me, com'r'ades, gold is not impo'r'tant."

"Songs are songs and gold is gold!" the comrade said. "You are supposed to turn in the gold; only traitors to the working class hide it. You betrayed the Party. You are a selfish bourgeois; an enemy, a foreign element on our Romanian shores."

Clara looked at us, terrified. Norah moved her hand very slowly to attract Clara's attention, then pointed at me with her elbow. Clara seemed confused, but Norah nodded, looking at me from the corner of her eyes, then pointed her elbow in my direction again. In a moment of inspiration Clara made the connection and, pointing at me, she yelled, "*She* has the gold! I gave he' the v'r'acelet, and she lost it." She said the words very fast, swallowing the *r* in her usual way. The only thing people could understand was that she was pointing to a person in the front row.

The town's political commissar asked me to the podium. I was a thin, seven-year-old child with curly red hair, dressed in the dark-blue clothes distributed by the Party. A man lifted me onto the top of the table, and the city's Party official asked, "What is your name, child?"

"Meia."

"And who are your parents?"

This was a confusing question. I was living with four adults, so I pointed them out one by one: "Him . . . and him, and her . . . and her, and . . . Comrade Stalin."

For a split second, everybody held their breath, then the room shattered with applause. Only a child raised in the true spirit of the Revolution could be *everybody's* child. At my house, everybody was a parent because I spoke their languages and, since I had to learn Russian, I assumed that Comrade Stalin was my father also. I saluted the people and started singing and dancing on the table.

> The call for morning wake-up
> Brings people lots of joy.
> The siren tells the workers:
> Be ready for the day,
> Love your faithful leaders
> And never disobey.

The political commissar pinched my cheek and handed me a medal, on which golden Cyrillic letters on a red background spelled, "A hero of the Socialist Revolution." The members of the politburo applauded. The comrades voted and Clara, too, became a member of the Communist Party.

The next day, the local newspaper published a black-and-white photograph of a little girl dancing on a table, one arm above her head, the other on her hips, surrounded by happy-looking people, a flag fluttering in the background. "A child shows love for the Communist Party," the caption read. Later on, socialist-realist painters used this scene over and over again, with only slight variations. Sometimes a red Party card is being handed to a man while the little girl is dancing. Sometimes a woman holding a red flag and looking like a well-fed peasant is gazing at the little girl.

To celebrate the event, Aram gave me a Russian watch with big red letters spelling *pobeda*, victory, and taught me how to tell time. Mendel taught me how to whistle, and Clara and Norah received me into the clan of women, showing me how to make potato dumplings.

Dumplings

Boil potatoes, as many as you can find.
Mash them to a paste.
Add as many eggs as you can put your hands on.
One is sufficient, two is luxury.
Form a dumpling and fill it with anything you can get:
A berry, a piece of apple, a prune, or nothing.
Boil them. Drain well.

Cover them with a mixture of breadcrumbs and sugar.
Of course, if you have butter . . .
But that is another story.

LESSONS FOR SALOMEIA

Following the Party meeting, Clara and Norah talked endlessly about the communists going fishing and the Germans replacing them to work in the factories. Remembering the old man's silly idea about teaching the Germans Romanian or sending them to Auschwitz made them burst into laughter. "I could teach them Yiddish," Clara said, and pointing a finger at an imaginary German, mockingly she asked, "What does *visbiden* mean?"

"*Visbiden* means the essence of nastiness," Mendel answered.

"Somebody whose natural inclination is hate, whose thoughts betray an evil disposition," Clara said.

"Somebody who can demonstrate what can be achieved with stupidity and a weapon," Norah added. "Precisely, a Nazi!"

A strong believer in the connection between language and behavior, Clara came up with a new solution to the German problem. "As war reparations, Germans should be ordered to convert to Judaism, speak only Yiddish, and take the identity of one of their victims. Only that would change the way they think."

"Sure," Aram offered, "conversion, assimilation, inquisition, and alienation; that is what the world is missing."

"Clara, you're crazy," Norah said, but she liked the idea. They laughed until their laughter became tears. This was the beginning of their attempt to talk about themselves while continuing to hide the past. Their identities before the war, their family life and links with other people had never been mentioned. But after the Party meeting, some change had settled in, and their conversations started to reveal memories of Jewish holidays, Jewish songs, and Jewish meals. They were not able to talk about their past, but they gave themselves permission to discuss Jewish subjects. These conversations were particularly intense.

"Walls have ears," Mendel would caution, discouraging talk about such subjects.

"Yes," Norah would agree, repeating the admonition in Hebrew: "*Oznayem lakotel.*"

"Besides," Mendel informed us, "we are not religious, so we are not Jewish. We don't believe in God. We believe in progress, and religion means oppression."

"Then, Mendel, if I don't believe in God, if I am not Jewish and I am not religious, why is Jewish written on my identity card?" Aram asked.

"So you can always remember what you're not," Norah replied with sarcasm.

"We are not Jewish because there is no official anti-Semitism in Romania," Clara concluded.

"What?" Norah shouted. "You mean to define my cultural heritage, my traditions, my beliefs, my existence, through the absence of hate? You mean that I can be Jewish only if somebody is there to kill me for it? Nonsense, Clara! I am Jewish because I was given a set of basic beliefs that are part of my culture as well as my religion."

"What basic beliefs? Do you respect any of the 613 laws? Do you light candles on the Sabbath?" Clara was shouting. "Do you ovse'f"—observe, she wanted to say—"the Jewish holidays?"

"I don't have to observe anything," Norah countered. "I am born of Jewish parents, themselves born of Jewish parents. This lineage alone makes me Jewish. That's it!"

"You are Jewish because the Germans told you so," Clara challenged. "They put a yellow star with 'Jude' on your arm, they stamped a J on your documents, they numbered you. True?"

"True," Norah said, looking at Aram for help. "They did. But it was not because I was or was not going to the synagogue. It is not *their* hate that makes me Jewish. It is for being *Jewish* that they hate me. They wanted me dead for my traditions."

"Jewish is a religion," Mendel intervened. "It is not a race. It is identity based on primitive beliefs. I personally, with all my strength, do not believe in God. I consider myself a first-generation assimilated Jew. If I change my name, nobody will remember in five years."

"Stop it, Mendel!" Aram yelled, to everyone's surprise. "Please, spare us your blindness! You are just denying your past. We were Jewish before Auschwitz, and that is why we ended up there. Whether we believed in God or not, whether we participated in economic and cultural progress or not, it didn't matter. We were destined to the Final Solution, as progressive a force as the Jews were in commerce, art, and sciences. And if now you believe in assimilation, later on you may want to deny life to anyone else who doesn't."

"I am Jewish because I say so, not because the Nazis put a mark on my arm. I was born that way," Norah said, addressing no one in particular. "Nothing obliges me to be Jewish except the memory of my parents—and they are dead. I am not confusing Judaism with mysticism. I am Jewish even if I believe that God's power to intervene in history is nonexistent."

"Norah, that is exactly what Sartre is deploring—you, the inauthentic Jew. Read *Réflexions sur la question juive*. In 1946, he defines anti-Semitism as a revolutionary democratic concept. Read it and you'll understand. He deplores the inauthentic Jews, the character that creates the anti-Semitic effect."

Aram turned to Mendel and put a hand on his arm. "Mendel, what happened to the French authentic Jews who didn't change their names, who didn't assimilate? Weren't they sent to extermination camps? And the inauthentic, the first generation to assimilate, who spoke French without accent, who supported arts and democracy, what happened to them, Mendel? They were found out because they had hooked noses, thick lips, large ears, moist and bulging eyes, curly hair, dark skin, and flat feet. And Sartre's 'Sarah, the beautiful Jewess'—'symbol of treachery and deception,' with her 'very special sexual significance,' and her 'seducing powers'—is troubling Sartre enough to embrace anti-Semitism. I read the book, Mendel. I know what Sartre thinks about Jews, women, and the Communist Party."

"Listen to me, you who hide behind words and never smile," Norah said, moving away from Mendel. "We were making bricks under the supervision of German soldiers. It was a spring day. The trees were warming up—some had green buds on their branches. Even the clay, which we had to scoop by hand, felt warmer. Nobody wanted to be alive, and nobody was alive for long. We were beyond despair. That day, our ankles deep in mud and our hands blistered, a whisper passed among us. 'Today is Passover.' And I, for whom tomorrow meant a body left to die in the mud, a body resented for the extra effort it took to go around it, I felt happy. Passing the mud bricks into the next hands in line, I said,

Este es el pan de la aflicción,	This is the bread of affliction,
Que comieron nuestros padres	Which our fathers ate
En tierra de Egipto.	In the land of Egypt.

"And always passing the mud bricks, the next person in line whispered to the next one:

| *Esto año aqui,* | This year here, |
| *El año qui viniere en tierra de Israel.* | Next year in the land of Israel. |

"The words rose above the guards, floated in the air, and returned with the sweet smell of apple blossoms. Each one of us continued to whisper to the next one in line:

Esto año aqui siervos,	This year slaves,
El año qui viniere libres	Next year free
En tierra de Israel.	In the land of Israel.

"I am Jewish because I belong to a history, because I resent those German murderers who wiped from the face of the earth the oldest and most flourishing Jewish communities, along with our culture and collective memories."

Aram, hearing in Norah's voice the pain of her confession, interrupted. "Let's not lie to ourselves, Mendel. The murder of the Jews was not a single, circumstantial event. Country by country, village by village, street after street, this was mass extermination with the aim of destroying the structure of the Jewish way of life for generations to come. We were killed one by one, person by person—one after the other, until six million had gone. The cultural exchanges and the trading for which the Jews in Europe were responsible are gone. The language, the humor, the manners, the customs of an entire civilization ended up in smoke."

This conversation proved to be a turning point in Norah's life. She had talked. She delivered some of her past. To show that she was Jewish she devised a system of dots which the educated eye would perceive as a Star of David. Six white buttons decorated her indigo blue dress and six pieces of rabbit fur enhanced the back of her winter coat.

"What are you doing?" Clara asked. "Are you crazy? Haven't you already had to wear a Jewish star?"

"If I was supposed to die because of this star, then now, if you don't mind, I want to live with it."

Norah baked her own round loaves of bread, a mixture of herbs and potatoes, and decorated them with six dots of red pepper. Pork was eliminated from her vocabulary and her diet. She cooked only vegetables or fish and never mixed milk and meat. Norah went back to her traditions without a word. She thanked God every morning for being able to see light. She set the table and lit candles on Friday. She stopped working on Saturday by invoking a doctor's treatment for women's problems. Every Saturday morning she walked to the hospital and walked back through the park, reciting a prayer. Norah was Jewish again.

The Party rewarded its new Communist members with new jobs. Clara was sent to teach at the school for gifted children. Norah was asked by the Party to open the first movie theater in town. Mendel was asked to translate Maxim Gorky's novels. Aram was sent to the Party's Youth Congress and returned home with a Medal of Honor, which added a monthly increase to his salary. He brought back a purple velvet dress for me and a round box of red fish eggs—*ikra*—for all of us to share. The salty dried fish eggs were inedible, but Norah used them as decoration, making red-orange Jewish stars on her plate.

15

Norah was given the job at the movie theater because nobody else in our neighborhood wanted it. To run the movie theater meant to be closely scrutinized by the Party's cultural commissar, whom people not only mistrusted but feared. Norah, who didn't know him, was glad for the challenge, and to celebrate, she bought sugar on the black market to make Turkish halva.

The commissar told Norah that working for the Party was an honor, then sent her to the people's warehouse, where goods requisitioned from bourgeois enemies were available to the revolutionary working class. Norah found a film projector, 104 chairs (no two alike), theater curtains, a discarded billboard, and an old van. The requisitions commissar offered her an ornate Venetian mirror that he himself had taken from the house of some bourgeois enemy.

"If you want it for the theater you should take it," he said. "You don't even have to put it on the list. Just give me something in exchange." Norah declined the offer.

During the same week, the Party's employment agency hired three more people to work at the movie theater: Silvia, a painter; Dima, a driver; and Victoria, a cashier. Norah met her new comrades in front of the kiosk, the place in town where the Party sold bread. They shook hands; exchanged some information about themselves, their families, their former jobs; told some jokes; then went to see Comrade Nico, the Commissar of Art, Culture, and Education. They walked the short distance to the Party's head office, then waited in line for the comrade to receive them.

Before the Revolution, the comrade, then known as Short Nico, was famous for taking bets at the cockfight pits. Now, with the change of regime, because of his excellent social origin and his experience with popular culture, he was appointed to this highly respected position.

Comrade Nico shook hands with them. "Comrades, the Politburo has rewarded us with a movie theater," he said triumphantly, pulling up his pants. "But first, you have to learn the 'Directives of the Communist Party Regarding Education.'"

> The immoral, reactionary bourgeoisie kept the movies only for the rich. This changed. Beautiful innocent girls were seduced with promises and with champagne, then abused and mistreated by the imperialist film industry. This also changed. We are united in the fight against oppression. None of that will happen in our free society. Our comrades have the right to a first-class education. Down with oppression!

Comrade Nico stood up, and Norah with her entire team followed his example.

"Down with champagne!" Victoria, the cashier, shouted.

"We received a movie from our brothers in the Soviet Union. I didn't see it yet but it is beautiful and heroic. For the well-being of our working class, this movie will run until everyone in town has seen it," Comrade Nico said, keeping his eyes for a second too long on Victoria's bosom. "You," he said, pointing at Norah. "You are the manager. You will show the movie six times a day, every day of the week. Many of our comrades at the Red Flag Company work in three shifts. They should be able to see the movie at any time. The first show starts at eleven in the morning and the last one ends at eleven at night. Is this clear?"

"Yes," Norah answered. "We will do the best to show our gratitude to the Party; we will project the movie every two hours, six times a day, seven days a week."

"Look here," Commissar Nico said, drawing directly on the top of his desk with a piece of chalk. "We have 104 seats. You, the driver, you have to arrange them in the room. Then write a number on each chair. Put the best chairs in the middle. You understand?"

"Yes," Dima answered. "I will put the best chairs in the middle because that is where the rich have to sit. They got fat exploiting the peasants and need bigger chairs."

"No!" Comrade Nico shouted at Dima. "There are no rich people anymore. We, the Communists have eliminated them and their class. Now we are all the same: peasants, workers, and women. We fight for peace, progress, and . . . the other one. How do they call it . . . , I think they call it parity or . . . paternity, something like that. You understand?"

"Yes," Victoria interrupted. "We sit the good-looking people in the middle rows. When the actors look at them they see how beautiful our nation is."

"Victoria!" the commissar yelled. "Have you ever seen a movie?"

"Yes, Comrade, I have, before the war. A Turk, from a place called India, came to our village and showed us a movie with women dancing and men on horses. We had to change seats all the time. Everybody wanted to be in the front row so the actors could see us one by one."

"Comrade Victoria," the commissar said, putting his arm around her shoulders. "First of all, there are no Turks in India, and second, the actors cannot see you. They are moving photographs. They are not there. The film will arrive in a box just like this one. You don't have to strive for the front row, because nobody is going to see you. Reserve the better seats in the center for the members of the Communist Party. Do you understand now?"

Comrade Nico had pushed Victoria's shoulders down toward his desk until her left breast was close to his hand. "And what is your job?" he said, leering at her. "Your job is to sell tickets. Each time that you sell a ticket, you put a cross on a piece of paper and take the money. That is why you are the cashier. For example, I come to the theater and ask you for two tickets. What do you do?"

"I tell you that we do not have champagne," Victoria answered, pulling slightly away from the desk.

"No, Comrade! You ask me where I want to sit, right? And I say to you, 'I want two seats in the middle of the row.'" With that, Commissar Nico stuck out his tongue, licked a finger, and—using his saliva—drew two crosses on the desk. "You give me two tickets, then put two crosses on the paper. At the end of the day we count the crosses and the money and know how many tickets were sold."

"Yes," Dima, the driver, said. "We put crosses on the paper like at the cemetery; you die, you get a cross."

"Every day Comrade Dima will bring the money to me, together with the crosses."

"Comrade," Norah intervened, "I think that a fallacy could occur in the system of crosses, no?"

"A fala—*what*?" Comrade Nico said. "What is that? Can't you speak the language of the Revolution? You work for the education project. Don't use the words of the treacherous reactionary class, words that no one understands."

"No, no, Comrade! She represents our Turkish minority and sometimes she uses Turkish words," Silvia, the painter, said, coming to Norah's rescue. "What she was trying to say is that she wants to make an *addition* to what you just said."

"Then call it by its name, Comrade. *Daca ai cuoaie, spune cuoaie*, if you have balls, call them balls!"

With a smile of superiority, Dima put his hand between his legs and rubbed his groin. Victoria blushed slightly.

Norah turned to Silvia with a look of nervous gratitude.

"Comrade Commissar Nico," Norah said, "you know best how to organize events. You want Dima to write letters on the rows and numbers on the chairs. Is this what you just said?"

Comrade Nico quickly realized the advantage of the system. To reinforce that it was his idea, he said, "Yes, this is exactly what I want. *A* should be the first row, and the chairs should be numbered from right to left. From the Oppressive Right to the Liberating Left, the spirit of the Bolshevik Revolution is everywhere! Is this clear?"

"This will also benefit the working class," Silvia added in a tone that she believed to be sincere. "Our comrades will also learn the numbers and the alphabet when they look for their seats. You will be in the front line of the fight against illiteracy. The Party will be proud. Row L, seats 4 and 5—two crosses."

Norah nodded in agreement, afraid that Silvia would start laughing at her own words.

Then Comrade Nico further explained their duties. Painting the title and an evocative scene from the film on a billboard above the entrance was Silvia's task. It was also her obligation, her expression of personal gratitude to the Party, and a true chance to put her talent at the service of the working class. Dima had to set up the chairs and drive the van to the collective farm, once a week, to bring people to the movie. Norah's job was to supervise everyone, to inform him of any irregularities, and to make sure that everyone in town saw the movie. "And Comrade Victoria, you should *stai pe cur si vinde bilete*, sit on your ass and sell tickets. The movie didn't arrive yet but we will send an engineer to work the projector," Comrade Nico concluded. "For me, of course, admission is always gratis. I am the culture and the culture is me."

Everyone understood. As they prepared to leave, Dima turned to the commissar and said, "Comrade, just between us men, what is the name of the movie?"

Comrade Nico, trying to disguise his own lack of knowledge, said, "Dima, when the Party wants you to know, the Party will inform you."

"Yes, Comrade Nico," Dima replied with a military salute. "The education is us."

The movie didn't arrive for a long time. In the meantime, Silvia taught Norah how to play ping-pong, Dima brought back food from the countryside, and Victoria knit scarves for all of them.

SILVIA

Silvia was tall and slender, with big blue eyes and soft blonde hair. With her hair tied up in two braids, she was the image of the perfect Aryan German girl, as seen in the Nazi propaganda posters. Silvia had an exotic air about her, which she cultivated with dignity. "The happy *Über* blonde," she described herself. Her face was round and delicate except for a raised, horizontal scar beneath the bridge of her nose. It was a nose with character. When I asked her about the scar, she touched it and laughingly told me that it was her lucky mark. "I used to have a different nose," she said, "a little wider, with a large bump. When the anti-Semitic laws were passed, a crooked nose was enough to get you arrested. A dentist friend of mine agreed to cut the bump on my nose to make it smaller. I was afraid that I looked too Jewish, especially in profile you know, like on the pamphlets put out by the government."

The dentist, who was forbidden to treat Jews, had performed the surgery at some risk. After the transformation, Sylvia obtained false identification papers from a friend and moved to the capital city. She rented a room from people she trusted and found a job painting dishes at the porcelain factory. In the city the hunting for Jews became systematic. Silvia was forewarned before the police made their house-to-house rounds to register the Jews on each street. She prepared for the visit in advance. She heated her room and put on a summer dress that was a little too tight. Her braids tied with red ribbons gave her the look of a mischievous teenager. When a policeman knocked at her door, Silvia invited him inside. Wearing an oversized winter uniform and appearing a little shy, he took off his cap and shifted from one foot to the other, asking to see her identity cards. Silvia called the other girls from their rooms, and they all sat down to talk. He showed them the required form to be filled out by Jews, foreigners, gypsies, and other people not registered with the police. Silvia's working permit was very recent and described her as a refugee, but a Romanian refugee. She had the right to travel, work, and receive food coupons.

"Why did you leave your home, Miss Silvia?" the policeman asked.

"What can we do, My Captain? My poor mother is dead, my father is fighting in the war, and I came to stay with my cousins," she said, looking into the policeman's eyes. "I am afraid to be at home alone."

"We are all afraid to live alone," Silvia's friends added. "Don't you see how many strangers are in the city?"

"*Adevarat*, true," the policeman felt obliged to say. "Times are difficult. I also left home and am here alone."

"Then you should come to visit us," one of the girls said. "We are scared. *Sa ne ajute Dumnezeu*, God help us!"

"*Da Dumneavoastra domnisoara Silvia, ce fel de religie aveti?* But you, Miss Silvia, what kind of religion do you have?"

Silvia was taken aback and glanced at her friends in fear.

"Why don't you ask me?" one of the girls chimed in. "You ask her because she is the prettiest one, right?"

The captain blushed. The girls giggled.

Twisting her mouth in a droll way, Silvia said, "They are just jealous of me because I am a natural blonde. *Eu am religia atea*, I am an atheist," she said very fast.

The policeman, a simple man, unfamiliar with the word *atea*, atheist, thought he heard her say *"a ta,"* meaning "yours."

"Ah! Mine," he said.

"Yes, yes, yes!" Silvia said. *"A ta,* yours!" then crossed her chest, as is the custom of the Greek Orthodox.

"Well, since we have the same religion, none of you need to register for identity cards," the policeman said. "Only the Jews."

"God forbid," one of her friends said, spitting on the floor in feigned disgust.

"If you know any Jews, tell them to come to the police."

"Why is that?" Silvia asked with naïve surprise.

"Not all Jews are recognizable. We have to stamp a *J* on their documents and give them new names: 'Sara' for women, 'Israel' for men."

"How about that!" Silvia replied.

"Yes, they know how to hide," the policeman said.

"Not from you," Silvia chortled, patting his hand. "Not from your eyes."

The policeman blushed. "Some are easier to find, but not all of them have long noses and curly red hair," he said.

"That is true!" Silvia said.

"But what happened to your nose?" he asked.

"Acident de bicicleta, a bicycle accident," she answered.

Thus a minor acoustical incident—the slight alteration of a single letter—saved Silvia's life. She alone of her entire family survived.

After the war, Silvia had married and moved in with her husband's family. There was no work for artists except painting buildings and fences. Silvia stayed home and painted icons of saints conversing with the Virgin Mary. Despite the Party's banishment of religion, her mother-in-law sold the icons in secret to the peasants from the *kolhoz*, the collective farms surrounding the city.

Silvia was a skilled painter who could reproduce almost anything, and painting movie scenes seemed far preferable to painting icons of illegal saints.

Almost half a year after the four comrades had started working together at the theater, the cultural commissar informed Norah of the imminent arrival of the movie. He gave her a written description of the film, provided by the Party.

Brave Soldier Ivanov's Visit Home

This famous film from our brothers in the Soviet Union depicts Private Ivanov, who single-handedly destroys several enemy tanks. For this heroic accomplishment, he is rewarded with a week's leave. Instead of going straight home to repair the roof of his mother's house, the private puts aside his personal needs to deliver letters from his comrades. The war hero stops to comfort an older couple who have just lost their son in battle. Finally, when he arrives in the village, he is welcomed by his beautiful, blonde girlfriend, and the Agrarian Revolution's Commissary. From the cornfield, his mother and other villagers run to him. They admire his war medals. However, the drama is that Private Ivanov has spent all his time on the road and has to return to his unit immediately upon his arrival. He cannot stay even for dinner—and he certainly has no time to repair the roof. He must return to fight in the war; the army needs him! Mother Russia first! His girlfriend is very proud of his heroic acts and encourages him to return to the front. His mother walks with him to the edge of the village. She watches him leave, as the narrator's voice tells the audience that the heroic soldier Ivanov—the courageous, generous, hardworking, honest, loyal, self-critical, tall, good-looking young man, the hero ready to put the interest of the country and the people above his own personal needs, the son prompted to sacrifice in order to help others, the patriot—will never return home.

In preparation for the film's arrival, Silvia went to the Party's warehouse to find whatever paint she could. She returned with several cans of paint, some of them already opened. She also brought back the ornate Venetian mirror, which she propped against the wall in her workspace. Reflected in the mirror, the long-abandoned backyard brought into Silvia's workspace a perfectly arranged, wild, and mysterious English garden.

"What did you give the warehouse manager in exchange for the mirror?" Norah asked Silvia.

"An icon, 'Jesus weeping over Jerusalem.'"

Dima repaired the billboard—four wooden doors nailed together with metal braces—and Silvia painted it white. Norah asked Comrade Nico what should be painted on the billboard.

"I want to see the blonde girl when she greets the soldier," Comrade Nico said.

"Make her beautiful, like one of our girls. Tell Silvia to give her a curvy form, like Victoria's." Then, thinking about the film that none of them had yet seen, he added, "Put in the mother, too, and a red flag."

Silvia painted a couple holding hands near a tank, an older woman offering them some bread, the city's orphanage on fire—to represent the devastation of war—and, in the background, our local monument to the Unknown Soldier.

One day, nearly three months later, the movie arrived. Silvia painted the title in orange-gold letters on the billboard, "Brave Soldier Ivanov's Visit Home," and Dima installed the billboard above the long canopy of the theater.

THE MOVIE THEATER

Comrade Nico, the Commissar of Art, Culture, and Education, officially opened the hall. The first couple of weeks, only members of the Communist Party were able to get tickets and see the movie. But an air of progress and happiness swept over the entire city and eventually every person in town had seen it.

What Norah and Silvia didn't know, however, was that for the next few years this would be the only film shown at the theater. Now and then a short documentary of news from around the country arrived, but these bland, ten-minute, Party-approved newsreels were hardly enough to entice the population to visit the theater again. And so the hall was empty most of the time.

Norah found herself in a critical position. The Party wanted glowing statistics of attendance, but she could not fill the hall. The Party might think she was sabotaging the education of the masses. She could be criticized and transferred to a lesser job. After numerous discussions with Dima, Victoria, and Silvia, it was decided that every month Silvia would paint a new scene on the billboard, as if a new movie had come to town. The city's residents looked at the billboard, commented on the scene, and then the rumor that it was the same movie circulated and no one came again. In the countryside, nobody wanted to see the movie either.

Only newcomers ventured in to see the film and then, only once. Nothing the four of them did brought people back to see the drama of Private Ivanov. Every evening when Norah sent the money to the commissar, she gave extravagant explanations why tickets could not be sold. Most chairs were wet from a leak in the roof. Due to a strong wind, the windows had opened by themselves and dust covered the screen. The chairs needed repair or had to be repainted. The curtains had caught fire. The key to the movie theater was lost, stolen, stuck in the lock. The film melted, the projector fell apart, the ladder to the projection booth was stolen. When Norah finally ran out of explanations, Victoria wrote that nobody came to the movie because people were choosing to wait in line at the kiosk to buy bread instead. Comrade Nico used his connections to recommend that bread be sold only to the people who had also bought tickets to the movie, but his request was denied. The theater crew also received great support from Silvia's mother-in-law, who knew everyone in town, arranged marriages, and spread rumors about the imminent arrival of Mamie Eisenhower, who she claimed was a remote cousin. The wife of the American president will be arriving with the American army to save the country from Communism and to take Silvia's mother-in-law to the White House. They will arrive on the morning bus from the airport. This extraordinary event was supposed to take place at the movie theater. "Everybody should be there. It will be a surprise," Silvia's mother-in-law told people in secret.

After that, Norah and Silvia played ping-pong, Dima painted the van, and Victoria, since she had nothing else to do, sat on her ass, as recommended, knitting all day in the theater's small ticket booth.

Victoria was from the countryside. Hidden as she was inside the ticket booth in the dark corridor of the movie theater, she grew nostalgic for seeing light and smelling the grass outdoors. Her nostalgia became depression, which she fought by knitting. In the beginning, people came to ask her about the movie, but later on, only friends, or friends of friends, came, and only to ask for favors or to gossip. They wanted to use the toilet, to store a suitcase before the arrival of a bus, to leave messages for other people in town, to leave the key to a friend's apartment for a secret lover. Victoria welcomed the visitors, took messages, and delivered packages.

One day, as she was complaining to a friend that the mulberry trees on the sidewalk changed from flowers to fruit without her even noticing, Victoria had an idea. She consulted with Dima.

They moved the chairs to the front of the room, keeping the last two rows for their personal use. After covering the seats with mulberry leaves, they installed a silkworm farm. The project kept both of them busy—and gave them a strong incentive to come to work. Every few days, reaching as high as he could with a ladder, Dima would cut new leaves from the city's mulberry trees to feed the silkworms. The sound of the larvae eating the fresh leaves gave Victoria an ecstatic sense of achievement. The worms were her little workers, the movie theater her collective farm, and, watching carefully that the cocoons did not open, Victoria spent her days designing silk scarves, ties, and brassieres.

Norah and Silvia played ping-pong in Silvia's workshop. Dima transported people and food to the city and, on the dashboard of his van, wrote a poem of his own that explained his view of the world:

Noi ne facem ca muncim	They pretend that we are paid,
Ei se fac ca ne platesc.	We pretend that we are working.

Norah, who had nothing to do, planted vegetables in the garden of the workshop. One day, sitting in the garden with a thermos of black Russian tea on her lap, Norah had an inspiration. It was the end of September and the air was chilly. There was a shortage of coal and, by decree of the Party, heat was allowed only in public buildings. Citizens were required to sacrifice their private comfort for the general well-being. Only people who held positions of importance or knew someone who knew someone were able to get wood for fuel. "Silvia," Norah shouted in joy, "we're open every day and our building is heated!"

Norah asked Victoria to move her silkworm farm to a winter location. She then asked Silvia to change the billboard. Silvia painted a comma after "Home"—the last word of the movie title—and wrote in large orange letters, "A Warm Place To Be." Norah heated the room well, put back all the chairs, reserved the front two rows for the commissar, kept the lights on, and let the movie play.

As autumn advanced and the nights became colder, word spread, and people began coming to warm up at the theater. They visited with friends and family, played cards, ate dinner, cut their hair, and sewed clothes. Children played hide-and-seek, grandmothers knitted, and everyone kept warm before going home to sleep when the movie theater closed at eleven.

Even though attendance was high, Silvia continued to paint new scenes on the billboard—if only out of boredom and for her own pleasure. She took increasing liberties to slowly transform the blonde. Her lips grew fuller. Her eyes took on an oriental slant. Her white blouse soon revealed cleavage. The hero's mother, in contrast, became increasingly disheveled. Endless interpretations circulated in the city. When Silvia's mother-in-law got sick, the billboard showed Ivanov crying, while from her deathbed the mother-in-law was pointing a finger at the blonde. From that moment on, people suspected that the paintings on the billboard were just as often about Silvia's relationship with her husband and mother-in-law as about the heroic Private Ivanov.

To attract more people, Silvia and Norah decided to go one step further and paint scenes that were not even remotely in the movie. On the International Day of Women, the blonde appeared dressed in a doctor's coat, holding a book and a microscope. The mother wore a dark blue dress for the occasion, along with a bright red scarf. On the International Day of Children, Ivanov and several children were pointing to the sky, where pink, magenta, and green letters spelled out the message:

In our schools
There is a teacher for every student
And a student for every teacher.

And when the blonde and the mother were shown embracing, next to a flag-draped tank, the local newspaper congratulated Silvia for her contribution to world peace.

RUSSIAN

By spring, everyone in town knew the lines from the movie by heart and was using them in daily conversations. When taking a bus, the driver might ask in Russian, "*Kuda ty napravlyaesh'sya, geroy?* Where are you going, my hero?" In the schoolyard children would tell each other, "*Da, ya geroiou*, I am a hero! *Ya poluchil razreshenie na visit domoy!* I've received permission to go home!" Speaking Russian was patriotic; using the movie's dialogue in Russian, was ironic. Norah would return from the market and say, "*Vot hleb*, I got bread," or "*A myasa n'et*, there is no meat." Visiting friends would declare, "*Ja prin'os zakuski*, I brought appetizers," or "*Ja prin'os vodku*, I brought vodka."

Like everyone else, I knew the entire movie by heart and made especially good use of the dialogue when Yuri Gagarin, the Soviet Union hero and first man to fly into space, came to visit our town. The pilot-cosmonaut was invited to inaugurate the first trolley line in the country. A metalworker by trade, Gagarin had been chosen to go into space for his correct social origin, mild manner, and good-looking physical features. His round, handsome face made an appealing centerpiece for Soviet propaganda. A better pilot named Major Titov had also competed for the flight but, being more educated and urbane than Gagarin, he was perceived as too removed from the Soviet working class. Colonel Gagarin, in contrast, was a farmer's son. His roots struck a chord in the heart of Comrade Khrushchev, himself a farmer's son. After taking a course in aeronautics, Gagarin replaced Laika, the dog who had had some success flying around the world on her own. The new space hero had silvery hair, blue eyes, pale white skin, and a small-framed body. Photographed in his cosmonaut outfit, Gagarin's was a face that everyone all over the world knew and admired.

My language skills made me the best candidate to welcome Gagarin to our school. After rehearsing a short welcoming speech in front of my fourth-grade classmates and our Russian-language teacher, I was granted the honor of giving Gagarin flowers. At home, I practiced declaiming the sentences, while Norah ironed the white blouse, blue skirt, and red triangular scarf of my Pioneer uniform. Silvia came to visit and tied two red bows on my braids.

The next day at school, when Gagarin arrived, the Russian teacher pushed me to stand up. I greeted Gagarin with the Pioneer salute, and Gagarin saluted me back. I recited the sentences learned by heart. Their meaning was revolutionary: "All the students in our school are ready to fly into space and bring Communism to the moon." As I handed him the flowers, and he kissed me on the cheek, I so identified with Ivanov's girlfriend that, in her exact words, I blurted out something I had not rehearsed: "*Ya ostav'lu samoe lychshee na potom*, I will keep the best for later."

Gagarin blushed, and the audience applauded. The Party's official painter enriched his repertoire with new socialist-realist vignettes. I was depicted welcoming Gagarin as he emerged from his space capsule. A radiant smile on his face, a grin on mine, I give him flowers, and he gives me a plastic model of the capsule. Sometimes I'd be shown embracing Gagarin. Sometimes the two of us would be riding the trolley toward an imaginary city on the edge of the moon. One newspaper photograph showed us at the moment of his kiss. I am totally abandoned in Gagarin's arms, just like Ivanov's blonde on the billboard. The heading reads: "Our Pioneers join the Hero Cosmonaut for a trip to success."

After another year of painting scenes from the life of Private Ivanov, Silvia felt entitled to change the plot. She painted on the billboard a wedding between the blonde and a doctor. Comrade Commissar Nico found the choice appealing—doctors are few and people give them bribes. Only his political supervisor believed the blonde's choice was disparaging of the peasant working class. Silvia should have married the blonde to a miner or a metal worker, not to a bourgeois intellectual. A red flag should have been painted in connection with the wedding. As it was, the painting on the billboard was not acceptable. It had to be repainted.

Silvia was called to make her self-criticism in front of the Party. She confessed that she was not a good-enough Communist. She felt compelled to change the actors' lives. She knew all the lines of the movie and felt responsible for the characters. She felt that her own life was a repetitive movie in which she was acting according to somebody else's script. The Party found her explanation to be self-centered. Silvia had failed to put the goals of the working class above her own personal issues. When asked whom she had consulted before deciding "to marry the blonde with an enemy of the working class," Silvia looked baffled. She could not say why she had painted that scene. It was not even in the movie. She had painted the blonde mechanically, rewarding her with a wedding dress and a tiara for the loss of Ivanov. Looking around the room for an answer, Silvia bit her lips and, in a moment of inspiration, shouted, "I consulted with the People!"

Surely the People couldn't be wrong, so everyone applauded. The Party instructed Silvia to paint only scenes that advanced the goals of the working class.

"If you say so," Silvia replied.

YELLOW PAINT

Soon after the billboard incident, the Party approved the screening of a new movie. *Angelica*, a film about a French woman who leads the people to kill the king and the aristocrats, was the first French movie to arrive in the country after the war. Everybody was eager to see the new film and to learn the dialogue. Silvia was especially enthusiastic. She now had a new repertoire to paint on the billboard: a queen, a palace, people riding on horses. To prepare for the arrival of the film, Silvia cleaned the workshop, moved the ping-pong table to a corner, found some new brushes, and sent her mother-in-law around town to find paint. The mother-in-law knew a person who had some yellow paint—a rarity at the time— so she acquired it in exchange for another "Jesus weeping over Jerusalem" icon.

Unacquainted with Silvia's talents, and much to everyone's surprise, the French sent hundreds of large, glossy, heavy-stock posters along with the film. In the poster Angelica is standing on a barricade waving the French flag. She's wearing a white blouse beneath a purple mantle that covers her body. In the chaos of the French Revolution, her breasts are exposed, and one of her legs is visible all the way to the hip. Her blonde hair floats in the wind. In the background, one can see the king's palace on fire. A young man falling backward off his white horse is raising an arm, a bullet hole spotting his white shirt.

Silvia found the posters banal. They didn't show interior drama. They evoked no emotions, nor had they any message for the working class. The best thing about the posters was the smell of the ink; otherwise, the painting was childish, and Angelica's costume frivolous. Silvia decided to repaint the posters to conform to the Party line. In exchange for a painting of the blonde kissing the soldier, Silvia's mother-in-law obtained two kilograms of salami from the Party's shop, which she bartered for some red dye from the flag factory. Silvia diluted the red dye and covered Angelica's exposed leg. With the recently acquired yellow, she covered the breasts. On the flag Silvia wrote a message for the working class: *"Comrades, look to the horizon—We have tractors!"*

Soon the city was covered with posters and Dima's van was making its way through the villages advertising the new film. Angelica became the new fashion in town. Purple pants, skirts, and stockings dyed at home with beet juice appeared everywhere. Since the color could not be chemically fixed, in rainy weather, bloody drops stained the sidewalks.

But the lusty red leg painted on the poster was not the reason Silvia was fired. Unbeknownst to her, the yellow paint she had used to cover the breasts was road paint. Visible from afar, two perfectly painted breasts, covered by a phosphorescent bra, glowed in the night, to the delight of the citizens.

Comrade Nico called for an emergency meeting.

"Comrade Silvia, after love for the Party and for our leaders, is there anything more important than a mother's breast?" Comrade Nico asked. "Anything?" he repeated, moving his hands in the air over two enormous imaginary breasts. Then, without waiting for an answer, he continued: "Are women in the factories or on the farms harnessed like that, with a bra? Why are you oppressing the masses, Comrade Silvia?"

"Comrade Nico," Silvia answered, "the bra is supposed to elevate the masses and keep them under control."

"So, have you ever seen a bra in our stores?"

"No," Silvia answered, "but we are not French."

"Your values are reactionary, Comrade Silvia. Our honest working-class women were once seduced with brassieres, silk stockings, jewelry, lipstick, high heels, and champagne. But our enemies were crushed. You celebrate the bra after the Bolshevik Revolution has eradicated all bourgeois values from our society! You offend our working class. You are indoctrinating our youth. You bring corruption to our nation. You are not an artist anymore. You are being transferred to the park. There you can learn the real values of the working class. Death to the bourgeoisie!"

THE PARK

Silvia started her new job with dedication. In her new function, she was required to put a lye solution on the tree trunks and to repaint the wooden benches in the park. But soon she got bored and used the lye to cover not only the tree trunks but also the first branches of each tree, forming a white arcade over the walkways. When it came to repainting the benches, Silvia could not restrain her artistic instinct. Soon, exquisitely rendered scenes of desert landscapes, pictures of the Kremlin and other known monuments of the world, as well as her cat, began appearing on the benches. Silvia could not stop. When she looked around the park, she saw dozens of white canvases. Every tree was a canvas. Encouraged by friends and passersby, pink flamingos, ostriches, and hordes of zebras, camels, and tigers were soon grazing in the park. A giraffe was eating the branches of the very tree on which it was painted. In time, a candelabrum, a teepee, a Chinese pagoda, Saint Zachariah, and people dancing and holding hands appeared on the trees. And since a directive from the Party specified that in public spaces only red flowers could be planted, Silvia painted bushes of red roses. For Norah's birthday, Silvia painted a phosphorescent birthday cake on the gate of the park. Two turtledoves kissed each other on the columns marking the entrance. The local newspaper called the park "an extraordinary example of the magical realism of Communism," and every week featured the progress of Silvia's boredom.

People called in sick only to meet their friends at the park. That year, for virtually the whole last week of December, the city came to a close. On Christmas day, people refused to go to work. They showed up early at the park, and when Silvia arrived to open the gates at precisely seven o'clock, a crowd applauded her. Led by Silvia, the city's population entered the park to see the paintings and the statue of the Unknown Soldier. Transformed for the holiday, the soldier wore Santa's red clothes. In his hand he carried a metal flag on which Silvia had written—in Russian, Romanian, Latin, Hungarian, Chinese, French, and Yiddish—a glowing yellow phosphorescent message: "Mom & Lenin."

The following summer, Bilu arrived.

16

B ilu was everybody's sister. Her visit was proof of our commitment to Socialism. We were not transient foreign elements.
We lived there and received visits from our family, in our own
apartment. Not only did I have an aunt but one who lived in the
Soviet Union! We were very proud. We cleaned the house, saved
food, and with great expectation, told everyone that our family
was coming to visit us. The day before Bilu's arrival, Clara bought
flowers. Mendel found wine, and Norah prepared her special eggplant salad. Aram was restless.

Bilu arrived by train. As the train pulled into the station, Aram
spotted her at a window and immediately bolted from us to help
her off the car. She and Aram tried to embrace, but other people
coming off the train were pushing, and they got separated. Bilu
was carrying a pair of red skis and many cardboard boxes. Mendel hurried to help Aram with the boxes, while Clara, Norah, and
I waited for Aram to bring her to us.

With her small chin, red hair, and big black eyes, Bilu looked
ugly to me. She was supposed to be elegant and gracious, to have
nice clothes. I had expected to see her wearing lipstick, a hat—
perhaps even white gloves. I had imagined her looking like an
actress. Instead, her clothes were the same as ours. Her shoes
were torn. Her cardboard suitcase was patched and tied up with
ropes. Her face was tired. How could I walk on the street with an
aunt that looked so disheveled? How could my only visiting family member betray me and look like everyone else around us? I did
not like Bilu.

Clara embraced her, both of them breaking into tears. Norah
moved closer. Clara disengaged herself from Bilu's arms and tried
to smile, pulling me to her. "Meia, Meia, this is your Aunt Bilu,

your father's sister," she said. "Give her a kiss—she is your real aunt!" Bilu bent to my height, took my head in her hands, looked into my eyes, and said to me in French, "You are a . . ." and before she could finish, I shouted, "ten-and-a-half years old!"

"Yes, you are a very pretty ten-and-a-half-year-old girl." Then she smiled and kissed me on the lips. Her smile covered the tears that covered the feelings that covered the words that had no voice. But the taste of her tears stayed with me.

Norah inched toward Bilu. "I am your sister-in-law. I am Norah!"

Bilu turned to her and took her in her arms. "I am so very happy that you are here! I am so glad that you chose Aram!"

"Are you glad for him or for me?" Norah asked in a sarcastic tone. Bilu disengaged from her arms, took a look at her, and said, "Right now, I am glad just for him! And if we become friends, I will be glad for you also!"

Norah went off to hire a carriage to take us home, returning moments later, happy to have found one for a good price. Mendel sat in front with the driver. Bilu sat next to Clara, with Aram and Norah in front of them. I sat on Clara's lap. Aram did not say anything, and Bilu kept crying and telling him, in Hungarian, how she could not believe they were together.

My father and his twin sister looked alike. They were the same height, but he seemed taller because he was slimmer than she. They had the same forehead, the same ears, the same oval nails, and the same shade of skin. The color was that of a golden sassafras leaf after the rain, a mixture of almond brown and milky white, a combination between dark Mediterranean and white northerner. Their dark eyes, their high cheekbones, the dimple on their chins, and their curly red hair were the clearest indications that they were twins. But Bilu's face looked alive, while my father's was rigid. When she talked, her eyes, mouth, and chin were vivid with emotion. Their smiles were alike, but my father rarely smiled.

Norah was busy with the pair of skis. Clara kept an arm around Bilu's shoulders. Their bodies were shaking as the carriage crossed the potholes in the city streets. When we arrived on our street, people came out to see the sister.

Upstairs in our apartment, Bilu visited every room. In Moscow, she told us, there was no running water in the house where she, my uncle Emil, and my cousin Tania lived—a former one-car garage. "In the summer when we pull the garage doors up, I look outside to the people passing and I think that I am at the theater." There was a toilet and a water pump in the courtyard. I thought that Bilu wasn't telling the truth. How could the mighty Soviet Union not have running water, and how could people as important as my uncle and aunt live like peasants who had just arrived in the city?

Bilu's gifts were mostly food that she had saved before leaving Moscow. For Norah and Clara, she brought a set of metal tableware and two bottles of perfume. On one of the bottles, under the word *Karmen*, written in red letters, a gypsy girl in a beautiful polka-dot dress was dancing the flamenco. On the other bottle was written *Pikovskaya Dama*, the Queen of Spades. Both had a very strong scent. "This was Adah's," she said to Aram, handing him a hair clip with a ruby stone. "I took it when we left Budapest."

I received a rubber alligator, a red toothbrush, and a blue velvet dress. The skis were for Aram, since the two of them used to go skiing together when they lived in Budapest. Bilu brought photographs of my cousin Tania, my uncle Emil, and my Great-Grandmother Julia. None of them was smiling.

Bilu slept in the hallway, in the bed left empty by Alisa. She slept for most of the first two days, but after that she moved the furniture, rearranged the books, and made curtains for the windows. Every morning she listened to music on the radio and sang Russian songs.

STORIES

Without anyone asking, Bilu told us stories from her childhood in Budapest.

"We had a cherry tree in our garden. It had the best yellow cherries that I have ever eaten. Remember, Aram, how one day Adah came from Vienna and together we picked cherries? She took some to make a soup and gave Aram and me each a handful. And I said, 'You gave him more! You always give him more!'"

"Were you always envious of your brother?" Norah asked.

"Wait, and Adah said, 'If that is how you feel, Bilu, why don't you count them?' I counted Aram's pile—and he counted mine. There was exactly the same number of cherries in each pile."

197

"It must have been by chance," Norah said.

"Of course," Clara added, "unless your mother had a sharp eye and a refined sense of proportion."

Aram listened to Bilu, unenthusiastically supplying some details. They both called their parents by name, but when I called my mother Norah, she said angrily, "'Mother,' to you." My father never talked about his past, he never mentioned his mother, so I was especially curious to hear Bilu's stories.

"We had always lived in Budapest with our grandparents. We left because of the anti-Semitism; grandfather was forced out of his job at the hospital," she said. "For Christmas 1939, the bank accounts of the Jews were frozen, to give you an example."

"I remember the radio screaming that Jews are involved in child prostitution and tax evasion," Aram added. "We also left to join Rafa'el and Adah in Palestine."

"And after the incident," Bilu said, looking directly at Aram, "Luca, who was with the Communists, told us that we should leave."

"What incident?" Norah interrupted. "And who is Luca?"

"A friend of ours," Aram said quickly.

"What incident?" Mendel asked.

Bilu turned toward Aram. "You never told them about the incident?" Her eyes caught his and they gazed at each other for a long moment. Aram lowered his eyes.

"If you have private things to say to each other," Norah said, "we can leave."

"No," Bilu answered, looking again at Aram. "Stay. Let me finish this story. I will tell you about the incident another time. One night Luca arrived with a friend. 'Next week we are all leaving,' he said. His friend dyed our hair black—remember, Aram?—and Luca took pictures for travel documents."

"Why did they help you?" Mendel asked.

"I don't know. I guess because they were Communists."

"There is no such thing," Norah said. "They helped you because your grandfather paid them."

"Probably," Mendel shrugged.

"Could be," Aram said.

"In any case, Luca got us travel documents."

"How?" Clara asked.

"I don't know! I only remember that he arrived and said, 'Tomorrow we leave!'"

"I know how," Aram said. "The Turkish government was neutral and in 1942 negotiated with the Reich to let all Turks living in Germany, Austria, and Hungary go back to Turkey. A transport was organized as far as Bucharest, and we left with fake documents."

Bilu's face was animated. She looked younger when she talked.

"Luca asked us to speak only broken German, but Aram learned several sentences in Turkish."

"Yes," Aram acknowledged, blushing, "*Affedersiniz ama his sigaram yok.*"

"What does it mean?" Clara asked.

"It means, 'I am sorry, I don't have any cigarettes,'" Norah said. "A useless sentence. First of all, if you were a Turk, you would have cigarettes, even if you didn't smoke. And second, you can always bribe a Turk."

"I forgot that you speak Turkish," Bilu said. "What a shame that you weren't with us. You would have known what to say, I am sure."

"We managed," Aram said, looking at Norah.

"We were nervous and afraid," Bilu continued.

"Yes, nervous and afraid," Aram repeated, then excused himself and left the room.

"How old were you then?" Norah asked Bilu.

"We must have been almost fifteen. Adah and Rafa'el were already in Palestine and we were trying to join them. Except for abandoning Moka, our cat, Aram and I were happy to leave Budapest.

"When we arrived at the train station, Hungarian soldiers verified our documents, and along with dozens of others, we boarded the crowded train. We were dressed like poor people: old hats, scarves, and layers of clothes. Aram looked like a day worker. I remember Grandpa's comment: 'The Carnival of Purim is early this year. I wonder how many of us travel disguised.'"

"What is Purim?" I asked.

"You don't know the Jewish Holy Days?" Bilu asked, surprised.

"We are not religious, we are Communists."

"Purim is the Mardi Gras Carnival of the Jews," Mendel offered. "People wear masks and dress in costumes. Before the Inquisition, the Purim in Zaragoza was a well-known celebration. There are carnivals in Italy, Brazil, America, and many other places."

Bilu took a deep breath and asked, "And you, Meia, are you Jewish?"

I looked around me and shrugged my shoulders. Norah looked offended. "What kind of question is that, Bilu? She is born to a Jewish mother."

"I know," Bilu answered, still looking at me.

Unaware of my question about Purim, Aram returned to the table and broke the silence. "Bucharest was full of refugees," he said.

"Then what did you do?" Mendel asked, happy to change the topic.

"Grandpa had a doctor friend who let him work at his clinic," Aram said. "He was taking a risk, since Jewish doctors were not allowed to practice."

"They were probably doing abortions," Norah said.

"I wouldn't doubt it," Mendel jumped in. "In the German territories, Aryan doctors weren't allowed to treat Jews. Some did, but only for large amounts of money, so he must have hired your grandfather to treat the Jews."

"Could be," Bilu answered, "but I doubt it. The doctor's family helped us, even after Grandpa died."

"I tried to find them when I returned, but they had left Romania," Aram said.

"Wait a second," Norah said. "Forget about the doctor. I want to know how you and Emil met, if this is not a secret."

Bilu shrugged.

"We were friends," Aram volunteered. "We shared the apartment, and he also worked at the clinic with our grandfather."

"He is from Antwerp," Bilu said. "He was in his last year of medical school when the Germans entered Belgium. He came to Romania hoping to cross the border into the Soviet Union. He believed that it was the only safe place for the Jews and persuaded Grandma and me to go with him."

"He wanted to experience the miracle of Bolshevism firsthand," Norah, who couldn't control her sarcasm, said. "You abandoned your brother to go to Russia with Emil?"

"I don't think you understand, Norah," Bilu said in frustration. "I was alone with an older woman who had just lost her husband, and then, as you said, my brother was taken. We were without travel documents in a hostile foreign country, where Jews were arrested, deported, or killed. Crossing the border into Russia was our only possible escape. And it was safer; and we were lucky."

"He looks old," Norah said, looking at Emil's picture.

"He is seven years older than me," Bilu said, shrugging her shoulders to make it clear that she didn't like the remark. Aram, who was still uncomfortable with all the talk about their past, took the opportunity to change the subject.

"I heard that the city of Samarqand is covered entirely in blue and gold mosaic," he said.

"Yes," Bilu answered, "it is a mysterious place. It always reminded me of the flamenco."

"What do you mean?" Norah asked, raising an eyebrow. "It reminds you of the flamenco. How can a city remind you of a dance?"

"Not of the dance, but the dancer," Bilu answered. "When you first see Samarqand, you are mesmerized by the colors and the skyline. You want to cry, to laugh, to never leave, to become one with the domes, as one becomes one with the dance of the flamenco. The dancer freezes in place and holds his breath. Then the music suddenly stops, and the silence falls abruptly, like a sharp pain. The drums start a rapid rhythm and the dancer moves in a trance-like tornado. The world around you becomes a mirage, and the dancer appears to be floating above the music. The desire of dancing between the domes and the minarets moves you from the ground. You see yourself levitating above the old walls of the city without realizing that you are holding your breath in the rhythm of drums that are everywhere. This is Samarqand."

"Very poetic, Bilu," Clara said.

"It is poetic," Mendel said. "But saying that the dance is the dancer is a very narrow, egocentric view, like saying that art is for art's sake. In our society, art is for the people. And dance celebrates our achievements, not only the pleasure of rhythm and movement."

Bilu seemed a little confused. "What does that have to do with anything? Do you know how it feels to dance the flamenco?"

"Don't tell me that you also dance?" Norah exclaimed, jumping from her seat. "I can't believe it. She cleans, she cooks, she makes clothes, falls in love, writes in her journal, raises a child, teaches mathematics, and dances the flamenco. *Über* woman! No, this is too much!"

Bilu stood up, ready to leave the room, but stopped in the doorway and, turning to us, said, "Yes, Norah, I know how to dance the flamenco." With that, she squinted her eyes and slowly moved one arm above her head, slightly twisting the other one toward her back. She curled her fingers and straightened her body. "You see?" she said. "You put up your arms like this. You start moving in a staccato rhythm until the music gets faster and faster and the dancer's steps get shorter." Extending her arms in front of her, Bilu then stamped her heels on the floor, making the sound of castanets with a click of her tongue. She stopped abruptly, frozen in that position, her chin up and her fingers curled in the air. After a short silence, she burst into a long cascade of anguished cries, "Ay-ay-ay-ay-ay!"

"Bilu," Aram said, "we believe you."

Aram appeared to avoid being alone with Bilu. But one afternoon she joined him while he was reading on the terrace. From my veranda I could hear their conversation.

"Times were difficult," Bilu said.

"They were difficult for everybody."

"Yes, entire regions were evacuated," Bilu continued. "Jews, as well as Russians, Poles, and Ukrainians, were all on the road. Only after we moved to Moscow did we feel some sense of security. People in Moscow are friendly. They like to listen to our stories. It plays to their Russian sense of drama. Of course, we keep some distance between ourselves and our most intimate friends. They can't really understand us. Sometimes I think about our life, and even I believe it is fiction. How can I tell my friends who I am? Raised in Budapest by my grandparents, born in Vienna of a Greek, Turkish, Italian, Spanish, Portuguese, Moroccan, Jewish father, himself born in Palestine, educated in Vienna, living in Israel—wait, I haven't finished!—and of a Viennese, Hungarian, Jewish-born mother. And now I live in Russia and visit my brother in Romania, and the only thing I want—this is a secret that I cannot tell anybody at home—the only thing I want is to go to Hanah's Paradise. On the rare occasions when I tell my story, I can see how people's eyes glaze over."

"Well, you have to pay attention to what you say and to whom."

"Aram," Bilu continued, "did you ever tell your story to anyone?"

"What story, Bilu? There is no story to tell. I wrote you everything."

"Aram, can I ask you something? What happened to the orange scarf?"

Aram didn't say anything. I heard him move from his chair and walk into the bedroom. The orange scarf was in a drawer. I had seen it many times. It was nothing more than a faded piece of fabric, stained here and there, thin and worn out, not much longer than a child's arm.

"You still have it," Bilu said softly when Aram returned.

"It was very useful. It was longer and a brighter orange."

"It was Emil's idea," Bilu said. "'Pack some sugar and lemons in a piece of cloth and try to give them to him.' I grabbed Adah's orange scarf and made a small bundle. Emil found out when your convoy was leaving, and the doctor took Grandma and me to the train station. We waited for hours. The prisoners finally arrived, but at first I couldn't see you. As the convoy passed near us, people were screaming, and with the pressure of the crowd behind us, Grandma and I were pushed very close to your group. I grabbed hold of a hand and pressed the small bundle into it: 'For Aram, Aram from Budapest,' I whispered. For years I wondered whether you got it."

Aram sighed. I heard tea being poured into a cup.

"As soon as we were on the train, somebody called my name and passed me the little bundle. Then the doors were locked and the train started moving. Panic was the only thing we all felt. People were yelling, screaming, crying, and slowly the screams gave way to whimpers, then to silence. Not going mad in that cattle car took enormous effort. I shut off my mind to isolate myself and leaned slightly on the body near me. For the first day, I stared at the light coming through the barred window in a state of shock. The fear was immense. I was empty of any other thought or emotion. A sensation of sleepiness fell over me, and the only thing I remember is a slight awareness of changes in the light coming through the small window. Morning, evening, night, morning again. After some time, I felt the bulge in my coat. I opened it slowly, not taking it out of my pocket. With my fingers I counted two lemons and fifty cubes of sugar. I counted them several times. Over the next four days I ate them, one by one, very slowly."

"Aram, why did you say you were a Communist when they arrested you?"

"Jews in transit were sent to German camps in Poland; the government had to supply a quota. Since I didn't have any documents with me, I declared myself a Communist from Budapest. Communists were only sent to forced labor, Jews were killed. I survived because the Communists helped me. When the Jews were transferred to another camp in Poland, no one denounced me. I was part of the information group. We were able to smuggle a radio into camp, and because I knew English and German, I was given the task of listening to and memorizing the news. Then I would relate the information to two other comrades, who would relate it to another two, and so on, until everyone in the camp received the news. We were never caught. Being Communist was more important than life. It kept us human. I taught my comrades English; they taught me Marxism."

"You know, I wrote to Luca, but I never got any answer."

"Bilu, the past is over. Let it be."

They sat in silence until Bilu said, "I keep looking at this orange piece of ragged silk—it is all we have from home."

"Home? We don't have a home," Aram said. "Hanah's Paradise is only a name."

"When we were in the Jewish Republic, in Birobidjhan," Bilu continued, "the Party allowed us to write, but we knew that the letters were kept on file—never sent. So I pretended, like everyone else. I wrote about the great life we were having in Birobidjhan, inviting Adah and Rafa'el to join us there. In my letters I condemned carved furniture, endless draperies, thick Persian carpets, and the wall coverings of the bourgeois home. I copied the slogans learned from the Party and I repudiated our class status. I committed my life to revolutionary Marxism. All of us refugees lived a double life. We were Bolsheviks eliminating class divisions and engaging in radical political activities, and also refugees dreaming of leaving the Soviet Union. Our social life was in Russian. Our private life was hidden, packed away with our hopes of going home. We weren't even allowed to speak in our native language. Could I have written about our impoverished everyday life when we knew that all letters were read? We covered up our dreams, our past, the longing for our own family. We were not deceiving the Party. We were not lying. We were surviving."

Communal life teaches strict boundaries, but soon after Bilu danced the flamenco in the kitchen, everyone began to gravitate to her. Tucked under the window, in the small corridor leading to the bedrooms, the bed that used to be Alisa's became her room. We all ended up there after dinner to drink black mulberry tea.

The first time we were all there, Clara and Bilu sat on the bed, Norah sat on a chair in front of them, and I sat on the floor near Bilu—my back against the bed. Aram and Mendel stood in the doorway, Mendel with his arms crossed, Aram with his hands in his pockets and a shoulder against the wall. Our only common language was French, so "How do you say this?" was often asked, and someone would translate. Bilu was telling us how she got to Asia.

"The war was going on, and we had no other place to go. The Communists were taking a convoy of refugees into the Soviet Union. We joined them, hoping that from there we could find a way to Hanah's Paradise. There were about fifty of us, and once we were on the Russian side we were taken to a collective farm and didn't have the right to move freely. Then they sent us to Asia. We had to walk there."

"At that time a lot of people went to the Soviet Union," Mendel explained.

"What do you mean you *walked to Asia*?" Norah asked. "Nobody *walks* to Asia!"

"We walked most of the time. We didn't speak the language and didn't know the geography. Sometimes we could find a train or a truck and went wherever it took us, as long as it was away from the war."

"We did the same thing leaving the *Lager*," Clara said. "That is how we got here."

"What is a *Lager*?" I asked.

"It's a work camp, Meia."

"Why didn't you leave a message for me? Or at least let them know at Hanah's Paradise that you were going to the Soviet Union?" Aram asked.

"I did. I did—as soon as we got on the other side. But the letter was returned."

"Really," Norah said, not without a hint of sarcasm.

"Really," Bilu answered, quite annoyed. "I saved it. But you don't seem to trust me. You don't know how horrible it feels to be cut off. We could neither send nor receive news. How could I have known that you would return here? I didn't think to leave you a message. I was desperate, hoping every moment for something to change our destiny. You don't know what it's like to be alone."

"Of course," Norah said. "You didn't leave him a message because you thought that he would die. As for being alone, how could we possibly know the feeling?"

Bilu blushed and looked at the floor. Once again she had offended Norah. She did that all the time without even knowing. Between the two of them, Norah had the monopoly on pain. She had to win.

"You saved a letter from 1943?" Clara asked, trying to protect Bilu.

Bilu bent to the floor, pulled her cardboard luggage from under the bed, and took out a book. She searched between the pages, found an envelope, and gave it to Norah.

"I can't read it," Norah said. "It's in Hungarian."

"This part is in English," Bilu said, and showed Norah the stamped envelope.

"'To the Office of the International Red Cross, Moscow USSR: Please forward this letter to Rafa'el Raveo at Hanah's Paradise in Palestine,'" Norah read. "And, 'Return to Sender,' stamped over it."

"Give me the letter," Clara said, reaching out to take it from Norah. "I can read it." She took out the letter and read it aloud, first in Hungarian, then translated it into French for all of us to understand.

> September 28, 1943,
> from Circik, in the Soviet Union

Dear Mama and Papa,

We are safe. Along with some other refugees we were put on a barge and floated on the Danube for three days, waiting for the Russians to signal us to land. We were all sick from the lack of food and the suffocating, humid heat in the hold of the barge. After we landed, we worked for some time in a fishing village, then we were sent to a village called Circik, near Tashkent. We work on a collective farm, waiting for an opportunity to go south, cross over into Iran and then join you. There are people here from Belgium, France, and Spain and from the German-occupied zones of Poland, Moldavia, Czechoslovakia, and Holland. There is also a group from India learning collective farming techniques. All together, we are about one hundred. We are very lucky that Emil is here with us. Because he is almost a doctor, he treats people in exchange for food. I keep turning my head, searching for Aram. Then I remember that he was taken away, and I see his shaved head and his eyes, looking at me before he climbed into the train. I am very lonely without him. There are rumors that Jews are being killed all over in Europe, and as the German army advances, refugees are pushed toward Asia. Can't anyone kill this Hitler? Why can't Papa come to take us from here?

We miss you very much and think about you and Aram every moment. Grandma is tired, but she is happy because now we have food and we can walk freely on the streets. We are thinking of you and send you all our love. May we soon be reunited! May God give Aram strength to find a way to you and to bring us all together again! Please write and send us some money at the Office of Refugees and Displaced Persons, Moscow Central Post, USSR.

Bilu

P.S. I wrote the other letter the night before leaving Romania. I wasn't able to send it earlier. I am sending it now.

Dear Mama and Papa,

I am writing in a rush to let you know that we have to leave. After a new Iron Guard pogrom, we are now at great risk. Jews have been taken to a slaughterhouse, killed, then hung in the windows. It is dangerous. Romania must send Germany their quota of Jews, and refugees are taken first. We can't wait for Aram here. There are controls on the street and door-to-door searches for Jews. We have to leave. Tonight we are crossing the border into the Soviet Union. The people organizing the passage are very confident of our success. We are joining a convoy of refugees heading for work on a collective farm. Emil, a refugee doctor from Antwerp, put us on the list. There is no other solution. We are going with him. At least we are not alone. From there, we will find a way to reach you. We heard that Aram is in a labor camp in Bessarabia, but Communists are being freed if they agree to join the army to fight against the Russians. He told the police that he was Communist so he may be freed as soon as next month. Grandma wants to stay here to wait for Aram but I would not leave without her. Together, we don't have to worry about each other. We know where we are. It feels like my soul is cut in half but Aram will find his way to Hanah's Paradise and we will all meet there. I will post this letter as soon as we cross the border. Please give everyone our love. Desperately missing you!

Bilu

"Why was the letter returned?" I asked.

"It didn't have enough stamps," Norah said.

"What a beautiful notebook," Clara whispered.

"Emil gave it to me to keep a journal. I take it with me everywhere. When Emil gave it to me, something extraordinary happened." Bilu's eyes lit up as she smiled broadly. "I looked at Emil and saw Adah's face. It was incredible! She was looking at me, and I felt very, very happy."

"Nice story," Clara said.

"I would like to see my mother's face, also," said Norah. "I forget how she looked."

"What does it say?" I asked Bilu, pointing at the intricate arabesque of gold Cyrillic letters on the cover of her journal. Above them, in a vignette painting, a couple was seated under a willow tree, a firebird flying above them.

"It says 'Svetlan and Rusalka.' It's a Russian folk tale."

"Is it a sad story?" I asked.

"Meia, you and I are alike. I asked Emil the same thing when he gave it to me," Bilu said and caressed my face.

"And?" Norah asked.

"His answer was—" and Bilu laughed "—'I hope not!'"

"Here," Bilu said, handing the book to Aram. "Read this page."

"'December 12, 1943,'" Aram began, making an effort to control his voice.

"'When I am next to Emil, I forget who he is and I think that he is Aram. Grandma feels the same. Sometimes we call him Aram by habit.

"'December 18, 1943. Today the People's Commissar of Refugee Affairs told us not to separate from our group. Until transportation is made available to move on we are asked to work at the farm. He also said that for security and defense purposes, mail is not leaving the country and we are not allowed to send any letters until further notice!'"

As he continued reading, Aram's voice became steadier.

"'January 1, 1944. Happy New Year . . . ,'" he read.

"January '44!" Clara interrupted. "I was still in Budapest. We were hiding. It became increasingly dangerous to leave the house. Jews were simply beaten up. But in March the systematic killing started."

"In the Soviet Union life was much easier," Bilu said. "We worked on farms, so there was always some food. Only after the war did our situation become difficult. Stalin started mass deportations."

"Let Aram read!" Norah objected.

"He doesn't have to read, I can tell you the story myself," Bilu said, and much to her brother's relief, she took the book away from him—and closed it.

"I remember that January very well. We danced to celebrate the New Year. There was an older man from Spain there, and when Grandma told him that I could dance the flamenco, he begged me to dance it. 'Please, Bilu. Try it!' Since it meant so much to him, I sang 'Verde Limon,' and a comrade from Poland played the guitar. It was difficult to dance without you, Aram. I had to improvise. I moved with despair, nudging the dress around my body. It wasn't me but my soul that was dancing. The *soleá* is the dance of solitude. I braced myself, I curved my arms, I held my breath—and I saw my wishes passing before my eyes."

"This is another beautiful story! All of you dancing. For some reason we didn't celebrate the New Year dancing in Bergen-Belsen, and we were also refugees. I am going to sleep. Good night," Norah said.

Bilu, by now used to Norah's sarcasm, replied, "Good night, dear."

From that point on, Clara got in the habit of climbing onto Bilu's bed in the evenings to talk about Budapest and read from the journal. Norah would come to ask for something and then would stay. Aram and Mendel joined us from time to time, but I was always there.

"'February 4, 1943,'" Bilu read. "'German forces are leaving Stalingrad.'"

"Bilu," Norah immediately interrupted her, "don't tell us about the Germans at Stalingrad; tell us how you fell in love with Emiliano, as you call him."

Bilu giggled and shifted her position, pushing the pillow against the wall.

THE WEDDING

"It was May of 1944. Emil and I walked to the river. It was a hot day, just like summer in Budapest, and it felt as though I was walking with Papa on the banks of the Danube. Emil put his hand on my shoulder, like Aram used to do, and it made me cry. Then, when I raised my head, I saw an extraordinary multitude of tears hanging from the branches of the cherry tree above us. The entire sky was full of pink and white tears. 'Look, Emil,' I said, 'those are my tears! It will take me an entire life to cry them all.' Emil took a branch from the tree, put all the white and pink flowers into his hands, and covered my tears with the petals. They stuck on my wet cheeks, and when he had covered my eyes, my nose, my lips—my entire face—he said, 'Bilu, if I share the tears with you, will you share the flowers?'"

"This can't be true," Norah said. "Nobody talks like that. You are describing a painting, a photograph—this is not real: the river, the cherry blossoms, refugees kissing, and the war roaring." Then she framed Bilu's face with her hands, like a camera. "You are inventing stories to show us your superiority for escaping concentration camp."

"If you were in love at seventeen you would have done the same thing, even though the world was at war—and even though you were in a labor camp. Does it hurt you to see me happy?" Bilu asked.

"You don't know what you are talking about, my dear," Norah said, holding her breath. "Falling in love in a concentration camp— are you crazy?"

Bilu didn't answer but opened her journal again: "'August 2, 1944. Today we kissed.'"

"You recorded that you kissed?" Norah interrupted. "You spent the war writing about your first kiss?"

"You don't understand. You should have kept your own journal if you don't like mine. For me this was important. After Emiliano kissed me, I didn't feel like a twin anymore."

"Of course you didn't. You weren't a kid anymore. You replaced one man with another one. Unfortunately you abandoned Aram. You betrayed your brother. As for keeping my own journal, look, it is written on my arm. It is so abstract that there are only numbers. It says a lot if you know how to read it," Norah insisted.

"Stop it, Norah!" Clara said. "It's not her fault."

"'Today, September 6, 1945, Emiliano and I got married,'" Bilu read and closed the journal. "It was a wonderful wedding and I wish that Aram and everyone else had been there. But they weren't. What should I have done, Norah, commit suicide, try to get captured by the Germans, volunteer for a labor camp so I could experience what Aram and you did? Well, I chose life. Emil was there, we fell in love, and we got married."

"I can see the movie: fear, separation, devastation, Prince Charming, adventures on the road, then the wedding," Norah said. "Did you have a dress and a tiara also?"

"You don't have to answer that," Clara intervened. "She was luckier than us and we were luckier than many others. Just statistics applied to circumstances."

"Emil took cotton sheets from the hospital, and the women from our group made me a dress, just by folding them. I can still see myself in it, although we didn't have a mirror. It had a square décolleté, and the skirt flared out at the back, forming a small bow. I put wildflowers between the threads of a burlap sack and made a shoulder wrap. Somebody made me a hat from jasmine flowers. *Comme ça, tu es très coquette! Comme ta mère.* You are very stylish with this hat. You look just like your mother,' Grandma told me. All the refugees from our group came to the wedding—about forty of them. We spread out blankets on the wheat field and set up a long table under some trees. The wheat was as yellow as the inside of a ripe apricot. Some people were lying on the grass, others were playing guitars, and a few were helping Emiliano build a *chuppah*, a wedding canopy. 'You have to get married under a canopy,' Grandma said. 'It symbolizes the wish to always have a roof over your head.' To scare away the evil spirits, I circled seven times around Emil with a tree branch in my hand. It is the custom of the Jews of Spain. Emil broke the traditional wedding glass, and *Zikim*, glimmers of light, souls of friends long gone, flew into the air like diamonds. Miguel, the refugee from Spain, married us. Then something so strange happened that people thought it was staged. Some Russian farmers had heard about the wedding and arrived with a priest. They were shouting, '*Bragoslavie, bragoslavie*, Be sanctified.' The priest blessed the sky and the earth, gave Emil a marriage certificate, then asked for money. The other peasants went under my *chuppah* and, holding onto each other, tried to dance. The priest sat on his knees in front of us, praying and making crosses in the air. I looked at the *chuppah*, the tables covered with berries, cheese, eggs, honey, bread, wine, and I started to cry. Miguel took me aside. He took my chin in his hands, forcing me to look into his eyes, and said, 'Bilu, *Nit'ater g'vee'ari v'radeem b'terem yibolu*, let us adorn ourselves with roses before they wither.'"

"Very nice," Clara commented, "a good lesson for life."

"I don't think so," Norah immediately intervened. "Too much vanity is not good."

"I like weddings," Clara said.

"You know, Bilu, this is quite offensive," Norah said, irritated. "While you were putting flowers on the table, we were eating grass. Your decoration was our staple. If we were lucky, and only in the spring, we ate bitter dandelion leaves. Boiled potatoes—this is luxury in Paradise. So excuse me for being so direct, but you are describing a nature trip in the countryside. You had only bread, cheese, eggs, and some berries! Poor Bilu, let us not talk about suffering," she said, then broke into a piercing laughter that made my ears hurt.

"Norah," Clara shouted, "I want to hear about her wedding, not about your anger. Please let me enjoy her story."

"After the wedding Emil and I went camping by the river," Bilu continued. "We arrived there late in the afternoon, and went for a swim."

"Naked," Norah said and giggled.

"He saw your body?" I asked.

"No, I couldn't take my clothes off. While we were still in Budapest some soldiers forced me to undress in the street. It was so horrible that even now when I remember my hands shake and I breathe with difficulty. No, I swam with my clothes on."

"How silly," Norah said with pleasure in her voice.

"You're wrong," Clara said. "For her being naked meant fear, hate, and humiliation. She couldn't look into his eyes without seeing the abuse. Only a lover can show you how beautiful you are, and she was afraid to know."

"Well, I couldn't take off my clothes. We swam out together, racing to a flat stone in the middle of the river. We arrived almost at the same time. Emil held onto the stone with one hand and brought my head near his with the other. He kissed my face and said, 'Bilu, I am really proud of you! You're a great swimmer.'

"When he returned to the shore to make a fire, I let myself float near the bed of the river. For the first time since 1937—after Adah and Rafa'el left—I felt happy. I knew that I would be able to live without them, and without Aram, and I shouted, 'Emiliano, I love you and I am scared.' 'Me too, my darling,' he said. 'But right now I am hungry!' Then I thought, Why should I deprive myself of pleasure? So I took off my clothes and stood naked by the fire, dripping with water. I was tan from working in the fields all summer. My hair was almost orange and I had freckles everywhere. Emil came up behind me and handed me a small package. 'Bilu, this is for you. If my mother were here she would have given you a gift. This is her wedding gift for you. Welcome to our family.' It was a silk blouse embroidered with red carnations—a typical peasant blouse from the area. I tried to put it on, but I was still so wet that the silk clung to my body. Emil straightened it with his hands. The silk was so fine that I looked covered with flowers. I felt the warmth of his body, and when I turned around and put my arms around his shoulders, his face caught the sun, his hair looked reddish, and at that moment, in his eyes, I saw Aram. I saw his face and I knew that he was alive and happy for me."

"What a talent you have to see people's faces when you need to," Norah commented.

"We lay by the fire until we fell asleep. When I woke up," Bilu continued, "the sun was down and the wildflowers around me looked like reverential magicians preparing for an evening incantation. I remembered a song that Rafa'el used to sing to Adah sometimes and I changed the name:

> Embraced by the arms of the Universe,
> I ascend along a diagonal path.
> To meet the love of my husband,
> Emil Neter the apple of my eye.

"Emiliano was cooking potatoes by the fire: 'There is nothing I can do about this stupid war! Nothing! So I am going to adorn myself with roses even if I never get to Hanah's Paradise and never see Aram again,' I shouted. This is the story of my wedding."

"My father would have given me a big wedding, with musicians and more than one hundred guests, for sure. I never thought about the dress. I mean, I never saw myself in a wedding dress but I imagined the food," Norah said, pulling up the sleeve of her blouse to study the tattooed number on her arm.

"Norah, if you want, we can celebrate your wedding now," Bilu said. "I can make you a dress. If you want a wedding, you should have a wedding, no matter the circumstances."

"I already had a wedding," Norah answered. "The guests wore gray-and-white-striped costumes of exquisite design. Everyone had gone to the hairdressers and looked very dignified with their shaven heads. We sat around big fireplaces. Only the line to the buffet was too long. Some guests didn't get any food," she said, twisting her hands in mock despair. "My older brothers would have built me a *chuppah*, but they were dead. Do you understand? Dead, dead, dead! They stayed too long by the fireplace and caught fire," she said, then laughed.

"Norah," Clara said, fixing her eyes on her, "*please*! This is *her* wedding. Why are you offended? She *didn't* go there. For her the word *wedding* is not a synonym for death."

"I am offended because what I hear is thoughtless and egotistical," Norah replied. "She was sad because her mommy wasn't at her wedding, annoyed by some peasants, scared to take her clothes off. She is telling that to me, knowing where my mommy is and what taking a shower means for us."

"Norah, I am sorry," Bilu said. "I am sorry for your suffering. Your past is a nightmare that I can't change. Nobody can. I wouldn't have survived. But you, Norah, did. Please don't be mean with me in the present because I don't share the cruelty of your past."

"I am not mean at all, but you are just ridiculous," Norah said defiantly.

"For God's sake, Norah," Clara said, "if you want to tell your story, go ahead, but don't insult her. Her life and yours don't coincide, Norah; they only intersect."

"I would have had a wedding under the *chuppah*, a dress, and a ring, if it wasn't for . . ."

"Here, take my wedding ring," Bilu interrupted her. "Grandma gave it to me. You can have it."

"Can I look at it?" I asked. It was a flat band of gold with a Hebrew inscription.

"'*Ani le dodah ve dodah li*, I am for my beloved and my beloved is for me,'" Bilu translated.

"When Clara got married, Guido sent her a gold bracelet," Norah said haughtily.

"All I can tell you," Bilu said, "is what Grandma told me. 'With or without a wedding, when you are with your husband, you are supposed to enjoy yourself; if you don't, then better talk to him about it.'"

"Great advice," Norah said, laughing. "That's what they told us when we arrived at Bergen-Belsen. 'You are supposed to enjoy yourself and if you don't, just tell us.'"

Bilu looked tense while Norah choked with laughter.

"You know, when you love someone, you share their pain. I suffered for Aram every moment. Now I am suffering for you also; for the loss of who you were before that experience. But Norah, please, don't punish me for your past."

The moment Bilu said that, my mother's face changed. Trying to control her anger all along, she had been biting her lips, and now in their place only a barely visible, fine blue line remained. Her face had no mouth. Her eyes started to roll, and her nose flared. She tightened her fists until they became blue. She sat up rigidly, opened her mouth, and screamed, *"Meeeersiiiiii!"* Then she burst into tears, hitting the chair with her fist.

My ears hurt and I covered them with my hands, waiting in silence.

When she finally stopped, Norah wiped her face with the sleeve of her blouse, took a sip of tea, and said, "I haven't cried since 1943 when . . ." She stood up to leave the room, but Bilu grabbed her hand and said, "Help me off the bed." As Norah pulled her up, Bilu adjusted her skirt for a second, then took Norah in her arms. Norah remained rigid, separated a bit from Bilu, who was beckoning Clara and me. This was quite unexpected. We all embraced, until Norah brusquely disengaged herself and left the room.

"Norah believes that hugging brings bad luck," Clara explained to Bilu. "She still speaks the language of the camp. 'To join' means to be sent to the crematory. You embrace before joining the line. For her, words have different meanings than the usual ones. This is called schizophrenia. It is the illness of meaning; the language of the poet, the king, the muse—and lunatics, like us. Don't take it personally," Clara continued and put an arm around Bilu. "I am glad you told us the story."

"I have my own bad-luck stories," Bilu said. "Whenever they enter my mind, I just remember how happy I was floating on the Syr Darya."

"That is such a beautiful name for a river," Clara said.

They sat in silence until Bilu said, "You must have a love story also, don't you, Clara?"

"My love story is from a distant past from which I am disconnected. The dates, the places, the people are the same, but the action is never in the present. Nothing is happening between characters now except the fragments of events in my memory. Even the role I used to play in my own love story seems foreign to me. It is a bizarre feeling, as though I am singing with a large orchestra. I know every instrument and my performance is right, except that the orchestra is in a photograph and doesn't make any sound. And although I can hear myself, we can't play together. Sometimes I recognize my parents and my sisters in other people's features and it hurts me. It must be what happens when you miss someone very much. Your mind searches for them."

"Yes," Bilu said, "you see them everywhere. I can see my mother's face in you, Meia. Your resemblance to her is remarkable."

At the time, I didn't realize how complex Norah's feelings toward Bilu were. I was witnessing a relationship that I didn't understand. Bilu's claim on Aram infuriated my mother. Bilu took liberties with him that Norah would never dare. In front of us she became his twin again, and their intimacy was that of people who know each other instinctively, who accept their connection as a biological fact. She would put her arms around Aram, take a pen from his pocket, taste the food from his plate, criticize his clothes, and interrupt him—all without Aram's ever objecting. Sometimes he made fun of her and they laughed together. Norah was jealous. Bilu ignored the jealousy, caring for Norah as one does for a loving, annoying child. She cut Norah's hair, made her several dresses, spoke to her in broken Ladino, and taught her how to dance the flamenco. But Bilu's affection didn't stop Norah's rivalry. She would come to Bilu's "room," sit on the chair, gesturing with her hands, raising her eyes to the ceiling, making faces, and commenting on Bilu's stories.

"The life of a refugee, another romantic episode, I assume."

"We were pretty divorced from what was happening in Europe at that time. News was only rumors," Bilu continued, ignoring Norah. "I was pregnant, Grandma was very depressed, and we were hoping to leave Russia at any moment. It was more difficult to travel with a child."

"You could have aborted," Norah said. "After all, your husband is a doctor."

"Norah, don't start again," Bilu said. "Being a refugee is not a great life either! There are sacrifices also."

"Norah," Clara said suddenly, "I couldn't figure out, the other night when you screamed 'meersii,' whether you were saying the French merci or the English mercy—compassion."

"I was asking for attention," Norah answered.

"The pregnancy wasn't difficult," Bilu said, again ignoring the interruption. "It's just that we had to walk and she was heavy, almost three kilograms."

"Three kilograms," Norah said in disbelief. "My God, you had that much food? We had very little to eat, so she was very small, and my delivery was easy. 'If she gains a hundred grams in one week,' the doctor said, 'she will live.' So I called her Meia—one hundred in Hebrew. The pregnancy was a nightmare. She made me sick every minute. At least she was premature, so she tortured me for only eight months," Norah said, pleased with herself, once again winning first prize in the competition of misfortunes.

"This child keeps alive the name of your own mother, and you call her hundred grams? That is very mean," Bilu said. "She is entitled to her name. Call her Salomeia, even if she was born premature and didn't weigh more than a cat."

"That is exactly what Aram told me when Meia was born," Norah said. "You both do think alike, don't you? Even after his cat in Budapest spent an entire night on top of a tree in the snow, Aram said, it looked better than his child."

"Was Tania born by the river?" I asked, simply to interrupt my mother. When she talked about me I always shriveled inside.

Tania had been born on the way to Birobidjhan, in a Red Cross field hospital. Shortly before her birth, Stalin had ordered all Jewish refugees to move there, to the First Jewish Autonomous Republic—Birobidjhan. Bilu, Emil, Tania, and my Great-Grandmother Julia lived there for many years. This is where they learned how to milk a camel and how to speak the Uzbek language, Bilu told me.

"What was it like there?" Clara asked.

"It was nothing like Budapest. The city of Bidzhan was a small village, with wood houses and only one paved road, when we arrived in late '46. But there was already a theater, a writers' club, and a school. We were given identity cards and allocated coupons for construction materials. Cement, wire, nails—there was a coupon for everything and we had to build our house with our own hands. We had a communal vegetable garden, and every street had a communal kitchen where we got food with coupons."

"We had a communal kitchen also, but no coupons," Norah said and left the room.

"Did you like living there?" Clara asked.

"I was with Emiliano and Grandma, I had a child, I was young, and yes, I liked it there," Bilu said. "It was exotic, it was revolutionary, and it was Stalin's propaganda at its best. Emiliano worked at the hospital. Grandma and I worked at the farm. We sorted fruit.

Waiting to leave for Hanah's Paradise, we got used to it. Only when we were required to attend the Workers' School, several evenings every week, did we start to doubt our possible escape."

Mendel, who had joined the conversation, asked, "What did you study?"

"Russian, history, and Marxism-Leninism."

"Is that true?" Mendel asked in disbelief. "They were teaching Marxism to the refugees?"

"Yes," Bilu said.

"Stalin was right to teach you the history of the Bolshevik Revolution," Mendel continued. "In Tsarist times, Russian Jews were small merchants and peddlers. They had bourgeois values, bourgeois psychology, and proletarian pockets. Comrade Stalin criticized them for being 'nationalists without roots.'"

"Sta-lin, Sta-lin," Norah chanted from the kitchen.

"Read," Clara said, pushing the journal into Bilu's hands. "I want to know about you, not about Stalin."

"'May 4, 1947. Again, the Party informed all foreigners that we should not write because mail can't leave the country. A letter could fall into enemy hands. With private information from us, spies could infiltrate the country.

"'May 9, 1947. Grandma has lost weight. The few clothes that she still has do not fit her anymore. Yesterday at the weekly meeting she was criticized for encouraging bourgeois affectation by reading a book in French. In the Soviet Union, we were told, even older people can learn Russian if they believe in Communism.'"

"You know, Bilu," Norah interrupted, "what you are reading doesn't make any sense. It is like we were on different planets. Isn't that true, Clara? What were you doing in April of '45?"

"What was I doing? We were already evacuated from the camp in Flossenbürg. It was the beginning of the death march," Clara answered, falling into Norah's trap.

"Listen," Bilu said with irritation. "Personally, I would prefer to hear your story instead of telling mine. It is not my fault, Norah. I am not responsible for what happened to you."

"Who says you are responsible? You always twist my words. I only asked a question."

Ignoring Norah, Mendel said, "Bilu, were there any Jews from Argentina when you were in Birobidjhan?"

"Yes, from 1928, from the beginning of the Jewish Autonomous Republic. After the Party condemned them for the construction of a synagogue, they disappeared. Emil was told in secret that they were 'subversive elements, enemies of the Proletarian Revolution.' They were probably sent to Siberia."

"How were they subversive?" Clara asked. "They were there to help."

"Building a synagogue is not exactly a Communist thing to do," Mendel said. "Religion keeps people in poverty. Communism is the new religion of the Bolsheviks."

"We had to read 'Fight against Religion, Fight for Socialism,' a book about slavery and economic exploitation of the working class. We went to the meetings, listened to the speeches, applauded the leaders, and promised to dedicate our work to building Socialism —while waiting to leave," Bilu said. "In fact, I am still waiting."

"At least we have that in common," Norah said from the doorway.

"Yes," Bilu answered, "that, and the fact that both of us are raising daughters, and both of us love Aram."

Norah looked as if a thin coating of ice had been put on her face. "If I had a brother, of course I would love him, like you do. As for children, that's what women do," she said, shrugging her shoulders. "They have children. But she was not desired," she said, pointing at me. "I can tell you that."

Bilu spoke Russian and French with me. She told me stories about Budapest and Asia, about my grandparents, my cousin, and her childhood. With Bilu, feelings had names. She braided my hair and made me a winter hat. Bilu thought I was pretty. When we walked in the streets, she always held my hand, and at home she covered me with kisses. Only Alisa used to kiss me. Silvia, too, but she rarely came to visit anymore. Clara, Mendel, and Aram usually kissed me on my birthday, or when they returned from some trip, but Norah, never.

"She does not kiss anyone because she wants to protect them. She thinks that hers is the kiss of death," Clara explained to Bilu and me one day. "But it has nothing to do with you, Meia."

Bilu believed that Norah was damaged. "She is mad," she would often say, "and her madness has to be forgiven."

To her credit, one day Norah asked Bilu to do something with her. She brought home some paint, and for several hours the two of them painted flowers and grapevines on the window of my verandah, all the while singing Ladino songs. They seemed to enjoy it. This happened only once.

"Bilu," Mendel asked her one day, "how did the Party transform the refugees into Bolsheviks?"

"We were all committed to political change. Every day we heard about equality, freedom, nondiscrimination, and the role of women as militant atheists—values that we all embraced."

"What kind of people were there with you?" Clara asked.

"There were two groups: Argentineans, Americans, and Jews from Palestine who arrived there in 1928 to build the Jewish Autonomous Republic, and the war refugees—Russians, Georgians, Tartars, Chinese, Kirkiz, Romanians, Polish, Armenians, Hungarians, Mongolians, Spaniards, Turks, English, Uzbeks, European Jews. Regardless of their status, nobody was allowed to leave. And to discourage nationalistic and reactionary attitudes, the Party required us to speak only in Russian, even in our own homes."

"To speak in another people's tongue is a form of exile," Mendel volunteered.

"That is precisely why Stalin wanted them to speak only Russian," Norah said, "to keep them in exile from themselves."

"Whatever it was, as early as 1945 the writers at our Yiddish newspaper, the *Birobidjhaner Shtern*, declared themselves proletarians and began writing in Russian, not in Yiddish. I remember the meeting. There it is," Bilu said, turning several pages of her journal:

With the help of the Party, we can change our way of thinking. Now we are workers; we are not confused intellectuals! The first step of Jewish colonists toward a new Jewish life is to become proletarians. The first step to become proletarian is to speak and write Russian—the language of the proletariat.

"We were constantly indoctrinated with slogans and political commentaries."

August 2, 1946. Economic progress will be our weapons. The Jewish institutions, controlled by the rabbis, were exploiting the poor and the women.

"In December 1947, a man from Moscow came to normalize the refugees' status. Since the war was over, we couldn't be war refugees. But since we had entered the Soviet Union illegally, we were not allowed to leave. Everyone's status had to be discussed with the political commissar. We went to see him, and when we entered his office, he yelled at me: 'Bilu is the name of a secret Zionist society, the acronym for *Beit Ia'acov Lekhu Unelekhah*, House of Jacob, Stand Up and Let Us Go.'

"'*Niet Tovaraschi*, no, Comrade, Bilu is the root for "crystal" in old Hebrew—*Beit, Lamed, Vav*,' Grandma said.

"The commissar disagreed. 'Crystal in Hebrew is *bedulah*: *Beit Dalet Lamed Ain*. In the Soviet Union semantics are important. In fact, unless you are Zionist spies, you should all take Russian names. This is my recommendation.' That is how I became Bella Emilianova Neterova and Grandma, Julia Antonova. We had no choice. We could not even change apartments or jobs without the Party's approval, let alone leave the city. Then we learned that refugees who had filed requests to leave the Soviet Union were arrested. 'The country needs you,' we were told. And this," Bilu said, handing me a photograph, "is from 1950. A photographer from Moscow came into town and I met him by chance. He took some shots of Grandma and Tania in front of our house. They look happy because it was Grandma's seventieth birthday and we had invited some people home to celebrate."

The picture was of an older woman with short curly hair and very light eyes, holding a big pocketbook in one hand and in the other, the hand of a small child. She was my father's grandmother. I wanted to slip my hand into hers, to feel her skin and the pressure of being held, but I couldn't. I took my hands and held them together as if it were she that was holding me.

"Tania was almost three. I made her the same dress as Grandma's. The dress was blue with a yellow silk bow. We had wine, smoked fish with boiled potatoes, red beets, mulberry jam, and cheesecake. It was the best party I had ever seen. Grandma was very beautiful. People were dressed in their best clothes. The ones from Moscow wore hats, gloves, and high heels. We danced in the garden."

I sat next to Bilu, looking at the journal. There were drawings, recipes, poems, newspaper clippings, lists of things to do, and pressed between pages some dried flowers. She had written mostly in Hungarian, sometimes in French. I read, as she turned the pages:

May 28, 1948. SHALOM ISRAEL! WE HAVE A COUNTRY NOW. Thank you, Comrade Stalin, father of the poor and the oppressed, for giving your vote to the establishment of the State of Israel. Next year in Jerusalem.

"Since Stalin was not opposed to the creation of the State of Israel, we requested permission to join our family there," Bilu said. "But then we heard rumors that there was a quota, so not everybody could leave at once. We decided to wait until we were sure that we could leave, then, on December 12, 1955, Grandma Julia died. She went to sleep and didn't wake up. It was terrible. I had never lived without her. I knew her better than my own mother. We were devastated. It was difficult to find ten men to say the Hebrew prayers. Such gatherings were forbidden. Emil and I said the prayer in secret:

Yit'gadal v'yit'kadash
Yit'barakh v'yish'tabach.

"I couldn't even inform my parents about Grandma's death. We didn't know where to turn or how to make decisions. Our family became smaller.

To add or to subtract
Is an act of mutilation.

"By March 1952," Bilu continued, "it became clear that we could no longer even hope to leave. We were summoned to a special meeting and told, 'In alliance with the USA, Israel is extending an aggressive dominance in the Middle East. The heroic Soviet people and Comrade Stalin are against this imperialist expansion. As

223

an outpost of American imperialism, Israel is the enemy of the working class.' And since the alliance with the enemy put the Jews from the Soviet Union on the wrong side, we were not allowed to emigrate. We resigned ourselves to living there. We could send letters only if they were written in Russian and only to Socialist countries. In any case, we knew that the Party censored the letters. We made good friends there and became each other's family. We shared everything, except our hopes. We were too afraid. People were disappearing and being tortured to confess false crimes. We wore the Communist mask as if our life were a play, as if every day were a carnival: 'Purim in Zaragoza,' my grandmother used to say. We watched the changing of the seasons on the banks of the Syr Darya and we went on with our lives, constantly and secretly dreaming of leaving.

"Then we learned about the Jewish writers in Moscow who conspired against Stalin. We understood very little about Stalin but felt thankful that he had rescued us from the Nazis. 'How could anybody be so ungrateful?' we asked ourselves."

"Stalin was very much loved here also," Mendel said. "We sang the same songs that you did and listened to the same speeches."

"Bilu," Norah asked, "did they force you to become a Communist, or did you join them for your own benefit?"

"I love to go to meetings, sit in the front row, and make eye contact with the speaker. That's why I joined them, Norah."

"Why do you have to be sarcastic with me? I can't even ask you a question?"

"I know, Norah. I can always count on you to say something nasty. I will tell you tomorrow. Now go to bed." When Bilu reprimanded her, Norah felt loved. She left without a word, only to return soon after.

September 6, 1952. Today the Party approved Emil's request to return to the university. We are very, very happy. At the Bolsheviks meeting, Dr. Yossif Babel, director of the hospital, talked about Emil's dedication to his work. "Comrade Emil Neter is a very careful and caring doctor. He helped build our hospital with his own hands. He is a much-respected comrade and knows medicine very well. I recommend that he be allowed to attend university." The audience applauded. Comrade Nazarov, the Party commissar, asked if there was any opposition. A man stood up. "Comrade Emil Neter is not a member of our Communist Party and is not making a sufficient effort to speak Russian. He went to school in Germany, and both of his parents are doctors. He grew up privileged and has an attitude of bourgeois intellectualism. I don't see why the working class should send him to university. Many others here have better social origins than he and are more deserving of going to study in Moscow." The commissar nodded his head. Emil stood there, his head down. "Anything you want to say in your defense?" the commissar asked. Emil said, "I am sorry. I am a war refugee. I want to be a good doctor, and for this I have to finish my studies." Then he sat down.

"I felt very bad for him," Bilu said as she closed her journal. "He worked night and day at the hospital. He wasn't a privileged intellectual. He was a medical student who had taken the oath to save people's lives. But the commissar didn't like his answer and said, 'That is very self-serving.' Emil looked baffled, then shook his head. 'No, Comrade. I want to finish school to be a better doctor.'

"'Neter, I don't think you understand,' the Party commissar told him. 'I don't hear you wanting to be a bricklayer or a miner! You want to go to school to receive a title, to distance yourself even more from the working class.'

"I was afraid for Emil," Bilu said, looking at us. "Then, in a surge of anger, I stood up and shouted, 'Comrades! Emil Neter, my husband, belongs to the working class. Yes, his parents were doctors. But what is the world of a doctor, comrades? It is not a world of leisure—even if it might have a bourgeois status! The world of the doctor, comrades, is the world of the emergency room, the world of life-and-death decisions, the world of suffering and hope. Doctors are workers in the service of health! A doctor works with his hands. He removes bullets from the wounded and repairs their limbs. He gives medicine and delivers children. A doctor heals. Comrades, can you imagine the devastation that takes place in a hospital if a doctor does not know how to operate? Can you imagine yourself sick, hoping for life, while a doctor who does not know what he is doing is operating on you? Can you, *can you*, comrades, allow that to happen to your family, to your friends, or to the working class? Can you take this responsibility? People go to school to learn skills from other, more experienced people. Comrades, do not die in the hands of the inexperienced!' I yelled this facing the crowd," Bilu said, and looked at us, her face radiant with pleasure.

Clara looked hypnotized by Bilu's words. Norah was playing with her hands, and Mendel nodded his head.

"'Comrade Nazarov,'" Bilu continued, "'I ask permission for Emil Neter to go to school to better serve the working class, to dedicate his knowledge to the poor, the oppressed, the farmers, and everyone discriminated against by the bourgeoisie of czarist Russia. Comrade Neter is a dedicated doctor.' I said all of that in Russian. I didn't even know until then how well I knew the language."

"*Que brava ragazza!*" Clara said, applauding. "You were so courageous. You were determined and spoke with persuasion. I would never have dared to speak like that."

"I was furious," Bilu answered. "After my speech, the comrades voted, and that is how Emil went to medical school in Moscow. But this is not how we joined the Communist Party, Norah."

"I am sure that you joined the Party only for the right reason," Norah responded.

"Yes, for a very good reason. It is called survival," Bilu said, and read again from her notebook:

November 1952—the beginning of a new purge. A band of Jewish doctors, spying for the Americans and the British, was discovered in Moscow. The year before, it was a group of prominent Jewish politicians and army generals. All were executed.

"We were all petrified. Again it became dangerous to be Jewish. The commissar asked to talk with Emil again. We didn't sleep all night. The next morning, when Emil went to the meeting, I went with him and waited for him in front of the City Hall. When Emil came out, we sat in the park and he told me what had happened.

"'Neter,' the commissar told him, 'you received approval to go to school in Moscow. This is a great honor. The Party believes in you, even though you are not Russian, you speak with a heavy accent, and you are not very friendly. But how can we trust you when you have sent letters to Belgium, Hungary, Israel, and America? We have reason to believe that you don't want to be here, that you have plans to leave the country. If you are not on our side, Neter, you must be on the enemy's side. A traitor, perhaps a spy! Should the Party send you to Siberia, instead of Moscow?'"

"How cruel," Clara said.

"They all are," Norah added. "It is in their job description."

"This reminds me of the meeting I once had with the commissar," Clara said. "I was so very scared that I cried."

"How did Emil respond?" Aram, who had joined us, asked.

"He told him the truth. When the war ended, refugees asked permission to return to their countries. At that time it seemed like a natural decision. But the commissar got really nasty and yelled at Emil. 'Comrade Neter, do you want to leave or do you want to go to school?'

"'I want to go to school, but I would also like to be with my family.'"

"How courageous of him," Clara said.

"The commissar was a brute. He said to Emil, 'Please, Neter, spare me your war tragedy. What you really want is to leave. As a second-best solution, you would do us the favor of going to our university. Why should we trust you? Nobody leaves Mother Russia, Neter! You understand? You have the retrograde attitude of a Jewish intellectual. We saved you from the Nazis! Millions died to defend you while you were taking a vacation in the Soviet Union. Now you want to go home? How convenient! Only traitors to the Bolshevik Revolution leave! We don't want secret medical research to fall into the hands of the enemy. The Party restricts the exit of Jews who are essential to the state. Don't you read the papers? Even Poland keeps their essential Jews—and you know how much they are hated there. And even if you could leave, your daughter can't. She was born here, a citizen of the Soviet Union. We want you to stay to build Socialism. It is your turn to do something for us. Did you ever consider that the workers' needs are more important than your mere personal drama? What about the families of the soldiers who died to defend you? What about the orphans and the old people who have no families anymore? Should they also leave? Neter, the Soviet Union is not a vacation summer camp, and I am saying this to you as a favor. I recommend that you ask forgiveness from the People and cancel your request to leave. If you confess your mistake, this time the Party will forgive you and let you go to Moscow. If you don't, we will have to send you to a reeducation camp.'

"Emil asked permission to talk with me about it, and the commissar agreed to give him one hour. I was waiting for him outside and right then we both agreed to cancel our request to leave the country. He went back, confessed that his attitude wasn't progressive, promised to be loyal to Communist ideals, and signed everything, including a request to join the Party."

"I would have signed it!" Norah jumped in.

"Me too," Clara said. "They could not leave the country in either case."

"At least they went to Moscow," Norah said approvingly.

"At first we felt that we had betrayed our families. Then we found out that people who hadn't signed were beaten. The image of Emiliano's face full of blood was something I couldn't bear. So this is how we joined the Communist Party and went to Moscow. And if I had to choose again I would do the same thing. 'Choose Life'—isn't that what God told Adam?"

"You mean," Norah said angrily, "that they let you choose without denouncing other people first, or promising to inform on anti-Communist activities? At Bergen-Belsen, if you denounced you got extra bread! And believe me, that was an incentive!"

Bilu shrugged her shoulders and, looking askance, said, "Norah, you are insinuating betrayal."

After that, nobody said anything.

Bilu sat on the bed with the journal open on her lap. Seated, next to her, I could read some of the notes.

"What is *Klub Kauchuk*?" I asked.

"Who gave you permission to read from her journal?" Norah snapped.

Bilu ignored her. "*Klub Kauchuk* is a community center in Moscow where the workers stage their own productions: theater, dance, and opera. We saw *The Battleship Potemkin* there once. It was a beautiful production. Afterward we took a walk to the river. When we passed a Georgian restaurant, *Pirosmani*, Emil said, 'Let's go in!' Stalin was from Georgia, and in his time, it was the only restaurant in Moscow that legally served wine. The food there was very good. It was the first time ever, we went to a restaurant. I felt so embarrassed at being served that I wanted to help with the cleaning."

"In Georgia they cook with walnuts," Norah jumped in, happy to know something more than Bilu did. "Everything is stuffed with walnuts or covered in walnut sauce."

"Really?" Aram said.

"I used to have an uncle who did business in Tbilisi and married a woman from there. When they visited she made goose neck stuffed with walnuts. I never told you about my cousins in Georgia?"

"You never, ever, mentioned having a cousin. Only your parents and brothers," Clara said. "What else do you have and are not telling us about?"

"I forget what I used to have."

"And when we drank the thick red Georgian wine," Bilu continued, "Emiliano raised his glass and said, 'Happy Birthday—to Bilu and Aram.' It was our birthday and I had completely forgotten." Looking into Aram's eyes, she closed her journal.

That journal was for me an unexpected link to my family. Bilu's notes, anecdotes, and stories brought me closer to people for whom I felt affection, even if I had never met them. I wanted to enter inside the words, to change their destination and hear them addressed to me. I wanted this journal to be mine.

One afternoon when nobody was home, I took it out of Bilu's cardboard box. It was about my family, and I felt entitled to know. If Norah never talked about her side of the family, at least from Bilu's journal I could learn about my father's. So I sat on Bilu's bed and I read from it alone.

April 29, 1953. We are still mourning the death of our beloved hero, Comrade Stalin. It is a loss for all humanity. People cry with grief. Our father Yossif Vissarionovich Stalin has left us, but his spirit will always remain in our hearts.

No father cherished his children more.
We treasured him more than our harvest.
We will fight to death to save his name.
We will work harder in his memory.

September 24, 1953. Our new father, Comrade Khrushchev, spoke on the radio and condemned an initiative taken by Comrade Stalin to send all Jews to Siberia. The lists had been prepared and the trains were ready. Stalin died the day before we were supposed to be deported. We are stunned! Comrade Khrushchev revoked the order. Some Russians believe that by sending the Jews to Siberia, Stalin, in his generosity, was giving them a chance to show their love for Mother Russia. But he was a criminal! Thank you, Comrade Khrushchev, for not sending us to our death!

January 18, 1956. Stalin's statues are demolished! People spit on his pictures. Political prisoners are freed. Factories, schools, hospitals, and libraries are changing their names. Stalin Plaza is now called "The Heroic Field."

September 14, 1956. ARAM IS ALIVE! MY ARAM IS ALIVE! We received an answer from the Red Cross. Aram is living in Romania, near us! Only ten days away! We cried from happiness when we received the news. Aram, alive! I knew it all the time! I sang "Verde Limon" all day. *Mi Limon, mi limonero!* Will he recognize me after almost fourteen years? How will it feel to be together again?

I read the entire afternoon. I read everything, even her cooking recipes and her lists of things to do. Putting together Bilu's words, I constructed my family. I learned about my father and his parents at Hanah's Paradise.

BILU AND CLARA

The week before Bilu took the train back to Moscow, Clara invited her to visit the music school where she was teaching. Bilu put a blue ribbon in her hair for the occasion. We walked there together. Clara took us into the recital hall, played the piano, and sang only for Bilu and me. Bilu asked her to play "Verde Limon," and when Clara played it, she sang along. Afterward, Clara invited us for lunch in a bodega. It was not exactly a restaurant. It was more of a corridor where people could eat standing up around several tall round tables. On a stone counter along the wall, small pies were lined up for sale. They were made of thin layers of dough filled with melted cheese, greasy and hot—wonderful with a glass of cold buttermilk. We waited until a place became available, then Clara bought a pie for us to share. She and Bilu talked mostly in Hungarian, giving each other advice about their hair and their skin. They talked about their lives with a directness that I had never seen in my family.

"Is he busy, or does he come home late because I am here?" Bilu asked Clara, referring to Aram.

"No," Clara said, "he is the same as always."

"He is strange," Bilu said. "He never told you anything about Budapest?"

"He doesn't talk about himself. He just brings up facts. 'We used to have a cat,' or, 'A friend helped me,' nothing more."

"That is not true," I said. "He told Mama about the cat. He said the cat was prettier than me."

"No, Salomeia," Clara said. "He said that you were as cute as Moka, his cat. That is what he said, trust me. I was there."

"What happened to the cat?" I asked.

"Oh, it's a long story. We called her Moka because she had soft, chocolate-colored fur. Aram brought her home and Grandma let us keep her. She was cute, but she got us into trouble." Bilu paused to drink some buttermilk.

"Aram and I were home alone when Moka escaped. Aram went to look for her and found her on a branch of the linden tree on the corner of the street, three houses down from ours. If I stretched my neck I could see her through the window. Aram tried to climb the tree, but he kept sliding off. It was December and the tree was full of ice. Some boys passing by threw snowballs at Moka, but instead of coming down, she got even more scared. Two others tried to help Aram climb up and he almost made it, but his hat fell off, and when they saw his red hair, one of them yelled, 'I know him. He's a Jew. I know him from swimming class. His *pipi* is cut off!'

"'Up, little Jew,' the boy started shouting, 'get up so we can hang you!'

"Aram pushed himself up the tree, and just as he got hold of Moka, he fell to the sidewalk. The sound of the branches as they snapped under his body is still in my ears. I ran out of the house screaming, 'Leave him alone! Leave him alone! He's my brother!' When I arrived at the corner, one of the boys caught me and bent my arms behind my back. Aram, stunned by the fall, was on his back on the sidewalk, and three of the boys were holding him down.

"'This is his sister,' the one who held me shouted. 'Let's put a Jewish star on their foreheads so we can always recognize the dirty Jews!'

"'Yes!' another one said. 'They won't be able to hide anymore!' He bent and held Aram's head on the sidewalk. Then one of them pulled out a pocketknife and went to scratch a star on Aram's forehead. Aram screamed and tried to turn his face to the sidewalk but the others were holding him down. I was screaming, 'Leave him alone. Let him go!'

"Alerted by the noise, Viorel, our next-door neighbor, came out. The boy let go of me and I ran toward Viorel screaming, 'Moka, Moka, Aram.'

"'What is happening?' he shouted.

"'There is a Jew here. We have to break his horns!' a woman passing by shouted.

"The neighbor, a sturdy man who was a sculptor, picked up a broken branch from the tree and pushed the boys away, yelling, 'Move, make space, move, move!'

"'He is a Jew,' the boys shouted defiantly.

"'I know who he is,' Viorel shouted back. 'But who are you?'

"The question remained unanswered until the woman said, 'We have to help our country. The Jew is Satan. Why are you defending them? Why don't you report them to the police, you Jew lover!'

"'Yes,' the boys shouted. 'Both of them are Jews.'

"Viorel pulled Aram up and, still brandishing the branch, said, 'Enough now. All of you go home! They've learned their lesson!'

"He walked us back to our house. He washed Aram's cuts with iodine and advised us not to go out in the street anymore. When our grandparents returned home, Grandma wanted to report the incident, but Viorel said, 'Forget it, Julia, the police won't do anything for you.' It was our first encounter with hate."

"How old were you then?" Clara asked.

"It was after the Jewish Law, so we must have been about twelve or thirteen, I think. Aram never told you about the scars on his forehead?"

"He told me once that his cat had scratched him."

"I didn't realize that he had kept his past and the incident secret. Soon after I arrived here I mentioned that his scars look like small wrinkles. Nobody can notice them anymore, I said. 'I can,' he answered. 'I know exactly what they mean.'"

I had always wondered about my father's scars. In the summertime, as his skin tanned, two white lines formed an irregular X on his forehead. Bilu's story scared me. I couldn't look at my father's face anymore without seeing him beaten up, covered with blood. Norah, I told myself, doesn't know the story. She still thinks it was the cat.

In the days before Bilu's departure, she and Aram went to the Portuguese cemetery to visit their grandfather's grave. Mendel took all of us to the circus, and Norah prepared the best food she could find. Clara gave Bilu everything she could—a pair of her shoes, some cotton to make a dress, and some food to take back home—gifts from people who had nothing.

The night before her departure, all of us met again in the corridor near her bed. Bilu stood by the piano. Clara played a song, then another one, and after a while Bilu turned to Aram and said, "Do you remember 'Verde Limon'?" Then, very proudly, she added, "Aram and I used to dance the flamenco together."

"Aram danced the flamenco?" Norah asked in disbelief. "With you?"

"Yes, he did! We took lessons. I even had a black ruffled dress with red polka dots. Remember, Aram?"

Aram nodded his head.

"Can you still dance it?"

Aram looked confused. He blushed, then smiled with embarrassment. "No, Bilu! I've danced the flamenco too many times already. I cannot do it anymore."

"I would like to see you dance the flamenco, unless you dance only for your secret muses," Norah said, laughing. But Aram didn't answer.

"Dance is a unique form of connecting space with time and movement," Mendel said, breaking the silence.

Bilu, ignoring the remark, asked Clara to play "Verde Limon." She stood up and started the first steps of the dance. With one hand she pulled up her skirt, simultaneously moving the fingers of her other hand in the air above her head as she beat the rhythm with her feet. Aram kept a frozen smile on his face. Beads of sweat were forming on his forehead. As Bilu arrived near him, she turned enough so that her shoulder touched his, her fingers dancing rapidly in front of his eyes. Aram did not move. His face was contorted. Singing and moving in short steps, Bilu brought her body even closer to Aram's. As she was about to pass directly in front of him, he grabbed her arm and pushed her aside.

"Enough, Bilu! Stop it!"

The anger in his voice took her by surprise. She seemed confused; hurt filled her eyes. She covered her face with her hands and started crying. Her body jerked with convulsions as she moved slowly away from him. She folded one arm on her forehead, turned toward the wall, and leaned there. Clara also started crying. Norah said good night, pushing me and Aram out of the room.

From my bed in the small alcove, I could hear everything my parents said. I was separated from their bedroom by a white cotton sheet. Aram often worked at a table near the curtain. That night, they sat there drinking tea.

"Why did she cry like that?" I heard Norah asking. "Is it just because you didn't want to dance with her?"

"She's always been like that," Aram answered.

"Like what?"

"Resentful and nagging, until she got her way."

"Aram, what happened to you and Bilu in Budapest? You have to tell me."

I also wanted to know, but Aram remained silent for a while. Then he said, "It is not my story, it is Bilu's story. You have to ask her."

Norah didn't like his answer. "If this story concerns you, it is your story, and you are going to tell me everything because you live with me, not with Bilu. I am losing patience with your private jokes, private stories, dance lessons, Hanah's Paradise, and everything else."

Aram started to walk the length of the room, then in a whisper, as if afraid that Bilu might hear him, he told the story of the incident in Budapest.

"Bilu and I were walking home from the library, when several German soldiers walked out from a restaurant and saw her. 'You there, with the red hair, what are you hiding under your clothes,' a soldier shouted, pointing at her. I was caught in the sidewalk traffic, several steps behind her. 'Let's see where else she has red hair,' another soldier said, grabbing her arm. People came out of their shops to see what was happening, and a small group formed around Bilu.

"'A Jew tried to hide in the church,' a woman said. 'Her hair is red because she drinks blood.'

"'Please let me go, I have nothing to hide.' Bilu said very politely, in German. The soldier laughed and said, 'Listen to this *Jude* shit. She has nothing to hide. Let's see if she's lying to us.' A soldier ordered Bilu to take off her clothes. She tried to unbutton her coat but her hands were shaking. They started to shove her back and forth between them. One of them inserted the barrel of his rifle in the seam between the buttons of her coat. As she pulled away, the buttons popped off, striking the sidewalk one by one. 'What is happening?' a man shouted from across the street. 'A dirty Jew, a prostitute,' a woman answered. 'No,' another man said. 'She stole from a store and they are taking her to the police.'

"The soldier ripped off her clothes and Bilu was naked on the sidewalk. Her arms were lifeless limbs. She looked down, trying to move her feet from the cold stone onto her clothes. Tears were falling down her face. One of the soldiers put his rifle between her legs, pushed them apart, and said, 'She is not hiding anything. She has red hair everywhere!' A woman near the soldiers yelled, '*Curvo!* Whore! Jewish whore, you should be hanged!' A soldier grabbed Bilu by her braids. Her body twisted in pain. As he held her, another one jumped from the side and cut them off with a knife. '*Kessenem szepen*, thank you,' a woman jeered. 'She won't need to use our soap to wash her hair.'

"I knew I should do something, but a tremendous weakness went through my body and I almost fell over. I moved away from the circle and started to vomit. Then, from the restaurant, a couple ran out, waving their arms in all directions. '*Tüz! Tüz! Tüz van a piazon*, Fire! Fire! There's a fire at the market!' People ran away shouting, 'Fire! Fire at the market!' One of the soldiers pushed Bilu aside and punched her under the belly. Bilu fell backward, hit her head and fainted. He spat on her, then joined the others running to the market. The couple helped Bilu up. Somebody had taken her clothes and I covered her up with my own."

"Don't tell me you are ashamed for not fighting them," Norah interrupted. "You couldn't have helped her. If you had tried, you would have been beaten up and probably arrested. The fire saved you both."

"It was not a real fire. The couple had yelled 'fire' hoping to divert the soldiers from abusing Bilu."

"Is that the couple that helped your grandparents leave Budapest?"

"Yes. Luca and Ana Senesz, brother and sister; they were with the Communists."

"I am glad you didn't help her," Norah said. "Both of you would have been killed."

Early the next morning, after three months with us, Bilu left. We took her to the train station. Before she boarded, we embraced. Bilu held Aram in her arms and cried. He stood rigidly next to her, one arm around her shoulders, the other at his side, the hand in his pocket. "We will see each other soon," he kept repeating.

Once aboard, Bilu came to an open window. "I am going home," she said laughing.

"What's happening?" Clara asked. "Why are you laughing?"

Bilu chased away a strand of hair from her face and said, "I am going home but I don't have the key." Clara and Mendel exchanged glances, but before they could say anything, Bilu continued. "In Russia it is illegal to make copies of keys, and if you lose yours, you are . . ." she started laughing again, ". . . you are . . ."

"Fucked," I shouted.

"Yes," Bilu said. "You are fucked."

"What a word," Norah said in disgust, turning toward me. "You don't even know what it means."

"It's a great word!" Bilu shouted.

Then Norah opened her mouth, curled her body, and with her hands on her stomach, laughed. "Yes, fucked," she said. "We are all fucked. None of us has the keys to our home."

The whistle separated us. As the train jerked forward, Aram took Bilu's hand through the window and ran along to the end of the platform. We waited for him to return.

On the street, I walked between Aram and Mendel. Clara and Norah walked arm-in-arm in front of us. Nobody said anything.

17

The morning of her departure, Bilu had put a large box of candies on the table. "A gift for the house," she said. "I got it at the Russian army store. They let me in."

There were two layers of candies wrapped in individual papers, fifty of them per layer. On the red cardboard box, in gold Cyrillic letters, was written:

> With the Party leading us
> Our victory is a must.

On the wrappings, printed on silvery paper, were reproductions of Soviet art from before and after the Bolshevik Revolution. Each wrapping was unique. They were arranged in the box thematically, to show contrast. Broken trees, charred darkness, and desolation were Imperial Russia. Sturdy white poplars, fields of wheat, blue lakes, and bright sunshine were present-day Soviet Russia. A ragged, famished peasant, pushing his plow, contrasted with a robust young woman behind the wheel of a red tractor. The centerpiece showed the wedding of two poor peasants and their Soviet counterparts. The poor walk in the muddy streets of the village. The man is holding a bottle of wine, the woman has a chicken in her arms. Two fiddlers walk behind them, nobody smiles. The Communist wedding shows two workers under a vine canopy, and colorful banners. People dance around a table full of foods, flowers, gifts, and casks of wine.

Aram divided the candies into five equal shares. Clara asked for two candies from each of us to take to the orphanage. In exchange for the silver wrappings of her candies, I gave her the cardboard box. I wanted to collect the wrappings and look at the paintings.

Norah studied her candies one by one. She opened some, re-wrapped them, opened them again, smelled them, and compared them, never eating a single one. Then she picked one and held it in her closed hand—very tight. "This one I'm saving for me; you can have all the others, Meia."

Norah put all the candies in a metal container and locked it in the kitchen cupboard. I was entitled to one candy every day. She would give it to me.

The candy-a-day law lasted until I found the key. Seldom was I home alone, but at those times I would pull over a chair, open the glass door of the cupboard, and reach for the shelf above my head. If I stood on my tiptoes and stretched my arm, I could reach the container, tilt up the cover, curl my fingers over the edge, grab a candy, lock the cupboard, put back the chair, and return the key.

One day, much, much later, Norah wanted her candy. She took the container into the bedroom and asked me not to disturb her. Seconds later, she stormed out of the room shouting, "My candy. Where's my candy?"

I shrugged my shoulders.

"The one I saved!" she cried.

I showed her my empty hands. "I don't know."

"Where is it?" She had emptied the container on the bed to find her candy. "I cannot believe it! Someone took my only piece of candy." She kept looking at the candies in disbelief.

"Meia, show me your wrappings," she said.

I brought my collection and she looked at them until she found the wrapping of the beautiful Communist wedding.

"You took something that was mine, you thief! You found the key and stole the candy, you Nazi snake."

"You didn't know which one was mine and you took it." She cursed me in Turkish, threw the other candies at me, and slapped me on the face.

Clara heard the screaming and opened the door. Norah was sobbing into her pillow, hitting the mattress with her fist.

"She took my candy," I heard her whimpering in answer to Clara's question.

When Aram and Mendel arrived home, they found Nora in her bed and Clara sitting on the floor next to me.

"She hit Meia," Clara told Aram.

"What did you do, Meia?"

"She found the key to the cupboard and ate Nora's candy," Clara answered for me.

"Norah wouldn't hit her over some candy," Aram said. "What happened?"

From the bed Norah yelled, "You want to know what happened. I'll tell you what happened! I licked the Nazis' pots! That's what happened! And do you think that I cared about anyone else starving around me? Not a bit! Just like *her*," she said. "I took the last drop of soup, turned my head the other way and said, 'Poor Jews, they are so hungry! Look what is happening to them!' And 'them' was *me*! But I didn't have to die in the mud pit, making bricks. I was in the kitchen, cooking for the camp commander. And how did I get to be so lucky? *Because of a piece of candy—you understand?* I owe my life to one miserable piece of hard candy wrapped in colored cellophane."

"I understand, Norah," Aram said and sat down on the bed next to her.

"He wanted to celebrate Christmas '44 with the Jews," Norah sobbed. "He kept us waiting in the cold to give us candies."

"I understand, Norah, I understand," Aram said.

"No! You don't understand! He watched while a soldier gave each of us a candy. When my turn arrived, I couldn't stick out my hand. '*Danke schön*,' I said. The soldier looked at me with disgust, then turned to his superior. 'I have to report that *eine Figure*, a number here, refuses the candy, *mein Kommandant*.' When all the candies were distributed, the *Kommandant* wished everyone a Merry Christmas and ordered me to report to his office. 'How stupid can I be?' I thought. 'He will deny my food ration for disobeying.' Whipping was the punishment I feared most, and suddenly something snapped in my mind. What I saw and where I was didn't match. I saw guards, dogs, barbed wire, people in uniforms, barracks, watch towers, everything in its right place, perfectly displayed in the mud, like cows in the meadow or trees on a hill. Like a scene from a folk painting—a Nazi version of the Jewish Garden of Paradise."

Norah stopped to drink some water. She drank it with such thirst that her throat made a convulsive sound when she swallowed.

"It was beautiful, the stillness felt eternal. I will take this image with me in death, I thought.

"I wasn't punished. I was sent to work in the kitchen. To him, not taking the candy meant not stealing his food. I never ate a candy after that. I didn't want to eat it even now. I wanted to keep my savior in my hand. I feel that as long as I have this candy nothing bad can happen to me."

"Just take another one and use your wrapping—they all taste the same," Clara said softly.

"It's over," Aram said. "I don't see the reason for your guilt. You didn't kill anyone. You didn't steal from anyone. You didn't denounce anyone. So forget it, Norah, I can get you candies from the Party's shop."

"Norah," Mendel said, "don't fall into that trap. We've all done things that make us feel ashamed; things that we would never do now. But we were *there*. And *there*, there was no moral code. There is no lucky candy, Norah. There is only survival, and this is an instinct that you should never judge."

"It was the candy with the beautiful wedding. It was the only one I wanted."

"It seems to me that it is about the wedding, not the candy," Aram said, "don't you think, Clara?"

"I know you don't want to know how I survived," Clara said in an angry tone, "even if you ask yourselves this question each time you see me. We know better than to ask questions, don't we? I am reminding you of you, as you are reminding me of me.

"Should I tell you about the famous Russian clown who performed under Nazi rifles in his circus costume? And I don't have to tell you who he was making laugh with his big nose and funny makeup. The famished, scared children, in line to enter the gas chambers! Letting the Jewish children laugh before their death was a gift, a nice thing to do! Uncle Fritz taking the children to the circus! And what did I do? I sang '*O mein liebe Augustin*'! The clown was crying under his makeup, making amusing gestures till the very end, and the children were clapping their hands, applauding the arrival of their death. He was killed after them. But I wasn't. I amused them. I sang their Nazi songs. I sang with passion. My eyes joined theirs. My face, my body, my arms and hands welcomed their requests. I smiled at them as if I were singing for an audition at the opera in Paris. The role I was auditioning for was called 'Life.' I performed to the delight of whoever wanted to hear the lovely sound of German music—'*Wie einst, Lili Marlene,*' I sang, and the soldiers cried. Sometimes the sentimental ones left food in front of me.

"And you don't know what it means to be afraid and to sing. You can't imagine the sacrifice. How can you sing about love when you are about to lose your life? There is no voice then. But I forced myself to separate from the words and from the place, and I was an abject human being in an abject situation. I did nothing that is worth living for, believe me."

As I grew up, my relationship with my mother became more and more distant, until she ignored me completely. Clara bought my clothes, corrected my homework, and took care of me. It was only on my birthdays that Norah ever displayed some affection, at least in her tone of voice. Even then she reminded everyone how difficult her pregnancy had been. Year after year she would offer me the same gift: the promise of a trip to Paris when the visa came. I saved money to buy my own gifts. I made up stories about her life. I described her to my friends as an eccentric artist, a woman of culture and authority, a priest's daughter who informed the Party of her father's illegal religious activities, an orphan raised by a gypsy fortune-teller, an opera singer who lost her voice, a certified lunatic, a nasty stepmother.

During those years Norah became obsessed with designing funerary monuments for her parents. She made hundreds of drawings and several clay models. "They are not dead," she corrected me one day. "They are departed."

Aram wrote more books and developed a new economic plan, basing its success on the promise of everyone's being employed. The doctrines of the reactionary financial bourgeoisie were abandoned. Theoretically there was no unemployment in the country. Everybody worked for the state, and everybody was the state. There was no fierce competition. The price of labor was kept stable. Our economy was a success. In his statistics, Aram did not take into account the millions who were in jail or in forced labor colonies, nor did he count the hundreds of thousands of professionals sent to work in fields or in factories as punishment for their bourgeois education, upbringing, or convictions. From his job at the university, Aram received a medal. He was an asset to the country. A loyal Jew saved from death by the Communists.

Over the years Aram fell in love often and brought every one of his loves home to meet the family. If any had a husband or children, they, too, were included. Aram fell in love with the passion of a teenager amazed at discovering his own desires. It was clear to everybody that he had to make an effort not to shout, *I am in love! Look at me! I am capable of loving. Aren't you happy for me?* His love for other women was a gift to Norah, an emotion he wanted to share with her. "Norah, this is wonderful," he wanted to say. "Falling in love is an extraordinary experience. Everything— time, light, colors, smells, even words, everything, including yourself—is different when you are in love."

We all understood that Aram fell in love to escape his numbness. Being in love was his connection with life—a private way of warding off his past.

Every time it happened, Norah would regress into the world of superstitions. In secret, she would knot one of Aram's socks around the leg of a chair "to hold him at home." She would put a strand of pubic hair on the other woman's coat to bring her bad luck. "To make a man love you," she told Clara, "put a drop of your menstrual blood in his food."

"If you don't stop this," Clara finally told her, "you will soon join the group of single women; you know—the widows, the divorced, the abandoned. You are alive. That's what counts."

"You mean I should accept everything just because I am alive? What would you do if Mendel brought home a mistress?"

"Norah," Clara said, "they are not mistresses. His love is melancholic, desperate, impossible, and platonic. He is looking for intimacy, not for love. Except Alisa, every woman he brought here was married."

"I can't even divorce. The Party won't let me—divorce is reactionary."

"Listen, from what I understand, his mother was never there. The only woman close to him was his sister. And he is trying to find her again."

"But now he has a wife—isn't that enough? He should protect *me*, and stop the nonsense of falling in love."

My father had a passion for topographical maps and mountain guide books. He studied them in detail. He knew all the lakes, remembered the names of the guides, and knew the location of cabins for refuge in case the weather turned. From him I learned to use my sense of orientation. I can find my way in any city, no matter how complex.

Every year my father organized long hikes in the mountains. All of us, along with all our friends and his present and former mistresses—including their husbands, children, friends, and relatives—some forty people, would climb the mountains in the summer for several weeks. Every year more people joined this group. He probably could have crossed the border illegally with the entire group, but that would have only brought us to a different Communist country. It wasn't worth it.

"There is only desperation in his mountain trips," my mother told Clara.

"It is a sort of pilgrimage. Every year he is crossing the mountains to take us to Hanah's Paradise. Just accept it, Norah."

SALOMEIA

When I was a child my father used to tell me stories from Hanah's Paradise, stories that he knew from his father—my grandfather Rafa'el. They were about remote cousins who traveled the world to go to Hanah's Paradise. When he knew the language, my father recounted the cousins' tales in their own native tongues, to make me aware of the ways different languages sound. I learned my love of languages from him. When the time arrived for me to go to university, my father encouraged me to study languages and literature.

My mother had a different idea. "No. Jews study science. Science doesn't have to conform to the Party. Mathematicians are not arrested, whereas journalists, writers, and translators are."

But I wanted to study architecture. It offered the promise of change. There was only one type of housing in the entire country, designed by Soviet planners. As far as the eye could see, dilapidated ten-story reinforced-concrete buildings provided shelter for the working class. They were the same everywhere. The only difference between the buildings was the number on the entrance door. If I couldn't change my life, I could at least dream about new cities.

To attend the university, one faced a fierce competition for the very few seats allowed by the Party according to the country's needs. My admission to the Institute of Architecture came as a surprise to everyone. I didn't have the right social origin, my parents were foreigners, and I didn't draw particularly well. I was accepted because of my imagination. My simplistic drawings were whimsical and caught the eyes of the professors. The drawing board became a universe under my total control. I could imagine and draw ideal cities for ideal governments. Life on paper rewarded me with the freedom that was missing from life on the streets.

When a group of French journalists visited the Institute, I was asked to show them around. The journalists, five men in their thirties, marveled at my language skills, taught me slang words, and gave me books, records, and French chocolates. I was in love with all of them. They showed me their passports; I had never seen one before. They had visas and could come and go as they liked. They could say what they thought. They were free.

The journalists invited me to travel with them and, lying, I assured my parents that I had received permission to do so from the Institute. There were rooms available for them in every hotel; Romanian travelers slept on benches at the train station. There was food in every restaurant we entered; Romanians had to wait in line for rationed bread. The French could buy gas for their car, but Romanians couldn't buy heating oil. I had never stayed in a hotel before. I had never been to a restaurant. These were new experiences that none of my friends had ever had. Those places were only for the Russians, not for us.

Wherever I went with the French visitors, people looked surprised. It was rare for Romanians to see foreigners in the streets, other than Russian military. Approaching foreigners was punishable by imprisonment. The French were easily recognizable. For one thing they wore clothes in colors other than dark blue. Their shoes were made of real leather. They also spoke out loud. Sometimes a courageous citizen would look around to be sure that no one was watching, then quickly shake hands with one of the Frenchmen. *"Bonjour, vive la France!"* he would say and feel dignified. Everyone loved the Frenchmen and wanted to touch them, as if something from their free country might rub off on the miserable Romanians in their blue Party coats and rubber boots.

The Frenchmen were revered. One night our car knocked down an elderly woman walking along the road. It was the driver's fault. He had failed to see her. At night the unlit roads, full of potholes, teemed with animals, people walking or on bicycles, tractors, and horse-drawn carts driving without lights. The woman was only slightly injured and asked the Frenchmen to forgive her for being in their way. People gathered. A man pushed her around and called her names. *"Timpito,* idiot," he said to her, "death is looking for you at home, and you walk along the road in the middle of the night like the plague. *Du-te dracului acasa, baba nebuna!* Get the hell home, you old fool!" The woman looked apologetic.

The French journalists could not understand. It was their fault and they offered to take her to the hospital. "Let's be serious, Mister Frenchman. She should kiss your hand, *dobitoaca,* the animal," a man said, raising his hand to hit her, the way one does to get rid of a cow. "Go to hell, *putuareo,* lazy whore! *Scroafa batrina,* old swine," he yelled. The woman flinched in anticipation of the blow and limped aside, holding her shoulder. The man turned his attention to the Frenchmen, gesturing for some cigarettes. "Don't you have some of your type of cigarettes, the kind that smell good, since our tobacco . . ." He left the sentence in the air. The Frenchmen gave him a pack of cigarettes, then stuffed some money and a piece of soap into the woman's hands. As we left, she waved to us, smiling and holding the soap to her breast. Why did I feel ashamed? "Dignity is not a quality to be acquired under oppression," one of my new friends said.

In meeting the French journalists I understood that life was not the same everywhere. My experience confirmed that the criticism and propaganda learned at school were false. Freedom of speech was not a bourgeois attitude but a right that, until then, I didn't know one could have. But my journalist friends had to leave in a rush. Students in Paris had taken over the streets.

Their departure left me disoriented. I missed their vivid descriptions of life on the other side. But with them in mind, I could now look at the empty food stalls at the market and fill them with descriptions of bounty at the market in Aix. I could look at a bleak apartment and see Le Corbusier's open-plan Villa Savoye. I could walk in the mud of the unlit streets of Bucharest and see the Champs-Elysées. *Vive la France*—and me, too, because I understood that to obey means to lose.

Three months later, just before my sixteenth birthday, a policeman in civilian clothes rang our bell and asked to talk to me. Mendel let him in. I was doing my homework in the kitchen. The man identified himself, asked if I was Salomeia Ravea, then requested that I follow him to the police station to answer some questions.

"She is a minor," Mendel said. "I will come with her."

"No, that will not be necessary," the plainclothes officer said.

Outside, a black Russian car with yellow curtains covering the back and side windows was waiting for us. After a short drive, we arrived at police headquarters, where another officer in a gray uniform showed me into a room.

The officer pointed to a desk and put in front of me several pages ripped from a school notebook. "You have been traveling with some French journalists. We need to know from you the exact details of what they did, where they went, whom they met, and what was talked about. Sit down here and write everything. When you finish, I'll read your declaration. Then you can go."

"They didn't meet anyone. Some people approached them but they only said hello."

"Just write everything in detail." The officer left.

It was a small room that looked out onto a courtyard. A political map of the world covered one wall. "Learning is the Mother of Knowledge," a quotation from Lenin, was written in red letters above the door. I looked around for a while, then sat at the desk and began writing.

At the request of our dean, I showed our French guests the projects designed by our Institute of Architecture. They commented on the progress made in our country in developing new techniques of construction with reinforced concrete to build large, spacious, and adequate houses for our working class. Since our French guests didn't speak Romanian I was asked to travel with them for a week. They were grateful to our dean for allowing me to translate for them. We went to visit many of the world-renowned treasures of our glorious past. Our honored guests commented on the political awareness, and the commitment to world peace, of our working class. Weapons such as lances, bows-and-arrows, and hatchets were erased from the former saints' hands in all the medieval church frescoes that we saw. In some monasteries, these have already been replaced with the hammer and sickle. The other comment that I recall was about the halos around the heads of former saints. In the fight against bigotry, the halos had been removed from paintings, mosaics, and sculptures. Our honorable guests were very pleased to see the progress of the former saints, who, thanks to the lessons of our glorious Party and to the teachings of Marxism-Leninism, looked like normal citizens, ready to build Socialism.

Except for a visit to the Memorial of the Unknown Soldier, where they spoke with a couple and their children, the only other conversation that I can recall was when an old woman walking on the road inadvertently hit the car in which our honored guests were traveling. Comrades from the village arrived immediately to reprimand the woman. They welcomed our honored guests with bread and salt. The discussions on the road were mostly about the rapid progress made by our country, moving from an agrarian, feudal system of exploitation to a progressive Marxist economy in which the Party asks from everybody whatever they are able to give while giving back to them according to their needs. I personally discussed many questions of linguistics, learning from our honored guests a vocabulary that better describes our country's fight for progress and peace. I gave the dean a list of gifts I received from our honored guests. This statement is true and signed by me, Salomeia Ravea.

My declaration was made up of sentences learned in school, heard on the radio, and written in newspapers.

The officer returned, stood on the other side of the metal desk, and read my confession. I felt as though an enormous clamp was holding every muscle of my face.

"Do you belong to the Communist Youth Party?" he asked.

"No, I wasn't selected yet." I said the words very fast, trying to get rid of them and to retreat into the silence of my fear.

"Were you a Pioneer in high school?"

Not able to talk, I nodded my head.

"And who taught you how to lie?"

His question took me by surprise.

"Why don't you write your story again, and this time tell us the truth."

I revised my confession.

I have traveled with French journalists, who I now understand are enemies of our country. They accused us of vandalism when they saw the painted-over frescoes of the old churches. They complained about our roads and commented negatively on our working class when they saw women doing heavy work—digging on construction sites. I tried to contradict them but they didn't believe me. I am sorry if I ever said anything that could compromise anybody because whatever I said was words that they put into my mouth. I did not have any subversive discussions with the French on any subject. The French insisted on coming to my family's house and I couldn't refuse. I lied to my parents, assuring them that I had permission from the Institute. At our house they drank tea and admired our collection of Russian books. I am a good student and I love my country, and from my soul I ask the Party to forgive me if I made any mistakes. Except for a minor accident on the road, the French didn't meet with anyone in my presence. They just criticized everything because that is how the French are.

The officer returned, read the second confession, and said, "You were asked to show them around the Institute. You were not permited to go with them to restaurants and hotels. You were not allowed to travel with them."

"I was reluctant to go with them but the French visitors asked our political commissar to approve the travel. They needed me to translate for them. They told me that their request was granted."

"It is a crime to have private conversations with nationals from capitalist countries. It is a crime to lie to the Party. Stay here until I return, and I will tell you what will happen next."

When he left the room, the fear that had been with me all day reached full force. The realization that I could be arrested and put in jail left me in shock. I wanted to cry, but I couldn't. Instead, I drew on a piece of paper a garden that in my imagination was Hanah's Paradise.

Late in the night, Aram came for me. He was allowed to take me home but was asked to return the next day to sign papers for me since I was still a minor. On the tramway I fell asleep.

The next day Mendel and Aram returned to the police station. They were allowed to speak with an officer.

"*Tovarasi*, Comrades, your daughter traveled in the country without a permit. She had contact with foreign nationals. She received gifts from them. She lied that there is no heat and no food in our country. She lied about the workers and engaged in anti-Communist defamations. For slandering the government of the people, she will be judged by the People's Court. Until then she is under house arrest."

When Aram arrived home I was alone in the kitchen. He sat down and very calmly explained the consequences of my betrayal. "You lied to me. You said that several students and teachers from the Institute had permission to travel with the French visitors when, in fact, you went alone. You also lied to us when you brought them home. You told us that you had permission, which you didn't. You will be punished!"

Aram stood up, took off his leather belt, and began swinging it at me. His lips a quivering line of rage, his eyes nearly shut, he pushed me into a corner.

Stuck between the table and the wall, I dove under the table, barely avoiding the first blow. Aram struck the edge of the table with his belt, not uttering a word. No insults, no screaming, just lashing away blindly. He was delivering blows without asking himself to feel what it was like to inflict pain.

The table, a four-legged pinewood epitome of Socialist simplicity, was very sturdy. But the sound of the belt repeatedly hitting the wood amplified my terror. Could he break the table? Would he bend down and pull me out? I crouched under the table. When I heard Mendel at the door, I screamed for help.

Mendel stormed in as Aram was lashing at the table.

"What's going on?" He tried to stop my father, but Aram pushed him into the wall. Mendel rebounded, then, without any warning, slapped Aram hard in the face. "*Figur, du lass das, verstanden? Du lass das!* Number, you stop that, you understand? Stop it!" Aram recoiled, dropping the belt on the floor. I crawled out from under the table. "Get out," Mendel yelled at me. I glanced at Aram before bolting to the terrace. He was gazing at Mendel in a stupor.

I went outside but stayed near the door, watching them through the glass. Aram looked at his hands for a moment, then fixed his eyes on the belt at his feet. Mendel shoved him brutally onto a chair, slapped him again, and yelled, "*Raus, du Schwein*, Out of here, you pig!"

Aram buried his head in his hands and started crying. "Forgive me, please," he begged, his voice quivering. "Don't hit me, don't hit me." Mendel noticed me at the door and yelled, "Leave!" I moved back.

"Talk," Mendel shouted, "talk, you shameless pig, you clown!"

"I don't have the strength," Aram said between sobs. "And anything I say would only be a parody of reality."

"Talk," Mendel shouted again, walking back and forth in the kitchen. Carefully, controlling his words, Aram started to talk.

"What can I tell you? I was hungry. I was humiliated. Yes, those are the words. Do they render anything of the absurdity of life in the Nazi camp? Can I speak the language of that misery? Does terror have a name? Whatever I say is fated to be incomplete. Any attempt to reconstruct my story would be a useless, grotesque spectacle. What can I say to Meia? That I used to be a dangerous microbe named *Jew*? That to protect the world from these germs, the Nazis tried to kill them all? That her father and mother and some of their friends survived? Would this help Meia understand what it was like? Suicide would say it best."

"Listen," Mendel said angrily, "don't ask for pity—I was there too! I looked above the gates and the barbed wire and I thought about freedom—a dream borrowed from the dead by the living. Only death was freedom. Every day was an eternity. It could have ended at any time. 'Never' was what we called 'tomorrow.' And you, you took me back there. You repeated what you learned from them. I saw your look when you were hitting the table. You are cruel. You are still attached to the Nazis and to your pain."

"What do you want me to do, Mendel?" Aram said, calmer now. "I was not even fifteen when I was sent to the camp. My life has meaning only in pain. This is what the Nazis did to me—and to Meia also. Talking about the horror would be an act of voyeurism."

"Aram, none of us can forget! The effort is trying not to remember. I am constantly purging my brain of unbearable scenes. Can I say it was horrible? Everyone knows that. Can I say that although the Nazis were savage brutes, if you were compliant and worked hard, if you had a little wisdom—and if you were lucky—you survived? But wouldn't saying that make the horror tolerable? And when horror becomes tolerable it enters into our habits and very soon is part of our life. If I accept terror as an attribute of civilization, I will no longer be able to be indignant at any injustice. But if I don't accept it, the only place for me to live is death. So I have invented an intellectual, esoteric order to stay alive. Translating words from one language into another is giving life to death. I am killing a word in one language to give it life in a new one. It is my way of being exiled from my feelings. This is why I cannot write. I published four books of poetry before the camp but returned without words. Is my life now a dream? I ask this question every day."

I wanted to come back into the kitchen, but when Mendel saw me near the door again, he shook his head. I stepped back and sat on the terrace floor with my back to the wall, holding my knees in my arms. I could hear Mendel preparing tea.

"People like us," Mendel said, "are the result of a dilemma. Life is the leftover of death. We know this intimately. Death is normal, life is the surprise."

"I don't know how to name the impossible," Aram said, still crying. "Every day we walked the four kilometers from the camp to the factory. As I walked, I tried to find something to hold on to, the morning light falling on a tree, a stone with a funny shape, a broken branch, a bend in the road! It kept me human. In my mind I was walking to Hanah's Paradise to meet my father, not to the camp to meet death. *I am getting closer,* I would say to myself. A detail of some sort was enough to make me believe that I was walking each day on a different road. 'Look,' I would say, 'today I walked more than yesterday. There is a village at the end of the road, and I will spend the night there.'

"I walked, I worked, and I pretended not to be there. We walked in rows of three. Walking in line with me were two brothers from Moldavia. We looked after each other. One day they escaped. My row was short two men. I was put in jail, guilty of not having reported them. They were found the next day walking in the vicinity of a different camp. They didn't know the area. When they were brought back, they were beaten, stripped naked, and even though they insisted that I hadn't known of their plan, we were locked in the same cell to await execution. We shared my prisoner's uniform to keep warm. 'What can you take from life when you go to death?' I asked myself. You can take only something that you don't have, something that defies reality, that stops time—anything that keeps the present longer. One of the brothers recalled a passage from a prayer. We translated it from Hebrew into French and Italian, into Hungarian and Spanish and Moldavian, and into every other bit of language that we knew.

> The Master of All,
> Took Abraham, our father,
> May he rest in peace, to His bosom,
> Kissed him on his head, and called him
> 'Abraham, my beloved.'

"I sang 'Verde Limon,' the song that Bilu wanted me to dance when she was here. In the morning, soldiers led us out from the cell. Three camp musicians walked in front of us, playing one of those uplifting Moldavian melodies. I looked at my naked friends walking in the cold. They had put their hands over their genitalia. It crossed my mind that death doesn't care to see them naked. They covered themselves in order not to offend the viewers. They were still human. Then I did the same thing. I put my hands on the same place over the prison uniform—as evidence that the Nazis were killing not a number but a human being. In the cen-

253

ter of the camp, the other inmate slaves were standing and watching, resenting us for keeping them in the cold. They knew their turn would also come. We climbed the execution platform and waited as a camp commander read our sentence. I couldn't figure out what he was saying. I just heard empty words: 'punishment,' 'hanged,' 'example for others'—and that is when I lost my mind. 'Verde Limon' was ringing in my ears, and without thinking, I started singing it with all the strength I could muster. The two brothers joined in, marking the rhythm with their feet. And I, demented as I was, waiting for my death, I began to dance the flamenco. You can imagine the scene: a skeleton in prison uniform dancing the flamenco under the noose of a rope, and two other naked men, skeletons just like him, singing 'Verde Limon.'

"The guards were laughing and slapping their hands on their thighs, looking at these rejects of humanity in their last bit of life. The musicians picked up the melody. What better way is there to isolate oneself from reality than by singing? The hundreds of other inmates looked on silently as I sang and danced the flamenco once, twice, three times. I couldn't see anything but the gray sky. I wasn't dancing to prolong my life. I was entering the world to come, dancing.

"A soldier wearing black leather gloves ordered the older brother to slip a noose over his brother's head. He refused. The German whipped him until he fell to the ground, then shot him. He then ordered me to slip the noose over my friend's head. I knew I could not do it. I felt the whip and heard the German scream, 'Pig! Do it, now!' Then I heard my father's voice saying, 'Shalom, Abraham, my beloved,' and I felt his hand touching the back of my head. My hands disobeyed my heart and slipped the noose over my friend's head. The whipping stopped. They let me live; my compensation for killing a man! I survived because I was young enough to learn cruelty, to became pitiless, to lie."

"Life is stronger than we are," Mendel said. "It sometimes makes decisions against us. You blame yourself for being alive! It is not you, Aram. It is Hitler who killed him. Hitler and all the Germans who believed in his madness and helped him achieve it!"

"How can I tell Meia what I have done? Could she hate me less than I hate myself? How could I have gone to Hanah's Paradise and looked into my father's eyes?"

"You are angry at historical events that transformed your life into a nightmare, Aram."

"But my life is full of deceptions. Do I really want to build Socialism? Did we return from concentration camps looking forward to life, embracing it with joy? The answer is no! This is where the lie is. There is no returning from the camp, Mendel. Ever!"

"There is no escape, Aram, but we survived. This is essential. We don't have a future or a present. Only Meia does."

SALOMEIA'S FUTURE

Until my case was judged, I stayed inside the house, translating for Mendel. The decision arrived by mail. In observance of the government's policy, political enemies of the Party were stripped of their rights. No education, no food coupons, no identity card, no right to travel in the country, restricted to live in a void, not included in any statistics. They were nonpeople. If another country offered them asylum, they could leave, joining the exodus of intellectuals and artists in exile from dictatorial countries. If not, they were sent into a restricted area in the swamps of the Danube delta. This mosquito-infected area was the forced residence for all political prisoners.

I was given ten days to leave, if I could obtain an entry visa to another country.

"Israel," Clara said, with her common sense, "we have to ask for a visa to Israel."

"They need people with skills there," Aram said, "and she has no skills."

"She is Jewish, and she will get her skills there," Norah said.

"How is she Jewish?" Mendel asked. "She doesn't know the culture, she doesn't know the traditions, she doesn't speak Hebrew—how is she Jewish?"

"She just is," Norah answered, "and that's enough. There is no other alternative."

Mendel took me to the Israeli agency, a small office opened with the hope of future diplomatic relations. An Israeli man wearing a kipa brought us into a small windowless office. He gestured to us to sit, then turned up the volume on his radio. "Microphones," he wrote on a piece of paper.

Mendel showed him the letter from the tribunal. "She has nine more days," he wrote.

"Your parents are Jewish?" he wrote back, passing the paper to me.

"Yes," I nodded.

"Who do you have in Israel?"

"My grandfather, my aunts, my cousins. Everyone is there at Hanah's Paradise," I wrote.

He called somebody into the room, talked into his ear, then wrote down, "Okay. We are giving her an entry visa to Israel but she needs the exit visa from the police here. There is a plane only once a month. She can leave for Tel Aviv in two days, if she can obtain the exit visa."

Mendel started crying. He felt tremendous gratitude toward this man who accepted me and, because I was Jewish, let me into his country. The evidence was the name of my parents, not my religious beliefs. The name—this private identity, this unique way of knowing who I am—would take me to freedom, and Mendel was moved. But the same name had taken my father to a death camp. The name meant a different thing then, although the spelling hadn't changed.

The Israeli handed me a sheet of information and an airline voucher written in both Romanian and Hebrew and sent us on our way.

Back on the street, Mendel bought flowers from a gypsy girl, then took me to the park.

"I would like to tell you, Meia, that your parents care about you. Growing up with people like us makes you also see life in our way. We do not say it, but we are afraid of life. We are always in pain, sorry for ourselves, lost in memories we do not want to remember. Clara and her sister hid for several months in a secret concrete cubicle in the lower basement of her piano teacher's home. Until they were found and deported, every sound, every new voice, every step was a death sentence. For a year they were slaves in a factory. In the first days of 1945, as the Soviet Army approached, two thousand of the factory women were marched in the freezing cold from Poland to Czechoslovakia. Clara was among them.

When her sister couldn't walk anymore and was shot, Clara took her shoes and clothes, left her naked body in the snow, and kept moving. We are damaged people, Meia! We carry with us images that we want to forget and cannot. We have only one prayer: 'Please, God, help me believe that it was not true.' We are angry to be thankful for being alive, ashamed of having to be grateful to exist. You, too, have shared with us the horror of the unspeakable. It makes you different from other children. You grew up with the questions we brought back from death. Every day we confront the idea that we have to survive, only to say to ourselves, 'Survive for what?' From us you learned lies and strangled hopes."

ADIEU, BUCHAREST

My departure became the mirror of everyone's life, and their reactions to this event ruptured the seams of their well-sewn discourse. These four people who had lived their adult lives in a make-believe story, who tried to survive by faking a passion that in time they confused with reality, who had learned the language and customs of a geographical place that they were not attached to, who had made friends and lost friends—these four people were now confronted with the exit visa that, all along, they had denied they were waiting for. In an ironic twist, without even asking for it, I had everything my family could not obtain. I could leave the country. It did not seem to bother any of them that, at sixteen, I was entering a world for which I was not prepared. Just like Norah, Clara, Mendel, and Aram after the war, I, too, became a displaced person.

I returned my birth certificate and library card to the police. I presented the letter from the tribunal and requested an exit visa. The policeman looked at the papers, put them in front of Norah, and with a look of disappointment, showed us his empty hands. Norah understood. She took back the papers and slipped some money between the pages. Since paper clips were not available in the Marxist economy, she clipped everything together with a Chinese hairpin. Suddenly my exit visa was ready.

That night Norah put a small pillow and a yellow blanket into a brown cardboard box. It was what she had taken with her when the Jews of her little island were rounded up. Mendel gave me his

Russian pins collection. With great formality Clara handed me the gold bracelet. Aram gave me a small pocketknife.

I felt sorry for them. It was a new feeling, and I was afraid they would notice it. "Poor people," I thought. "They waited all these years for an exit visa, and I received it." Clara and Mendel felt happy for me. I was escaping Communism, and although the possibility of our being together again was very slim, they hoped that we would see each other again. Aram talked about his parents and siblings, and Norah drifted even more into magic, making sure that I learned from her the formula for seeing destiny.

To see your destiny:
Enter the house of a happy couple at midnight, and without saying even one word, go straight to the fireplace and remove some ashes from the hearth. Take the ashes to your house. Sit on the threshold with your back to the door, facing the world. Put the ashes in a sieve. Sift the ashes behind your back into a flat dish. Place a glass of water on the dish. Drop the wedding band of a loving husband into the glass of water. Keep your eyes on the ring. The face of your beloved will look back at you and your future will unfold.

On the day of my departure, Silvia joined us on the bus trip to the airport. Aram carried the cardboard box. Mendel sat next to me, taking advantage of our last moments together to explain the grammatical structure of Hebrew: "This is a very simple language. There are seven possible verbal constructions, all derived from three roots. From each of them, you can build a variety of verbs." Clara wrote down Mendel's comments. Silvia sat in front of us, eating roasted pumpkin seeds. Norah looked silently at the road, and Aram wrote a last-minute note to his father. They could not hide their tears. Even my mother, Norah! But why were they crying? Isn't this what they had always dreamed about for themselves? Couldn't they, for once, be happy for me? Were they crying for themselves for being left behind? They didn't seem to be anxious about my future. They were lost in their thoughts and their sadness. After today, I would remember them, I would miss them, and I hoped that I would be able to visit them, but our separation was definitive.

Rain was beating on the roof of the bus, and every so often mud would splash on the windows. The wind stole an oak leaf and slapped it with fury on the window next to me. The leaf—a yellow-red patch of fall—fluttered passionately against the window, then flew away, only to twist again and return to the same spot. It did this several times. Silvia, who had been watching the leaf, laughed.

At the airport, the departure lounge was closed. We waited in the corridor. Aram put the orange scarf around me. "Your grandfather will recognize you with this." Mendel took me aside and said, "You are a very courageous girl, and I will miss you." Silvia surprised me with a painting of our kitchen—no bigger than my hand. Everyone, including her, was sitting at the table. Clara held me in her arms until soldiers with dogs and machine guns came to escort passengers to the airplane. We embraced. Even Norah faked kissing me on the forehead, then wiped my face to clean it from her kiss. I made a turban from my father's orange scarf and left them in a hurry. I didn't want them to see how happy I was. "Adieu, Bucharest," I yelled from the tarmac. "Adieu, empty stores. Adieu, fear of speaking up. Adieu, propaganda, uniforms, shame of being Jewish, abuse of women, lack of human rights, desperation at being watched, fear to trust a friend, terror of your absurd police state. I am leaving everything here: my Russian books, my Pioneer uniform, my picture with Gagarin, my pain from discrimination, my resentment, my anger. Adieu."

18

From the airplane I could see in the distance *ir levana*, the white city of Tel Aviv. My curiosity left no room for apprehension. My life was starting now as we flew over the Mediterranean and over the streets of the city. Before the plane taxied to the gate, I moved to an empty seat at the very front. I wanted to be the first one to touch the ground.

When the airplane door opened, the heat took me by surprise. First one to leave the plane, I walked slowly down the metal stairs and across the hot asphalt of the tarmac. The sun was already setting and the velvet indigo-blue of the Tel Aviv sky was rapidly covering the horizon. The humid air of the Mediterranean left a film on my skin and filled my eyes with mist. The smell of lemon and jasmine, the shadows of the jacaranda trees, and the taste of salty air on my lips were welcoming. From a terrace, people were waving and I waved back at them. A welcome shout broke the humid evening air and a dance began on the terrace. This spontaneous joy was a gift to everyone arriving to Israel. Happiness could not be restrained! As we walked toward the airport building to meet our families, one of the arriving passengers started singing in the twilight:

> *Heyveynu Shalom Alechem*
> We will bring peace to you
> *Heyveynu Shalom Alechem*
> *Heyveynu Shalom Shalom Shalom Alechem.*

The airport was packed. On their fathers' shoulders, children held signs above their heads with the names of arriving relatives. Could one recognize a sister not seen for twenty years?

I entered the immigration booth with dread. What if they didn't let me into the country? But a female soldier, a little older than I, took me to an office, where I was given a temporary identity card. As we walked, she introduced herself. "Ronit," she said. She looked especially comfortable in her army uniform, a short straight skirt and a jacket. She carried a machine gun strapped on her shoulder with a gas mask dangling from it. She asked me questions about my life and my family, and with great deliberation drew on a piece of paper the letters for the word MIKLAT, "shelter," in Hebrew. "There is one in every street and in every house. When you hear the siren, you go there immediately and keep the mask on your face. This is important. Remember how this word looks, and wherever you go, always identify the shelter first so you'll know where to run should there be an attack. Keep the mask with you at all times, even when you go to sleep—especially then."

Ronit walked me through the building, and I admired her way of being: sure of herself, she exuded power. Several soldiers approached us, and when she stopped to talk with them, she introduced me. "This is Salomeia," she told them. "*Olah khadashah*, a newly arrived immigrant."

"*Shalom*," one of them said, "welcome," and I blushed. I had never felt so much love and so much confusion at the same time. The meaning of "soldier," a word that I knew only to fear and despise, changed. An epistemological shift took place. Israelis are citizen-soldiers, in an army of defense. It is their way of life. Their reality is neither imaginary nor symbolic. It represents the asymmetrical exploitation of a present with an uncertain future. Gas masks and machine guns are as matter-of-fact as umbrellas and hats are to people in a tropical climate. I was enthralled with the Israeli soldiers and Ronit had to pull me away from the group. I walked holding her arm, my head turned toward them. After several corridors, stairways, and escalators, she led me to the terrace of the arrival hall.

I stayed near the door, uncertain of what to expect. A young man in a military uniform caught my eye and shouted my name, "Salomeia?" I nodded. He motioned to me and shouted my name again. A large group of people walked in my direction. The entire family was there to receive Aram's daughter! I was passed from arm to arm, kissed on my hair, my lips, my cheeks. I was pulled to meet an older woman; I was shown a newborn baby. Children ran around me as flowers and bags of fruit were thrust into my arms.

A tall man came toward me. "She's here, she's here," people shouted and moved out of his way to let him pass. He walked slowly, carrying an ivory cane with a silver top. He used it as a mark of distinction, not support. A black cape over his shoulders and an embroidered Arab shirt distinguished him from the mass of people waiting on the terrace of Ben Gurion Airport.

Grandpa Rafa'el stood in front of me. He was taller than my father. He took my hand, put it on his heart, looked deep into my eyes, then took me into his arms. We stood there as other arms covered our bodies and shared the tears of our embrace. When we were able to separate ourselves from the others, he kept moving with me between aunts, uncles, and the wives and children of cousins. Aram's younger brother, my uncle Oded, had the jovial face of a man made of smiles and pleasure, along with the remoteness that Aram and everyone else in the family seemed to have, including me.

Around me, words in Hebrew, Ladino, Greek, French, Spanish, German, English, Portuguese, Italian, Hungarian, Russian, Hindu, and Farsi jostled together in every sentence. In this linguistically fragmented world, when somebody made a joke, people would laugh in waves, as the translation made its way to them. I could understand a word here and there, but I couldn't make sense of their laughter. I could not answer their questions. The three-hour flight had taken me out of a world that had no meaning for them. How was I related to this cousin? Whose child was holding my hand, and why were they all talking at the same time? I was drunk with the present. When the Yemenite cousins spread a blanket on the floor and lit a fire to make tea, the airport security moved us outside.

On the drive to Grandpa's house, we passed through Tel Aviv and the old port of Jaffa. A mixture of white Bauhaus buildings and domed Arab houses surrounded a market. Meats, clothing, and mountains of fruits that I had never seen before were being sold in the street. Large trees with blue and red flowers shadowed the city. Neon signs gave the early evening a festive air. It was the first time I had ever seen a palm tree.

RAFA'EL

My grandfather lived in one of the houses built by his great-grandfather at Hanah's Paradise. It had three wings to accommodate the large family. Thick walls enclosed an octagonal courtyard, where orange trees grew in large pots. Inside the house, arched doors separated the rooms, and from small skylights in the domed ceilings, the daylight gave objects a crisp blue cast. The walls were covered with small ceramic tiles decorated with geometric and floral motifs. Turkish and Arabic rosewood furniture occupied the hallway and the living room. I was given my cousin Ruth's former bedroom. It opened onto a gallery overlooking the reception hall, a large space between four columns. The stone floor was covered with rugs. Flower pots, pillows, and small tables were displayed along the walls. Light streaming through intricate wooden screens played on the whitewashed walls. Could happiness be measured in shades of light, in the number of orange trees in one's garden, in the intricacy of floor patterns? Could freedom be learned from the anxiety of having so many choices? Freedom was complex. I felt the guilt of abundance. I felt sorry for my past. I felt sorry for my father and my Aunt Bilu. They would never see this place.

My grandfather looked after me as I tried to understand the reality of my new life in Israel. Visitors stopped by every day, but since I spoke Hebrew hesitantly, I was often left out of their conversations. A kind of comic opera would take place in front of me, with me as the supporting witness. People would come and go, deliver packages, ask for a sandwich, throw their keys on the table, use the phone, take naps, answer questions, offer advice—and then leave. All of them were my family. Their interactions with me were reduced to two questions, for which nobody ever waited for an answer: *"Ma hadash?* What's new?" and *"Ma nishmah?* How are you doing?" By the time I had found the words to answer, they were gone.

On the weekends, my Grandpa taught me Hebrew and showed me how to sort the records belonging to my family at Hanah's Paradise. He liked to sit in the garden on a square Egyptian chair, holding his hands on the silver top of his cane. He could stay like that for hours, moving one hand or the other to lift his cup of coffee. Grandpa had elegant hands. They were bony and energetic. They were the hands of a musician. On the third finger of his left hand he wore a heavy silver ring. It was a gift from his best friend, Sinan.

"You speak Hebrew now, Salomeia," he said one day; "you have made friends, you are going to the university. What do you think about us and about life here?"

"I still don't know yet, Grandpa. I love it here," I said without hesitation. "I love the things that for you are ordinary: the streets, the markets, the colors, the smells, the abundance! When I walk, I still keep turning my head back, looking at the window of the last shop."

"I know, Salomeia. This is how we recognize the immigrants. The shock of seeing such abundance gives them a radiant smile. They are lightheaded. They immediately learn two magic sentences in Hebrew: *'Eifo kanita*, Where did you buy it?' and *'Ve kama ze ole*, How much did it cost?'"

"Well, there is everything here, and nobody is waiting in line. But from what I have seen, there is not a moment of quiet in Israel, Grandpa. Everyone has opinions and asks for yours only to reject them."

"Unity, Salomeia, is not an existential requirement. We are a very confused people, very confused! The orthodox Jews live here, considering themselves a community in exile. They don't recognize the State of Israel. They don't recognize as a Jew anyone who is not deeply religious, not even the Holocaust survivors—once destined for extermination. This is one type of madness. Then there are the survivors of pogroms, of Stalin's and Hitler's outrageous raping of Europe. Some of them have gone totally mad, while others are bitterly angry. The new immigrants are also confused. For years they dreamed about Israel, and now that they're here, they miss their old country. They still speak in the language of the people who kicked them out. They cook the foods of the lands where their families were decimated. They talk for hours about the taste of a pickle or the aroma of marmalade 'from there.' For five thousand years they were punished for being Jewish. They returned to the land of their prayers as Poles or Hungarians. They do not intermarry with Jews from Romania because they lost Transylvania to the Romanians in 1918. The Bulgarians also lost territory to the Romanians, so they hate each other. The Russians are despised; they did not fight Stalin and Communism. These complex connections between people become pretexts for all kinds of feuds. Russian cousins have German cousins, who have Polish cousins, who have Turkish cousins, who have French wives and children born in Canada. The society is split into small communities of people living in their own enclaves. All those confused Jews join forces, only to hate the Arabs. I, too, have trouble understanding it all."

"But, Grandpa, the immigrants are committed to unity! It is just that we are faced with a question for which there is no answer. If our lives have been so different for five thousand years—and what we have in common is only an unfortunate past—what makes us alike? Mysticism? How can a Jew from Casablanca relate to one from Vienna?"

"But if for five thousand years they prayed to be 'next year in Jerusalem,'" Grandpa said, laughing, "then why is it that once they arrive here they want to move to America?"

"Maybe they don't like Jerusalem," I said. We both laughed.

"That is impossible. Jerusalem is special. People walk around the city in awe, expecting something extraordinary to happen."

"Is it magic?"

"The magic, Salomeia, is the light. It gives a mystical yellow cast to the sky and to the city's white stone buildings. Night descends early and fast, and the low sky makes one feel closer to Heaven. In the Souk, steep stairways go from someplace to nowhere. Alleys end up in somebody's courtyard. After entering the Old City through one of the gates, you find yourself in the Jewish, Armenian, Moslem, or Christian Quarter, where the dress code, the language, and the food are distinctly different. The smell of spices, vegetables, manure; the dry, dusty air; the stones of the walls and the churches; the noise and madness of reality are almost a biblical vision. It obliges you to constantly look at the sky, to make sure that you are not missing the vision of God, who, in Jerusalem, comes very close to life. In Jerusalem one always looks up; and without noticing, this is what you will also do. There is nothing on Earth as magnificent as Jerusalem!"

"Not even Rome?"

"No comparison, Salomeia. And near the arch of Bab el Khalil, a friend of mine makes the best roasted pigeons in the Middle East. I will take you there."

Grandpa Rafa'el dedicated his time to me. He told me stories about Aram and Bilu and walked with me through Hanah's Paradise at different times of the day. He read me the inscriptions and described the connections between families. But a young girl who has escaped the dreary life of Communism does not want to think about the past. A young girl has time on her side, but this is something she cannot understand. What is time for somebody who has never learned to dream? Only now, as I am writing the story of my family, can I truly feel the love and the generosity of my grandfather.

"Salomeia," Grandpa said one evening when we were alone in the courtyard, "when you arrived here you were wearing an orange scarf. I would like to have it."

"You want the orange scarf? But it is faded and torn!"

"I want it because it belonged to Adah."

For me, my grandmother Adah was just another abstraction. I grew up knowing of her existence, but I had no connection with her except that piece of orange cloth my father had asked me to wear when I left.

Grandpa's eyes were on the sky. After a moment, softly, as if talking louder might disturb the stars, he said, "Your grandmother and I met at a Zionist meeting in Vienna in 1926. She wore the orange scarf around her shoulders and a large, ridiculous blue hat. She confronted a rabbi, and in response, he insulted her, but she fought back. She was incredible. She stood in the middle of the room, staring at him. Then, after a moment, she took off her hat. She had long orange hair, and it flew into the air, catching people's eyes. It was so extraordinary that an unimaginable wave of orange light swept the room. Everyone became silent. I was seated in the first row of the balcony and when I looked at her, a vision unfolded before my eyes. The downstairs became the Mediterranean; the balcony, a steep cliff, from where I could see the waves. From afar, a young girl threw me an orange. It came toward me, but as it reached the peak of its trajectory, it remained suspended in the sky, an orange dot between the yellow sand and the blue sky. I felt a surge of happiness and whispered, '*Mode ani*, thank you.' When

I looked back to the room, people were fighting. Adah was hitting an old rabbi."

Grandpa took a small ring from his pocket and put it in my hand.

"I gave this ring to Adah soon after we got married—the day after our wedding, in fact. I think you should have it now. It's a sapphire. I am giving it to you because you look so much like your grandmother, and I know she would have liked you to have it."

I wanted to show him my appreciation, but I had never experienced such feelings and was embarrassed. I said, "Thank you," and held the ring tight in my hand. I didn't know how to receive his gifts. I looked into Rafa'el's eyes, trying to hide how overwhelming his affection was for me. In the soft evening light, his eyes were almost green, and speckles of gold flickered on his face.

THE DAY OF REMEMBRANCE

Grandpa Rafa'el had an old French car, and he taught me how to drive. Whenever I was free from my classes at the university, we took turns driving to see family and friends. We went through Druze farms, Arab villages, new Israeli settlements, and Bedouin markets.

On the Day of Remembrance we left in the early morning for the old city of Safed, in Upper Galilee. It was a trip that Grandpa had often taken. He liked the sweeping views of Mount Meron along the way. Terraced fields of cedars, orange groves, and pine forests put Safed in an unsurpassed setting. In Talmudic times, a beacon of burning fire from Safed would herald the beginning of the new moon, but almost two thousand years had passed since then.

"Safed used to be a city of textiles and metaphysics, built around a citadel and many synagogues," Grandpa said. "Now it is a city of artists."

Walking between domed houses, taking in the view of the valley below, we wandered up and down narrow cobblestone alleys until we came to the main market. Windows, doors, and balconies were painted the turquoise-blue color of Heaven to protect the inhabitants from the evil eye—and also mosquitoes. The air was hot but dry, and the silvery leaves of the olive trees made the valley shimmer like water. On either side of the narrow, arched passageways of the artists' quarter, paintings were displayed on whitewashed walls.

At the old post office, an exhibition featured historical documents about the city. Two black-and-white documentaries played in a continuous loop. What made us stop to look at the screens was the uncommonly slow speed of the projection, and also the silence. There was no sound track. The slowness of the images gave the impression of enormous fatigue. Two people seemed to be talking, but they looked rigid, as if talking required all the strength they had. They were wearing prison uniforms, with blankets over their shoulders. What was most extraordinary was seeing their lifeless faces. Their lips were moving very slowly, forming soundless syllables on the screen. If you looked carefully, you could decipher their words: "Father? Is it you? You're alive?" It was the encounter of two men leaving a death camp after liberation. The movie was only a few minutes long.

The other film showed a group of prisoners walking on a bridge, looking indifferent to their surroundings. At the slow speed of the projection, we could see the individual particles of dust raised by the marching convoy. And there he is—frail, emaciated, his sunken eyes looking around, a piece of cloth wrapped around his head, like a turban. There is something familiar about this man; perhaps the dimple on his chin, or maybe his way of looking, as if searching for someone. He stops in front of the cameraman, looks straight into the lens, and his lips form words we cannot hear. Who is he? Where do I know him from?

I looked at Grandpa. His face had lost its contour. It had become a white mask with hollow eyes and only a sliver of an opening for the mouth. He bent his head toward me, put his hand on my shoulder, and said, "This is Aram—I am sure it's him!" His voice broke, and I started to cry.

I took Grandpa's hand and squeezed it. "It can't be," I said.

We watched the movie again and again. When his face appeared on the screen, we followed his lips. It was him. "Bilu, I am alive," he is saying, "I have the scarf," and with his hand he touches the rag on his head. "I am going home to Hanah's Paradise." It was my father, for sure. When he talked, his eyebrows arched and the scar on his forehead appeared between the wrinkles.

His words were pounding in my head, his face was haunting. "My God," I said out loud, "I have to leave. I'll meet you later."

I ran down the crooked main street of Safed. When I lost my breath, I sat down. The stone felt cold. I sat for a long time, staring in front of me, until my father's face appeared, projected on the wall. I saw his lips forming the syllables: *Bi-Lu*. I saw my father walking home. I saw him running alongside the train, holding Bilu's hand. I saw him reading me stories. I saw him at the meeting when he received the Communist red card. I saw him crying in the kitchen when Mendel slapped him. "This is my father, Aram!" I screamed at the wall and threw a stone against it. "Let his pain, and mine, be remembered."

Grandpa was waiting for me at the bottom of a narrow street leading down into the old Jewish Quarter. He motioned for me to sit on the bench next to him. The sun was setting over the mountains of Lebanon. In the distance I could see the Sea of Galilee, dazzling in the last sliver of sun. Safed was turning dark beneath the velvet indigo sky.

Grandpa sat, his hands resting on the cane one over the other, his long fingers moving slightly. "I have looked for Aram and Bilu in every document, in every movie, in every photograph. Always! And this is the first time I have seen my son in over thirty years. He was not even ten when we left him in Budapest.

"We knew that he was arrested, that my father-in-law, Anton, died, but we didn't know anything about Bilu and Julia in the Soviet Union. Then, for three years, until 1945, when Aram sent a cable, we didn't know if they were alive or dead. We had no other communication with them until 1958. Somebody smuggled out some photographs with a letter from him, and we learned about Bilu in Moscow, and about Tania and you. Aram was forbidden to contact us and asked us not to write him again. He renounced his own father. It was a letter of tremendous pain."

When I told my grandfather that I wanted to go back to see my parents, he objected. But I needed to talk to my father. I wanted to put together the hidden fragments of his life, and to free myself from his silence and pain. Grandpa was afraid that I would not be able to return and that he would lose me.

19

Bucharest was being terrorized by packs of wild dogs roaming the streets. People carried sticks and walked only in groups. The fireman assigned to protect Silvia from the dogs was severely bitten. After that, she could no longer work in the park. She stayed home and again painted portraits of saints. Beggars and abandoned children controlled the city. The unlit streets were piled with garbage, water ran for only two hours every other day, and electricity was cut off every evening at seven. There was a lack of food and a lack of hope. No aspirin, no soap.

Every friend, every neighbor, every teacher from my school came to visit. "I heard that Meia is here," someone would say, opening the door. They came to ask for favors. Could I send them medicine, glasses, dental instruments, needles for sewing machines, food, clothes, and books? As deprived as they were, they waited for the bus, spent the money for the ticket, and came to visit with me, always bringing a gift. Generous and loving, they came to dream. For an afternoon they could identify with me and delight in the descriptions of the cities I had visited, the people I had encountered, the colors, the smells, and the feeling of living in Israel. They smiled with sadness when they talked about themselves and asked whether I could find sugar and meat there. They touched my clothes, admired my shoes, and looked at the photographs I had brought with me.

Norah put herself in charge of distributing the gifts I brought. Each neighbor would get a razor blade from the box I brought for Aram.

"Even the ones with beards?" Clara asked.

"Why not?" Norah said. "Everything can be bartered."

"What about the other people, the doctor, the hairdresser, the neighbor who stands in line for us—what about them?" Clara asked.

"We have the boxes with powdered soup and the big box of matches."

"We should keep some soap and aspirin for Silvia. And maybe some coffee for the doctor," Clara said. One by one all the things that I had brought with me, even my personal objects—my eye-drops, my scissors, my notebook, my face cream, and a silver pin—were examined and given away. There was nothing in Romania. Nothing!

The shops were empty. In total boredom the vendors stood around for eight hours a day, talking and drinking tea. Plaster models of hams and salami hung in the windows. At the market, people were selling things they could no longer afford to keep. A man was hawking an old coat. When a young boy asked to try it on, I watched the man caress the coat with affection and ask its forgiveness for selling it. Light bulbs now controlled the black market, in the barter economy.

"Are there no light bulbs in the country?" I asked in dismay.

"No," Clara said. "And you know what else is difficult to find? Paper, ordinary writing paper! I'll show you," she said, handing me a box.

Inside the box were several sheets of paper. I took one out.

"Look how inventive people are. They cut off the margins of books and glue the strips together. Norah bought them at the black market. We have a lot of books. They all have one or two empty pages so we don't miss paper; aspirin is what we need the most. And of course the coffee and the sugar that you brought are really a treat. Thank you, Meia."

I hugged her frail body with all the strength that she could take. The image of the food stalls in Tel Aviv came to mind. How would she feel if she could see the market there? All the olives—small, long, black, green, stuffed with garlic or almonds, mixed with hot peppers—smoked meats, smoked fish, white bread, black bread—even sesame bread—exotic fruits, dried fruits, limes and lemons, pickled eggplants, mounds of spices, almonds, raisins. What would

Clara do? She would stand on the sidewalk staring at all that food, just as I did, until a vendor—used to seeing immigrants staring at his stall—would invite her to taste the fruits one by one, teaching her their Hebrew names. I didn't tell Clara about the food, but I did tell her that in Israel you can find pastel-colored toilet seats.

"How elegant," she said, laughing.

For Norah, I brought a box of pastries. "Baklava!" she said immediately. "My mother used to make this. I remember her pulling the dough until it became a thin, transparent layer. It looked like a white bedsheet covering the entire table. Then she covered it with chopped walnuts. One time—I must have been about four or five—I kept eating the walnuts off the dough. 'Norah, take your hands off the walnuts!' my older sister admonished me. So I put my hands behind my back, bent my head over the table, and picked up the walnuts with my mouth. My mother and sister laughed so much!" Norah said, eating a piece of baklava.

"What sister?" Clara asked her. "You never told me you had a sister."

Norah looked around the room and mumbled something about somebody that was her sister but had gone away and wasn't her sister because she was shot by the Nazis when they came to the island. The more she talked, the more confused she became, until, full of rage, she yelled, "She's gone. You understand? She's gone! She was my sister as long as she was alive. After she was killed I told myself that I never had a sister, so I don't have to miss her. She only came to my mind right now because of this pastry, but I forgot about her completely."

"Did she have a name?" Clara insisted.

"Of course she had a name. But she is gone and so is her name."

"So after she was murdered, you got rid of all the memories you had of her? You decided never to think about her again? Norah, you are a crazy liar," Clara said. "Tell me her name. Give her a chance to be remembered for her life instead of ignoring her for her death. What's her name?"

"Why do you care? Why should I think about somebody who no longer lives? She's gone like everyone else is. No names, no faces, no memories, no pain. The past is the past. Gone, you understand? Gone."

Clara stood up from her chair, covered her eyes with her hands, and started to pray in the middle of the kitchen:

Remember, God, that a woman was murdered
For respecting her traditions, and let us remember her name

"Sarah," Norah whispered and covered her face with her hands. "Sarah," Clara repeated.

After spending time with my grandfather, I had forgotten how, in my family, words were carefully chosen to keep their meanings vague, referential, and ultimately hidden. The tension created between my trying to understand what they were not saying and their trying to hide their past was the essence of our exchange. When they talked about their lives, they refused to fill in the gaps. Denial was the weapon, ambiguity their reality. Why was it that Norah refused to tell me about the tattooed number on her arm? Why did I have to learn its meaning from others? And why didn't I dare to ask them what had happened? They didn't talk about their past; they endured it. The separation created by their silence couldn't be bridged. Since there was so much they couldn't share with me, we couldn't be intimate.

The first time Aram called me "dear," he blushed. We were all in the kitchen, soon after my arrival. Norah laughed and said, "Sounds like he missed you."

Aram made an effort to spend time with me, alone. We looked at the photographs I had brought with me: the family, the house, the garden at Hanah's Paradise, the stone on his mother's grave.

Aram had a look of resignation on his face. He felt betrayed by Communism. He couldn't figure out whether it was the theory or the abuse of power that had brought the country down. Those were dangerous questions for which he could have been sent to jail. He shared his thoughts only with Mendel. I was coming from the Western world, from the capitalist side, and each time I compared the two systems, Aram, as deceived as he felt, defended Marxism. Capitalism was simply bad. Not only as an economic position but morally, too, it was corrupt and wrong. By then, I was my own person, so I wasn't afraid to contradict him.

"With all that you see around you, don't you think that the worker's paradise is dissolving in front of your eyes? The free market gives incentive."

"Along with exploitation," he said immediately. "There is no job security in a free market, after all." I could see how painful it was for him to accept the bankruptcy of a system in which he still believed.

Aram wanted to start a friendship with me, and those conversations were a point of encounter. It was a fatherly thing to do, but we weren't intimate. We went to visit the grave of his grandfather. It felt awkward to take his arm. We simply walked next to each other.

"Do you like living in Israel, Meia?" he asked.

"It's home," I replied. "There is a comfort in not being different from the others."

We walked silently for a little while, then I continued: "Even if we do live in a constant state of anxiety."

"Does it really matter where you live?" Aram said, looking above the trees lining the central walkway of the cemetery. "I am alive, surviving in a foreign country—it doesn't matter."

"Other people left," I said.

"Yes, to a displaced persons camp in Austria, to hear German spoken around me, again? No, I couldn't do it. I stayed here."

"You could have gone to Hanah's Paradise, as you told Bilu. I saw the movie, I recognized you. 'Bilu, I have the scarf. Come home to Hanah's Paradise'—that's what you said."

"You saw the clips?"

"At an exhibition about Liberation."

"The Russians showed it everywhere after the war. Each time I saw it I felt ashamed: for being deported, for abandoning Bilu and Grandma Julia, and for surviving. Yes, I wanted to go to Hanah's Paradise. But I felt damaged, and guilty and afraid to be with them. I can't explain it. It is the fear of hiding the truth. You wouldn't understand. We don't hide the past, Meia, we hide the pain. We are fearful of survival. That is the tragedy." His voice broke, and when he started to cry, he sat down on a bench, then covered his face with his hands. "We are not people of courage, Meia. I am sorry."

I sat next to him. I took a pebble from the ground and played with it, moving it from one hand to the other. I felt sorry, but I knew not to say anything. I waited. He sat there sobbing, witnessed by the names on the funerary stones. When he became calmer, he took the pebble from my hand and started to talk.

"After Grandpa Anton died, our connection from Budapest, who helped us leave, sent a message and I went to meet him. But there was a riot in front of the King's Palace. The police closed off the streets and arrested about fifty people. I didn't have any identification with me and spoke no Romanian. In the truck that took us to the jail, somebody who spoke German said that the Jews were to be deported to a concentration camp in Poland; the others were to be sent to jail.

"I gave the police a false name. I didn't tell anyone that I was Jewish. The next morning we were separated into two groups. The Jews were taken away and the Communists were kept in jail to await prosecution. After a mock trial the entire group of Communists was sentenced to two years of forced labor. We were sent to Vapniarka in Bessarabia, where some fifty labor camps were controlled by the Germans. After two years, I was sent to the Grossulova camp. I was there until the Soviet Army arrived, over a year later, in 1945.

"I returned to Romania in September and started to look for Bilu and Grandma, and for aid to leave for Palestine. When I met your mother, we did try to leave, you know, but the borders were closed already, even those with the Soviet Union. Yes, if I had been a little more courageous or more determined I could have left. But I was afraid to meet my parents and Bilu. When she finally was allowed to visit us, I could see how disappointed she was—I wasn't the same person she had known.

"We used to be very close then, when we were children. Now we relate to life differently. She could not feel my sorrow. I felt ashamed, discarded, incompetent, while begging for her sympathy. She wanted to be intimate in a way that I am unable to experience anymore; to dance the flamenco. It was a very painful reunion, and an even more painful separation. And if I had been with my parents, they, too, would have asked me to dance the flamenco. Perhaps it is better that I stayed. Here I am doing what I learned to do: surviving."

How can you be so selfish? I wanted to scream. In Israel we are also surviving, but we fight for it. And you, little scared Jew, you do what you are told and accept whatever happens to you—for one hundred grams of bread! Yes, stay here and cry over your horror stories. Why don't you fight to make sure that what happened to you will not happen again? And what about me? How do you think it feels to grow up alone, alienated, ashamed of my name and my parents' past? How do you think it feels to be the daughter of survivors? For you, affection means food and a roof above your child's head. Nobody is hitting me for not working fast enough, for talking, for breathing, for thinking, or for being Jewish. This is what you believe to be life. All of you are mad, angry people, damaged by your own inability to love, covering up your true desires and hopes for death.

But I said nothing.

It was on the return trip from visiting my parents that the Romanian policeman stopped me at the airport before I could board the plane. The slogans on the radio, the bartender's vulgar remarks, the depressed environment of the airport were reminders of the grim reality. Dictators kill life, I told myself, and I understood why my parents refused to talk about their past. Just like them, I wanted never, never to remember the time I spent in Romania. Even the beautifully expressive language felt oppressive, even the good and generous friends seemed cold and depressed.

How detached I became because of their sufferings! How fast I forgot! How much I changed in the years I lived without my parents and became my own person! I went to school, I worked, I made friends, and I spent every weekend with my grandfather at Hanah's Paradise.

"I believe that God, should He exist, enjoys Hanah's Paradise," Grandpa said to me one day after my return. We were walking in the garden in the late afternoon. "It celebrates intelligence. I look at the beauty and history around me and I can imagine our garden cut off from this land and lifted up to Heaven by God. It will be floating up there where that cloud is now. The trees will be in flower, and exotic birds will be singing, and He will read the inscriptions left by so many lives."

"Not a chance," I said. "It is not written in the Books. It can't happen—gravity."

"Then He said unto Ezekiel, 'Son of man, these bones are the whole House of Israel,'" Grandpa recited.

Behold, they say. Our bones are dried up, and our Hope is lost. . . .

O my people . . . you shall live, and I will place you in your own land. . . . I will take the people of Israel from among the Nations. . . . I will gather them on every side. I will bring them to their own Land, I will make them one nation upon the mountains of Israel. . . . And they shall dwell in the land that I have given to My servant Jacob. . . . They and their children and their children's children shall dwell there forever.

"'Our bones are dried up and our hope is lost!'" Grandpa repeated. "We used to come to Hanah's Paradise in the evenings, Adah and I. We would talk constantly about Bilu and Aram. We felt guilty for not seeing the war coming. We were active in the Zionist cause. I even named my daughter Bilu from the words in the Torah, *'Beit Ya'acov lekhu unelekhah*, House of Jacob, stand up and let us go.' There are no words to describe the loss. After Aram was arrested and the letters from Bilu stopped arriving, Adah became very militant. She took aerial photographs for the British and copied them for the *Hagganah*, the Jewish underground. She knew every inch of the border and helped to smuggle in refugees crossing over by land from Lebanon and Syria.

"Even if we ourselves did not go to a concentration camp, our lives and our children's lives were affected. The other children were here, fighting for Israel, vaguely remembering Bilu and Aram and their grandparents. But the missing children were more real to our emotions. It is impossible to think that somebody close to you is not there anymore. Every day we hoped for news. Every morning I would say, 'Aram, my son, come to my bosom.' I remembered him only as a young boy. Little gestures stayed with me all those years: the look in his eyes when I would ruffle his hair; the time when we left and I put my hand on his neck and squeezed it slightly. I was standing on the step of the train and I said, 'Good-bye, Aram, my beloved.' This is how I remember him. Then I saw his face in the documentary. Aram my beloved was leaving death to come to Hanah's Paradise and never arrived. Has he seen the movie?"

"Yes, and he is ashamed of himself. He feels tortured. He says that he is capable only of surviving but he can't live. Deep, deep in his soul he is violent and angry, still caring about the piece of bread at the end of the day. He wasn't able to let go and resents himself for it."

"You are cruel and unjust, Salomeia. You are angry at your parents and at their past. You know, Salomeia, when you first arrived here you were afraid to talk, or to take an extra piece of food. Gifts embarrassed you, affection made you shy. You had no opinions, no desires, no initiatives. You were like your parents: a survivor."

"Not anymore, Grandpa. The people I grew up with are terrorized by the past, destitute in the present, and alone in the future. Not me, Grandpa—not anymore."

20

Nothing can describe Hanah's Paradise; not the sound of the bamboo leaves moving in the wind, not the poems on the stones, not the color of the light, not the smell of the pomegranate flowers, not even the silence of the sand. But if nothing can describe the place, the sense of walking through a personal history is readily present. The mystical realism of Hanah's Paradise is my home, and that of my cousin Ehud and his wife, Cila. It also belongs to my cousins Lyora and Karen, Dina, Yoram, David, Eli, Tova, Menahem, Ruth, Avram, and Zipora, and to all the others who wander through the garden and find their family name written on the stones.

SABBATH DINNER

Grandpa took me to Afula, where he owned some land. He had once hoped to build an opera house there, he told me, but after Adah's death, he planted an orchard. We picked apricots, *mishmish*, to make a dish invented by Aishe, my great-grandmother's famous cook. It was also a favorite of my grandmother Adah's. Whenever apricots were in season, this delicacy was served at Grandpa's house for Friday night dinner.

Mishmish

Keep the apricots in boiling water for a minute.
Remove their skins and discard the pits without separating
   the halves.
Fill in the apricots with toasted almonds or pistachios.
Close the two halves with cloves from Zanzibar.
Poach them for one minute in syrup of white wine and honey.

Every Friday several long tables were set up in the courtyard for the Sabbath dinner. Children were seated apart at a lower table. People would come for dinner or simply stop by to meet newly arrived immigrants, newborn children, or recently married couples. Grandpa sat at the head of the table, and the most recently arrived family member was seated next to him. Nurit, our cousin from Yemen, put herself in charge of Grandpa's house, deciding on the menu for every dinner. On Fridays she baked *challah* and prepared small dishes of pickled radishes in beet juice; spicy olives; roasted eggplant with garlic; cucumbers and tomatoes in sesame sauce; *petrosilia*, a sauce of chopped parsley with tahini and garlic; and, best of all, she made hummus. The hummus always made me hungry. It was a dense paste of chickpeas that she spread around a large flat plate. She sprinkled it with parsley and poured over it a heavy, dark olive oil, leaving a sinuous green line on the ivory hummus paste. I always associated this image with the Hebrew word *hushanah*, sensuous.

Fridays before sundown, people met to prepare dinner. We cooked the same meal—each family bringing the spices and the recipes from the places from where they came.

When chicken was on the menu, the Moroccans made *Daphna de poulet*, a chicken stew with pickled lemons and green olives; the Spanish family cooked chicken with almonds, lemons, and apricots; the Egyptians cooked it with walnuts and mint leaves. The Russian cousins roasted it with onion, garlic, and peppers. The Polish stuffed it with mushrooms. The cousin from Budapest made a goulash with sweet paprika. The Greek answer was chicken with olives and marjoram. The Indian cousins used curry and tomato chutney. The Iranians used pomegranate syrup, the French produced *Poulet Basquais*, the Americans barbequed the breast, and the Germans made *Schnitzel*. I created my own recipe:

Cold Chicken in Lemon Aspic
Cut a chicken into small pieces
Add onions, garlic, and pickled lemons
Cook everything until tender
Discard bones, fat, and skin
Add spices and herbs, cool it in a mold
Decorate with pistachios and sliced fruits.

At each dinner, Grandpa offered advice, settled disputes, and made sure that promises were kept. He remembered everyone's name and knew each person's connection and place in the family. There were my cousins Ygal, a shoemaker; Yossi, a banker; Leah, a doctor. There was Aunt Sarah, a musician; Rebecca, a clothing designer; Lenke, a painter; and Helen, an actress. There were my cousins Ehud, an architect; Nathaniel, a filmmaker; Olga, a journalist; and Karina, a dealer in luxury linen.

Once candles had been lit, prayers said, and food served, arguments about us *Yehudim*, Jews, took over the room. No matter what else we might be talking about, the subject surfaced each time: What is it to be Jewish? How Jewish are we? What makes us Jewish if we do not believe in God? Which Jews should we befriend, and which Jews should be kept at a distance?

"Salomeia," my aunt Rebecca said one evening, "Do me a favor. Talk to your cousin Zipora. Tell her that Moroccans are pimps. She won't listen to me. She will end up with ten children, while he smokes hashish and plays cards. You are the same age, she'll listen to you."

"Some people here at the table are from Morocco and are not pimps," her husband said.

"There are exceptions," Rebecca retorted. "It is known that Moroccan men don't like to work. They beat up their wives, then cover them with jewelry; 'love your mother, beat up your wife' syndrome."

"Stop it!" her husband said. "Last week you were against the Romanians."

"Well, *Rumanim ganavim*, Romanians are thieves; even they say it. Sorry, Salomeia, you are Romanian, but this is what people believe here—and they are right. They always cheat!"

"I am not Romanian," I said. "I am Jewish!"

"Don't listen to her, Salomeia," Rebecca's brother advised. "She is always upset. She is angry with Emperor Constantine for converting to Christianity. She forgets that even if we have our differences, we are here because we are Jews."

Inevitably the subject would move from some personal grievance to general questions concerning the Jews and the Germans; the Jews and the Poles; the French, who were philo-Arab; the Palestinians, who hated the Jews; and the Americans, who were being too lenient with the Palestinians.

"*Ma atem hoshvim*, What do you think?" my cousin Avital asked. "What are the Palestinians fighting for?" He paused, looked around the table, then answered his own question.

"First, guilty after the Holocaust, the big powers gave us the land of Israel and forgot the Palestinians—fenced inside refugees' camps. Now they are threatening the Arab countries that took them in, the State of Israel, and Western civilization. I believe that they should have their own state and stop fighting for the Pan-Arabic partition of the world—a myth."

"Avital, you don't know what you are talking about!" my cousin Moshe said.

"The Palestinians are crazy! I saw it in the army. They come close to the checkpoint, open their arms, and scream, 'Kill me! Kill me! Allah is great!' They throw stones at us to provoke the shooting. They all have the same story. In Heaven, their mullah said, each martyr will have seventy-two black-eyed virgins serving them nipples cooked in honey. Shows you how sexually repressed they are! They actually think it's true."

"Cannibalistic!" Aunt Rina declared.

"Could be, but nonetheless, they don't have a country, and they live from handouts. We should have given them a lot of money in '48 for them to stay and prosper. But we kicked them out and now we have inherited the problems we ourselves created."

"Bad *kalkul*," somebody said, meaning calculation. "Look at the demographics. If they had stayed here, we would be the minority by now."

"They are still better off than the ones who live in Egypt or Iraq," someone interrupted. "At least they have food, schools, medical care, and a lot of attention from the Western world. You think the Arabs in Syria are doing better, even if they have a country?"

"The Muslims want control over this part of the world," a voice from the end of the table broke in.

"None of the Arab countries want peace. They want us out of here—that's what they want!"

"*Ata lo mevin*, You don't understand," Avner, a border police officer, jumped in. "You don't know the Arabs! I talk to them every day. They come from Jordan to sell their products, and we at the border have orders not to let them in. How do you think they feel when the Israelis keep a truckload of their ripe tomatoes in the sun for several days, then tell them they can't cross the bridge into Israel? Not only is the market in Amman small, but in Israel they get better prices."

"So what if their tomatoes rot?" Avner's sister Ariel yelled at him. "They, too, should rot in the sun! They come with tomatoes but end up selling hashish. You guys at the checkpoint are taking a cut, I'm sure."

"Let me finish my story, Ariel," Avner shouted back. "What you say is so ridiculous that it is not worth answering! So, instead of having them rot, Israelis move the products into their trucks, take them over the bridge, and sell them to the market in Jerusalem. They return the next day with the money. This shows you the power of commerce! Arabs want peace just as we do. It's better for them to be integrated into our economy."

"We can't integrate them!" Rahel, his mother, said. "The more you trust them, the sooner you will end up with explosives in the tomato truck and a knife in your back. They have a different mentality. They provoke incidents at the border, call in the journalists, then complain."

"I am on your side, Rahel," Yossi the banker said. "Look at their leaders—if you can call those corrupt lunatics by that name. Instead of economic development, it is occupation by the Israelis that defines their whole political movement. What an excuse for not building jobs and democracy! It is the poor bastards who suffer! And the myth that without the American support, Israel would . . ."

I could not remember all the names and relationships between people, but as I moved around the table to refill a dish or bring some bread, I heard snippets of conversation. By the end of the evening people would be yelling from one end of the table to the other, interrupting to give their opinions, banging their fists, jumping to their feet, or shouting insults. Sentences crossed each other in the air, leaving trails of emotions scattered over the table. "In our family," Grandpa said, "we tolerate madness."

While people were arguing, Grandpa Rafa'el would taste each dish, compliment the cook, and—remembering recipes from Aishe, the Turkish cook—offer his suggestions. Once the evening became dark and people's arguments too extreme, Grandpa would usually thank everyone by name for coming, and tell a story he had just read from the records at Hanah's Paradise.

"*Chaverim*, my friends, our own family has lived on this land, coming and going, for over eight hundred years. The stones at Hanah's Paradise attest to it. We are not ambivalent about being here. Our spiritual, religious, and national character has been shaped here. This is the place where we have created a culture of universal significance and given the world the laws of communal life. In the countries of our dispersion, we continued to keep our faith in this land, with the hope of returning to revive our political freedom. We find ourselves now facing the catastrophe of Palestinians' hatred and violence. We need to offer the Arabs different choices. We lived with them in Spain, in North Africa, in the Arabian Desert—and together we prospered. The Arab world also wants economic progress. There is no profit from war anymore. Economic growth and peace are around the corner."

"*Alevay*, if only!" my Aunt Yael said. "I wish I could be as optimistic as you are. But I don't think you realize how deep the hatred runs. You stay here at Hanah's Paradise, detached from our world, not noticing the panic, the confusion, and the fear that we feel. In Israel we are living on a precipice all the time. You are a romantic, Rafa'el, and don't see the madness of the Arab world."

"Yael, *motek sheli*, my dear, I look out the window at the beauty of our land that for thousands of years has suffered attacks, vandalism, sieges, and I know that Israel will survive. I too—I am nervous when I see a young Arab entering the supermarket. Every hour I listen to the news. Every hour I hold my breath hoping that nobody was killed. But let us not generalize! I have Arab friends with whom I fought against the Turks—and even against the British. They are happy to be living in Israel, to have work, and to send their kids to a good school. Not all Arabs are terrorists."

"Nobody said anything to the contrary," Aunt Ruth broke in, surprising her father. "I can tell you that I had a meeting last week with the principal of an Arab school financed by our government. He is a moderate Israeli Arab, leader of a major Arab party represented in the Parliament. He told us that, despite minor disagreements with other mainstream Arab Israelis, his party also wants peace and coexistence. He is happy to have a voice in the government, yet he himself believes that there is no difference between an Arab-Israeli citizen and a Palestinian from a refugee camp. He would like to be called a Palestinian-Arab rather than an Israeli-Arab. He also insists that his brothers be given the right of return in a Palestinian state, with Jerusalem as its capital."

"Nonsense!" Aris, my cousin from Corfu, said. "There is no right of return! There is no Arab Jerusalem! We keep everything, build more housing, and get rid of the Arabs. This is what we need to do."

"Are you crazy?" his wife exclaimed. "This is extended occupation! It can only rot the soul of the country."

"Then maybe we should force them to convert. They did that to us numerous times."

"You are a sick man," his brother Gady said.

"Give them back everything," Gilmor, my cousin from Tel Aviv, said. "Abandon the settlements and stop the killing! If we want to preserve our Jewish democracy, we need to make peace. That requires sacrifice."

"*Ma ata omer*, what are you talking about?" Nathan, who lived on a kibbutz, shouted from the other end of the table. "You want to give up Jerusalem and all the territories? You think that God is a left-wing intellectual? I, too, wanted to help the Arabs, and they almost killed me."

"Why do we have any more rights over this land than they do?" Gilmor shouted back. "Look at how we treat their civilian population!"

"So," said Ephraim, another cousin, raising his voice, "do you remember when I went to the aid of villagers in the West Bank? I already told the story! There we were, some fifty students with shovels and barrels, protesting our government, filling in the enormous trench dug by *our* army to close off the village. As we were working, Arabs from the village that we were helping were shooting at us and throwing stones. How crazy can they be? Arabs don't understand compromise. It is not part of their vocabulary. They are psychotic. They believe in death, not in life."

"I told you then, *yaqir*, my dear," Ephraim's mother said, "that helping Arabs is the kiss of death, a noble and absurd idea, even if helping is a Jewish thing to do."

Menahem, the oldest rabbi in the family, tried to be conciliatory. "We fight because we are similar. We are cousins, after all. We look alike and keep similar customs. God in His Mercy will make sure that we don't bother them and they don't bother us. Separation is the only solution. God will guide us in our prayers."

"We've prayed enough already, Grandpa!" a cousin whose name I couldn't remember said. "They don't want to live with us, so we should kick them out of here."

"If it were up to you, you would shoot them all," another cousin put in.

"Siberia is the answer," Arkady, my cousin from Kishinev, said. "Send the Palestinians to Siberia and let them fight among themselves. There is nobody around for five thousand kilometers!"

"How horrible," a voice shouted. "You're worse than the Palestinians! You'd be happy to go there to sell them mint tea."

"Listen," somebody else said, jumping up. "If we work together to develop their economic system, there will be peace. They need roads and schools. There is nothing wrong with integrating their traditions with ours."

"Sit down, David, you're dreaming!" arose a new voice. "We already got together with the Arabs. We've already integrated our traditions, built schools, hospitals, roads, factories, and an airport. We irrigated their fields, bought their products, accepted them into our universities—and? Did the killing stop? No! Do you really believe that the Arabs are crying for the extra land taken by Jewish settlers? Not that I agree, but there is so much land in this part of the world that they could just rent it out to us and make some money in the deal. It is not about territory. It is about us being here by virtue of national and historic right."

"What do you want?" an older man asked. "Aren't the settlers colonizing the land? Don't you think that their existence—not to mention their opulence—is provocative? Big houses, huge gardens, tax deductions, military escorts to go shopping. They would rather *die* than live like us in cramped apartments!"

"*Lama ata medaber shtuyiot*, what you say is stupid," a woman shouted at him. "You mean to say that the settlers deserve to be killed because they have big houses and don't pay taxes?"

"The settlers are developing the desert. Their settlements are the cities of tomorrow," Asher, an anthropologist who rarely disagreed with anyone, said.

"I think the settlers see themselves more as a Zionist avantgarde than as modern traders," Ehud, my favorite cousin, said. "Theirs is a historical mission: to establish permanent borders by the plow, not by the sword. 'In Samaria, we don't fight, we build,' as the saying goes."

"Absolutely," someone across the table from Ehud agreed. "That is how they took over the Jordan Valley. They displaced the Bedouins and diverted the water for their own use. The Arabs lost their fields and the Bedouins lost the grazing for their flocks. How happy can they be?"

"Don't say that," a cousin named Shai objected. "We didn't settle the land for greed or for security reasons. We worked west of the Jordan River to recreate the pioneering experience of the first immigrants. We had a strong desire to be like them, but after a while it felt unreal, so I left."

"Sure, you left! You were part of the fanatic religious Zionists *Gush Emunim*, the Core of the Faithful," Zafira, my cousin from Johannesburg, said, removing her infant daughter from her breast.

"You weren't there, so how can you talk?" Shai answered. "We were living in harmony with the Arabs. We also helped them to clear their land. For us, it was a project of hope."

"What hope?" said Eitan, a younger cousin from Kfar Saba. "To kick them out and take over the entire Biblical Land of Israel?"

"Darling," Olga, my cousin from Athens, said, with a hint of cynicism, "we live at the beginning of messianic times. The redemption of the Land of Israel is necessary for the redemption of the world."

"Amen," the old rabbi said.

Hadassa, an aunt from America, jabbed her finger at Shai and said, "Don't tell me that you still believe in the redemption of the world, when all we ever hear from your group is, 'It's either us or them,' meaning, 'let's make sure that *we* get rid of *them.*'"

"The *Gush Emunim* acted according to a divine plan," Sharon, a rabbi's wife, interjected.

"People like that are fanatics," said Michal, who was famous for helping family members paint their houses. "They call themselves *mitnahelim*, the possessors of inheritance, like in Joshua: 'For you shall cause them to inherit the land.'"

"They are not crazy, they are nostalgic," Hadassa corrected him.

"They are both," Eitan said. "And they are pretty determined. They sleep in bulletproof clothes and travel in armored chariots. They live in mobile homes, surrounded by concrete fences topped with barbed wire. Even if they *are* developing the desert, is that a life?"

"We have to live together with the Arabs," Grandpa said as he turned an apricot in his hand. "They are going through their Counter-Reformation. We can only hope that they move toward Enlightenment. It will take some time—and we have to help them."

Nurit brought to the table some mint tea, roasted almonds, and dates. The argument continued as we began clearing the table.

"Well," Noah, the cousin every girl in the family loved, said as he slung his M-16 over his shoulder, "another Friday night dinner when, once more, we agreed to disagree! If anybody needs a ride, I am driving an army jeep and I am ready to leave. It is getting late. *Shabbat Shalom*, everyone! Thank you for dinner! Good night, Grandpa."

The next day we were told that Naftali, a grandson whom Grandpa had raised and loved very much, had been murdered near his house in Hebron. Naftali and his left-wing wife believed in coexistence. As an expression of tolerance and integration, they spoke fluent Arabic and gave their daughter an ancient Islamic name, Hagar. A very gentle man, Naftali was a musician who recorded Ladino songs and poetry. Grandpa mourned alone in his room.

Yit'gadal v'yit'kadash	magnified and sanctified
Yit'barakh v'yish'tabach	blessed and praised

SINAN

Several weeks later, Grandpa took me with him to visit an old friend of his in Tamra, an Arab village in the Lower Galilee. The village was only forty minutes away by car, but twelve military checkpoints—one every two kilometers—made the trip last almost two hours. We left the car at the last Israeli checkpoint and walked the ruined streets of Tamra to Grandpa's friend's house.

Tamra used to be a village of bleached stone houses and blue doors, famous for its vegetable market. Barbed wire now blocked off the main street, and stones littered the sidewalks. Several palm trees were dying on the median strip. Two faded billboards promoted frozen orange juice and flights to Mecca. Fire-gutted trucks were scattered along the road, and the fountain in the center of the village was filled with stones and burned tires. A short distance ahead of us, at the checkpoint, Israeli soldiers in a jeep were listening to the radio.

Dressed in white Turkish pants and shirt, with a black cape around his shoulders and his ivory cane in hand, Grandpa looked impressive. Older people greeted us on the way. "Keep the scarf on your head, Salomeia," Grandpa said. "It is the custom here."

As we walked, avoiding debris, a small group of children walked alongside us, laughing and pushing each other. Grandpa spoke with them in Arabic and they came closer to us. The children, most about eight or nine years old, were dressed in handed-down clothes: T-shirts, pajama pants, old sneakers or flip-flop sandals. A few younger ones tagged along. Some were barefooted, others naked, except for a shirt. They asked for money, for pens and candies. The children walked with us until we arrived at the home of Grandpa's friend.

The house was a two-story concrete cube with iron bars on the windows. High walls enclosed a garden, and when we knocked at the door, a young boy answered and led us into a courtyard where several chickens pecked away under the shadow of a lemon tree. A woman in an embroidered Arab dress was cooking on an open fire pit.

"Israfil!" she shouted with joy when she saw us, then dried her hands on her dress and ran to us. "*As Salâm Aleicum*, good day, Israfil."

"*Aleicum Salâm*, Ayala," Rafa'el replied. Pointing his finger to his chest, he said to me, "Israfil is my Arabic name, Salomeia."

"We received your postcard and were waiting for you. I am so glad to see you! And who is this young woman? She looks like a village girl with that scarf on her head."

"This is Salomeia, my son Aram's daughter, the one who stayed behind," Grandpa said. "She is with me now, at Hanah's Paradise."

"Welcome to our house, Salomeia. I have my niece Saïda with us also. Her parents are in France. And you—how are you, Israfil?"

"I am well, Ayala. I am well and very pleased to be here. We miss you at Hanah's Paradise."

"Oh, Israfil, it is too difficult to travel. Too many checkpoints, and also I don't want to leave Sinan alone."

"He would hardly be alone," Grandpa said, glancing around the courtyard, where several women and children were smiling at us, holding onto each other. "I see your daughter is here and some of your grandchildren."

Grandpa and I walked toward the house and said hello to Ayala's daughter, who introduced her five children to us. A short man dressed in a white *djelaba* arrived in the doorway and pushed the children away.

"Israfil!" he shouted. "*As Salâm Aleicum.* My old friend Israfil—you're here!"

"*Aleicum Salâm*, Sinan," Grandpa replied, opening his arms.

"*Zayak innaharda*, how are you, my friend?" Sinan said, and they embraced.

"How good to see you, Sinan! This is Salomeia, my son Aram's daughter."

"*Ahlan wa-sahlan*, welcome," Sinan said, then rapidly touched his chest, forehead, and lips with his right hand.

"It is the Arab way to say, 'What is in my heart is in my mind and on my lips,'" Grandpa explained.

Over blue pants, Sinan was wearing a long white cotton shirt. The straight collar of his shirt mounted almost to his chin. Sinan had green-brown eyes with gold speckles, exactly the same color as the mother-of-pearl buttons of his open shirt. With his receding hairline, thin gray hair, and well-trimmed moustache—all bleached by the sun—he had the look of a scholar.

"You must be so happy to be with your granddaughter, Israfil. She looks very much like Adah. But please, come inside! My home is your home!"

We followed him into a dark room. "We've blocked the windows with sandbags," Sinan explained. "A stray bullet can do a lot of damage. Difficult times, Israfil, difficult times! Come and sit down! We have so much to talk about."

Through the windows, a sliver of light was shimmering on the floor—a reminder of the sunshine outside. Once accustomed to the darkness, I could see several pillows arranged under a window in front of a low table. The ray of light found its way through the sandbags and when it landed on a painting, a gold-orange sunset erupted on the wall. Sinan said something in Arabic and a young girl came into the room.

"Go, Salomeia," Sinan said. "Go with Saïda."

Saïda looked a few years younger than me. She had dark hair and wore white pants. On her T-shirt, *Friday* was written in turquoise letters.

Saïda led me across the courtyard and into the summer kitchen, where Ayala was cooking. I could smell fresh bread. Ayala moved with surprising lightness for her size. Her large breasts were sagging down to her waist. Her legs were short and her ankles swollen. She wore a pair of old slippers. Strands of thin, henna-colored hair were constantly escaping from under her scarf. She had beautiful deep-green lavender eyes. I sat on a chair looking at her. She smiled and said in French, "*Tu veux manger quelque chose, ma fille*, would you like to eat something, my daughter?"

"*Non merci*," I answered. I liked that she called me her daughter.

Ayala put in front of me a dish with olives and a glass of tea with mint leaves. Submerged in the liquid, the branch of mint took on a luscious dark-green color. "*Na'ana*," she said and pointed at the mint.

Saïda put a basket of lima beans on the table and started shelling them. I pulled some in front of me and we worked together in silence. When we finished Ayala said something in Arabic, and Saïda gestured for me to go with her to the house.

We sat on the steps to the entrance of the room where Grandpa was talking with Sinan. "*Ona*," she said pointing to herself, "*Ona*, Saïda."

"*Ona*, Salomeia," I said. We both laughed. Saïda took a fine-haired paintbrush and a small bottle of black henna out of her pocket. She studied my hands for a minute or so, then began tracing the lines of an intricate motif on my hands. She knew exactly where to draw the flowers, leaves, and dots. She worked unhurriedly, filling in the lines of an imaginary painting, as I sat in the soft shadow of the house, smelling the cumin and coriander from the outdoor kitchen, listening to the men's voices from the other room.

With a large tray on her head, Ayala traversed the courtyard, left her slippers at the door, and entered the room where my grandfather and Sinan were talking. They were speaking in English, Grandpa wanting to avoid Hebrew—the language of occupation.

"Thank you for coming, Israfil," Ayala interrupted them. "This is a great day. Make yourself comfortable on the pillows and please eat. I made your favorite *shakshuka*."

"Ayala, *ma chérie, tu ne peux pas imaginer le plaisir que j'ai à te voir*, you cannot imagine, my dear, how happy I am to see you," Grandpa said. "Not only do you have the most beautiful eyes I've ever seen, but nobody makes *shakshuka* like you do. It has a soul! The eggs are so light that I can taste the herbs eaten by the chickens."

"Thank you, Israfil. But don't offer compliments before eating!"

"I'm sorry I arrived late. I didn't expect the drive to take so long."

"I know! We pray not to get sick; I don't know how we would travel. It takes hours just to find a ride. But eat before the food gets cold; I will join you later for coffee," she said and left the room. Ayala put on her slippers, admired my hands, walked around the lemon tree to cross the courtyard, and went back to the kitchen.

"I miss Hanah's Paradise, and I have missed you," I heard Sinan saying from the room. "It's been almost two years now since I last left the village. Let me push aside a sandbag from the window so we can see each other. I hope that no one shoots at us. Tell me the news, Israfil."

"Sinan, I brought you oil paints, some canvases, and Egyptian cigarettes," Grandpa said. "Better tobacco than what we used to smuggle from Jordan! And this is for Ayala, and here is some candy for the children."

"You are a generous man, Israfil. *Mutashakir geddan*, thank you. You take after your father. When I finished art school, your father bought my first ten paintings. Who had ever heard of a poor boy from an Arab village going to art school? My parents were simple people."

"I know, but when you became a teacher they were very proud. I remember the celebration."

"I wish we had something to celebrate now," Sinan lamented. "Around me, all I see is pain. Nobody in the village has any work. We are cut off from other cities. We cannot work in Israel and cannot travel. The young people are desperate. Now I have time to paint, but there is so much death and desolation around me that I don't feel like painting anymore. Who would have thought that it would be so hard for our people to reach an agreement?"

"If it were up to you and me, Sinan, we would have peace by now."

"I don't know anymore, Israfil. I don't know what side I am on—or for what reasons. I keep changing my mind as friends and relatives get killed."

"I feel the same way myself. My grandson Naftali, the musician, was killed in Hebron last month."

"Is he the one who had red hair and spoke Arabic?"

"Yes. He was a left-wing peacenik. He lived in Hebron. Somebody cut his throat."

"Puppets in the hands of fundamentalists! I am sorry to hear this, Israfil. May his soul rest in peace. I know you loved him very much. He played for me once at your house, and I taught him 'Isefra Va Vvainou Va, The Night Voyage.' How cruel our people have become. We too have lost several members of our family in the last year, including my daughter Fatumata's husband."

"Is this why she is with you now? I saw her in the courtyard. What a tragedy! I remember her wedding. We all live with losses now."

"Israfil, my friend, our family is breaking apart. Our lives are pretty much shattered. Out of eight children, only my daughters are here. The boys are all gone, the six of them scattered all over the world. I would like to have them around me, but when I am on the phone with them, I tell them not to return. How can I insist they come when they don't have any opportunities here? Do I want to see them living under curfews, with sandbags against the windows? Do I want to look into their eyes and see anger? I am a painter, Israfil, I am trained to paint expressions. But all I can see around me are helpless Arabs. They smile subserviently at the soldiers, wishing to enter Israel for menial work. They try to make nice with the enemy for a piece of bread. I see them standing in line at the checkpoint sometimes for days. They have the fake smile of the abused servant who has no place to go, who can't do without you and hates you for it. You must understand that, Israfil. Your people have lived like this for centuries. That is why I don't want my boys to return, even for a short visit. I prefer missing them to seeing them at the checkpoint, with forced smiles, faked eagerness, and covered-up fear.

"They are angry with the Arabs for choosing violence, and with the Israelis for responding with force."

"Yes, it is not the way we envisioned things to be. The personal and the historical are intimately connected. Everyone suffers. You too, from a well-known Israeli-Arab painter, you've become a recluse—a village painter promoting the art of miniature and calligraphy."

"First, nobody buys paintings now. Second—and I hope I am not offending you, Israfil—I'm more of a Palestinian-Arab than I am an Israeli-Arab. Third, I have a house here."

"But you don't have to live like this! You choose to stay here to paint the Arab village in a time of absurd conflict. It is not for me to say so, but perhaps you can leave here—and paint something else."

"You mean I should come on your side and paint the streets and the harbor in Haifa. It occurred to me, but then my grandchildren would have to go to an Israeli-Arab school and be taught Zionist literature. What kind of Arabs will they grow up to be if they are not allowed to study Darwish, our most celebrated Palestinian poet? My sons-in-law are opposed."

"Well, perhaps it is better for them to study Zionist literature than not to study at all. At least they can read Darwish at home. That is how you and I learned Turkish, Sinan. At least we got to go to school."

From outside, I could hear Sinan's laughter. It circled the room, squeezed between the sandbags, and burst into the courtyard—just as a lemon broke off from a branch and, swimming between leaves, fell to the ground with the sound of a kiss. *Verde limon, mi limonero*, I sang to myself, remembering Bilu.

"That is why I love you, Israfil. You are an expedient dreamer, like your grandmother. Remember what she said to me when my parents decided that I should marry my first cousin, Salima? 'For a first wife'"—at this Sinan choked with laughter—"'for a first wife,' your grandmother said, 'she is not bad.' Like her, you always make me see the world from a lighter place, Israfil. Of course, better Turkish school than no school at all, but why not a Palestinian-Arab school? We have our own history to teach, don't you think? And if we throw enough stones, perhaps one day we will have our own schools also."

"What do people in the village think, Sinan?" Grandpa asked. "Is it possible to stop the killing? If we give back the territories, would we have peace?"

"Israfil, my beloved friend, if you believe that a peace treaty between us will change anything, then you don't understand the Middle East."

"You don't want peace?"

"Israfil, you were born here and so were your parents and grandparents, but you still don't understand us. We Arabs are a very angry, uneducated people. Enlightenment, progress, and modernity passed us by. We didn't have an Industrial Revolution. Islam is our Bolshevism. Was colonialism better for us? Perhaps! But should it continue? No!"

"But you do agree that a democratic, humanist Islam could benefit more people?"

"You think that our self-perception is playing a trick on us. If Islam is the ideal religion, then why are we so miserable, so poor, so uneducated? You mean to say that the gap between our self-perception as the superior Oriental race and our reality of repression is the source of our rage? Could be, Israfil, could be! If the Islamic way of life is not God's highest achievement, should we convert—to Judaism perhaps?"

"Sinan, this is a defiant position. You don't have to convert but to educate, to participate, to change. The Muslim world is fighting democracy."

"See, you don't understand," Sinan answered, irritated. "We don't want democracy; we want Muslim unity. The Middle East is Muslim! From North Africa, across the Arabian Peninsula, then north to Turkey, Iran, Afghanistan, across the Caspian Sea, passing through the entire length of the former Soviet Union, then south to the Indian subcontinent, then east to Malaysia, Singapore, Indonesia, then north again to Bangladesh, Mongolia, and parts of China—all this is Muslim land! What is Israel and its democratic government to the Muslim world? Nothing! It is a small Jewish state that ultimately will also be Muslim! Open your eyes, Israfil! The entire territory of Palestine is ours. It is *Waaf*, a Muslim religious entity, an endowment of the Prophet, not subject to any transaction. It means that unless our religious laws are changed, this land is ours, and only Muslims can live here."

"And you don't think that Islam has to be rescued from the monopoly of fundamentalist thinking? You don't believe in a thriving new Islam?"

"Again, you don't understand. Listen to me! We, the Arabs, are believers. We are obstinate and intolerant. If you understand the Arab mind, you will know that the negotiations about the Temple Mount are simply ridiculous. If the Israeli left thinks that withdrawing from the settlements will change anything, they must be insane. All parts of this land are *Waaf*, endowed. Every inch of Israel is ours. This is the truth! This is what the people in the village believe, and this is why there will never be peace."

"Sinan, your people are denied economic progress."

"Oh, we have our own cottage industry: the 'martyrs of Allah.'"

"So, in your opinion, Sinan, the Arabs don't believe that we have the capacity to protect ourselves, to make sure that history doesn't repeat itself?"

"Sure you can protect yourself! But so what if you have the capacity? We are many, and a lot of us are pressing for the right of return."

"So you don't think the Jews have a fundamental right to a place here that is their own. If your prophet gave you this land, what is wrong with our God giving it to us, before?"

"Only you can think that way. This is the fundamental difference between a group that is defined by others and a group that defines itself."

"Sinan, my friend, not to disappoint you, and not to tell you anything that you don't know already, even if every sliver of this country is a battleground, we will never leave."

"Israfil, this 'sliver of a country' is surrounded by the Muslim world. If they wanted to have peace, it would have been done by now. You know what Israel is to us? Nothing! A molecule of fat on the watery chicken soup of the Arab world!"

"Sinan, what would Islam gain by our not being here?"

"Is it better to have Israel around? From my point of view, yes! But does it matter? No."

"You mean to say that the Arab world can't compromise? That you are many, and if some of you die now fighting against us, you are not losing much?"

"The martyrs are our heroes, Israfil, and our leaders gave them the chance to achieve something in death—rather than nothing in life."

"A pointless life versus a glorious death!"

"Well, if you are an angry, hopeless, depressed young man, if you have no hope whatsoever, why not become *shaheed*, a martyr?"

"How can you reconcile yourself with a civilization that uses its children as weapons? How can you stay here and witness the inhumanity of adults fabricating martyrs on a conveyor belt?"

"It is abhorrent to me. I'm vehemently opposed. I am sickened by the sight of those women dancing in the streets, ululating in happiness over the death of a child. Then they put in a claim and wait for the money. They are proud mothers. With the money they have power and status. They get a TV or a new couch, even a new apartment. 'The wedding of my beloved child with a Black-Eyed Virgin was celebrated in Heaven' is how a suicide is announced in the newspapers. Can you, with your rational mind, understand that this is the new economy of refugee camps—martyrdom as a commodity? The honor of dying gloriously, while destroying you, is what people dream of."

"Sinan, we could reduce you to dust. We could unleash a tremendous war and win."

"But there is nothing to win, Israfil! You kill us and we kill you. How long can that continue? To win, you will have to wipe us out, and although the Israelis have the means, they are not going to do it. It is not a Jewish thing to do. This is going to be a very long war and you will get tired of it, Israfil."

"You mean to say that after fighting to have our own country, the Jews will just leave?"

"I mean to say that millions of Arab children are growing up hating the Jews. The rage is so tremendous that they will come out and kill you one by one—every day a few more—until all of you are gone. Jerusalem will be empty. How long will it take for your people to say, 'I don't want any more of my children to die'? You will leave, Israfil. You will become tired of being scared, of losing your friends and your family. Because the Arabs don't mind dying! I love you, Israfil, and you know that. Sometimes I love you as a father and sometimes as a child, but I always love you as a friend. You just don't understand what is happening. Even if you give us East Jerusalem, even if we have a Palestinian state, Israel will disappear. It could happen next year or in twenty years or in a hundred years, but it is going to happen. There is nothing to contemplate or to negotiate. And this is what you don't understand. Nobody wants you here, even though you do have some historical and political rights. Time, Israfil, is not in your favor, and you will have to accept the inevitable. You should leave, Israfil! Israel and the Jews should leave. The sooner you accept this reality, the sooner the region will be at peace—then everyone can go about their personal business. This is Muslim land, and we want it only for the Muslims. This is what the mullah and the villagers think."

Rafa'el paused, then, in very carefully chosen English, pronouncing each word with theatrical affectation, he said: "Thank you, Sinan, for being so open-minded. But you forget just one thing; dictators also die. The Arab leaders will change. Fundamentalism won't rule. People want rights to education and to freedom."

Sinan laughed and answered with similar affectation: "Yes, my dear fellow, we are indeed a strange people. When we kill our brother, we raise his children. We can give you our best horse, then cut your throat from behind your back. We Muslims are promised a great life in Heaven, and what makes you and me such good friends is that we don't believe in Heaven."

For a while they sat in silence. Saïda was drawing the last lines of a flower on my hand. Ayala was still cooking. In that warm afternoon silence, I felt a surge of new love for my grandfather. I had listened to their conversation and noticed the disappointment in his voice. Sinan was his oldest and most precious friend. I could hear how sad Grandpa became. The King's English of the last sentences must have been a game they often played. With feigned formality, they told each other hurtful thoughts.

"Let's have coffee in the garden before the sun goes down and the shooting starts," Sinan finally said.

They moved outside. Ayala brought them coffee laced with cardamom pods. Saïda took the dishes back to the kitchen, then called me in to eat. I sat near her, trying to eat with my right hand, the Arab way, and when Saïda laughed at my attempts, I felt her camaraderie.

Before we left, Grandpa chose a painting, a village scene in which a woman is milking a cow while a young man under the shade of a Lebanese cypress is pressing olives. In the background several gazelles wander among a host of pomegranate trees and an Israeli tank.

"And this, Salomeia," Sinan said, handing me a box, "is my gift for you."

It was a lampshade, made from three concentric cylinders of parchment inserted one inside the other. Each depicted a series of different scenes so that when rotated, they told a separate story. Through the transparency of the parchment, people and landscapes appeared in various combinations.

"This is your grandfather, and this one here is me," Sinan explained. "The Turks arrested us and we were in jail together for a week. See, this is the jail, and this is your great-grandfather, who bailed us out. If you turn the shade in that way, you can see the house, and Aishe, the greatest cook on earth. Now move the shade the other way. What is Aishe doing? She serves Israfil coffee and sweets. Turn it again and she is dancing. This is when Israfil and I went to Masada to signal the arrival of a British convoy bringing arms. And this one is when I visited Israfil in Vienna. Here is my cousin Lulu, a famous opera singer, and this is a view of Hanah's Paradise. This is Adah, your grandmother, talking with Madame Sal'it, your great-grandmother."

I was delighted with Sinan's amazing gift. After we said goodbye to Ayala and Saïda, Sinan walked with us to the Israeli checkpoint, talking with Grandpa, wanting to prolong his friend's visit a few minutes more.

"If you want to understand our society, Israfil, you have to compare our present with our past. We Arabs were a very advanced culture. In the twelfth century, the University of Cairo was famous—Cambridge and the Sorbonne had not even been founded. We studied the sky and became good navigators, we developed chemistry and medicine. But now we are in the Dark Ages and we don't believe in Enlightenment. We believe in public executions. We don't have laws, we have customs. You in the West want us to build airplanes—and all we want is to learn how to hijack them."

At the Israeli checkpoint, we embraced.

"Sinan, why do you stay here?" Grandpa asked, just before starting the car.

Sinan's deep laughter echoed off the metal of the Israeli tank, then became a hiss. "*Dafka*, Israfil," he said in Hebrew, "for spite!" Then he turned his back and started walking toward the village, every so often glancing back at us as he sang in Arabic:

> Our homes are overflowing with blood.
> The assailant desecrates our land.
> We will fight and not be deterred
> Until the enemy leaves or is dead.

"It is a poem by Yusuf Abu Hilalah, a Palestinian," Grandpa explained. "Sinan has changed some of the lines, but the meaning is quite clear."

The rest of the way home, Grandpa was silent. We crossed the many checkpoints, stopped for coffee, and arrived at Hanah's Paradise late in the night.

After the death of Naftali and the visit to Sinan, Grandpa spent more time at Hanah's Paradise. For the first time in his life, and to everyone's surprise, he traded his black cape and long Arab shirt for European clothes. He continued to read the Arabic newspaper every morning and spent the evenings looking at old maps, realigning the borders of the country, making lists of archeological sites, libraries, museums, markets, and historic monuments. He listened over and over again to my cousin Naftali's record, sometimes forgetting himself and singing aloud the words of the sad melody:

> Embraced by the Universe
> I ascend a diagonal path.
> As I leave
> *Kohev aval lo pashut*
> It hurts, but it doesn't matter.
> The world is waiting for me.

21

That Friday evening the air was so humid that we ate late, hoping for a breeze. The menu was decided quickly. "On hot days my mother made cold yogurt soup, so I made the yogurt," Nurit informed the cousins as they came into the kitchen to prepare dinner.

Yogurt Soup

Make yogurt in a thick ceramic pot.
Store it in a cool dark place.
To serve, spoon several ladles into a bowl.
Add to it the following:

Mint, diced cucumbers, and raisins
If you are from Buchara and Samarqand.
From Greece, mix in olive oil, salt, and wild marjoram.
From Egypt, add fresh mint, onions, and hard-
    boiled eggs.
The Turks squeeze the juice of a large onion, add salt,
    pepper, and cinnamon.
From Hungary, diced beets and paprika.
The Tunisians mix in hot pepper, lemon juice, caraway,
    coriander, salt, and olive oil.
From Lebanon, sprinkle sumac over the soup just
    before serving.
To make a Jewish Burmese yogurt soup, add grated
    ginger and coriander.
In Yemen, they crush in some garlic.
The Jews from Tehran mix in dried sour cherries.
The Iraqis eat the soup with dates.

In Georgia, they make the soup with walnuts and
    pomegranates.
For a universal Jewish dessert, sprinkle honey and warm
    pistachios over the cold yogurt.

We had finished eating and were making a place on the table for
coffee, when Grandpa stood up.

"*Haverim*, my friends," Rafa'el said, "*Haya'ly hulom*, I had a
dream last night. I dreamed that I was sitting on a stone on the
French side of the Carmel, looking out at the harbor. Above me
were hanging the gardens of Hanah's Paradise. All of you were
in the garden going about your business and I, with my two arms
stretched above me, I was trying to reach the garden to come
to you. Some of you noticed me and put a ladder down, but I
couldn't reach it. I tried and tried, until I tired. In my dream I
fell asleep and had another dream, where all of us were at a wedding. To become a bride, every woman had to run naked between
two lines of barbed wire, as policemen with dogs chased them.
As I approached a bride, a bomb was thrown at me. It exploded
with great noise and a wall of fire came forth. In the midst of the
gleaming red flames, I saw a form—with the likeness of a human.
I thought that it was a miracle and I knelt. When I heard, 'Son
of man, stand upon your feet, and I will speak to you,' I woke up
from both dreams."

"You dreamed Ezekiel's vision from the Torah," Nahum, a musician, said, "except that Ezekiel sees a chariot of fire with four
wheels. Even the words are his, 'Son of man. . . .'"

"This is a dream about anxiety," his daughter Dinah said. "It
is a pretty simplistic dream, with banal metaphors. The fire and
the garden have to do with intercourse. He tried to reach but the
ladder is too small and he can't really 'come' to the garden. The
two lines of barbed wire, according to Freud, are the lines of the
vagina dentata; when men come close to it, their grenades burst."

"Dinah, you are rude."

"Well, at your age, Grandpa, there is nothing wrong with not
being able to reach satisfaction. People learn to sublimate."

"Dinah," her father shouted, "apologize to him now!"

"You are dead wrong," Dinah's cousin Amos said. "This is about
separation. Don't you see? The suspended garden separated from

the land, men separated from women, Rafa'el separated from us, a dream in a dream enclosing a vision. Structurally you are wrong."

"It is not about separation, it is about evolution," Tamar, a scientist, explained. "Rafa'el doesn't reach the garden because there is no garden. Everything is a vision. The only reality is biology. He had two dreams like concentric circles. He regressed twice, and when he became just a molecule of energy—fire—he told himself, 'Stand upon your feet,' in other words, grow."

"But the dream is the dreamer," Rafa'el said, to everyone's surprise, "and I dreamed the agony of our time. For generations every firstborn has come to Hanah's Paradise, and continuity has been rewarded. But what has happened to our country and to our hopes? We are desperate. We fight among ourselves as we try to disentangle from the Muslims. How did we create this situation? Brothers," Rafa'el's voice started breaking, "brothers . . . , the dream is about us . . . it is telling us that . . . Messiah has arrived!"

In the sullen silence that followed, his words remained suspended between his lips. Perhaps it was the rabbi who first moved from his chair, perhaps we all felt the need to do something, but without a word being spoken everyone stood up. We looked at Rafa'el, waiting for more words. In the shock of the surprise, we couldn't find our own. Still poised in the doorway holding a tray of fruit above her head, Nurit started crying.

"Yes," Rafa'el continued. "Messiah has arrived to take us to a new land. This is the meaning of my dream. We will leave."

Around the table, frowns, stupor, shock, even bemused smiles showed on people's faces as we all began shifting plates or glasses on the table. At the children's table someone was rubbing a wet finger on the edge of a glass—the high-pitched sounds broke the silence.

"There is no peace for us here," Rafa'el continued. "Our life is full of uncertainties, and the intensity of our situation is no longer tolerable. We fought to fulfill the Zionist dream, but many millions of Arabs don't want us in this part of the world. We have to accept that this country may not survive here. Created from the enormous guilt and sympathy following a slaughter, the whole idea of a Jewish state in Palestine is perhaps just a failed experiment. I too want to believe that we can't walk away from here, that somehow we will make it, because we have to. But I feel the deep Arab hatred. I too want to say that maybe next year everything will be better—isn't that what we have been saying for five thousand years? But the inevitable has to be said. Peace is not on the horizon anymore. A Palestinian state with which we could have peaceful relations is an illusion. Are we willing to give up the Temple Mount? Do we leave or fight? Do we fight to drag the Arabs into a modernity that they don't want? But if it takes giving up our land for the Arabs to stop the killing, then we should go."

The sun was down by now. A last bit of light was playing on Rafa'el's face.

"To even think that we could leave is a blasphemy! It is insulting and unacceptable. It is a horror. But there is no end to the conflict. The Palestinians' grievance is, and will always be, inconsolable. Millions of Palestinians believe that this land is destined, endowed Muslim land. There is no peace to be had here."

We looked at one another in disbelief. Dasha, Grandpa's niece from Riga, was about to scream but instinctively covered her mouth with her hand, realizing the horror of her gasp. In the arch of the doorway, Nurit, still holding the tray above her head, moved slowly, twisting her slim body in a pas de deux. When she became just a line under the tray of fruit, she banged the tray down on the table. "No! This is *not* Muslim land," she said.

Grandpa pushed the tray of fruit toward Nurit, then said to her, "You and I, Nurit, will stay. We are too old to go."

"Rafa'el!" the rabbi screamed, as if woken from a nightmare. "This is blasphemy! Only the Jewish state can ensure the survival of Judaism, and if the Jewish people leave, we will be assimilated in not more than two generations. This is a stupid, shallow conversation. You are insulting *Him*. You are disrespectful of the laws, you are . . . are . . ." and failing to find words for the anger that engulfed him, the rabbi took off his wide-rimmed black hat and threw it on the table. Somebody handed him a glass of water. "*Pulssa de Nura*, a curse on you," the rabbi said, coughing. "I'll put a curse on you—you will all diiiiiiie!"

Grandpa moved his cane into his other hand, bent his body toward the rabbi's bald head, and said, "But you, Shmuel, you live in New York!"

"We are being killed even without your curse, Rabbi, so don't make any effort," Tuvia, a dark-skinned cousin from Venezuela, added. "Put a curse on the martyrs, so they explode before entering the city."

"And if you are so good at cursing, why don't you put a curse on all the Arabs?" Fanya, a right-wing extremist, said. "They die, we stay."

Ashnouar, the head of the Ethiopian side of the family, shook his head and simply said, "*Gmar chatimah tovah*, All good things to you, Rafa'el, but if it weren't for the Israeli army who lifted us from Eritrea, we would all be dead. We can't just abandon the country and go."

"The Palestinians will never stop the war," Rafa'el answered. "Let us be open-minded and understand that the sooner we leave this land, the sooner there will be peace."

"We, the Ethiopian Jews, we all revere Hanah's Paradise," Ashnouar continued. "When we arrived here, all of you took us in and brought our hearts together. We were so poor in our village that the Palestinian refugee camps seemed luxurious. We had one cow for fourteen people. And that was it. No tools, no clothes— just rudimentary shelter. And in less then two hours we traveled a thousand years. Strangers took us into their homes to teach us how to use a modern toilet, how to cook on a stove, how to use a refrigerator, how to cross a street. Doctors took care of us and teachers taught us how to read. But what affected us most was seeing the women in the army. And our children, who before coming here could at most hope for milking the cow, are now going to the university. For us, this is a miracle. And if you, Rafa'el, had the chance to be part of a miracle, don't believe for a second that you can walk away from it."

Rafa'el nodded his head. "We will take the miracle with us. We will find another place."

"We can go to Australia," my cousin Ygal, eager for a new adventure, shouted.

"Yes," Raisa, his latest girlfriend, said. "There is the ocean, there is the desert—and the men are gorgeous!" Ygal put his hand over her mouth.

"There is even a Dead Sea in Australia," somebody said.

"Are you all crazy?" Erika from Budapest screamed. "We finally have a country, and you want to give it up and move! Are you sick? You expect me to go around the city telling my friends and everyone at work that we should pack up and leave? Are you demented, all of you?"

Grandpa listened to Erika, his eyes focused on a peach in front of him. When she stopped talking, he looked up and said to her, in Hungarian: "In Australia, apparently, men are gorgeous." Erika blushed.

"You know, this is not a bad idea," Arkady reflected. "We were thinking of moving to the States, but if everyone goes to Australia, we will go there with you."

"*Habibi*, my friend," Ehud, my architect cousin, said, "what a chance to build a new city. Can you imagine?! *La Nuova Gerusaleme!* The city of the century! This is a fantastic proposition."

"Friends," Grandpa called out, "how much more death should we witness? For five thousand years, dispersal has always been the norm. We must build a Jewish life outside of Zion!"

"This is insane! And coming from you, Rafa'el, I am more than surprised—I am insulted. What about the sacrifices we made to have a country?" Absalon, a physician, said.

"But that is just it, Absalon! I am thinking about the sacrifices. That is what we have to stop!"

"I married a rabbi," Sharon said. "Do you think that he will say, 'Sure, let's pack up the view from my house and leave'?"

"You know, that can be done!" said Akim, a cousin from Brazil and the computer genius of the family. "I could put in cameras and record the view in all seasons and at all times of the day and night. Then you can store the images and project them on your windows."

"*Ze nahon*, is it true?" Odelia, a choreographer, asked. "Could I be in my room dancing on top of the Temple Mount?"

"As long as you don't open the window," I said.

But Odelia didn't hear the humor. In her head, she was already choreographing *The Arabian Nights*.

"I can see the costumes for Scheherazade," she said to no one in particular. "This is incredible. I could dance in front of the al-Aqsa Mosque."

"We can take every stone of Jerusalem and rebuild the city some other place," Cila said, reinforcing the view of her architect husband.

"The archeological sites have not yet been explored," Claudele, the cousin from Switzerland, said. "We have to take them with us."

"If I understand correctly, you want to build a theme park in Australia and call it 'New Jerusalem,'" Marius, a classics philosopher, yelled. "This is ridiculous! Should the Egyptians have dismantled their temples?"

"Well, if the choice is death or mythology, *Gzl*," Issachar, a lawyer seated at the middle of the table, said, "I will leave."

Hearing the consonants forming the word *gazelle*, the family signal that food was stuck on one's lips, or between one's teeth, everyone wiped their mouth. Grandpa rested his cane against his chair and began to eat a yellow persimmon.

The idea of leaving was outlandish. After the initial surprise, everyone started to argue. The split between generations was immediate. *Sabras*, the generation born in Israel, were ready to leave. Their parents, all immigrants, stubbornly wanted to stay.

"Besides," said a voice rising above the argument, "did you ever ask yourself why we are the Chosen People? We have been chosen to bring peace to the nations. And you can't be chosen and also have it easy. It is asking too much."

"Maybe God gave us this land only to promote a stateless nation."

"Had He given us the Laws and not brought us to the Land of Israel, it would have been enough."

"*Day dayyenu*, it would have been enough," a voice near the wall chanted the Passover song.

"I'd rather stay and build a fence between us and them," Ariel, a cousin from Cape Verde, said.

"Yes, and if you build the fence, you might as well show an act of will and determine your own borders," somebody seated across from her answered. "Just make sure you triple the actual size of the country."

"What separation? What wall? This is all empty talk. We should stop blaming the Arabs and find a respectable solution for all of us," Ygal, the shoemaker who wanted to be a politician, said.

"Didn't we already find a respectable solution?" someone added, jumping in.

"We didn't, because we will not give up Jerusalem, nor would we accept the Arabs' right of return!" Saul shouted in his heavy Turkish accent. "The Arabs want everything, and they also want us out of here. There is no respectable solution."

"Can they convert to Judaism? It would make things a lot easier. They are the children of Abraham, after all," Nurit said.

"Arabs are so *shasta*, stubborn," Beth, a middle-aged cousin, said, using a Yiddish word from Brooklyn.

"Jews don't leave Israel!" Dasha finally yelled.

"If they could, they would!" Marina shouted back. "Believe me! We from Russia would not be here if we had another place to go."

"I wouldn't mind moving to Spain," Eva said. "After all, my name is Toledano."

I wondered why Grandpa had provoked this conversation tonight. He could have let us talk about the Polish, the French, or the Germans, as we always did. Why did he have to tell everyone what Sinan had told him? Was Grandpa serious when he said that we should leave?

"What about . . . Hanah's Paradise, Grandpa?" I asked timidly. But before he could answer, Noah said, "Rafa'el, this land is our state and our history. It is here that we conceived of monotheism. We are a nation; we cannot live without our past."

"Once we contemplate the possibility of leaving and establishing ourselves in another place, the rest is only details," Rina countered.

"Perhaps monotheism is not such a great idea after all. It allows for too much ecstatic violence," my cousin Eugenia from Latvia said.

"If we leave, we will lose our identity. We will not know who we are anymore. The deep emotional attachment to this land is what has kept us alive for five thousand years," the rabbi retorted, outraged.

"You don't believe that we should fight until death, do you?" Sulamit, my cousin Nathaniel's daughter, said. "Masada, Episode Two! You can't be serious. I personally prefer to accommodate the Palestinians if that stops the fighting. If not, I don't mind leaving. After all, our state relies too much on historic references."

"Rafa'el, this is folly," the rabbi said. "You are denying the loss of the Temple and its deep meaning to every Jew. You are truly a corrupt and degenerate individual."

"You cannot speak to him like that," my cousin Ruth objected, "even if you don't like what he is saying. Apologize!"

"This land was given to us by God. Messiah can arrive only here," the rabbi said, moaning a prayer:

> Have mercy, Adonai, on Israel,
> On Thy People, on Jerusalem,
> Thy City of Holiness,
> Rebuild Jerusalem in our days, O God.

"Change the name in the prayers," Susan Rose, a cousin from America, said. "You can say, 'Have mercy, Adonai, on Brooklyn, Thy City.'"

"This is brilliant," Amos, her brother, said. "And please add to the prayer, 'Blessed art Thou who permits us forbidden things.'"

"Rafa'el, this is heresy!" the rabbi shouted. "You know the Books! The special Revelation of the Torah will happen only in the Land of Israel. Our Lord, may His majesty increase, will reveal Himself to us only here."

"Can you imagine, if only for a second, Rabbi, that not all of us are waiting for His revelations?" a cousin visiting from Ukraine said. "It is better for us to spread out into different countries; if a lunatic drops a bomb on Israel, we would all be gone."

"Jews are civilization's dust, whose particles try to cling to each other," somebody said, paraphrasing Ben-Gurion.

"We should not simply leave," Miriam, who was a business student, said. "We should sell ourselves to countries in need of restoring their Jewish past. We will go to the highest bidder: Spain, Poland, Germany, Portugal, Russia, whomever."

"Baja California would be the best place," Yony observed.

"It is paradise," his wife, Simone, contributed.

"It would be a great thing for the Mexicans, also," Yoram, an economist, added.

"I personally request my right of return to Spain or Portugal. My name is Belmonte. We must be from there."

"At least from the linguistic point of view," I said.

"You know, we are tired of the constant fighting for this land," Rivka, my cousin from Ashdod, said, her frustration starting to show. "Let's leave. Let the Land of Israel return to peace and dust. This place does not serve us well."

"Right," Seth, a sculptor, agreed. "Why should we be the keepers of history when Western civilization cares only about the last two thousand years? We bulldoze all the monuments, level the cities, reduce the area to desert dust—then leave. Perhaps our state is the state of permanent exile."

"Anyone who gives away or sacrifices the land of Israel deserves death," the rabbi said. "You have to win the war for Messiah to come."

"Rabbi, why are the religious students not fighting for the land? Have you noticed how many Israelis are dying so the students can pray, waiting for Messiah?"

"They pray for Israel several times every day! They say *Tehilim* for all of us. The Psalms will protect our soldiers and deliver our land. You too should recite them: 20, 83, 121, 130, and 142. The power of prayers is immense."

The sky had darkened. Early moonlight found its way between the bamboos, and a line of light shimmered on the table. Grandpa stood up again. He glowed in the softness of the garden's shadows.

"Dear friends!" he began. "From Paradise, God sent Adam into exile, and man is still in exile. We are a modern nation; we have a state and a political voice. In Israel we have achieved historical unity. We revived our language and our traditions. We revived a culture and established a new identity. Metaphorically, the tribes have been reunited. But does Israel have to be here? Do we have to be tied up by the past? *Higya zman*, the time has arrived for us to go on. *Yihye lanu makom aher*, we will have a different place. Perhaps exile is the answer to our continuity. As for the religion, more people go to synagogue in New Delhi than in Tel Aviv. Our traditions would be stronger, our country would be the world, and our holidays would be remembered. There is something powerful and poetic about exile. It sets us apart. Why not accept it? A nation of expatriates! Isn't that what modern man is? Isn't the idea of state, country, and nation insufficient for what we have become? We are the global connection. Stand up and leave! We, the Israelis, are returning from the Land of Moses and Abraham to live as we always did—in exile."

Stand up and leave? I thought. No, not again. Please, no more separations. I love living in Israel. I love the intensity of life here.

The directness born from the lack of ambiguity in the meaning of words, the arrogance of survival inherited from repeated threats of death, the softness of the affection when tomorrow is not certain, the hands leaning an M-16 against a wall to free themselves for an embrace, this I love. How would people fall in love if there were no war? If we cannot say, "Love me now, for tomorrow I may be killed," falling in love may take forever.

Stand up and leave? What are we to do, start a new exodus? Define the laws of a new Diaspora, be a stateless nation? Was the wandering Jew destined to become an expatriate Israeli? Grandpa, the dispersed tribes returned home to create this country. We are not only Jewish, Grandpa, we are also Israeli. This is our identity. Being threatened is part of it. Maybe we *can* live side by side with the Palestinians. Perhaps coexistence is not a fiction. After all, they, too, feel that they are in exile.

But what if it is fiction and we can't live side by side? To stay, we will have to fight forever. If we leave, we can again say, "Next year in Jerusalem" and remain permanently in paradise—no matter where we are. My cousins born in Israel don't mind living abroad, and some of them already do. They keep falafel stands in New York and kosher restaurants in Budapest. They reenact the Zionistic movement in exile, hoping to return one day to the land they left not so long ago. And like them, when I am not in Israel, I constantly look at the clouds, waiting for the sky to become the velvet indigo-blue that descends every night over Tel Aviv. I drive on a narrow road and suddenly I smell orange blossoms. The white stone of Jerusalem will be in front of me at the turn of a corner, and the silvery leaves of a lonely cypress will bring to mind the winding road to Safed. But people don't fight wars to avoid nostalgia. I shook my head and said softly, so only he could hear it, "No, Grandpa, we can't leave. This is our story."

"Our story, Salomeia, is in the inscriptions left at Hanah's Paradise. Everything that happened is there: continuity, separation, secret lives, and the price of survival. You read the story of Don Simeon and Don Alfonso. You saw how many times they stood up and left. Remember Doña Reina and Doña Isabel? You recorded their songs, their poems, their cooking traditions. You wrote the story of Aram and Bilu. Now we can go. We will take our bamboo, and wherever we may be in the world, when the bamboo flowers, everyone in our family will remember Hanah's Paradise."

ADIEU, JERUSALEM

One by one, the pebbles, the stones, the inscriptions, the gates, and the trees of Hanah's Paradise were packed. The bamboo was divided among family members. The *luz*, the almond-like bones that belong to our family, were kept by Rafa'el. From each city, square by square, tree-lined streets, schools, banks, parks, corner shops, street lights and benches, gardens, houses, old buildings, coffee shops, newsstands, art galleries, libraries, museums, theaters, restaurants, and archeological sites were dismantled and packed. From Jaffa we took the clock tower, the flea market, and the stone where Poseidon chained Andromeda. From Tel Aviv we took the monument to Rabin, the falafel stand near the corner of Allenby and Shenkin, the artists' Sunday market on Nahlat Binyamin, the Bauhaus buildings, Geula Street, the Carmel market, the smell of the chocolate factory, and the mist from the promenade along the beach where the waves break and scatter on the sand. My cousin Ruth took the view from her corner window and the white waves of the Mediterranean. Some took their olive trees; some took crates of sand, orchards, and arched stone houses. Some took the hills of Judea, the Sea of Galilee, the stones of Masada, the inscriptions on the monuments, the sound of explosions, of moving tanks, of helicopters, of rocks hitting the windshields of their cars, the fear of bombs. Some took only the view from their terrace and their tears. And some left everything behind.

Our five thousand years of memories and hopes were numbered and packed. Adieu, *Terre Sainte!* Adieu, the white stones of Jerusalem, the Montefiore windmill, the quince tree at the corner of Jaffa Road and Makhane Yehudah; adieu, the stone arches by the Pool of the Patriarchs, the caper bushes on the road to Jericho, the afternoon light from the Mediterranean, the rooftops of the Old City, the Crusader tower, the King David Hotel, the wind from the Arabian peninsula, the color of cactus flowers, the smell of the desert after rain—adieu. We are leaving behind a religious world, a thousand names for God, the many beginnings, the wars, the pain, the love of this land, the hope to be here—we are leaving all this behind. We are wandering again toward a New Jerusalem, but now we are a nation. We will live in other lands as we have done so many times before. We, the tribe of Israel, the Hebrew slaves, the tortured *Marranos*, the slaughtered Jews, the impatient Israelis, united in our language and in our history, are leaving our own country.

For peace is more important than history.
And life, more precious than God.

The ships with our memories left the land of Moses and Abraham. From the empty shores, we heard Rafa'el's voice rising above the waves, following us around the harbor, whispering to each of us in the language of our fathers:

Im eshkaeh Yierushalaim
tishkah yemini,
If ever I forget you, O Jerusalem,
Let my right hand wither.

22

S eated at a small table, they were facing each other. I sat a bit
away from them, my chair leaning against a tree, listening to
their conversation. In his gentlemanly way, Sinan was speaking
Hebrew, the language of his host.

Sinan had arrived at Hanah's Paradise with his sons: six middle-aged men in suits and ties. They looked familiar—they had
their mother's lavender eyes. They came to visit with Rafa'el. After
they drank the ritual coffee, they left. Sinan stayed on to spend
some time with his old friend.

"That was quite a dream," Sinan said. "I am sorry I wasn't there
to see people's faces: 'Messiah has arrived and we shall leave.'
What a vision!"

"Yes, you should have heard the shouting. It was even suggested,
Sinan, that since Israelis and Arabs are cousins, we should unite
forces and . . ."

"Stop it, Rafa'el, stop it," Sinan interrupted, his body shaking
with laughter. "You mean to say that when I go to the mosque, I
should wait for the end of prayers, and, with people still on their
knees, incite them to join with you and riot against Christianity?
Rafa'el, you are still crazy; and still wonderful! You are an artist!
We have to reform Islam, not start a war against the Vatican."

"How did you convince them to return?" Grandpa asked.

"I didn't convince them; I asked them to come back. We Palestinians have been misguided, betrayed, manipulated by the world,
by history, by our leaders—even by our father Abraham when he
sent Hagar away. 'You have to come back to teach us coexistence,
not with the Jews but with the world,' I said to them. And if they
tell this to their friends, and to their friends' friends, then we may
have a chance."

"Sinan," Grandpa said, "what happened that made you change your mind?"

Sinan poured some coffee into his cup, opened some pistachios, and made a pile of shells and a pile of yellow-greenish nuts in front of him. He started talking, interrupting himself every once in a while to eat a pistachio.

"I knew four teenaged boys—brothers, very close in age. Their father had been my student. After he died of an illness, I took some interest in them. A month ago they came to visit and say good-bye. Each of them was getting married to the Black-Eyed Virgin—all four at once. It had all been arranged. They would explode at the same moment and, in as much time as it takes to smile, be reunited in Paradise. They promised to send me messages from there. They were going around saying good-bye to their friends, inviting them to the celebration following the wedding. They were embracing each other, bonded by an immeasurable love. Never had they felt so intimate, so close to each other; never had their words been so attended to as now. Life had guided them to their happiness. Their unshakable belief in the reality of an after-life was inebriating. The annihilation of others was only secondary.

"I took them into my studio, where I have a drawing by their father. 'Before you go,' I said, 'I want to show you something. Your father was the best student I ever had. He could see the hidden life of things. Other people could also draw, but he—he could feel. He was a master. Once, your father painted the world to come. It was a beautiful painting. After he finished it, he sat in front of it for a day and a night, then burned it. "The world to come," he said, "is a dark, beautiful night, but a night without soul. Darkness is wrong; the Essence of God is brightness."'

"As I was talking, one of them drew a cube, shadowed its hidden side to emphasize the third dimension, and said, 'We are going to be the soul of the night.'

"'Which one of you decided first?' I asked. They elbowed each other, giggling. The oldest one said, 'We will be Allah's guests. We are bringing Him messages from His land.'

"'Allah is here,' I said, pointing to their father's drawing on the wall. 'This piece of paper was once only a flat surface, not even a void. Your father put a line on it and created a form. He trans-

315

formed the world with this line. Creation is the true act of God. Your father loved God and his love gave meaning to the void.'"

Sinan stopped talking to rearrange his *kafiah*. He was quiet for a time. Then he said, "I kept the drawing of the cube."

"What a loss," Rafa'el said. "We lose, they lose, the whole of humanity loses."

"After the villagers celebrated their martyrdom, I had a terrible thought. What if the world regressed, and states became nations defined not by political and lawful agreements but by customs and religious beliefs?"

"This is also the dilemma of the Jewish state."

"The thought that fanaticism could become our only way to live is frightening," Sinan said.

They sat in silence. Around us, purple shadows moved slowly over the garden. Hanah's Paradise took on a mystical glow. The walls, the paths, the squares, the bamboo—everything had a deeper color. A peacock, a gift to Rafa'el from our firstborn cousin Soussan, from Persia, opened its tail. Even birds celebrate the end of the day, I thought. The peacock walked with majesty toward us, turned around, and spread his green-blue-gold feathers in a perfectly adjusted half circle. Above his iridescent feathers, I could see an inscription left long ago by one of my firstborn cousins. I couldn't read the name, but the words were well chiseled, and when I read what they said, I wondered whether it had been a woman or a man who had written:

> With only a few rules
> In logical manipulation,
> We build
> Increasing complexities
> And call them
> Life.

"And very often love," someone had added underneath.

Acknowledgments

To David, who shares with me his passion for jazz, painting, and literature; to Rosalie Siegel, who taught me perseverance while representing the book; to Ruth Greenstein, who taught me delight while editing the book; to Bernard Sthele—man *heroicus sublimus*—who advised me on the book; to Claudia Suter, who shared with me her elegant friendship; to Paco Villegas and Simone Kuoni, my Spanish publishers; to Jean Michel Rabate for encouraging me to write; to Susan Behr, Nathaniel Kahn, Karina Sotnik, Kevin Platt, and Jean Patrice Netter, who kept me focused; to my sister Corina; to my children Priscille, Avram, Clara, and Dorothée—thank you all.

To Dina Wind, Antoine Grumbach and Lena Sofer, Francis Nordemann, Anne Chapoutot and George Bloch, Ehud and Cila Kory, Robert Aresnault, Sarita and Morris Gocial, Carol Klein, Larry Spitz, Werner Graf, Harold and Yassue Slovic, Michaela and Viorel Farcas, Debra Werblund, Yvette and Jean Jacques Terrin, Liliane Weissberg, Bavat Marom, Nadia and Jean Michel Hoyet, Sandy and John Moore, Cora R. Levy, David Sanders, Ann de Forest, Louis Greenstein, Mark Lyons, Debra Leigh Scott, Diane Burko, Linda and Daniel Gross, Jill Sablovsky, Lucile Bertrand, Toby Lerner, Debby King, John Wind and Kirk Kirkpatrick, Pamela Martin, Debby Smith, Anca and Daniel Constantinescu, Kathryn and Stewart Rome, and Edith Newhall; to my parents Odelia and Avram; to my dear cousins Monzi, David, Rina, Tova, Yael, Zipora, Marius, and Yossy at Pardes Hannah; to all my dear friends and sometimes readers who went out of their way to give me friendship and tremendous joy, thank you.

Special thanks to David Walters for his work on the cover, to Miriam Seidel for her help and support, and to Doug Gordon for pulling everything together.

LaVergne, TN USA
29 April 2010
180967LV00001B/296/P